ReVenge Unleashed

SENJA LAAKSO

ReVenge Unleashed

SENJA LAAKSO

REVENGE UNLEASHED
Book 2 in Revenge Series

Copyright © 2024 Senja Laakso

ISBN 978-952-69809-3-5 (hardcover)
ISBN 978-952-69809-4-2 (softcover)
ISBN 978-952-69809-5-9 (EPUB)

First published January 2024, by Stoorily

www.SenjaLaakso.com

Cover: Stoorily

Also by
Senja Laakso

Revenge Series

Revenge Undone
Revenge Unleashed

See all books and learn more at:
senjalaakso.com

NOTE FOR READERS

This novel contains grief, manipulation,
therapy, violence, and other content that may be
triggering to some. Reader discretion is advised.
For full list of content warnings,
visit the author's website:
senjalaakso.com.

This book is written in British English.

*To my grandmother,
you're the one I still miss*

1

Liam's hands shot out, his fingers curling and uncurling in a desperate attempt to reach Ciara. *Too slow.*

There, right in front of Liam, were her brown eyes, glistening with tears. And then, they weren't. She vanished, slipping through his fingers. Like time through an hourglass.

Their sand—their time—had slipped through. Everything was over.

Liam stumbled, the sharp pain of his knees hitting the hard, unforgiving wooden floor jolting through his body. He deserved it. Clenching his fists, he tried to steady his shaking body.

No. Please, no.

The storm of feelings overwhelmed him, and his knee was the unfortunate target of his sudden outburst. He grimaced at the dull pain. The physical pain was nothing compared to the ache inside his ribcage.

He had never intended to hurt Ciara. All he had ever wanted was to keep her safe—far from harm and those who would bring harm with them.

He hadn't realised how badly she would be hurt, but he should have. It was all his fault.

Liam sighed, but his fingers twitched. That sick murderer—Theo—had never deserved Ciara. Not for a second.

Liam had been there to see what Theo's *death* had done to her. That man had shattered her and left others to pick up the pieces. Ciara deserved better.

Ciara deserved everything.

Liam was determined to make the bastard—Theo—pay for everything he had put her through.

Liam opened his hands, sighing. The floor was cool to the touch as Liam rested his palms against it.

He was too much like Theo himself. Liam had also hurt Ciara.

He had known the truth since the moment he had seen Theo kill Doherty. He should have told Ciara. Because of Liam, she had discovered the truth in such a cruel way.

Liam wished he could have turned back in time and told the truth.

The problem was that moving back in time was tricky—nearly impossible. It wasn't an option.

Still, somehow, Liam would fix everything. An apology would be a good start, but it was going to have to wait.

Liam had to go back to the hospital. His father and ex-fiancée were fighting for their lives, and Jenna's condition had barely improved.

The fate of Bill was a mystery to everyone. Even the doctors.

Liam's family came first, so he had to put everything else on hold, even if it killed him not to go and talk to Ciara.

She didn't want to see him. No matter how much he hated it, he would give her space.

Liam stood up. As tears welled up in his eyes, the messy room became a hazy blur. He dragged his feet to the bathroom through his trashed room, turned on the faucet, and threw cold water at his face. Coolness washed over him, but he didn't feel any better. He wet his hand under the rushing water and raked his fingers through his hair.

After he closed the tap, he looked up and met his own gaze. He looked into the hazel abyss of his puffy eyes, and he hated them. He hated himself for what he had done.

He had fucked up. Badly.

Liam grabbed his wand but then halted. His thoughts crept back to the hospital and what was waiting for him there.

Would there be news?

He had no choice but to go back there, even though he wasn't ready. He never would be.

His fingers tightened around his wand, knuckles turning white. A part of him still longed to follow Ciara. He bit down on his lip, forcing himself to stand still.

He wanted to go after Ciara. It wasn't fair to leave her alone. She had been through so much. He needed to talk to her and to be there for her.

But she wouldn't listen. Going there wouldn't make a difference. She didn't want him there, and it was his own fault.

He had to go to the hospital.

Sitting and waiting for news of his dad's survival—or death—was going to be excruciating. Liam already knew that.

But Liam had witnessed his siblings and mother break down upon hearing about the attack. His father couldn't be there for his family, so someone had to be. Liam had to be.

He would stay strong. For his father. For his family.

He had to.

With that in mind, he shoved his feelings to the farthest corner of his mind. Ciara would have to wait.

He would fix everything later. His primary concern was getting his family through the difficult days that lay ahead.

2

"**L**et's talk about my American cousin whom you killed two years ago." He paused. "And don't be so surprised. I told you something would happen soon. Or, *very soon*."

The room spun around Ciara. Jesse had almost told her he was the witch hunter behind the threat notes, and she hadn't realised. He had played her, and she had let him gain the upper hand.

But Jesse's cousin? "I don't know any of your cousins, Jesse. I—"

"Enough with the bullshit!" An uncontrollable rage consumed the once composed lethality. Jesse's grip tightened around the knife, and the blade dug deeper into her throat. It was enough to draw blood.

Not a fatal cut. *Not yet.*

But it stung. Ciara bit her teeth together to stifle the hiss of pain. She had been through worse before.

The flat, once filled with love and warmth, now felt eerie.

Coldness had seeped in through cracks that she hadn't noticed. She hadn't seen the warning signs flashing red right in front of her.

Something about everything going on around her didn't sit right. Even within the walls of her own home, she was in danger. Even in the presence of her friends, lies had been as common as the air she breathed.

Ciara was alone.

The uneasy feeling in her stomach told her that things were only going to get worse with Jesse. The iron scent of her blood wafted through the air, and it was only the beginning.

Ciara didn't dare to speak. Jesse seemed to have plans that included slicing her throat, and she didn't want to encourage him. It would have been like sealing her own fate. It would have been suicide.

"Two years ago." Rage and grief trembled in Jesse's voice.

Ciara didn't recognise this Jesse. He wasn't the boy she had once dated. Not the boy she had once, maybe, known.

"You killed a guy. Kyle Kingston."

The name rang no bells. Had Ciara killed this person?

Two years ago, she repeated Jesse's words in her head.

Two years prior, she had been working on one case. Only one. She had been working undercover in the United States, inside the witch hunters' terrorist organisation.

She hadn't killed more than three witch hunters around that time. Four men had caught her reporting back to her boss. Theo had been undercover with her, and he had killed the fourth man.

"Your cousin was a witch hunter?" Ciara had known Jesse had relatives in America. But witch hunters?

"Yes. Working for the good and—"

"Good?" The word spilled out. It was unfathomable to Ciara how someone could genuinely claim that the witch hunters' cause was good and just. They were terrorists and murderers. The night's events had proven that. Her friends were in the hospital, hooked up to machines and surrounded by beeping monitors, their lives hanging in the balance because of them.

No one good would do such things. Hearing Jesse claim otherwise made Ciara's insides fume with anger.

"Yes! Good!" Jesse snapped. "We're fighting for justice."

That was it.

"You sound insane, Jesse." She was still in shock. She had never doubted Jesse. Yet there he was, a knife at her throat.

He huffed out, unphased by the use of his name. "You want to know what's insane?"

Ciara pursed her lips, unsure if she should reply. Jesse still had the blade pressed against her neck. A single slice through the air and she'd be finished.

She had just made it out of the warehouse, and she refused to die now. But if she wanted to survive, she had to stay calm. Jesse's taunts were like a flame, but she refused to let them ignite her anger.

"It's insane that—"

With a quick snap of her fingers, Ciara sent the knife hurtling across the room. It lodged itself in the wall of Ciara's living room. Her heart racing, she leaped up and spun around only to find a wand mere inches from her face.

Before she could raise her hand, Jesse flicked his wand. She was sent flying across the room, slamming into the wall with a jarring jolt. Her head throbbed relentlessly, like a hammer pounding against her skull. The overwhelming fatigue made her consider dropping to the floor. But it would have been the last thing she did, so she couldn't.

The knife was only an arm's length away from her. She tried to reach for it, but ropes appeared out of thin air and snaked around her wrists. The scratchy rope tightened, burning her skin as it did.

She tried to cast a spell, but the magic was weak and fizzled out. The magic-binding ties glowed faintly around her wrists, showing their power to trap her magic.

She inhaled sharply, the sudden understanding hitting

her like a ton of bricks. Her hands were tied, rendering her magic useless until someone untied her. She found herself at Jesse's mercy, completely trapped.

Jesse smirked. Not the Jesse from Ciara's memories. This Jesse scared her. His dirty blond hair was a tangled mess, and his eyes were wild, like a predator on the hunt.

He grabbed the knife, hung it off his belt and grabbed Ciara by her hair. He practically threw her onto the sofa, making sure she was seated before releasing his hold.

Her eyes narrowed at him. "You're going to get caught."

Jesse shook his head, fiddling with his wand. "Nah, I don't think so. After I kill you, Elliott will reward me with protection."

Elliott? Ciara didn't know anyone called Elliott.

"Now...where were we?" Jesse smirked at Ciara again. Not arrogantly, not vainly, but like a cold-blooded killer.

Ciara made a mental note to move out if she lived through the night. She didn't have to wonder how Jesse had got his hands on the flat's key. His friend owned the flat. Jesse had helped Ciara to get the flat.

It had to be all part of his plan. A plan Ciara hadn't been aware of until he had shoved a knife at her throat.

Ciara glanced out through one of the windows and saw nothing but an abyss of darkness and a hint of a reflection of what was inside the flat. The night had already lasted an eternity, so dawn had to come soon. It was January, so the sun would rise before eight o'clock.

Would someone look for me by then? Ciara had to survive alone. She couldn't count on anyone to come looking for her.

Not after all the lies. As she had found out that very night, she had no one to count on.

"Ah, right. The insane part." Jesse's smirk didn't fade. "You trusted me since the beginning."

She had known him since their school years. "I didn't kill anyone when we were sti—"

"Don't pretend to be stupid!" The smirk dropped, and Jesse's eyes burned with fury. "The speed dating event! You think a guy like me needs an event like that to get company?" Jesse laughed, gesturing to his body—his abs, arm muscles, all of it. "Nope. I could have any girl I want. Including you, it seems."

He had planned *all* of it. It had all been a game since the beginning. He had played her for months.

And she had naively let him.

"Then why am I still alive?" Ciara locked eyes with her ex-boyfriend, his crazed expression sending shivers down her spine. She refused to cower in front of him. Even if he was going to kill her, she wouldn't go down without a fight.

She wasn't sure she could live with herself after what she had done to Theo in the warehouse. But no matter how tempting death was, she hadn't finished what she had started yet.

"I chickened out." Jesse shrugged. "Stupid me, I know. That's why I drugged you after we had sex."

Drugged. The word hit Ciara like a slap. She had slept in at Jesse's flat after they had spent the night together.

She *never* slept in.

Except that time.

She felt a dull, persistent buzz in her head as she struggled to make sense of the past few months.

"Fuck." The word slipped out.

She could have died months ago. She was only alive because of Jesse's cowardliness, and that terrified her.

Perhaps he would be a coward again. But that chance was slim. Slimmer than Ciara would have liked.

"Then, at the gym, every time I thought about it, someone called you. You, of course, told them where you were." Frustration boiled inside Jesse, his teeth gritted and his eyes blazing like flames.

Ciara had to get out of the binds, or she was going to die. But no matter how she tried to pull, they held—and they burned her skin like hot iron, leaving marks on her skin.

"They would have figured out who killed you. Same problem when you stayed over at my place." His eyes narrowed as if piercing through her. "Then the party..." He sighed. "Couldn't kill you there, either. Too many witnesses to deal with after."

Nausea hit Ciara again, listening to Jesse list all the times he could have killed her—and had thought of killing her. And she had trusted him.

She should have seen the signs.

Like at the supermarket before Christmas. Jesse had been there. He had worn a hoodie that day. Exactly like the witch hunter she had caught a glimpse of.

The notes. The witch hunter at the supermarket had left one of them. Right after Jesse had showed up, wearing the exact hoodie—just the hood down.

"Why did you leave the notes?" Ciara's hoarse voice cracked as she stared up at her ex-boyfriend. Jesse's lips curled into a wicked smirk, pleased with her reaction.

"Just two of them. Theo left the first one."

They—or apparently Theo—had threatened Liam on the first note. *Someone who's alone and unaware might get hurt unless you stop.* That had been the first note.

The second one had been one word. *Soon.*

The last note had been two words. *Very soon.*

Only the first note had been there to look out for Liam. The last two notes—the ones from Jesse—had been there to tell her that her own end was coming.

"Maybe Theo was jealous?"

Ciara shuddered at the mention of Theo—her fiancé. The man she had once loved.

The same man she had killed with her own hands only hours ago.

"Theo..." Jesse laughed, eyes distant, as if reminiscing a memory. "Ah, he was pissed when he found out about the time I broke into your hotel room."

Ciara's brows furrowed. *Hotel room?*

"Yes." Jesse smirked, as if her silent reaction excited him. "I went through your stuff. You know, to make sure I wasn't in a wrong room. I don't like to kill innocents, unlike some of us." His eyes hardened, the smirk long gone. "Luckily, I got help with a cloaking spell before you came with your friends."

Ciara had stayed in a hotel after she and Doherty had come back from their work trip to America. "That was before the speed dating."

"I know." Jesse was enjoying it. All of it. Seeing her in shock, playing with her.

But he was buying time. Rambling on. Was he hesitating?

Ciara was still alive. It had to mean something. When she had to kill someone, she didn't stick around to play. She went straight for the kill.

Jesse wasn't used to killing.

"I'm surprised you didn't even notice this. Guess my spell worked." He pulled his shirt up enough to reveal the tattooed witch hunter mark on his muscled chest. "We match." He gestured to her burnt witch hunter mark. The one Theo had left on her shoulder.

It was a flame-like symbol with a straight line in the middle. A mark of killers. A mark Ciara longed to erase from the entire world.

Ciara still hadn't figured what her mark was there for. Not that she had even had time to spare much thought to it.

But she wasn't a witch hunter, even if Theo had wished her to become one.

Jesse stepped closer and leaned down. He pulled her shirt aside enough to see the entire mark on her shoulder. Ciara recoiled at his closeness, turning her face away.

"Guess I should have asked Theo to help with the cloaking spell. But then again, I doubt he would have." Jesse chuckled, still not stepping away. "He hates how I speak about you. Or rather, *hated*."

"Don't talk about him!" Ciara snapped. Jesse was inches away, but she still turned and locked eyes with him.

"I told him about our night together. I swear he wanted to kill me after that. You should've seen the way his fingers clenched around his wand. How his hands shook with the rage of knowing—"

"Shut up."

"Nah, I'm not done." Jesse shook his head, not making one move to pull away.

Ciara pretended to shudder, casting her gaze down.

"You know—"

Her head connected with his nose, and she heard a sickening crunch.

That was her chance. She leapt to her feet, her adrenaline pumping, and sprinted towards the door. If she got out of the flat and called for help, she could make it out alive.

So close. A few more steps and she would reach the doorknob.

But pain shot through her scalp, and she hit the floor. The pain was excruciating as Jesse's fingers dug into her scalp, and her head hit the wooden floor again.

Her vision blurred, but she could still make out Jesse's outline.

"Dumb move." His voice was deep and growling, an indication of his animalistic rage.

He had kept his calm around her for months and, by doing so, had fooled her. He had been so calculated.

That composure was long gone, overtaken by his rage.

"Jesse—"

He yanked her up by her hair. His fingers didn't ease their grip, and he dragged her back to the living room.

Ciara's head pulsed with pain, but her vision was clearing.

As soon as he released her, she felt a sudden push on her shoulder, sending her down to her knees.

She tried to cast magic, but it didn't work. The magic-binding rope held tight.

Jesse's hand shot out, gripping her chin tightly and forcing her to look up. Something warm and sticky coated his hand.

When the iron stench filled Ciara's nostrils, she realised she was bleeding. And it wasn't the minor cut on her neck from before.

3

Taking a shaky breath, Liam flicked his wand. The bathroom shifted, slowly disappearing, and the bustling front of the hospital materialised before him.

He walked in, and the blinding brightness of the endless white walls made him squint. The ceiling was too low for his liking. As if the building was closing in on him.

The pit of his stomach burned, and his throat closed. He willed his stiff muscles into action, pushing himself to move. One step at a time, his feet carried him down the corridor, and soon he found himself jogging.

But at the door of his father's hospital room, he froze. Taking a deep breath, he tried to calm his trembling hands. Someone had to stay strong. *He* had to stay strong.

He shoved his emotions aside for the rest of the night and pushed the door open.

It was like the ceiling crumbled down on him, suffocating him. His two twin sisters sobbed, clinging onto one another.

Gabriel hugged their mother. They both shook with soundless cries, fighting against their sobs.

Henry wasn't there. He had to be with Jenna, who at least was awake. Liam knew his younger brother would come see their father when he could.

Their father was unconscious, and Jenna was awake. She had only briefly passed out when River had brought her to the hospital. She had to be traumatised, and she needed Henry—in that moment more than their father needed Henry's presence.

Liam shut the door silently. He didn't want to startle anyone.

He walked closer, and his eyes fell on his father. Laid on the bed, pale and unconscious. Despite the surgery being over, he still appeared pale and weak. He looked *half-dead*.

Liam shuddered at the thought.

"Oh, Liam." His mother raised her gaze and noticed him first.

Gabriel pulled away from their mother and ran to his oldest brother. Liam wrapped his arms around Gabe, surprised by how tall he was, and then the younger Rossler broke into loud sobs.

The sight was enough to make their mother lose her composure. A sob passed her lips, and tears stained her face. Polly and Poppy rushed to hug their mother, but Liam remained hugging his little brother.

He vowed to get them through the nightmare they were forced to live through. He would do it for their father.

He had to.

⁂

Liam left the hospital room, closing the door behind him. It was like stepping out of a burning house. As if suddenly he could breathe.

It made him lightheaded. He had to halt for a moment before heading to another hospital room to see his ex-fiancée.

When he walked in, there was a healer checking on Iris.

The blonde woman—Iris—was still unconscious on the wretched hospital bed. At least she looked calm. Though still pale, some colour had returned to her cheeks.

"H-how is she?" Liam asked the Southeast Asian healer. He had seen the healer before—probably had met her through Iris—but couldn't remember her name.

"More stable, but we're monitoring her every breath." The healer glanced at Iris. They probably knew each other since they both worked as healers in the same hospital. "We haven't reached her parents yet, but we'll try again. It's early, so we assume they might still be asleep."

"I'm sure they'll come here the second they hear about this."

The healer nodded. "You're her ex-fiancé." It wasn't a question; the healer knew.

"I am." Liam looked down at Iris. He felt sorry for leaving her alone, even if she was unconscious. "We're friends now. I brought her here after the attack."

The group had claimed to be attacked by the witch hunters. Kellan had instructed them to do so. After all, MPG—Magical Protection Group—and their missions were illegal. They couldn't tell anyone they had gone after the witch hunters on purpose. Kellan, Ciara, and her team— they would all lose their jobs for working with the group. As for the MPG members, they would likely all go to jail if someone found out about the missions.

"She seems to be getting better," the healer said, reassuring Liam. "It's only been a few hours. I can't say anything for certain yet, but she's a fighter."

Liam smiled. Even if he and Iris weren't as close anymore, he knew her.

She would fight through it. She would get better.

The healer left the room in silence, and Liam sat down on a chair next to Iris's bed.

The least he owed Iris, even just because of their history, was a bit of time. She didn't deserve to be lying on a hospital bed with no family or friends—even if she was still unconscious.

After visiting Iris, Liam needed coffee. Both he and his mother did.

He shut the hospital room's door, sparing one more glance at Iris. She didn't deserve to be left alone after what she had been through, but he had to go be with his family.

Liam's footsteps echoed through the only deserted hallway of the hospital until he halted, narrowly avoiding running into a man. And not just anyone, but Kellan, who was anxiously pacing outside Bill's hospital room. Liam had never seen him look so pale.

"Hey." Liam stiffened as Kellan pivoted to look at him. The redness in Kellan's eyes was impossible to miss. "Bill... is he..."

"The same." Kellan's voice was rough and tired.

"So w—"

"Do you know where Ciara is?" Kellan asked, brows furrowed.

"She went home." Liam let out a deep breath, but the tightness in his chest remained. "We broke up."

Kellan nodded, his expression remaining the same. "She's at her flat then."

"That's where she went a couple of hours ago."

Kellan's haunted expression deepened as he glanced at the closed door of Bill's hospital room. "I would have thought she'd come see Bill."

Liam frowned. Kellan was right. Although Ciara was actively avoiding Liam, her desire to visit the hospital—visit Bill and the others—hadn't changed. "You sure she's not here? In Jenna's room or something."

"I checked," Kellan said. "Your brother was there with

Jenna's parents. No Ciara."

"Last night was rough for her." Liam was also to blame for that, and they both knew it.

Kellan hummed, agreeing.

"I'm sure she'll come when she can. Perhaps she's still drained and needs rest before she'll come."

Hugo and Shawn had told Liam how much of her magic Ciara had drained. Ciara hadn't even been able to teleport herself away from the warehouse. After her magic's outburst at the warehouse, though, Liam wasn't surprised.

But he was worried.

Though the witch hunters were still a looming threat, the likelihood of another attack so soon was slim. They had to be tired and worn out as well. Going after Ciara, not knowing if the team would show up, would have been too much of a risk for them.

Kellan's frown eased. "You're right."

Liam nodded. Ciara was safe at her flat. She had to be.

The two men didn't say goodbye, but they went their separate ways. Kellan headed back in to see Bill, and Liam headed for the coffee machine.

He was dying for caffeine—or rest. But the latter wasn't an option.

Once he had two brown paper cups filled with coffee, he headed back to his father's hospital room.

Nothing had changed while he had been gone. Polly was asleep in the armchair. Poppy chewed on her nails, sitting on a wooden chair. Their mother and Gabriel sat beside one another on a bench, shoulders hunched.

Sleep and rest would have been better than caffeine. *Time for sleep later, time for caffeine now.* Liam wasn't ready to let himself sleep. After the talk with Kellan, he grew more worried about Ciara.

But the witch hunters had also sustained injuries. They wouldn't attack again so soon. Liam was well aware of the facts, but still, an anxious feeling gnawed at him.

That worry was swiftly replaced by another when their father's breathing changed to almost non-existent. The room filled with the bitter smell of stale coffee as their mother rushed to press the emergency button, her cup spilling onto the floor.

As soon as the alarm sounded, healers and doctors swarmed the room, teleporting inside the room.

Even the most skilled witches and wizards couldn't teleport inside buildings. Not normally. From inside a house, one could teleport outside, but not the other way around. The hospital's staff—healers and doctors—used emergency teleportation devices for that.

Liam hardly noticed when a healer pushed him back. His gaze remained fixed on his father until a throng of doctors and healers blocked his view.

4

Ciara's hands shook. Even if she could free her wrists, she knew she was no match for Jesse. Not with magic or otherwise. Exhaustion had taken over Ciara.

Jesse's fingers released her chin, and she let out a deep sigh, her eyes closing in exhaustion and her head dropping. She never saw it coming when his fist slammed into her face. The sharp pain that coursed through her body added to the already unbearable agony she was experiencing.

She braced herself for the next hit as Jesse's hand shot out once more. But it never came. She felt his fingers dig into her shoulder as he held her steady, preventing her from collapsing onto the floor.

"That's for killing Kyle."

Ciara had never thought of witch hunters as someone's family. But they were. Knowing what it was like to lose someone, she wanted to apologise to Jesse. But she didn't; apologising wouldn't help.

Jesse was going to kill her.

"It's almost funny how your ex-boyfriends have such perfect timings." Jesse couldn't help but chuckle and shake his head at the situation. "I was supposed to poison you the night Liam got wasted at that pub."

It wasn't enough to surprise her anymore. Jesse had been planning her death for so long. She had been blind and naïve, but that was on her. She hadn't seen the signs even when they had been screaming at her face.

"Then this one time," Jesse said, "Theo saw me leaving. You should have seen the look on his face when I told him I was coming to see you. He didn't even know I planned to kill you that day, but still made a big deal out of it. Made a whole scene, and even Elliott got furious."

That name again. Ciara had no idea who Elliott was, but Jesse had already mentioned his name twice.

He had to be important.

Elliott had to be a witch hunter, and Ciara had to tell the others about that. But without magic—and about to die in Jesse's hands—she couldn't.

She would never get to tell anyone anything.

The sky was turning pink and orange and the hues were creeping into the flat through the windows, a sign that the sunrise was nearing. The light was gradually seeping in, casting shadows on the walls. Ciara hoped her team would realise something was amiss. They had to know there were very few things that could stop her from going to see Bill. Her time was running out. Someone had to come to her rescue, or else it would be too late.

Perhaps by the time someone would look for her, Jesse would be long gone. Perhaps no one would ever find out he had been the one to kill her.

Ciara's lip hurt. Likely bust from the punch. She gagged, something itching her throat, as the overpowering stench of blood reached her nostrils.

The smell triggered a rush of images from her past. Ciara's heart pounded as she recalled plunging her knife into Theo's abdomen. The memory of his pained, hurt expression haunted her. It replayed in her mind again and again.

The overpowering taste of vomit flooded Ciara's senses. She barely registered Jesse's next punch. Jesse's fingers tangled in her hair, the blood-stiffened strands pulling painfully.

Was he going to beat her to death?

Perhaps she deserved it for what she had done to Theo. Even if he had been a witch hunter, it was still Theo. Her Theo.

"Thought you would fight back." Jesse's rage-filled demeanour wavered.

"Your cousin didn't." Ciara spat at Jesse's feet. The spit was mixed with blood, and it stained his shoes.

Ciara recognised the pain in her bottom lip, the same pain she had felt when she fell off her bike as a child. As she ran her tongue over her lip, she could feel the split skin.

His fingers curled tightly around the handle of the knife as the unhinged rage returned to his eyes. He used his free hand to lift Ciara from the ground and pressed her against the wall near the kitchen doorway. "Don't talk about him," he growled at her.

It had been a stupid move. Instead of motivating him to kill her right away, she should have been stalling him.

But the night's events left her completely drained. There was no spot on her body that didn't ache. There was only pain, unbearable both mentally and physically.

"You've always had anger issues." Her voice was rough, and her mouth had gone dry. Only the iron taste of blood lingered.

Even when they had dated back in school, Jesse had had odd outbursts. Often out of jealousy. But he had never been violent back then.

"Shut up." He wavered again.

"You thought I liked Liam. Even back when we dated."

"Doesn't matter." His voice remained ruthless, but the rage in his eyes had eased.

Jesse wasn't a killer. Not like Ciara. He hesitated.

Perhaps she still had a chance. If only someone came looking for her...

She prayed Liam would follow her to her flat. She had said horrible things to him. They both had hurt one another. *But maybe, just maybe...*

She didn't think he would actually come.

It seemed she had been right about one thing. She didn't have friends. The people she had called friend had all lied to her.

Nobody had bothered to tell her the truth about Theo being alive.

The only things keeping Ciara standing were Jesse's grip and the wall he had shoved her against. Her legs shook, ready to collapse when given the chance.

"Guess not." Ciara's sigh turned into a wince. "You know, I always thought—"

"Enough!" He realised what she was doing—that she was buying herself more time by reminiscing about their past.

She didn't want to think about the past. Not after all the lies, the violence, and the manipulation. Even Jesse wasn't stupid enough to believe she wanted to talk about their past. Not in the situation they were in.

"You're going to pay," he snarled at her, the insanity returning to his eyes. He gripped the knife so hard his knuckles turned white.

"Do it." Ciara had to tell her team about that name— Elliott. She couldn't die before that. If she encouraged Jesse, perhaps he would hesitate more.

If only for one more moment...

Cold rushed through Ciara's body from her abdomen, pain pulsing where there was a red spot on her shirt.

The blade clattered to the ground, and Jesse released his grip on Ciara. Her legs didn't hold, not even with the wall behind her offering support. She slumped down, knees hitting the cold, hard floor.

Her hand moved to the wound, and warm liquid coated her hand. Warm, like Theo's blood when she had stabbed him.

Had he felt as cold?

She didn't have enough strength to press on the wound. The blood kept spilling out, and all she could do was watch.

She tried to form words, but only whimpers came out.

Jesse stood still. As if frozen. The knife which he had dropped lay on the ground. Bloody.

There was so much blood.

All of it hers.

Only hers.

Her muscles gave in, and she dropped on her side in a pool of her own blood. With the blood loss, she would pass out soon.

Click.

She raised her gaze just enough to see the door fly open. "Hey!" *Kellan.*

Jesse ran. Stepping on her blood and painting his footprints on the floor, he ran out to the balcony.

Ciara couldn't see more than that. Her hand dropped from her wound.

Everything around her was blurry. The voices had to be near, but they sounded quiet enough to come from a mile away.

"Ciara." Definitely Kellan, except his voice rarely reached such a soft tone.

"Elliott," Ciara tried to say. She couldn't feel her lips. Were they even moving?

"Press on the wound!" Another man's voice. Liam? Henry? Someone else?

She couldn't tell, and her vision faded. And finally, darkness embraced her.

5

Liam paced near his father's hospital room. They had forced the family out while the doctors and healers treated Ray. It had already been over an hour, but they still weren't allowed in. A healer had stopped by to say Ray was alive, and that was it.

Liam supposed it was the best they could expect in the situation. The doctors and healers were doing the best they could, even though it didn't feel like it.

"She's been beaten and stabbed by an uncaught, hostile criminal. I will need to remain near her for everyone's safety." The familiar, booming voice filled the corridor.

Liam spun around to see healers, doctors, his brother, and Kellan. In the middle of the chaos was a wheeled stretcher with someone on it.

A woman.

Liam's eyes locked onto her dark hair and bloodstained clothes, and he didn't hesitate to start running beside the stretcher. "W-wha..." He couldn't form words, trying to keep up.

"Henry, stay here and tell him." Kellan didn't leave room for arguments.

Ciara's shirt was soaked with warm, crimson blood that had seeped from her abdomen. She lay there, unmoving and unresponsive. She was so still that it was hard to tell if her chest was rising and falling at all. Her skin was so pale that it appeared almost ghostly to Liam. Except for the red, bloody marks on her wrists.

Someone stabbed her. "Is she—"

Henry's fingers dug into Liam's arm, bringing him to an abrupt stop. Liam tried to wrestle out of his brother's grip. A wave of fear washed over him. He could only watch as Ciara was wheeled off to surgery, surrounded by doctors, healers, and Kellan.

When she was no longer in his sight, all his strength drained out of him. His legs were on the verge of giving out, and every muscle in his body trembled.

He should have gone after her when she had left the house. He could have prevented *that*.

"Liam."

Ciara.

"Liam!"

He faced Henry, who kept repeating his name, but Liam was unable to form words.

"You need to sit down. You look as pale as Ciara." Henry's voice was hoarse, as if he had been screaming.

Liam's imagination ran wild as he envisioned it. His brother screaming for Ciara to wake up. Her blood all over, and not just on her, but all over the flat. A bloody knife abandoned next to her. Even knowing no details, picturing it in his head wasn't hard.

"Was that Ciara?" Poppy asked, her voice shaky, when Henry pushed Liam onto a chair next to the rest of the family.

"Y-yes." Henry had to pause to keep his voice from

breaking. "Someone attacked her."

"Who?" Liam demanded to know, his voice hoarse and his fingers gripping the edge of his seat.

He could have prevented the attack.

"Calm down," Henry said.

"As if you could calm down, either. Tell me what happened!" He didn't mean to raise his voice, but the panic overwhelmed him. With panicked tears streaming down his face, he struggled to see his brother clearly.

"Her ex—"

"Theo."

"No." Henry swallowed as if hesitating. "It...it was...it was Jesse Kingston."

It was like a punch to the gut. Out of everyone, Jesse Kingston?

"He beat and stabbed her. There was *so much blood.*" Henry's voice filled with dread and his eyes widened, as if he was reliving the moment.

"Oh, no. No." Their mother let out a sob, and her eyes watered.

Liam's stomach churned with nausea. He would have dashed for the bathroom if his legs had worked. The news had hit him like a ton of bricks, and he couldn't move a muscle.

Not Ciara. Not her.

For a moment, he thought he would hurl his guts up right then and there. But miraculously, he didn't.

"Kellan is staying with her, so Jesse won't get in here and..." Henry shook his head. "Niles is tracking Jesse but...but he escaped. Jumped from the balcony and teleported mid-air. It looks like he got away. It looks bad."

Liam swore to kill Jesse if he ever got the chance. He wouldn't say it out loud, but that monster would pay with his life.

"I need to tell Jenna," Henry said, and this time his voice broke.

Gabriel jumped up and hugged Henry, who slumped into his younger brother's arms.

Liam didn't feel his hands. Nor his arms or legs. He hardly registered Poppy clinging onto his arm. He couldn't move. Not even to hug his sister.

He had sworn to stay strong, but this was too much for him.

The memory of Ciara's limp body on the stretcher haunted him. He would never get the image out of his mind, no matter how briefly he had seen her. Her hair tangled and stiff with dried blood. Her lip split. There had been blood everywhere. On her clothes, on her skin, her hair.

And a burn mark. Identical to the witch hunters' mark.

Jesse would be dead if Liam ever got his hands on the guy.

Liam wept silently, oblivious to the tears streaming down his face, until his sister's touch brought him back to reality. Poppy brushed away his tears, and he hated himself for not being strong for her.

Not Ciara.

♕♕♕

The moment Liam got the chance to see his father, he rushed in with his family. Except for Henry, who had gone to tell Jenna the bad news.

Liam didn't stay in the room for long. He left the room once he knew his father was okay and ran off to find Ciara. After sneaking past a healer, he found Kellan outside an operating room.

"She's still in surgery."

"H-how bad is it?" Liam glanced at the doors behind Kellan. There were no windows—which was good. He wished to never see Ciara in that state again.

"Bad." Kellan's voice lowered, and the worry shone through.

Liam closed his eyes. If Kellan showed his worry, it had

to be a new level of bad. "And Niles…"

"He's searching around Ciara's flat. Declan is with Bill since he can't go out in the field. He's still recovering from the incident at the manor. Owen is doing research, and he's supposed to stay in contact with our American colleagues."

Liam opened his eyes. "Like Josh?"

Kellan nodded. "Yeah. River is with another team. They're searching Jesse's gym and flat."

"Nothing so far then."

Kellan was silent for a moment before he sighed, defeat painted on his face. "Nothing so far."

Cold rushed through Liam, seeping into his heart. Liam had let Ciara leave on her own. He had known where she was. Had known something was off when she hadn't shown up at the hospital.

And worst of all, her last thoughts of him had to be about how he had pushed her away. How he had hurt her. Lied to her.

He was no better than Theo.

Liam couldn't help but wonder if that monster had had something to do with Jesse's actions. If they both were witch hunters, they had to know one another.

Liam's hands tightened into fists. "Was Theo there?"

"No. But we have one more name."

"A witch hunter?"

"No idea." Kellan's brows knitted together. "Does the name *Elliott* say anything?"

"No," Liam said and looked at the operating room's door, hoping the operation would end soon. "Ciara said something about an Elliott?"

"Just before she passed out. It's the only thing she said." Kellan's hardened expression flashed with pain, but he hurriedly re-fixed the mask he always wore—a calm and calculated expression.

Liam opened his mouth to tell Kellan that Ciara would tell more when she woke up. But then the realisation sunk in.

There was no guarantee Ciara would ever wake up.

Ciara shuddered. Cold pulsed in her veins, and her entire body ached.

"Elliott." It was her own voice, echoing in her head. But her lips moved this time.

Someone's breath hitched, but it wasn't her.

She opened her eyes but saw nothing. Darkness swam in her vision. Her mind was like a puzzle. She struggled to fit the pieces together. Some pieces were missing.

"Hey." A soft male voice.

Not Jesse. Not him. No. Panic rushed through her, and something pressed on her chest. Her fingers clutched onto something.

Something warm.

"Ouch." Same voice.

But it wasn't Jesse's.

She blinked, and the darkness faded into mist. It was like fog clouding her vision. Like a veil over her eyes. She couldn't quite make out whose hand she was holding. All she saw was a silhouette.

"Next time, don't stab me."

Impossible.

"Theo?" Her hoarse voice nearly broke.

He shushed her and caressed the back of her hand. "Everything's okay."

Her cheeks became wet. Tears, maybe. "Am I dead?"

"No."

She wanted to roll her eyes. Instead, she closed them as a surge of pain rushed through her.

"I'm sorry," he said.

"*No.* I'm sorry. I...I..." She couldn't say it out loud, no matter how much she wanted to apologise for stabbing him.

He shushed her again. "I know."

She opened her eyes again, and this time she could make out his face. The olive skin, the grey eyes, all of it. Fresh tears blurred her vision.

He was alive, and she couldn't believe it.

"Jesse said—"

"We don't have to talk about it." His voice remained soft, but there was a strain this time. Anger boiling somewhere deep within him. He tried to keep it there, so she wouldn't see.

But she saw right through his façade.

Ciara didn't want to talk about Jesse either. She blinked, and her vision cleared again. She couldn't trust her sight. Theo was still standing there, holding her hand.

"What happened?" she asked.

"You're in the hospital."

Henry... She had heard his voice. And Kellan's. They had saved her.

Unless it was all a dream.

She had stabbed Theo, but still he stood there as if nothing had happened. It couldn't have been *that* long since the ambush at the warehouse.

"But if you're here..." It couldn't be real. If she was at the hospital—where her team was too—Theo couldn't be there. The team would have caught him.

It was a hallucination. Her imagination.

Theo was dead.

⚜ ⚜ ⚜

Ciara's eyes snapped open, and panic soared through her.

Theo!

"Whoa there!"

Ciara's head spun. Still, she tried to get up.

Only to be stopped. Fingers tightened around her forearms, and her mind started screaming at her, telling her to get out. To free herself.

I have to get out or I'll die.

"Ciara!"

She blinked, her eyes focusing on the man in the room. Not Theo. Not Jesse.

Her muscles gave in. Without his hold on her, she would have collapsed back onto her back. "Kellan," she breathed out, exhaustion hitting her like an asteroid.

Kellan eased her back down. "You're safe."

Safe. A surge of the opposite feeling hit her, and her eyes widened. "Jesse! Is he—"

"We won't stop looking for him." Kellan's blue eyes turned icier, and it wasn't just the colour.

They hadn't caught Jesse.

"I..." Ciara's throat closed, and it took every bit of her strength to utter out the next words. "He's a witch hunter."

She still couldn't believe it. She had gone to him for comfort when she had been struggling with adjusting to her life in England. Jesse had been a friend—an escape for her. She couldn't believe how stupid she had been.

Her own judgment had betrayed her. She had betrayed herself. She had more or less handed herself over to the enemy—to Jesse.

"You okay?"

32

"No." Ciara's voice broke, and she raised her hands shakily to her eyes. Kellan didn't need to see the tears that started rolling down her face. She didn't want his pity.

"Stop that." Firmness and gentleness mixed in his voice. He brushed his fingers against hers before prying her hands away from her face. "You've been through a lot and more. If I were you, Ciara, I'd be a mess."

She sniffled. "I am a mess." Her voice broke, and she cursed herself in her mind for it.

She was enough of a mess to have hallucinated Theo. The man she had once loved, had lost, and had, in the end, killed with her own knife.

"Not compared to what you've been through." Kellan shook his head, lips thinning into a line.

Ciara looked up at the ceiling. The bright lights and the white colour of the ceiling mixed into a blur that made her squint. Her head ached, and so did most of her muscles.

"What time is it?"

"The next morning. You were out for one whole day."

"Was Henry with you?" She could have sworn she had heard Henry before she had passed out the previous morning when they had found her. Had it been a hallucination too?

"Yes."

She sighed. She wished Henry wouldn't have seen her that way—covered in her own blood.

"How bad was it?"

Kellan flinched, and for a moment, remnants of panic washed over his face. "*Bad.*" That voice wasn't his usual one; it was rawer and scratchier.

He had been worried.

"That bad then." Ciara closed her eyes, a wave of drowsiness washing over. Like a wave, trying to drown her in the sea of sleep. After all the horrors, even the hospital bed's mattress felt nice and welcoming.

"You're tired."

"Wait." Her voice was fading. She blinked, trying to keep

her eyes open. But fighting the sleep became harder and harder.

"I'll be here when you wake up."

"No, Kellan. I must tell you about..." It was like a fog creeping over her mind. "Jesse said...Elliott..."

"Who is he?"

"He's..."

"Who?" Kellan's voice grew louder, echoing inside Ciara's head.

She tried to utter out another word, but it was too late. The exhaustion won.

⁂

"Fuck you, Kellan! I'm going to see her now."

The door slammed open, and the bang startled Ciara. She bolted up, pain shooting through her. She yelped out, her hand flying to her abdomen, as she watched two men turn to her.

"Ciara!" Henry rushed to her side. "What are you doing up? Stay on your back!" He helped her lie back down, the pain in her abdomen increasing momentarily.

"Hi, Henry." A smile crossed her lips.

He didn't smile back. Like he hadn't that day back in Seattle—when he had come looking for her.

But it wasn't shock on his face. It was pain. His face was drained of blood, and he had dark circles under his eyes. If it had been Halloween, someone could have easily mistaken him for a man in a corpse costume.

"Your Dad and Jenna—"

Henry shushed Ciara. "Jenna will be fine. All you need to worry about is yourself."

"And Bill—" Ciara's eyes shifted to Kellan, who stood near the door.

Kellan's lips pursed together, and he hesitated to say anything.

"No—"

"He's not dead."

The solemness in Kellan's eyes was enough to tell it wasn't good news. Bill wasn't dead *yet*.

Henry brushed Ciara's hair off her face, and she realised the strands were sticking to her skin. First, her heart jumped, remembering the sticky feeling of her own blood mixed in her hair. But it was just sweat that covered her forehead.

"What were you two fighting about?" Her throat ached a little. She tried to wet her tongue, but her mouth was dry.

"Nothing of importance," Henry said and reached for something on the table beside the hospital bed. A glass of water. He helped Ciara take a sip, and she hoped she would never have to live through a moment like that again. She had never been so helpless. It was humiliating.

"Who's Elliott?" Kellan asked.

"Not now." Henry's words were a hiss, and he narrowed his eyes at Kellan.

"No, Henry, it's important." Ciara shuddered. She couldn't tell if it was from the cold or from the memory of what had happened.

"What's important is your wellbeing."

"Elliott is the name of a witch hunter," Ciara said, ignoring Henry's comment. "I think he's important. Jesse kept talking about him and..." Her breath caught in her throat.

Not again. Even thinking about Jesse made her mind a blur of memories. He had been planning his attack for so long. She kept thinking back to any signs she should have noticed. There had been so many.

"Ciara!"

Henry's voice pulled her back to reality. She raised her gaze, locking eyes with him. "I'm fine."

"No, you're not. You went through hell."

What had happened with Jesse invaded Ciara's mind first. But the physical pain was nothing compared to the anguish in her heart. For a second, it felt like someone was crushing her lungs.

"I stabbed him," she rasped out.

"Jesse?" Henry asked.

Ciara shook her head, eyes burning and tears building up. "N-no."

"What do you..." It didn't take him longer than that to fall silent, realisation dawning on him. "Oh, Ciara."

Even Kellan's face twisted in pity.

She had killed Theo—her fiancé.

7

The healers and doctors walked in and out, running tests on Ciara. Exhaustion blurred her mind. She was too tired to even acknowledge all the doctors and healers coming in and going out.

They had given her painkillers. The pills didn't kill the real pain, though. She had been stabbed before. She had been shot, cursed, and many other things. None of that was new, and she could get through that. But getting through what really hurt was impossible.

Ciara had stabbed Theo to save the people who had lied to her. They—the people closest to her, all of them—had lied to her for months.

"Miss. Miss. Miss!"

She snapped out of her thoughts, gaze settling on the healer. "Y-yes?" Her mouth had gone dry again.

The healer smiled. She tried to appear friendly, but the pity shone through.

Ciara hated it.

"We are done with the tests. Everything seems to be in order for now. The medicine should speed up the healing, but you must remain on bed rest."

"When can I go see my friend?" She wanted to see Bill. Whatever Theo had done to Bill, it was bad.

"Not today."

"Tomorrow?"

"Maybe."

Ciara sighed in defeat. "Okay, thanks."

She hated hospitals. And more than anything, she hated being trapped in the wretched hospital bed.

"Let me see her!"

Ciara's eyes snapped open. She reached for her knife until she realised it wasn't there. She was in the hospital, wearing stupid hospital clothes, trapped in a stupid hospital bed.

She wasn't home.

But she was safe.

"If she asks for you—"

"You know that won't happen!" The desperation cracked in Liam's voice.

For a split second, she wanted to ask him in. She was dying for the comfort—for Liam's arms wrapped around her. For so long, he had been her rock. She had never needed someone to lean on so badly.

But Liam had lied to her about Theo. Liam *and* everyone else.

"Walk away." It was Kellan, who Liam was talking to on the other side of the door.

"I just need to see her!"

The door opened, and Liam rushed in. Kellan was about to grab Liam, but they both halted at the door.

Ciara's eyes met Liam's exhausted gaze.

He looked worse than Henry, with his hair all over the

place. His skin was pale like a ghost's, and he had dark circles under his eyes, aging him by ten years. He still wore the same clothes—the ones he had worn at the warehouse.

Ciara's throat tightened. Her eyes travelled back up to meet his gaze. His eyes were glassy, as if he had been crying—or as if he was about to burst into tears.

They were both tired and hurt. Ciara wanted to excuse Liam's earlier actions. Neither one of them had the energy to fight.

"Are you okay?" he asked, voice almost cracking. He still cared, and Ciara wanted to forgive him everything, but she wasn't ready.

"I'm fine."

"No, you're not."

She had to bite her tongue. Liam had no right to read her like that. He had broken her heart enough times.

"Time for you to go," Kellan said to Liam.

Liam shot a sharp glare at Kellan and turned his attention back to Ciara.

Her heart broke, seeing him in such despair. She wanted to ask about his father. Henry had refused to talk about it when she had asked. She wanted to tell Liam everything would be okay. And even more so, she wanted to hug him—cling onto him and never let go.

"Liam, go," she said and looked down. "I'm fine."

"Ciara—"

"You heard her. Get out," Kellan said.

"I just need a minute," Liam pleaded.

Ciara wanted to ask him how he was, but she already knew the answer. He wasn't fine. No one was after everything they had been through because of the witch hunters.

"You saw her. She's fine. Now get out," Kellan said.

Ciara didn't have to look up to know Liam had left the room. The door closed behind him, leaving Ciara alone with Kellan.

"Have you found anything? About the witch hunter?

Elliott?" Ciara asked and looked up.

Kellan shook his head. "Stop thinking about work."

"I can't. It's not just work, and you know that."

"It's personal for you."

"They tried to kill me in my flat. My home, Kellan!" Ciara clenched her jaw. "Jesse had been planning my death for months."

"I'm sorry you had to go through that." His voice softened, and for a moment, he didn't sound like himself. "The night before yesterday...I can't even imagine all the things you went through. And not just with Jesse."

"I killed my fiancé. You can say it out loud. It's not like I could stop thinking about it for more than a split second, anyway."

"I'm so sorry."

"You should have told me. At least one of you should have." Ciara shook her head. "Did everyone know?"

"Pretty much."

"Bill?"

"I had to tell them before the mission. They didn't know until Monday." That was the day of the mission. That night they had fought witch hunters at the warehouse.

"But my friends did, didn't they?" Ciara said.

"I think so."

Henry, Jenna, Shawn, Hugo, Mary, Ray... They all had known, and no one had told her.

"How is everyone?" Ciara asked Kellan. "Bill..."

"He's the same. Alive, just barely. It's not exactly a coma. This is worse. It's like a killing curse, but it kills slowly. Like some poison or..." Kellan sighed. "The doctors can't do anything to help him."

"And Ray?"

"You should ask Henry."

"He won't tell me."

"It's bad, Ciara."

"How bad?" she demanded to know, nausea building up.

"He's in a coma."

Coma? It explained everything. How Henry was so distressed. And Liam too.

For a split second, Ciara wished she hadn't pushed Liam away. He was going through a lot, and she wanted to be there for him. But she had a feeling he wanted more. Her forgiveness. Ciara wasn't ready to give that yet.

She needed a moment to find her voice again. "And Iris?"

"She's getting better, I believe."

Ciara nodded. She had a headache brewing, and the news only made it worse.

She would have killed for a cigarette and a bottle of whiskey. It had been weeks since the last time she had smoked, but a lot had changed in less than two days.

Her eyes burned thinking about it, but she didn't let the tears break through the surface. She had cried enough.

Theo's grey eyes flashed in her mind, and she flinched. The hurt in his eyes—when she had stabbed him—played on repeat inside her head, and she didn't have the stop button. Not even the pause button.

Estella—Theo's mother—deserved to know. Ciara owed her an explanation. But how could she tell Estella what had happened? There was no right way to tell a mother that her presumedly dead son had been alive after all. Only for his fiancée to kill him.

As if reading her, Kellan started talking. "I didn't choose to hide the truth from you, Ciara. About Theo, I mean."

"I don't want to talk about him." Her voice wavered, but she steeled herself and refused to break down. "I stabbed him so we could get out of there. I won't make the same mistake twice because I can't."

Kellan was silent for a moment before he said, "I would never expect you to."

She should have been faster. Her hesitation had cost too much. Bill was dying because of her. Everyone could have walked out of there in perfect condition if she had gone with

Theo.

She had blood on her hands. The kind that could never be washed off.

"Ciara!" Jenna rushed in, but she couldn't quite run. The awkward hospital robes hung on her body like they did on Ciara's, a reminder of their injuries and of the nightmare they both had gone through.

Jenna's arms enveloped Ciara in a tight hug. For a split second, the sudden warmth of Jenna's arms comforted her, but then the image of Theo tainted it. He had been that close to her when she had stabbed him.

Jesse had been that close when he had stabbed her.

Ciara panicked and pushed Jenna away.

"Ciara—"

"I'm sorry." Ciara's eyes widened, and she raised her gaze up to meet Jenna's. "I..."

"It's okay." Jenna's face told enough. She knew something was wrong.

It was a new day. Ciara had been on the edge all morning. As if Jesse would run in and kill her, even though Kellan and River had been at her room's door the whole time. They wouldn't let anyone suspicious pass them. They had even checked most of the healers and doctors before allowing them to walk in.

Ciara was safe. Still, her heart jumped at every sudden sound.

If nothing else, Jesse had taken away a part of her. The part that got through everything on her own.

Shortly after Jenna's arrival, Henry came in with his mother and younger siblings. It took everything in Ciara not to push the twins away when the girls hugged her. Mary hugged Ciara and burst out crying—over Ray and everything that had happened.

Mary had lost two of her friends the night of the mission. The witch hunters had killed Eric and Hannah.

⚜ ⚜ ⚜

After the Rosslers and Jenna left, Kellan walked in. He looked Ciara up and down, which she hated. The hospital robes were far from glamorous and did nothing to improve her mood.

Kellan sat on the chair next to the hospital bed. "You look tired."

"Thanks. What a compliment."

"You seem more like yourself today." Kellan paused. "But I think the mission and what happened at your flat left wounds. And I don't mean the physical kind."

Ciara's mask had never wavered the way it had after the warehouse mission. "I don't know if I can continue the fight."

Hurt flashed in Kellan's eyes. "They poisoned Theo's mind. They—"

"Don't say his name," Ciara pleaded. She didn't care how weak Kellan thought she was. Not anymore. He had already seen her at her worst.

"I'm sorry."

Ciara shivered and wrapped her arms around herself. Ciara wondered if she was imagining the sudden drop in temperature—if her mind played tricks on her again. "I can't continue."

"Do you want to quit? I can get you another position in another department or—"

"No." Ciara's brows furrowed. "I don't know."

Kellan sighed. "We will *all* take time off. After everything that happened...we need that." He paused, eyes trailing down, so he was no longer facing Ciara. "We can talk about work matters later. Weeks from now."

"Okay."

She wasn't in the state to make decisions. The witch hunters deserved to be washed off the face of the world, and she wanted to keep fighting. But after everything, how could she?

She hadn't even seen the signs with Jesse. She needed to step up her game if she wanted to keep working as a hit witch. If she didn't even notice crucial details when they were flashing right in front of her, how could she notice subtle details on a mission where lives were at risk?

Kellan's voice pulled her away from her thoughts. "Do you need therapist appointments?"

"No!" Ciara forced herself to sit up, even though pain shot through her abdomen.

"Ciara." Kellan's voice had a stern edge to it, and his eyes narrowed ever so slightly.

"No." Ciara shook her head, her long hair swaying with the movement. "All I need is time. Talking to a stranger won't help me."

"But—"

"I'll tell you if I change my mind." And that was the end of it.

Kellan sighed. "Think about it. For real. After what Theresa did and..."

Ciara gritted her teeth. *That bitch.* Her name made Ciara see red. Theresa was as much a traitor as Jesse was.

"We all trusted her."

"We shouldn't have," Ciara hissed.

"It's too late for that now."

Kellan was right. Of course he was. They had already made the mistake, and it was too late to fix it. The witch hunters had the upper hand. They were one step ahead, as they always had been.

"But I swear it was the last time something like this happens." Kellan's voice was laced with fiery determination. "Not even one witch hunter will get in from now on. I'll ensure it myself. I already have a full-on search inside the entire department. From now on, our recruits will go through dozens of tests to prove their loyalty. No spy will get through."

Ciara's fingers brushed against Kellan's broad shoulder as she reached out to touch him. "A few days of rest wouldn't hurt you, either."

Kellan was the glue of the team, even if he wasn't officially part of it anymore. He was the cornerstone of the department, holding everything and everyone together. He was so focused on taking care of others that he often neglected his own needs.

Ciara had had her moments when she had despised him. But he was a lot like her. Stubborn and annoying to no end. She wouldn't hold that against him. As long as his heart was in the right place.

He was doing his best. That was enough.

"Do you want to go see Bill?" Kellan asked.

Liam walked out of his father's hospital room, desperate for a break. Not that the corridor full of people was much better. But it was taking all he had not to break in front of his family.

It took all his willpower to stay away from Ciara, too. He was dying to see her. But despite his desire to see her, he understood she needed space.

There was one place Liam could go to. He headed to see Iris.

His breath hitched when his eyes met a familiar set of blue eyes the moment he stepped into the room. "You're awake."

Iris smiled. Weakly, but at least it was a smile. "Yeah, I'm awake."

Liam's gaze moved to the middle-aged couple sitting beside the bed. Iris's parents—Elijah and Lydia Lamont. "Mr and Mrs Lamont," he said in greeting.

As Mrs Lamont stood up, the sound of her chair scraping against the floor filled the room. She smiled warmly at Liam and hugged him. "It's Lydia and Elijah to you, Liam."

He hadn't seen Iris's parents after their break-up. Not even when he had lived with Iris for a little while.

"We'll let you two talk," Elijah said, smiling at Liam first and then turning to his daughter.

"We'll be right back, sweetie," Lydia said to Iris before she and Elijah walked out.

Liam settled into the wooden chair with a creak, eyes locking with Iris's. "I'm glad you're awake."

Although Iris smiled, the fatigue in her eyes was evident. "I feel better."

"You kept passing out."

"So I heard." Iris shuddered. "I barely remember it, though."

"I'm sorry—"

Iris raised her hand to silence Liam. "No. If you're going to apologise or say this is your fault, stop. The only ones to blame are the witch hunters."

"In hindsight, a lot should have been done differently."

Iris reached out and squeezed Liam's hand tightly. "All is good now."

But that wasn't true.

As Iris's eyes darkened, her smile faded into a frown. "Or not? What's wrong? Is it your dad?"

"He's in a coma." When Liam talked, it was like he was running out of air. As if the words tried to block his airways.

Iris's hand instinctively flew to her mouth as tears welled up in her eyes. "Oh, my…I'm so sorry, Liam. I didn't…"

"The doctors are doing what they can." The tears threatened to spill again, but Liam kept blinking to try and force them away.

"A-and everyone else? How is everyone?"

"Mum, Polly, Poppy, Gabe, and Henry are all shaken, but physically fine. Jenna is recovering. Shawn and Hugo are fine. But Bill is…" Liam hesitated. "The doctors said he's somewhere between death and coma. I don't know how that's even possible, but he's slipping."

"A-and Ciara?"

Liam winced at the name.

Iris's eyes widened. "Is she okay?"

"Jesse Kingston tried to kill her." Liam's head spun as another wave of rage washed over him. "She's awake now, but for a while it looked…bad. They thought she wouldn't make it."

"Jesse Kingston. Her ex? Why would he…"

"He's a witch hunter."

For a moment, Iris remained silent, eyes still wide in horror. "She must be in shock."

"I…I don't know. She refuses to talk to me."

"She's your girlfriend."

"Not anymore." Liam grimaced. "She broke up with me. For lying to her. A-and she had every right to."

"I'm sorry."

Unsure of what to say, Liam simply nodded.

"Maybe she'll forgive you. It just takes a little time." Iris took Liam's hand in hers. "You were trying to protect her from Theo, that's all."

"She doesn't think so."

"Make her see your reasons."

"I'll try."

After seeing Theo kill Doherty, Liam had tried to tell himself it hadn't been real. That it hadn't been Theo, but someone else. But he had known, and he should have told Ciara, despite knowing how much the truth would hurt.

Theo was a witch hunter. He had killed many people. Someone like him didn't deserve Ciara's affection.

Liam's thoughts drifted back to Ciara and his father, his mood turning sour.

Her fingers quivered as she reached out to grab the doorknob, her breaths becoming shallow. Kellan was faster and opened the hospital door. He let her walk in first.

Someone had dimmed the lights in the room. The entire team was there—Bill on the bed and the others standing near his bed—but no one talked. Silence hung thick in the air. With so many people, the small room became suffocating.

The team—River, Declan, Owen, Niles—turned to face Ciara. She knew what they saw—puffy eyes, dark circles, and messy hair.

Bill lay motionless on the bed like a statue. His face colourless and eyes closed. His breathing uneven. The dark brown strands of his hair fell on the pillow. If Ciara hadn't heard his breaths in the silent room, she could have mistaken him for dead.

Seeing him like that was enough to make Ciara's blood boil. Theo had hurt Bill, and Ciara hated it.

But she wasn't sure she could hate Theo.

Ciara shifted her gaze from Bill to the rest of her team. She had no words.

River walked up to Ciara, surprising her when his warm, brown arms encircled her. But she returned the gesture, needing the comfort.

To her surprise, she didn't panic this time, even though River was close to her, hugging her. Being so close to anyone had been hard since the mission, and it still wasn't easy. It helped to realise that River needed the hug more than she did.

One by one, each team member hugged her. Declan, Niles, and Owen.

River stayed by Ciara's side, but the others retreated to their former spots.

Bill had been her closest friend on the team, followed by Theresa. She didn't have either by her side anymore. Bill was barely alive, and Theresa had turned out to be a witch hunter.

She couldn't wrap her head around how fast everything had changed. She had woken up in Liam's arms on Monday. It felt like weeks instead of a few days.

It wasn't the first time Ciara had been in a hospital room, watching a colleague slip away. Die.

This time, she prayed for a miracle. She always wished for one, but this time, she *needed* it. Bill was too important. She had let him become more than a team member. She knew she shouldn't have, but somehow Bill had done it—had become dear to her. Like any of her friends. Like Henry or Jenna—if they still were her friends after all the lies.

Bill's forehead shone with sweat. Some of his hair stuck to his skin. His face was twisted in discomfort, far from the peaceful look she had hoped to see.

When Ciara found the strength to talk, she asked what the doctors had told the team to make sure she hadn't missed anything. But there wasn't much to know. The doctors didn't know what was wrong with Bill, and therefore couldn't heal him.

Theo could have. That gnawed at Ciara's heart. If Theo had somehow survived...

She shuddered, even daring to think about that. She had stabbed him. But she hadn't seen his final breath. Just maybe...

She shook off all hope, refusing to let herself believe he was alive. Hope would only break her apart.

Ciara stayed in Bill's hospital room for hours, even though her original plan had been a quick visit. One by one, the team members left. Only Kellan stayed with her.

"Do you feel better?"

"No."

Kellan nodded.

"I need Bill." Her voice cracked. A habit she had to get rid of around Kellan.

"We all need him." Kellan placed a hand on her shoulder, giving a comforting squeeze.

"Theo did this." The words clung to her throat like spikes.

"I don't think it brings you any joy, but you got revenge then."

Ciara laughed in her head—but not out loud. She had tried to avenge Theo's death. Instead, she had killed him and avenged Bill's fate.

Ciara was hesitant to leave Bill alone. Knowing he was with someone soothed her.

"W-what about Bill's family?" Ciara asked when she and Kellan walked out of the darkened room.

"He doesn't have any."

"W-what? None?"

She knew that Bill's parents had been murdered, but she had assumed that he had someone—an uncle, an aunt, a cousin, a grandparent, or anyone.

"I think the team is the closest thing to a family he has."

"And we'll be there for him."

"Until the end."

Ciara closed her eyes. "He's not..." She couldn't form the word. Not out loud.

Dead.

But they both knew Bill was dying.

After visiting Bill, Ciara and Kellan stopped by at Ray's room. Only Mary was there. The younger Rosslers and Liam were home resting, and Henry kept Jenna company.

Seeing Ray—pale and still—lay on the bed made everything snap into place. New determination filled Ciara. She found a new reason to fight.

Theo wasn't killed by witch hunters; he was one himself. And he was dead. The revenge for his *death* had been in vain.

But that didn't mean the witch hunters would go unpunished. The MPG—Magical Protection Group—had lost two people because of them. More people were still fighting for their lives.

The witch hunters would regret ever laying a finger on any of them.

Liam had called Ciara's colleagues. He had helped with the search. He had worked on his own and with some of the hit wizards from Ciara's team.

They couldn't find Jesse. No matter how hard they tried, he was nowhere to be found.

He had jumped off Ciara's balcony and teleported. No one had seen him since.

Perhaps it was a good thing. Liam was going to end Jesse's life if he ever saw the bastard again. Jesse deserved a lot worse after what he had done to Ciara.

Liam wouldn't rest until Jesse got what he deserved. He was going to spend every minute he had to spare searching for that man.

Liam's twin sisters, Polly and Poppy, and his brother Gabriel didn't go back to school when the Christmas break was over. They were allowed to stay home a little longer, considering their father's state.

Their mother took time off, too. Mary went to the hospital every day, just not for work.

Jenna got to go home after a week, and Henry stayed

home with her.

They released Ciara from the hospital too, but Liam didn't know about her whereabouts. They didn't allow anyone to enter her flat, as it was still a crime scene.

Iris was still in the hospital two weeks after the warehouse mission. She had fallen in short-term coma twice after waking up, so the doctors were keeping her under their watch until they were sure it was safe for her to go home.

Liam's father didn't get any better, but he also didn't get any worse. It was an endless but steady nightmare.

Bill's state hadn't improved either. He was stuck in his near-death state, hanging in there. His heart had crashed once, but the doctors had brought him back.

Liam went to see Bill rarely. He didn't know Bill that well, and Ciara was often there, visiting Bill. Liam saw her almost every time he went to the hospital.

She didn't bother to even acknowledge Liam, so they didn't talk. He was dying to at least hear her voice, but he kept his distance.

Even after a month, Ciara still avoided Liam. According to Henry, she had distanced herself from him as well. But Henry had at least had a chance to apologise.

Shawn and Hugo had apologised too when they had seen her at the hospital.

But Liam never got the chance to explain and tell her how sorry he was.

After the month had passed, Liam was back at work, but he stopped by at the hospital every day. Even though he could have found a flat for himself, he stayed with his mother at the family house. Otherwise, Mary would have been alone because the younger children had returned to school.

They released Iris from the hospital, but she wasn't ready to go back to work. She had asked Liam to move back in with her. He had declined, and she understood.

A month after the warehouse mission that had ended badly, Mary was working again. She usually had shorter workdays, but it was better than nothing. Work was an excellent distraction, or so she told Liam.

That became Liam's everyday life. Sleeping, working, seeing his dad at the hospital, going home with his mum, calling Henry, eating, trying to find Jesse to make him pay, sleeping.

But the worst part was that Ray wasn't getting any better. There wasn't a glimmer of hope in sight.

9

Ciara's phone buzzed the second she stepped out to the street to go for a walk. It was a message from Henry. He was asking her to stop by at an address he had sent. An address Ciara didn't recognise.

She had barely talked with Henry recently. He had apologised for not telling the truth about Theo, but she still had trust issues.

Out of all the people, Henry should have backed her up. But Liam was Henry's brother, and family came first.

Ciara had been staying at a safe house of sorts. It was luxurious, even though she didn't have to pay a penny for it. It even had a home gym. Not that Ciara could use it yet.

She had used the bar in the kitchen more.

Ciara stared at her phone screen and sighed. Henry was going through a lot. Even if she was, too, he deserved to have his best friend there for him. Especially after how horribly she had left him once—when she had left England and moved to America. He had still been there for her after that.

Perhaps he had been a horrible friend for lying, but she had also been a horrible friend in the past. Ciara had come back in June, and it was February. She had only meant to visit, but it looked like she was staying for good.

She texted Henry back, telling him she was on her way. With a wave of her hand and by concentrating on the address, she teleported.

It was harder to teleport to places you hadn't been to before, but Ciara found the right place.

The Creature Sanctuary of England. A sign with those words hung above huge metal gates—the entrance to the sanctuary. Walls surrounded the area to keep the creatures inside—and to keep non-magics out. It was the biggest creature sanctuary in England, as far as Ciara knew. Henry and Jenna worked there. Henry was a creature trainer, and Jenna worked in research.

But Ciara had no idea why Henry would want to meet her there. They could have met after his workday was over. Ciara had never—not once—visited Henry at work. Especially after the recent events, it was odd to be there. Their friendship wasn't the same. It had been through a lot in the past, but the recent events had been like an axe cutting halfway through their bond.

Nothing was the same anymore.

Ciara walked closer to the metal gates, through the half-empty parking area. She wasn't sure if any witch or wizard actually drove to work or if the cars were there just for a show for the non-magics.

Before Ciara even made it to the enormous gates, they opened. It was Henry, coming to get her.

He smiled when he saw Ciara. "You ready to see Roan?"

Ciara's eyes widened, and a small smile played at the corners of her lips. "Roan is here?"

"Yes."

She hadn't seen the dragon in months. "Of course, I want to see him!"

Henry chuckled—something he hadn't done in a while. Not with everything going on. And Ciara smiled, knowing he could forget the terrors. Even if it was for only a moment.

She couldn't. The terrors followed her to the depths of her mind.

She followed Henry, her hand coming up to her neck where she had a necklace. Or rather, a ring hanging off a chain. It was her engagement ring. She had started wearing it after Theo's *actual* death.

No one had heard anything about the witch hunters. People, even in the States and in Canada, had been keeping an extra careful eye in case someone spotted Theo anywhere in the world.

But he was gone. She had killed him. Otherwise, he would have shown up already.

Estella didn't know. She had tried to call Ciara once, but Ciara hadn't been able to answer the phone. Not after killing Estella's son.

Henry led Ciara in. Within the creature sanctuary's walls, creatures could roam free. But only the harmless ones. Some of them could fly, though, and Ciara wondered how they didn't escape.

Of course, Henry had an answer. There was a shield enchantment keeping them inside the walls—for everyone's good. The shield spell also made sure non-magics couldn't get in. They couldn't even see inside.

Any non-magic would freak out if they saw an adult dragon flying around and breathing fire. That was why revealing the magical world to a non-magic was illegal and punishable.

There was a path leading up to an enormous building. It crossed through the lands where the harmless creatures roamed free, running around, lying in the sun and what not.

Walking past a purple ostrich-like creature with horns, Ciara asked, "How's Jenna?"

"I can take you to her office, so you can ask her." Henry

stopped for a second and patted another ostrich-like creature. This one was green but otherwise like the purple one.

"Jenna's working already?" That brought a smile to Ciara's face, but it didn't reach her eyes. One victory couldn't erase all the loss.

"Since Monday. But today is her first full day back."

Ciara didn't recognise all the creatures roaming around the grounds. They had been taught about creatures in school, but she didn't remember everything. She was no Henry. She loved creatures, but they weren't her passion like they were Henry's.

For once, she also didn't feel like asking about the creatures. Something was broken between her and Henry. Repairing that lost bond was going to take time.

"A-are you going to the hospital today?" Ciara wasn't sure if she should have asked.

"After work."

Ciara placed a hand on Henry's shoulder, and they stopped walking. "How are you, Henry?"

They hadn't talked recently. It was mostly Ciara's fault, and she regretted leaving her best friend like that. She would have to figure out a way to hang out with him and Jenna. A movie night perhaps.

She just needed a little time. Henry and Jenna had known about Theo too, and neither had told Ciara the truth. They had broken her trust—just like the others—and broken things weren't easy to mend.

Henry cleared his throat. "I've been better. But with Jenna recovering so fast, it's a little easier."

Ciara nodded. Henry needed a break from looking after everyone.

"A-and you? Knowing *he* is..."

"Knowing I killed Theo at the warehouse?" Ciara's voice trembled with emotion. Henry knew about what she had done already, but they hadn't talked about it. "Or knowing he was a witch hunter?"

Henry pulled Ciara into an embrace, surprising her. "You should have never had to go through that."

"People were dying. I had to do something." Ciara kept her voice stern. A mask to keep her from breaking. "It's done and in the past. Now I have to find a way to tell Estella."

Henry pulled away, releasing Ciara from the hug. "You were just prote—"

Ciara raised her hand to cut Henry off. "I know, but it doesn't help." Her eyes glistened with fresh tears, but she wiped them off as if they were boiling water on her skin. "He chose his side. A-and I chose mine. I chose other people over him, and I'll have to live with that."

"Do you regret it?"

Ciara stared at him, the only sounds coming from the surrounding creatures. Meows, roars, and weird squeaks.

"I wish there had been another way."

"I'm sorry."

"Not your fault." *But you should have never lied to me.*

Henry gestured to the building as if to ask if they should keep going, and Ciara nodded.

"When will you go back to work?" His eyes moved between her and the path ahead.

The two of them halted in their steps to give way to a galloping, golden brown creature that reminded Ciara of a lion but that moved more like a horse. Watching the creature's fur glitter in the sunlight made her realise how fascinating Henry's job had to be.

She had known his job was fascinating to begin with, but she had never witnessed it firsthand.

They continued to walk, and Ciara glanced at Henry. "Kellan is back. But with Bill's condition and everything, he doesn't think the team is ready to go back. For once, I don't mind."

"You lost your reason to fight."

"For a moment, I did. But I think I found a new one."

Ciara looked around the field filled with stunning creatures. Animals—or creatures, as magical animals were called— had a calming effect on people. "The witch hunters won't get away with what they've done. To Bill, to your father, to Jenna, to Iris. They killed Hannah and Eric, and they've killed many more. One day they'll regret it."

Henry hummed as if agreeing. "The group can help."

"We'll be fine without the group, especially for now. If we need you, we'll ask for help. But you should focus on everything else." *Like Ray.* Ciara wanted to say that out loud, but she didn't.

"*But* if you need us, we'll help."

"I'll let Kellan know."

"And Jesse?"

Ciara bit the inside of her cheek. She could have sworn the scar from the stab wound stung for a moment—or it was just her imagination. "No one found him."

The two walked to the grey door leading inside the building—the actual sanctuary. Henry opened it, and Ciara turned to look at all the creatures they had passed on their way from the gate to the building.

"You sure you don't want to come work here?" Henry asked and grinned.

Ciara smiled. "I could come visit again."

They stepped inside, and Henry led Ciara along the corridors. It surprised Ciara how much it looked like an office building. However, some of the glass-walled offices were more like little cages for tiny animals or animals going through treatment.

Each worker who passed by smiled and greeted Henry. One colleague also called him a dragon trainer jokingly. He had that effect on people. And in a place full of people who loved magical creatures, he fit right in.

Ciara and Henry stopped by at a dark brown wooden door with Jenna's name and title on it. *Jenna Tilley, junior researcher of magical creatures.* The title surprised Ciara. They had promoted Jenna from a research assistant.

Henry knocked but didn't wait for a reply. He and Ciara peeked in.

"What is it?" Jenna didn't look up from the papers she was going through, as if she knew it was Henry.

"We have a visitor." Henry gestured for Ciara to step inside, so she did.

Jenna looked up, and her eyes went round. Her mouth curled into a smile, and she dropped the papers onto her desk. "Ciara!"

"Hi, Jenna." Ciara smiled. "It's good to see you're back at work already."

"I would've been here weeks ago if the doctors and Henry would have let me."

Ciara's smile grew, and she gestured at the door. "Because of the promotion?"

Jenna's eyes widened. "They already changed the title on the door?"

"They sure did."

"It happened yesterday." Jenna's eyes twinkled with excitement. "The promotion, I mean. They were happy with my results from autumn."

"Congrats. You worked for it and definitely earned it."

Henry and Jenna gave their lives to their jobs. It wasn't just like any job. It was about the creatures—their rights and, even more importantly, their lives.

Ciara wished Henry and Jenna had even spent a hint of that devotion on their friendship with Ciara instead of lying to her.

Ciara and Henry chatted with Jenna for a moment, but Jenna was too busy to join them. They had to go see Roan without Jenna.

Henry led the way to the other side of the enormous sanctuary building where the dragons were. First, there was a sort of department for baby dragons.

Ciara had the most experience with baby dragons. After all, she had lived in the same flat with Henry and Roan when Roan had still been a baby.

The baby dragons were together in an enormous cage with glass walls. Well, there were a few such cages, all more or less filled with baby dragons.

There were dragons of various colours, sizes, and other qualities. Some were bigger, some were smaller. They were unique individuals, just like humans were. There were unique characteristics. Some had freckles on their scales, some didn't. Some were blue, some red, black, or almost any colour. There were even bronze and green dragons. Their eyes, too, were different. Ciara saw so many colours she was convinced dragons could be any colour—and so could their eyes.

She expressed it out loud, making Henry laugh.

"Well, I've never seen a pink dragon."

"But there is a purple."

"Purple ones exist, yes." Henry nodded, smiling.

"There's a white one." Ciara pointed at the blue-eyed white dragon.

"Yes."

"There is an orange dragon. A yellow dragon."

"But no pink dragons."

"Is that the only colour?"

Henry shrugged. "Pretty much."

A brown baby dragon with metallic red—almost bronze—freckles roared and spit out fire. As soon as the corner of the cage was lit up, sprinklers—that were *everywhere*, even on the walls—spat out water.

Clearly, fires were a real problem in the department. Remembering how Roan had been at Henry's flat, Ciara wasn't surprised.

After seeing the baby dragons, Henry took Ciara to see the other dragons. They were in cages in their own department.

"They look smaller than they are."

Henry meant the cages, not the enormous dragons. Some of them were closer to the size of a detached house, while others were barely the size of an armchair.

"They're all adults. Too big to be with the youngest ones. You know how some dogs don't like puppies? Dragons aren't that different. But the problem here is, dragons don't bark. When they want to get a message across, they spit fire. As you saw with the baby dragons."

"A fire hazard."

Henry laughed. "It sure is! But less so with the youngest ones in a separate section. Besides, the youngest dragons are even more of a fire hazard. And the ones that people have used wrongly in fights and such."

Ciara looked around. The grey ceiling was miles away, or so it felt. "Are the cages enchanted?" she asked. She glanced behind a dragon and saw an endless cage. Not that it looked much like a cage except at the front. There was grass, rocks, and trees. It looked like there was even a cave further in the cage.

"Yes. You can't see the back of the cages. We have to enchant them to be enormous, so the dragons can fly however much they want...or can."

They passed by a cage with a greyish blue dragon laying on the ground. A wingless dragon.

Ciara's eyes widened.

They stopped, and Henry turned to look at the blue dragon with pain in his eyes. "He was saved in southern Asia. A poacher had cut his wings off and sold them. Or just the scales. People pay sick amounts to have dragon scales or wings in their houses."

"Disgusting."

Henry's gaze blazed with rage. His lips pursed together as if trying not to break into ranting about how he wanted to cut the poacher's arms off.

Ciara wouldn't have minded listening. Creatures actually had perhaps originally connected her and Henry.

When they had still been in school, Henry and Ciara had been on a walk outside when they had seen a gang of other students throw stones at a garden gnome. Not the ceramic kind, but an actual gnome that tended to gardens, growing vegetables, and watering flowers with their gnome magic. A brown, cute creature that looked more like a living vegetable than a clay garden gnome.

Because of the law to keep the magical world hidden, Ciara rarely saw gnomes. There had been gnomes and such in the school grounds because non-magics didn't go there.

Ciara and Henry walked silently past the cages. The wingless dragon wasn't the only one injured. The ones that didn't have injuries were sick or unable to adjust to their natural habitats again.

Some dragons had small wings. Others had big ones. Ciara had never realised how many different dragons existed. Not even with Henry as her best friend, and Henry couldn't shut up about dragons—or creatures in general.

The scales of the dragons were different colours. Some were black or grey, some brown, others were red or blue. But none had the scales Roan had. Red with bronze freckles.

Until one did. *Roan.*

Ciara wouldn't have recognised the dragon without his red scales, nor his golden eyes. He had grown so much since the last time she had seen it.

"He's huge," she breathed out in awe.

Henry chuckled. "He sure is."

Even without Roan's wings and tail, the dragon was the size of a minibus. He couldn't go home with Henry anymore.

"Do you want to go in?"

Ciara eyed the enormous dragon inside the cage. She wasn't sure if Roan even recognised her. "You sure he won't eat me? Or spit fire at me?"

Henry rolled his eyes. "Remember the time you had to ride a dragon?"

"That was a long time ago."

"You'll be fine." Henry unlocked a small door leading into the cage.

Ciara took a deep breath and followed Henry in. She bit the inside of her cheek until she tasted iron, wondering how safe it was to walk into a dragon cage.

10

Roan lowered his head to sniff Ciara. Then the dragon hummed. The sound like a low rumble.

But Ciara didn't feel threatened. It was like a cat purring contently instead of a warning.

"He recognises you." Henry reached out and let Roan move his head to touch his hand. The dragon's muscles relaxed under the familiar touch, his eyes drifting shut.

"He's beautiful."

The golden eyes, bright and alert, opened and snapped at Ciara.

Henry grinned. "He prefers to be called handsome."

Ciara looked over at the creature, his eyes shining like gold, and gave a sheepish grin. "Sorry, Roan."

The dragon moved his head closer to Ciara, his hot breath washing over her face. She tentatively extended her hand, feeling the rough texture of the dragon's scales as he nudged his snout against her. His scales were sturdy and warm under her palm.

"Hi, Roan." Ciara's voice was barely audible, coming out as a breathy whisper. She was in shock, petting a full-grown dragon. The touch of the magnificent creature filled her with an overwhelming feeling of empowerment.

Even though Ciara wasn't into creatures like Henry, she loved animals and creatures—magical or not. But she had to admit, dragons had a special spot in her heart.

No other creature had taken her breath away.

Ciara's fingers tingled with the memory of the texture of Roan's scales as he moved away from her. The dragon's tail was like a whip, and as he turned, he made sure not to strike Ciara or Henry with the tail. Then he broke into a run.

Ciara gasped, mesmerised, as she watched the dragon jump into the air. Roan was flying. At first he headed away from Henry and Ciara, towards the back of the endless cage, but eventually they saw the dragon turn around and head back towards them.

"He likes to show off." Henry chuckled, watching the dragon with pride. Without a doubt, Roan had a special place in his heart.

With a heavy thud, the dragon landed at a safe distance, and the ground beneath him trembled. Roan walked back to where Henry and Ciara were. His spikes rose menacingly from his snout to the tip of his tail.

Roan hadn't had spikes when he had been younger. But he wasn't a baby dragon anymore.

"Like I said, he's a show-off." With a smile, Henry shifted his attention to Ciara. Gradually, his face darkened, and the smile faded away. "This is why I invited you here. B-because this is how I stay sane when everything around me is crumbling into pieces. Creatures are sometimes better company than humans can be. They're empathetic. It's like therapy."

Ciara's lips curved into a gentle smile. It was even scientifically true—as far as Ciara was aware—that being around creatures eased stress and all its negative symptoms.

For Ciara, the creatures were an escape, too. And although it was temporary, she welcomed it with open arms.

"Thank you for inviting me." She meant it more than she could express with mere words.

But Henry nodded as if he understood. "I know creatures are more my thing. They're such a huge part of my life, and I know they're not the same for you. But I know anyone with a good heart will have their mind eased in the company of a creature. Honestly, if I were to determine someone's character without knowing them, I would use creatures. They are better readers of character, believe it or not."

Henry halted, eyes fixed on Roan.

"His mother knew it."

Ciara's eyes grew bigger at those words. "Roan's mother?"

Henry swallowed thickly. "Y-yeah. They found Roan with his mother. His mother was barely alive, and his father was already dead. But Roan's mother had wrapped her body around Roan to protect her baby. The poachers hadn't found Roan all thanks to her mother. Poachers, human beings, likely witches and wizards in this case." Henry's shoulders jumped up and dropped right away as if a sudden coldness had engulfed him. "Still, when I, along with a research group, found him on a trip overseas...the mother dragon trusted me. I just stared for a while, unsure if I should move. Her injury could have made her attack me." Henry shook his head, eyes prickling with tears. "Yet she didn't. She looked at me, tilting her head as much as she could in her condition. Then she made way for me. She even pushed Roan closer to me with her snout. He was tiny back then. Like a big puppy in my arms. I carried him away to take care of him after the mother had given him one last sniff."

Henry stopped speaking, but Ciara didn't dare to talk. The story wasn't finished yet. Henry just needed a pause as he was telling the horrendous story.

"Roan's mother died only minutes later. Her injuries were too severe. We couldn't save her."

Ciara's heart broke. For Roan, for Henry—and everyone else included. But not for the poachers. Never for such cruel people.

She gazed at Roan, tilting her head. He didn't look at her with hate. His eyes held wonder, perhaps even sympathy.

For a moment, she wanted to believe Roan was right. Only for a moment she would believe that she was a good person—not the killer she had painted herself as in her own mind.

Ciara left before Henry's workday was over, so he could get back to work. Once she was out of the sanctuary, she focused on the thought of the safe house and teleported.

She walked in, hung her coat, and headed for the kitchen. Walking past the living room, she halted.

A scream pierced through the air, and her phone slipped from her hands. It hit the floor, and the screen cracked. Her hands flew up to her mouth, and her throat closed.

She was hallucinating. She had to be. Because there was no way it was real. What she saw.

Not real.

Her bottom lip quivered. It didn't make any sense. He had been gone for *so* long.

"I've been waiting for hours." He smiled at her. Not wickedly, but as if he was glad to see her.

Shock still wearing on her, she cleared her throat before getting any words out. "H-how?"

Theo rose from the sofa and walked closer. Ciara's throat closed, and her muscles turned to stone. She couldn't move.

He couldn't be real.

Theo knelt down in front of her to grab the phone from the ground. Taking his wand out of his pocket and flicking it, he fixed the screen.

Ciara couldn't look away from his face. The face she had once memorised, thinking it had been the last time she would see him. His gaze locked with hers, and his arm snaked around her. Holding her gaze, he slid her phone into her back pocket—because her jeans didn't have front pockets.

Her eyes burned, thinking about the last time she had looked into those stormy grey eyes. She had tried to kill him.

If he wanted to kill her for it, she would let him. She would have to. She swore to herself that she would never cause him harm again, even if he remained her enemy. She couldn't.

Her head buzzed, her mind still processing what she was seeing. His gaze bore into hers, leaving her feeling exposed and vulnerable. She had no idea what he was thinking, even though it was one of the few times she was dying to know.

Did he hate her? Probably.

Theo broke the eye contact, lowering his gaze. But it stopped at her neck.

She knew why. The engagement ring hung from the thin chain around her neck. The ring he had proposed with.

His eyes flew back up to meet hers. This time, his eyes had widened and his lips parted. It was the face of her fiancé—an expression she recognised.

She wanted to say something. She had a jumble of words in her mind, but none of them felt right. She didn't know where to start, so she stayed silent.

So did he.

The closeness of their bodies made her acutely aware of his every breath on her skin. Like at the warehouse. She had nearly ended every breath of his.

"I'm so sorry." Ciara's words were a hurried gasp.

His strong arms wrapped around her, drawing her close to his firm chest. She clung onto his shirt, fingers trembling, as if he would disappear otherwise. She questioned whether he was a figment of her imagination or an actual person. Like the hallucination at the hospital.

His muscular, brown arms looked real. She felt their

warmth and solidness as they held her close. The feel of those arms around her was like coming home; they had embraced her so many times before.

"I forgive you." He leaned down and pressed his lips to the crown of her head, his fingers tangling in the ends of her hair as he stroked her back. "It's okay."

But it wasn't.

The images flashed through her mind. The red in her hands. His blood. Her shaky hands moved faster than her mind processed everything. She pushed Theo, forcing him to take a step back, and raised his shirt, revealing the red scar.

Her knife had made that scar. And not just her knife. *She* had scarred him—her fiancé.

Except he wasn't that. She didn't think he was. Not after his false death and her attempt to kill him. Their engagement was finished after what had happened.

She attempted to run her fingers over the scar, but he swiftly grabbed her hand and pushed his shirt back down. "It makes me look cool."

Ciara couldn't bring herself to look him in the eyes.

"Ciara."

Tears threatened to form in her eyes.

"Ciara." His voice was low and tender. Exactly like it had been on their late nights together.

She didn't deserve to have him to talk to her with such softness. She took a step back, releasing her hand from his hold. "I can't," she said, her voice barely above a whisper as her eyes locked with his.

"Ciara, I'm fine."

There was no way she would forgive herself, but that wasn't all of it. "You're one of *them*." One of the witch hunters. The word brought her back to her senses—back to the present and the reality.

Observing her face, Theo hesitated for a moment. "You're angry."

"Of course I am! Y-you...I thought you were dead. For a year."

"I'm sorry."

He had forgiven her for stabbing him. Forgiving him would have been the right thing to do. But how could she?

His expression turned stoic as his face hardened. "But I had to."

"You had to?" Ciara's expression shifted to one of disbelief as she looked at him. Her hands were shaking. It was too much. "Does your mother know?"

"No, and she can't know."

"Why not?"

His lips pursed together.

Ciara shook her head, silently signalling her disagreement. "She deserves to know."

"I know she does."

"Then why won't you—"

"I can't!" His voice rose, and his eyes grew stormy. Not just the colour, but the emotion behind that look.

He was hellbent on keeping his mother out of it, and Ciara could understand that. She was doing the same with her own mother. For her mother's safety.

What did Theo keep his mother away for? Ciara wasn't sure.

"She misses you."

His tough demeanour cracked. His eyes glazed and he froze. That was the Theo Ciara had fallen in love with.

Gathering himself, he looked away and cleared his voice. "Y-you've seen her."

"Yes. When I've visited *your* grave." Accusation was thick in her voice, but she didn't care.

Theo grimaced and closed his eyes. "Ciara, I'm sorry."

"I deserved to know." Her voice cracked, saying those words out loud to him. She had missed him *so much*.

"I know." He still refused to meet her gaze.

"Then why—"

"I can't tell you." His face grew cold once more, and he finally looked at her. His fingers traced a path down her arms on either side, and he let out a contented sigh. "One day you'll understand, and—"

"Understand what?" Ciara shook her head, trying to think of her next words. "Why you're...why..." She closed her eyes, took a deep breath, and then looked at him again. "Why you're one of them, huh?"

"That too." Theo sighed. His hands wandered to the hem of her shirt, and he raised the cloth enough to reveal her scarring stab wound.

How does he know?

He looked back up into her eyes. "You don't remember, do you?"

"Remember what?"

"At the hospital."

She blinked, processing the words. "It was real?"

His lips twitched, and for a moment he was smiling. "I had to see you after I found out..." His jaw tightened as he spoke through gritted teeth. "If I had known that Jesse..."

He still cared.

Ciara opened her mouth, but she didn't know what to say. For weeks, she had thought she had killed Theo. Knowing he was alive was relieving—but also overwhelming.

The thought nearly sent tears down her face, but she bit the inside of her cheek and forced herself to stay composed. Because even if he was alive, they were on opposing sides.

Theo was her enemy. He had hurt Bill.

Ciara's hands stopped shaking.

Bill.

Bill and Doherty. Theo had killed Doherty, and Bill was slowly dying because of Theo.

"How did you find the safe house?" Only few knew where Ciara was staying. Theo definitely wasn't one of them.

"Stalking."

Ciara didn't doubt that.

She opened her mouth to talk again, but this time her ringtone cut her off. She grabbed her phone. Switching it on, she saw the name on the screen.

Kellan.

She looked back up, expecting to see Theo, but he had already vanished.

"Hey!" she called out, but there was no reply. He was gone.

In fear of her telling Kellan? Ciara couldn't be sure. But she wouldn't have said anything.

She couldn't hurt Theo again. Not even when it wasn't her hand holding the blade.

With a deep breath, Ciara picked up the call. "Yes?"

11

The team, which included Ciara, had no choice but to attend therapy sessions as per Kellan's orders. Kellan's decision didn't surprise Ciara, but it still annoyed her. She had seen enough therapists for three lifetimes, as it was. She didn't need to see one again.

Especially knowing Theo was alive.

But Kellan didn't know that. Ciara hadn't told anyone. She couldn't.

If she did, the team would do something about it.

She had tried to kill Theo once, and she had regretted nothing as much in her life. Even if he wasn't the Theo she had been hoping to marry—even if she had never truly known him—she cared about him.

The team met in group therapy. The worst form of therapy Ciara had ever had to endure.

Kellan wasn't even there. Although he claimed to have work to do, Ciara was unconvinced. He was the only who had that excuse. In order to return to work, the team had to complete therapy sessions as per Kellan's requirements.

They all sat in a circle of six different chairs. Two were armchairs, one was a stool, one a wooden chair and two plastic chairs. To Ciara's left were Declan and Niles. To her right were River and Owen. On the chair, on the other side of the circle, was the therapist. A woman in her thirties with a low, tight hair bun.

Owen was the first person the therapist addressed. "Let's do a round, so I'll have a track of who's speaking. Would you start by saying your name?"

Ciara felt as if she was back in school.

Owen's hands fell to his lap, and he leaned back in his chair, his shoulders tight with stress. He had let his hair grow unusually long, and he was trying to blow a few blond strands off his face without making a sound. "Owen Blake."

With a nod of acknowledgment, the therapist shifted her attention to River.

Leaning back in his chair, hands in his pockets, River let out a deep sigh. He appeared the most comfortable, even with his lips pursed together. He didn't hurry with his name. Slowly, he pulled his hand out of his pocket and ran it through his dark brown hair. "River. River Bowers."

The woman's focus landed on Ciara. This time, she didn't even nod before her gaze moved to her next *victim*.

Ciara clenched her fists by her side to resist the urge to cross her arms. "Ciara Jareau."

The therapist's eyes lingered on Ciara, calculating, and Ciara couldn't wait to get out of there. The sooner, the better.

Finally, the therapist turned to Declan.

He straightened in his chair. "Declan Stark." He had to regret not shaving. The messy stubble he had was as dark as his black hair. It couldn't go unnoticed. Lucky for him, the therapist couldn't tell if it was a stylistic choice or the fact that Declan didn't bother to take care of his looks.

Declan hadn't had a stubble before. The rest of the team knew that.

Somehow Niles looked the most lively of them—even though he was fiddling with his fingers. Ciara wanted to blame it on his orangey red hair and freckles that brought warmth to his features. But it wasn't that. Even if Niles had to force it, he was smiling a little. "I'm Niles Wilkins," he said before the therapist even turned to him.

The woman smiled at Niles. "Great. I'm Vivianne, or rather just Viv."

Ciara wanted to roll her eyes, but she didn't. The woman could have at least told her full name like an adult. Ciara couldn't trust someone who kept more secrets than the others in the room.

"Would anyone like to start by telling about the mission? No details, but anything you want to say about that night. A minor detail, a thought. It can be anything."

Even Niles's smile dropped.

"It was a mission," River said. "Like any other."

"Do all your missions end with a teammate betraying you, then?" The therapist—Viv—raised her eyebrows in challenge. Ciara could only imagine Kellan had told her to take that approach, to get through to the team.

River's eyes narrowed. "No, but it was still a mission. We go on missions all the time."

"And you have nothing to say about the fact that one of your teammates is still in hospital?"

"I can't help it. What happened has already happened." Shrugging, River gave no indication of his actual thoughts on the matter.

Ciara nodded by accident, too focused on River's words.

"So you agree?" Viv asked her instantly.

"The doctors are doing what they can." Of course Ciara didn't think that. All she had been thinking about recently was how she was going to force Theo to fix what he had done. To heal Bill.

"Do any of you blame themselves?" Viv asked.

"The others weren't there," Ciara said. She could no

longer help but cross her arms.

"On the mission?"

"No. They were on the mission, but they weren't anywhere near when Bill got injured." All eyes were on Ciara, and she hated herself for opening her mouth. She should have stayed silent.

"Do you blame yourself?"

"I didn't do it."

Ciara glanced at River, whose brows were furrowed as he tried to read Ciara's expression. Owen seemed to focus on remaining out of the therapist's radar. Declan kept glancing at the door. Niles had turned to stare at the floor, shoulders slumped.

The group session couldn't end fast enough.

After the group therapy, Ciara had her own session with the therapist. The others had appointments scheduled on another day, but hers was right after the group session.

The therapist—Viv—tried to get Ciara to talk. She didn't want to. She repeated what she had said in group therapy.

But Viv didn't let it be. "I hear you killed someone."

Ciara looked at the therapist skeptically and raised an eyebrow. Every time the woman spoke, she felt a wave of irritation wash over her. *Viv* knew nothing about Ciara and what she had endured.

"I killed my fiancé." Ciara turned to look out through the window, hoping to seem troubled but not heartbroken.

She needed to appear sad to lose her fiancé. Yet she had to avoid showing too much heartbreak. Or someone—the therapist—could question her loyalty as a hit witch.

"So I heard."

"My boss told you?"

"Yes. It's for your own good to talk about these things." Perhaps the woman meant well, but Ciara didn't care for the whole therapy thing. It wasn't for her. Beating the shit out of a punching bag was more effective.

"I had a few breakdowns, but I haven't had one in a while." Ciara faced the therapist. "Can I go now?" She glanced at the door, dying to get out.

But she knew she would have to endure another half an hour.

"If you want to get back to work, we'll have to talk about these breakdowns."

Of course.

Ciara sighed. "What do you want to know?"

"What triggered them?"

"The memory of his blood. You know, warm, wet, sticky. Not that getting stabbed helped. But I haven't had a breakdown in a while."

The therapist hummed. "Do you blame yourself?"

"I did what I had to." Ciara shuddered at the memory— which was a good thing as it made her look mournful—but this time the reaction was real. "I saved my friends. My colleagues. It's part of the job and has always been. This time the price was higher, yes, but I had to do it. I-I would never do it under *any* less demanding circumstances."

The therapist seemed pleased with the answer.

Little by little, they went through that night. Ciara couldn't wait to get out of there, but she got through the entire hour. The therapist let Ciara leave once she had promised to reach out to a friend who had nothing to do with the horrors she had recently gone through. She had promised to call Josh— conveniently forgetting to mention that he was more or less involved in the witch hunter case.

Things looked good for Ciara as far as she could tell. The therapist would have to go through everything with Kellan, but Ciara was likely going to get back to work.

She just wasn't sure when that would be.

Ciara headed to see Bill straight from therapy. She teleported herself to the hospital and walked straight in. She could have walked to Bill's room with her eyes closed. Not that she did, but she knew the way *too* well.

She halted in the middle of the hospital corridor, seeing someone peek into Bill's room as if lost. Then she made her way over.

"Excuse me, mister."

The brown-haired, skinny, possibly Indian guy spun around, startled. His brown eyes were wide, and he stared at Ciara. He was handsome, Ciara noted, with sharp facial features and warm brown skin.

"This is my friend's room," Ciara said, gesturing to the door. "I didn't mean to startle you."

"B-Bill's room?"

Ciara's eyebrows rose. "You know Bill?"

"I'm...Paul." The man—based on his looks in his thirties— cleared his throat. "Paul Singh. Not that my name tells you much. Bill doesn't talk much about work when he's with me, and vice versa."

Ciara blinked. "I...I haven't seen you before. You're his..."

Paul looked uncomfortable, frowning and biting his cheek. "I'm his...boyfriend. Maybe, I'm not sure. We... we never discussed that." He cleared his throat again. "I-I thought he had moved out or was avoiding me when he never opened his door or answered his texts. But then I ran into...a guy at his door. I think it was his boss. Dark hair, a stubble." With the anxious—but not too nervous—fidgeting, Ciara trusted Paul was telling her the truth.

"And muscular? Good-looking? Tall?"

"Yes!"

Ciara smiled. "That's Kellan. He's the head of the department. I'm Ciara Jareau, Bill's team leader."

"So...he's in there." Paul's eyes shifted to the closed door.

"Yes. He's...not well."

"So I heard. I never realised something had happened." Fresh tears welled up in Paul's eyes, causing them to glaze over.

"Do you want to go in alone?" Ciara was dying to see Bill, but Paul was there to see Bill for the first time. If Paul needed time, Ciara would give him that.

"I...I wouldn't mind you coming in with me."

Ciara nodded. "I can come with you."

"I'd like that."

Ciara gestured for Paul to step in, and she followed him. Paul walked around the corner, his eyes falling on unconscious Bill.

Ciara closed the door, shutting out the noise from the corridor. The silence was suffocating in the room.

Bill's face was deadly white, and his breathing was as uneven as it had been since that wretched night at the warehouse. His face looked sunken, and he had lost weight—muscle, too.

It had to be rough for Paul to see Bill like that. When Ciara had seen Bill after the mission, it had been horrible. But at least Bill had looked more healthy—and more alive—back then.

Paul broke into tears, shaking with quiet sobs.

Ciara hesitated to reach out, but eventually she squeezed Paul's shoulder. The man looked like he needed comfort.

It took a while for Paul to stop crying, and then he moved to sit beside Bill, taking Bill's hand in his. Ciara watched him brush his fingers on Bill's—likely cool—skin. Paul's touch was gentle, as if Bill were a fragile glass figurine.

Ciara understood. Bill looked so fragile, laying there on the hospital bed.

Because of Theo.

Ciara sat with Paul and watched Bill in silence. The others didn't come. They had probably visited Bill earlier that day.

Paul and Ciara remained in silence for hours, and then Paul said he needed to get out. Ciara left the room with him.

"How are you?" Ciara asked, and the pair of them stopped in the corridor.

"Not great," Paul admitted. His face had drained of warmth. His brown skin had turned ashen over the hours he had sat with Bill. The length of his stay spoke volumes about how much he cared.

"If there's anything I can do..."

"No, but thanks. You did plenty by sitting with me." Paul nodded. "It helped more than you think."

"I'm glad I could help then. If I had known about you, I would have told you much earlier."

"Bill likes to keep private about some things. Work is such a big part of his life, or so he says. He wants to have something special outside of it."

Ciara smiled. "That sounds like Bill."

Paul smiled a little, too. "Do you visit him often?"

"Every day."

Paul exhaled, as if relieved by the news. "It's nice to know he hasn't been alone the past month."

"He hasn't, but I'm glad you found out what happened."

"Me too."

"Will you come tomorrow?"

"Yes."

"Same time?"

Paul nodded slowly. "Yeah, I think so."

"Then we'll see tomorrow."

They parted ways. Ciara went home, and she assumed Paul did the same—unless he was the type to go out and get a drink. It had been a rough day for the guy.

At home, Ciara still had one thing to do. She had promised to call Josh. At first she hadn't intended to, but the idea had begun to sound appealing.

So she dialled his number and waited until she heard Josh's voice. "Hey, Ciara! It's good to hear from you."

She sighed in relief, smiling. "Hi, Josh. It's good to hear your voice, too."

And it was.

Josh had been the colleague that had become Ciara's rock after she had lost Theo. It still meant a lot to her, and it always would.

Josh was the Canadian alternative to Bill. Not that either could ever replace the other. But currently Ciara couldn't talk to Bill, and she could talk to Josh.

She was always asking him to help with the witch hunters, and she owed him more than new requests. He had been her colleague in America, but he was also much more. He was her friend, and she was going to have to learn not to push her friends away when she needed them.

She always needed Josh—work-related or not.

"How are you?" He wanted a genuine answer.

"Overwhelmed."

"What have you been up to today?"

"Group therapy, individual therapy, then visiting Bill." Ciara swallowed. "It's been a long day."

"Do you want to talk about it?" Josh asked. "I know how much you despise therapy sessions," he added, to lighten the mood a little.

Ciara smiled, letting out a small chuckle. "Oh, it was torture!"

"I bet it was." Ciara could hear the smile in his voice. "Imagine if we had had group therapy here whenever something happened."

"I would have quit, so I pray this was only a onetime thing."

"Let's hope so then. Your team needs you."

"It was torture for them, too."

Josh laughed. "I wish someone had recorded it. I bet they could turn the first five minutes into a mini-comedy film."

"Oh, trust me, there would have been plenty of material. The therapist didn't even seem to live in the same world, or so it felt."

"Ouch, that doesn't sound good."

"Like I said, pure torture."

"So, is this an option two for therapy?" Josh asked.

"To be honest, the therapist insisted I call someone who wasn't involved that night. Almost everyone I know was."

"I was involved more or less, though."

"The therapist doesn't have to know that."

"Fair enough."

"But that's not the only reason. I mean, do I ever really listen to orders?"

"Not as often as you should."

"Exactly. I wasn't going to call anyone when she insisted. But I also realised that..."

It really sunk in.

"When horrible things happen, I know you're the one to talk to. No matter what, I've always been able to talk to you." Flashbacks of Theo's faked death and its aftermath played in Ciara's mind. "And you're my friend. I should call you more often. Well, I should call everyone more often."

"I'm glad you called. I *really* am. You tend to keep everything inside until you explode."

"Well, thanks for not letting me explode."

Josh chuckled, lightly humoured. "That's what friends are for. So, please unload everything on me. I know you didn't tell the entire truth in therapy."

Ciara couldn't tell everything. Not even to Josh. She didn't know how he would react if he knew the truth about Theo. But she told everything else.

She and Josh talked for hours. Work, recent events, Doherty, the rest of the American team—they talked about everything.

Ciara also asked for Josh's help on a matter that had been bothering her. She asked Josh to look into Jesse's cousin— the witch hunter whose death Jesse had blamed on Ciara.

Every day that week Ciara visited Bill with Paul. Every day, they met at the door and went in together. Towards the end of the week, Paul stayed longer than she did, though. He didn't mind sitting with Bill alone.

Apparently, Paul had also met some of the other team members when he had been sitting with Bill. River had given him quite a questioning, because Kellan had forgotten to inform the team about Paul's existence until Ciara had mentioned it. Sometimes even the smartest guys acted like dimwits.

By the end of the week, Ciara got answers from Josh. It seemed possible—even likely—that she or Theo had killed Jesse's cousin. Jesse hadn't lied about that. He had gone after her in revenge.

Sort of like she had gone after the witch hunters after Theo's fake death.

🜁🜁🜁

Ciara headed to see Bill on her own on the following week's Wednesday. She was unusually late because she had tried training for the first time since Jesse had stabbed her. The visiting hours were nearly over, but she had to see Bill.

The instant her eyes fell on Bill's fragile form, her stomach clenched. Seeing him reminded her of Theo's actions. She hated the person Theo had become. A witch hunter.

After the first visit, Theo hadn't come back. Not once. Ciara had had time to prepare for the next time she saw him. She had planned a speech for her ex-fiancé. A rather angry one. She wasn't going to hurt him, but he had to answer for his actions. For what he had done to Bill. And to Doherty.

Ciara didn't stay with Bill for long. She couldn't. Nausea and guilt hit her when she watched Bill.

She rushed out of the room, gasping for air.

"Ciara?"

It was the worst timing. For a second, she shut her eyes, hoping the floor would swallow her.

"Ciara."

She raised her gaze and met his hazel eyes. Liam had tried to talk to her, but she had got away every time. This time, he was already standing right in front of her. He was pale and had dark circles under his eyes. His stubble had grown too.

Ray hadn't got better. Ciara had stopped to see Ray a few times—when Henry had assured her Liam wouldn't be there. It was a rough time for all the Rosslers. Even the younger ones who couldn't come home from school to see their father as often as they would have liked. Luckily, the February break was beginning on Friday.

"Liam." Her voice was shaky. Not from Liam's presence—or so she told herself—but from seeing Bill.

"Are you okay?"

She hated how soothing his voice was. After the lies, he had no right to talk to her so tenderly. She couldn't believe that after all the lies, he still had a hold over her.

"Cut the crap. I have to go." She turned to walk away, but he grabbed her by the arm. His grip was loose enough for her to get away if she wanted to.

But Ciara didn't pull herself free from his grip. She should have, but she couldn't. A comforting warmth spread along her arm. His touch was so soothing.

"Okay, fine." Liam let his hand fall. "I'll get straight to the point."

She kept her gaze fixed on the ground, refusing to look at him. The memory of his hurtful words and actions lingered in her mind, like an open wound. He had lied to her about Theo repeatedly. Even when he could have come clean, he hadn't.

He had known Theo had killed Doherty. He had known so many things that Ciara would have deserved to know.

"I need you to give me five minutes so I can explain myself." His voice was laced with desperation, yet Ciara refused to be swayed by it.

"Frankly, Liam, I don't have to give you anything." As

soon as she met his gaze, a wave of regret washed over her.

She had avoided him for a long while. On purpose. Seeing him—especially in that state—was heartbreaking. She still cared about him.

But he had hurt her. Like Theo had.

"I have to go." She had to force the harshness in her voice.

"Ciara." He reached for her again, but she pushed his hand away.

"Stop." The harshness in her tone wavered. "Just stop." The latter came out as a low, pleading whisper.

Hurt crossed his face, and his eyes softened. "Ciara." It sounded as if he was gasping for air. "Just let me explain. Let me make it up to you. I will never again—"

"You already did." Her voice didn't come out strong. Instead, it was another whisper. But she tried her best to give him a hard look before she spun around and headed out.

He didn't stop there. He rushed after her, following her out of the hospital.

"Ciara!" His hand found hers just when she teleported, sending them both to the alley near the safe house—her new home.

"Liam, stop!" She stepped back.

"No, Ciara." His voice filled with determination, and his eyes turned ardent—with purpose, not anger. "I screwed up. I treated you horribly, and you didn't deserve that. One way or another, I'll make it up to you. I will never give up on you."

She closed her eyes for a second. "Stop." This time she could at least talk above a whisper, even though she didn't come out as strong as she would have liked. "We're over, Liam. I think we both made it pretty clear *that* night."

He flinched at the memory. She didn't have to look at his face to notice. A lot was packed in that one night—and the memory of it.

There was a moment of silence as Liam thought carefully about what to say next. "Ciara, I'm sorry I never told you that—"

"It's too late!" She raised her voice, looking him straight in the eye. The truth could have changed the course of events that had led her to stab Theo. Had Liam told her the truth to begin with, she could have at least prepared for it. "It's too fucking late, Liam. You screwed up, and we're over. That's it. That's *all* of it." And just like that, the harshness was back.

His eyes widened, and she could have sworn he fought back tears. But even the feeling of needles pinching her heart didn't make her waver.

"Ciara, just..." He cleared his voice, fighting to keep his voice stable. "I love you."

The tears cascaded down both their faces. Ciara wiped hers away with one swift movement.

"We're over," she rasped out. She couldn't handle the closeness. She had to get away. So she broke into a sprint, running away from him—as if it would solve anything.

12

Liam ran after Ciara, but he lost her in the crowd. He didn't know where she was staying, so he couldn't go looking for her. He lost his chance.

She had every right to stay away from him, but it still broke his heart. He had screwed up, and he knew that all too well. He was determined to make it up to her, willing to do whatever it took.

But she wouldn't let him, and he would never force her.

Liam jolted up, hearing his phone ring. It was Friday morning, but he had taken the day off from work because he had worked late the previous day.

The caller ID said *Mum*, and Liam picked up the call. "Mum? Why are you calling? I'm home. Is—"

"Come to the hospital now."

Liam's eyes widened, and in an instant he was out of bed, pulling on his jeans. "What is it?" He sounded as if he had been running a marathon, breath hitching in his throat. "Mum, what is it?" His voice grew louder, and he could feel the acidic burn of bile creeping up his throat.

"Your father. I—"

Please, no.

"Is he okay?" Liam screamed into the phone, panic filling his insides. He felt a sense of frustration as his trembling hands fumbled with the button on his jeans.

"He's awake, honey."

Liam ended the call without thinking. He finished getting dressed, not bothering to wash his teeth or brush his hair. He couldn't care less.

With a flick of his wand, he teleported to the front of the hospital. His heart pounding, he bolted through the hospital corridors, the sound of his laboured breath filling the air. He earned scoldings and dirty looks, but he barely registered them.

His father was awake. That was the only thought repeating in his head. His heart drummed in his chest—both from running and excitement.

For the first time in a long time, he was *happy*.

He pushed the door open, running in. The moment his eyes met his father's, he froze, out of breath. The one thing that made him realise he was crying was the salty taste of tears on his lips.

He lunged for the bed, hurrying past his mother to hug his father. "Dad!"

"Hey." His father's voice was feeble and hoarse. But it was a miracle he could even talk.

Pulling away from the hug, Liam noted how tired his father was. His eyes were barely open, as if he was struggling to stay awake.

"Your father's still tired." Liam's mother had noticed the worried look in Liam's eyes. She placed a comforting hand on his shoulder, eyes glistening with happy, relieved tears.

Upon hearing those words, Liam's tense muscles released,

a wave of relief coursing through his body. The tears refused to stop coming, but he didn't care. His eyes didn't leave his father for a second. "We missed you, Dad."

Ray smiled—although it was only a ghost of his usual smile. He was too tired to even use his facial muscles. "So I heard." He didn't sound like himself, but it didn't matter. Seeing his eyes open was enough to give Liam hope.

Not much later, Henry and Jenna ran in. To Liam's surprise, they weren't alone. Gabriel, Polly, and Poppy were with them—back from school. He moved aside to let his siblings hug their father.

Only minutes later, Ray fell back asleep. Polly panicked and started screaming, but Mary was quick to calm her down. It was normal for their father to be tired.

Soon the doctors arrived, and they confirmed that too. Even according to them, things were taking a turn for the better. For once, there was good news for the family.

Their father was getting better.

"I have to call Ciara," Henry said.

Liam's eyes flew to his brother. Jealousy gnawed inside him. Not from the thought of Henry and Ciara. But rather from the fact that they were okay. Ciara talked to Henry. Liam would have done anything to have her even look at him.

He could live with Ciara hating him, but he couldn't handle the fact he was like air to her—if even that.

Gabriel moved to stand beside Liam. He had grown quite a bit. He was taller and had even grown a stubble. Gabe looked more like a man than a boy already. His eighteenth birthday was coming up in just five days.

"You and Ciara still haven't talked?"

The question half-surprised Liam. He sometimes forgot how *adult* Gabriel was. Gabe was still more of a teen and a *little* brother in Liam's eyes.

"No. I've tried, but...she won't talk to me."

Henry had walked out to call Ciara, and all the women

were talking together.

Gabe's brows furrowed. "Are you okay?"

Liam smiled a little. "Don't worry about it."

"You're my brother."

"I'm the oldest, though. It's my job to worry, not yours."

"Either way, I worry."

Liam smiled at Gabe, but the smile evaporated in a matter of seconds. "I apologised. She barely let me. She can't stand talking to me. But she has every right to be angry."

"Do you still love her?"

"I do."

Gabe paused. "But does she know that?"

"She does, but I doubt she cares." It was Liam's fault he had lost Ciara, but it didn't make it any easier. His heart ached, and he had to clear his voice, which cracked with emotion, to continue talking. "So it's over. For good, I think."

"I'm sorry."

"It's my fault. I should never have lied to her. It wasn't my place to decide for her. Even if it was to protect her, I didn't even manage to do that. She went through hell either way."

"Your intentions were good."

"She doesn't know that. I don't think she'd even care."

Gabriel frowned, sympathy all over his face. "I wish I could help."

"Yeah." Liam took a deep breath and forced a small smile on his face. "But back to happy thoughts."

Gabriel's face broke into a smile. "I can't believe Dad's getting better."

"Me neither."

Henry returned to the room soon, telling everyone Ciara would stop by later. He had a hard time coming up with an excuse as to why she couldn't come straight away.

Liam could see right through it. Ciara was avoiding him. She wouldn't come see their father when Liam was there.

He didn't blame her, even though it hurt. He had just been trying to protect her from Theo. His intentions had never been to hurt her. But it was too late for that.

He had hurt her.

Ray started waking up here and there. The following day, he was awake for an hour straight.

It became a habit for the siblings to go visit their father whenever their mother alerted them about their father being awake. She was staying at the hospital day and night, barely going home to change clothes.

Liam could understand that. He would have done the same with Ciara—even though they weren't together anymore.

"Do you think Dad will be angry if I don't come with you?" Gabriel asked uneasily, hugging his arms around himself.

Liam and the twins were just grabbing their coats, almost ready to leave for the hospital.

Liam's brows furrowed. "You don't want to see Dad?"

"No, it's not that." Gabriel shook his head. "I just have something to do, and it's important."

"Don't tell me you're going to a pub," Liam said. "You won't be of age until tomorrow."

Gabe chuckled. "I'm not going to drink. I can wait one more day."

"Good."

"I just have something to do." It was clear Gabe didn't want to tell his brother what was up, so Liam didn't pry. Gabe was nearly an adult and could handle himself. Liam had no reason not to trust his youngest brother.

"You sure?"

"Yes."

Liam nodded. "Do you need me to get you somewhere or—"

"No, I'll be fine."

Liam left with Polly and Poppy to the hospital, wondering what was up with Gabe.

13

Ciara stared at the cigarette pack on the kitchen counter. She had mentioned smoking during her therapy session. The therapist had told her to find a better way to calm down. It was a good thing Ciara hadn't mentioned anything about her overuse of alcohol. It was only occasional, but she knew it was bad.

Like Doherty had once taught her, the bottom of the bottle wasn't an actual friend and cigarettes brought no real comfort. Ciara should have listened better. Addiction claimed many of her colleagues who couldn't handle everything that came with the job.

But it wasn't just the job for her. Her life outside work had become too much.

Ciara snapped out of her thoughts, like being pulled out of a trance, when her doorbell rang. She wasn't expecting anyone. If it was Kellan and work, she was going to *kill* him for working too much on his own. The team wouldn't go back until the beginning of March. Apparently, the others needed a little more time, and Ciara could understand that.

Her eyes reluctantly moved away from the cigarette pack as she let out a sigh. She compelled herself to move her feet and walked towards the door. The moment she opened the door, her eyes widened in surprise at the unexpected guest.

"Gabriel."

"Hi." The boy—or rather a young man—smiled sheepishly. "I hope I'm not bothering you or—"

"No, not at all." Ciara smiled. "Come on in."

He stepped in, and Ciara closed the door behind him.

"What brings you here?" She had no idea. Gabriel had never even been at the safe house—her current home. Henry knew the address, so he had likely given it to Gabriel.

Gabe went quiet. He opened his mouth, but it took him a moment to find the right words. "I'd like to talk to you."

Ciara nodded. "Do you want tea? Or coffee? Or water, apple juice, something?"

"Tea would be great."

They headed to the kitchen. Walking beside Gabriel, Ciara noticed how much he had grown. He was a lot taller than her. Nearly the same height as Liam—and Liam was *tall*. Gabe had even grown a stubble, looking less and less like a boy.

"Henry called about your father last week. And, well, he's been keeping me updated every day since then." Ciara smiled at Gabe. "I'm glad he's getting better."

Gabriel's face brightened with a smile. "Me too. He's awake most of the time already."

"Really? That's fantastic." Ciara grabbed a kettle and filled it with water.

Gabriel and Ciara talked about Ray, waiting for the tea to be ready. Ciara doubted it was what Gabriel had come from, but she was in no hurry and didn't feel like urging him to speak his mind.

It was good that he talked about his father. It meant he was processing his worry and grief. Perhaps it was easier to talk to someone other than his siblings or mother about it. Gabe was the kind of person who didn't want to make others worry—even when they likely had every reason to.

Once, when younger, he had said he got a cut on his arm. It hadn't been just a cut, but a deep wound. Of course, Mary had treated it, and it had healed. Still, Gabriel had played it off as nothing, so no one would have to worry about him.

When the tea was ready—filling the room with a pleasant scent—they sat at the table, and Gabriel fidgeted with his teacup. Again, the young man seemed to be at a loss for words.

"You wanted to talk to me?" Ciara didn't mean to push him, but it was clear something was up. Gabe seemed to need a bit of encouragement.

"I don't want you to hate me for asking about it."

"Gabe." Ciara smiled at the boy she had known for years and years. "I could never hate you. You're like *the least* hateable person I know."

Gabe smiled, but it vanished soon. "It's about Liam."

Ciara's lips pursed together, and her breath hitched. But she nodded, urging Gabe to continue.

He cleared his throat. "You won't talk to him."

"True."

"Why not?" Gabriel's brows furrowed. "It's obvious he loves you, and I know you realise it, too. He's..." He sighed. "He's an absolute wreck. And no, he didn't ask me to come here. He doesn't even know I'm here. I came because I wanted to. I'm worried about him. Not that I expect you to be *with* him again or...whatever. I just think you should talk to him. Or rather, I want to know..." He inhaled sharply. "Why won't you?"

Chills tingled across Ciara's skin. She missed Liam, but it didn't change anything.

His lies had led Ciara into a situation where she had stabbed her fiancé. He hadn't trusted her to be strong enough to handle the truth, and that hurt. His lack of belief in her hurt. Despite his intention to protect her, she didn't feel protected. Far from it.

Ciara glanced down at her tea to avoid direct eye contact with Gabe. "It's complicated." She raised her gaze back up hesitantly. "He hurt me. And not for the first time."

The situation didn't have anything to do with what had happened a few years before. That was the past. And back then, Liam's actions had been for a reason. A good reason.

Nevertheless, it hadn't been the first time Liam had hurt her.

"And I know others lied to me as well." Ciara's mouth dried. "Gabe, everyone lied to me about…"

"About your fiancé."

"About Theo, yes."

Gabe's face twitched, hearing the name.

"I loved Theo, and he hurt me. Same with Liam. Not that those two things have much to do with each other." Ciara paused to swallow. "It's just that Liam told everyone. Everyone *except* me. He had plenty of chances to come clean, but he didn't." Ciara ran a hand down her face. "If I had known the truth before that mission…" *A lot could have been done differently.* Ciara shook her head, thoughts of Theo's blood invading her mind as she held her hand against the warm teacup. She tried to focus on Gabe, but all she could see in her mind was red—blood. "I did something horrible to get everyone out of there." Her voice was a hollow shriek as she spoke those last words.

Theo was alive—thank goodness. But it didn't change the fact that Ciara had stabbed him. That night plagued her nightmares. Its weight lingered in her mind, even in her waking hours.

"Had I known the truth, everything could have been avoided. At the very least, a lot could have been avoided," Ciara said.

Gabriel's face twisted into a deep frown. He was about to open his mouth, but Ciara beat him to it.

"Besides, we just rushed back into a relationship. It was foolish of both of us." Ciara didn't believe her own words, but she didn't want to talk about the night of the warehouse mission.

"What did you do at the warehouse?"

Blood rushed off Ciara's face. Her eyes fixated on the steam rising from the teacup.

There was no point lying to Gabe. Henry knew, too. Gabe was old enough to handle what she was about to tell him.

"I stabbed Theo." Ciara looked at Gabe, worried he would look at her with terror in his eyes.

But his expression barely twitched. "I'm sorry."

"It has nothing to do with you."

"Does Liam know?"

"I haven't told him." She didn't know if Henry had, though. Even if she talked to Henry, things weren't the same as they had been. Henry had lied to her—just like Liam.

"But if he'd know—"

"It wouldn't change the past, Gabe."

His shoulders slumped. "A-are you okay?"

"Getting better." Ciara flashed a quick smile. "I'll be back at work soon."

"D-do you want to talk about it, though?"

"No. If you decide to take this career path, you'll see enough to worry about in your own time. You don't need to worry about my issues."

"I wouldn't mind."

Ciara smiled in appreciation. "I know, but I would."

Gabe nodded, allowing Ciara to switch the topic.

"Anyway, how is school?"

"Same old, I guess." Gabe shrugged. "I can't wait to graduate."

"I bet." Ciara's smile widened into a grin. "But a fair warning, life isn't all great after school either."

"I know."

"And how's life outside lessons?"

Gabe opened his mouth but hesitated to speak his mind.

Ciara raised an eyebrow. "Something interesting?"

"Well," Gabe bit his lip, "I haven't told anyone yet."

"You can tell me." Ciara spotted the nervous look in Gabe's eyes. "But you don't have to. It's your choice, of course."

"I'd like to." Gabe frowned, fidgeting with his fingers.

"Take your time. I'm listening."

Gabe had to take a few deep breaths, but Ciara stayed silent and waited patiently. She had time, and Gabe needed a little time.

With one more deep breath, he started talking. "There's a guy."

The moment before, Ciara had been worried. But her face broke into a smile the second she realised what was up.

"Does he have a name?" She sounded like an annoying aunt asking about their nephew's dating, but she didn't care. She wanted to know more about this guy.

"Tim."

Ciara nodded. "Tim. And you are…"

"We're not dating, but he knows I'm gay. He's gay, too."

"And you two talk?"

Gabe's cheeks turned pink, and he couldn't fight the smile creeping onto his face. "Yeah, we talk a lot. He's really great."

"Has your family met him?"

Gabe shook his head. "We're not dating yet. And no one knows I'm into guys. Except for Tim."

"You're worried about what your family will think?"

Gabe bit his lip. "A little."

"Well, I'd like to say I know your family pretty well." Although, after the lies, Ciara wasn't actually sure about that. "They would be happy to hear about Tim. All that matters to them is that you have someone who cares about you." That part Ciara was sure of. Gabe's family loved him and cared about him without conditions.

Gabe's lips twitched; he was struggling to hide his smile.

"I think Tim cares about me."

"Then I wouldn't be worried." Ciara smiled, excited for Gabe.

"It's still nerve-wrecking."

"It's a big thing."

Gabriel sighed. "Yeah."

"But if you need backup, I'm here."

"You'd help me tell them?"

"Of course."

"Tomorrow?"

Ciara's face fell. Henry had told her about Gabriel's birthday dinner at the Rosslers' house. The problem was that Liam would be there. "I..."

"You don't have to."

"Well, I'd like to, but I can't promise anything."

Hope danced in Gabe's eyes. "You'll think about it?"

Ciara nodded. "Yes."

The hope in his eyes turned to joy. He grinned and started thanking Ciara over and over again.

She prayed she could work up the courage to go to the Rosslers'. For Gabe's sake.

But she didn't voice her worries. Instead, she listened to Gabe tell more about Tim. Based on what he told her, Tim was a great guy. Ciara could see Gabe with someone like him.

Gabe stayed for a couple of hours. Then he left in a hurry, planning to see his father before the hospital's visiting hours were over.

Ciara closed the door when he left.

"Liam's brother?" The voice sent chills down Ciara's spine. It was *the worst* timing.

14

Ciara spun around, hands twitching and ready to cast a spell if she had to fight Theo. "Stay away from Gabe."

"I'm not here to hurt him. Or to hurt anyone for that matter." Theo's eyes softened, but Ciara didn't let her guard down.

"What are you here for? After vanishing on me three weeks ago." Her voice was thick with accusation.

Theo's lips twitched, revealing a hint of a smile. "You missed me?"

Ciara clenched her jaw. She had prepared herself for that exact moment, going through the speech in her mind dozens of times. There was no doubt what she wanted from him. "I want you to tell me how I can heal Bill."

Her friend was dying. She had already lost Doherty because of Theo. She wasn't willing to lose Bill if she could do something about it.

Theo's face hardened. "I can help you with that."

"And you're telling me now?" Ciara's voice rose, and she

walked up to Theo, fuelled by anger.

"He's still..."

"The same he was when Liam took him to the hospital," Ciara hissed, seething.

Theo nodded. "Then I can help, but I need to get to the hospital."

Ciara's brows furrowed. If Theo went to the hospital, someone would spot him. He would get caught. It was a miracle he had been able to visit her in secret after what had happened with Jesse. "You're willing to get caught?" Ciara wasn't even sure that Theo knew how to help Bill.

"I have a plan." He didn't smile, but there was smugness in his voice.

Ciara didn't ask about his plan, even though she was curious. He likely wouldn't tell her anything, anyway.

"Unless you tell your team about my whereabouts." He raised an eyebrow as if he had asked a question.

"They don't know anything."

His lips twitched again.

"How—"

"I'll help your friend tomorrow. He'll be fine."

Ciara's eyes narrowed. "How do I know I can trust you? How do I know he'll make it?"

Theo paused. "It's me, Ciara."

"That's my point. You're..." Ciara sighed—almost winced. "You're one of *them*."

Hurt flashed in Theo's eyes, but Ciara refused to let it bother her. He had let her down enough times to erode her trust in him.

"I never wanted to hurt you." His voice softened, and so did his expression. Sincerity shone through. He looked like the Theo he had been in Canada. The same Theo Ciara had fallen in love with.

"But you did."

"I'm sorry."

She sighed. Her hand moved to brush down his arm. The

moment she realised it, she pulled it away.

He wasn't complaining.

She had owned a house with him, had lived with him. They had been planning their future together. He had proposed, and they had started thinking about their wedding.

But he had ripped that all away by faking his death.

Ciara still didn't know why. He owed her an explanation, but she wasn't sure she would get it. She was, however, sure she couldn't trust him without one.

"I'm sorry about everything."

But the words meant nothing. He was a witch hunter. He killed innocents for his own cause—for the witch hunters' cause. His actions spoke louder than any words could.

"You're still with them."

"It's not..." He frowned and shook his head, but his eyes stayed on Ciara. He was looking for words, but didn't seem to find the right ones.

"It's not what?" Ciara sounded bitchy but she couldn't care less. She wanted answers.

"It's not as simple as you think it is. You...you don't understand, Ciara."

"Then help me understand!" She shook her head in disbelief. "You won't talk to me. Fuck! You even faked your own death and let me believe you were dead. What kind of person does that?"

"Ci—"

"For an entire year, Theo!" It wasn't until a moment later that she realised her cheeks were moist with tears.

She tried to hate him and even failed at that.

"I'm sorry. You'll understand everything soon, I swear." His eyes were feverish, pleading for her to understand.

"But you won't tell me anything now. Heck, you won't even help Bill *now*."

"I can't go to the hospital right now."

"You shouldn't have hurt him in the first place." Ciara's jaw clenched. The memory of Theo torturing Bill returned to her mind, and for a moment, she absolutely hated Theo.

"I'm sorry." He refused to look away. "He didn't deserve it, and I'll make up for it."

She didn't believe the latter, but there was no point in arguing. Especially not before Theo would actually help her with Bill. He was her only chance.

"You cursed him then?"

"Don't worry, it can be undone."

"And you'll undo it? You promise?"

His gaze darkened, not leaving hers. "I swear on my mother's life."

Ciara's eyebrows rose. Theo was serious. His mother meant everything to him. It had to be the only thing that hadn't changed since his false death.

"Will you ever tell her?" She ran her hand down his arm, dying to comfort him when she saw the troubled look in his eyes.

"We'll see." His shoulders slumped, but his hand reached out for Ciara's hand. He took it off his arm but didn't let go.

Holding hands together was familiar, and somehow it brought Ciara a sense of comfort. She had missed the little things about him, including holding hands. They were no longer a couple, and they had no future, but she let herself enjoy the moment while it lasted.

"I'm sorry." It wasn't the first time he apologised, but it was the most intimate apology. He gripped her hand firmly yet tenderly, his eyes locked onto hers. "If I ever get a chance, I will make things right. P-perhaps you'll understand why all of this had to happen. Not today, but...soon."

"Theo—"

His finger flew up to her lips, silencing her. The sensation tingled her lips, and her breath caught in her throat.

"I never wanted this to happen. I never, not once, wanted to hurt you, Ciara. And I know it's hard for you to believe that, but you'll see. I'm not...I'm...I'm still me. I'm still Theo, the same guy you once loved." His eyes glazed over with tears. "I have done terrible things. To you and to others. And I'm so sorry it all had to happen. I won't let anything hurt you again, Ciara. I swear it on my life."

His unexpected reaction puzzled her. A tear slid down his cheek, and he looked utterly hopeless.

"Theo—"

"Ciara."

She looked into his eyes, looking for an answer, but it wasn't there. Not on sight. He was still hiding something from her, but it would be useless to question him. He would tell her eventually—or so he kept saying.

"I'm sorry." Ciara's voice wavered. She wrapped her arms around his neck. She needed that hug—needed to feel his warmth. The same warmth she had nearly taken away.

His arms snaked around her, holding her against his hard chest. Seeking comfort, he nestled his head on her shoulder.

They barely talked, but they spent the day together. Theo even cooked.

Ciara didn't mind. She needed a break. A little flashback wouldn't hurt anyone.

Because it was just like old times at their house. Theo had always been the one to cook.

Except, in a way, everything was different. They used to talk a lot more. The silence was killing Ciara, but she couldn't talk about her friends. She didn't know if she could trust Theo with all that information.

She trusted him enough to let her own guard down little by little. After all, she was the only one who could get harmed if the situation went sideways.

He couldn't talk to her much, either. He stayed mostly silent until they were doing dishes in the kitchen.

"Cigarettes?"

Ciara turned around, spotting her cigarette pack in Theo's hand. "I don't smoke all the time." She tried to brush off the subject and continued to fill her dishwasher.

"But you smoke."

Ciara nodded.

"When did you start?"

"About a year ago." *Around the time you died.*

She heard his breath hitch. The pack landed on the kitchen counter, and soon Theo pulled her away from the dishwasher. He brushed her hair behind her ear, a frown crowning his facial features.

"Because of me? Because of what I did?"

"My life, my choice." Ciara moved away and continued to load the dishwasher. When she finished, she washed her hands and wiped them dry.

Only then she turned back to look at Theo, whose eyes were still on her, never having left.

"You still smoke."

Ciara shrugged. "Sometimes."

"And this?" Theo flung open a cupboard. The cupboard with all the liquor. The bottles took up all the space. Below the counter near the kitchen aisle, there were even more bottles.

Ciara snapped her fingers, and the cupboard door slammed shut. "Trust me, Kellan already lectured me about this. And so did my therapist. And…" Ciara sighed and rolled her eyes. "Point is, you're not the first."

Theo's frown didn't ease. The opposite. "You're playing with your safety."

"I don't go out and get wasted. I do it here, at home. So chill."

He had no right to lecture her. She had issues, but she was only hurting herself. Unlike he had been. He was the one to have caused a majority of her issues.

"Jesse attacked you at your own flat. It doesn't matter where you are. It's not safe." Theo's jaw clenched.

"The house is warded."

"So was your flat. Yet Jesse just walked in." Theo shook his head, flames of rage dancing in his eyes.

"His friend owned the flat." Ciara rubbed her arm, frowning at Theo. "And you...you knew he's a witch hunter. You knew I didn't know that and—"

"I nearly killed him for touching you." Theo's voice had gone lethally low, and every word coming out of his mouth sent chills down Ciara's spine. "If I had known what he was planning, I would have killed him. Next time I see him, he's dead."

Ciara found herself at a loss for words, overwhelmed by Theo's words and the impact they had.

"He'll never touch you again."

She had to lean against the kitchen counter. "So you know..."

"I know you slept with him. He didn't shut up about it."

Ciara wanted to hurl her guts up. The memory of her night with Jesse—and all the other moments spent with him—made her feel used.

"And I swear I wanted to kill him for it."

"He had been planning to kill me since summer. I think he had been waiting to get you out of the picture first."

"If I could have, I would have killed him last summer." Theo's fingers glided softly along the contours of her face. "If I had known about his plan...I would have come to your flat straight from the warehouse."

Ciara's gaze wandered down to where Theo's scar was hidden under his shirt as she said, "I had just stabbed you."

"Doesn't matter." Theo shook his head. "I would have come."

She looked back up. "I..."

"Are you okay, Ciara?" He frowned. "After what he did..." His eyes softened, but his jaw clenched. As if he was fighting back the anger, trying to shove it somewhere deep within himself.

"I'm okay right now." Ciara didn't look away, no matter how intense the moment was. Her heart thudded, and she thought her chest might explode. Everything had changed, but Theo still had some effect on her.

Which wasn't good.

"Good." His breath hit her skin, sending tingly sensations across her body. His hands rose to the sides of her neck, brushing her skin tenderly.

In the same instant, her hands flew up to his collar, pulling him in. His lips were rough—but even more so familiar. The same lips she had kissed every day in the past—when they had lived together.

His hands moved down, his arms wrapping around her securely. Her hands moved up to his hair, pulling him closer—if it even was possible. They gasped for air between kisses, but his lips were back on hers in a flash.

Her hands roamed down, but she froze when her hand reached his abdomen—the spot of the stab wound from when she had stabbed him.

He pulled away, knowing what was going on. His fingers intertwined with hers, and he squeezed her hands. "I'm fine. It's fine."

"I can't believe I..."

His hands moved to cup her face. "I know why you did it. You were protecting your friends, and I can live with that."

"What if *I* can't?" She hated what she had done. Had it even been necessary?

He leaned his forehead against hers. "Maybe you can after I do this."

Her brows furrowed, and he pulled away. She was about to ask what Theo was talking about, but then she spotted the object in his hand. His wand.

"Theo, w—"

He pressed the wand against her palm, his hand closing around hers. Ciara's vision went blank.

For a moment, there was nothing. All she could see was white. Perhaps a bright light.

When she regained her vision, Theo was gone.

15

A wave of guilt hit Ciara, and she tried to raise her hand to her chest.

Her hand didn't budge. She wasn't paralysed. She couldn't be because she was still standing.

But no matter which muscle she tried to move, nothing happened.

"I'm sorry." The words echoed around her.

No, not around. They were in her head.

Ciara expected herself to panic, but her heartbeats remained calm. Something was terribly wrong.

"I need to do this to protect you." The words echoed inside her head again.

"What the hell is this?" she screamed. Her mouth didn't move, but she could hear her own words—her own voice—in her mind.

She was aware of her surroundings, but she couldn't move. Trying to lift her arm, she failed. Her body didn't react.

Had Theo frozen her?

No. His wand was in her hand. She was clinging onto it.

His wand, not hers. She wouldn't have even needed a wand, but he did.

He didn't have the gift of wandless magic; she did.

Panic rushed through Ciara, but still her body didn't react. She tried and tried, but nothing.

"Theo?"

"I'm sorry."

"Stop this instant!" She tried her hardest to let go of the wand, but nothing happened. It was a spell—an enchantment of sorts.

"I'm not going to hurt you."

"Get the hell out of me!" Struggling wasn't going to help her. She had let him in by trusting him.

He had played her, and she had let herself be played like a fool.

Her body moved. But not under her control. He controlled her body—her every move. Only thing he couldn't control was her mind.

"I didn't play you. This is how I'll help your friend. No one will know it's me," Theo said, his voice once again inside her head.

"You will help Bill?" Hope blossomed inside Ciara—not that her body reacted to it.

"Yes." Theo pulled something out of Ciara's pocket—with her hand, using her body. Her second pack of cigarettes.

"Will you let me go then?"

"No." Theo tossed the cigarettes away and then did the same for the other cigarette pack on the kitchen counter. But for once, Ciara didn't care about them. She had something more important to think about.

"At least you didn't lie this time."

"I can't lie to you now, but you can't lie to me either. One could say that we share all our thoughts right now. Feelings, more or less, too."

The guilt. It was Theo's.

And guilt and secrets were never a good mix.

It was way past visiting hours. Theo either didn't know or he didn't care. As he walked to the front desk of the hospital—in Ciara's body—she figured out his plan.

He started shaking, acting upset. Ciara didn't know the healer at the front desk, and the said woman was happy to let her in, even outside visiting hours.

"Guess she didn't know you." Theo's act hadn't been perfect. It wouldn't have worked on anyone Ciara knew. She wasn't the emotional type.

"She didn't."

Theo—in Ciara's body—headed towards Bill's room. Thanks to Ciara's thoughts, he seemed to know the way.

"Wanna know how I got control of you so easily?"

"I foolishly trusted you."

"I enforced the spell for future uses at the warehouse when you stabbed me." He was playing the long game while she had forgotten all about the reality—the fact he was the enemy.

"In case I would try to stab you again?" Was that why she also had the mark on her?

"You wouldn't stab me again. I could see it in your face when you first did."

Theo was right. Of course he was. He knew her inside and out.

"I do, and the spell has nothing to do with the mark," he said inside her head.

He could sense all her thoughts—or hear them. She couldn't quite explain how it worked. It was the first time she shared a body with someone.

It was tricky magic. Undoubtedly, Theo had been training his magic during his fake death. Ciara wished she didn't know how, but she did. Training magic was like training sports. If you wanted to become a better runner, you had to run.

If you wanted to be good at taking over somebody's body, you had to do that. Again and again.

"I don't agree with the torture," Theo said, speaking inside Ciara's head again. "But we deserve to be a visible part of this world without punishment. Just like non-magics. We should have equal rights."

Theo agreed with the witch hunters. But he didn't seem to agree with their methods. Ciara didn't know what to make of it.

The time spent with the witch hunters had affected him. Yet he was still Theo. Perhaps with more flaws, but Theo nonetheless.

Ciara's hand—controlled by Theo—reached for the doorknob and opened Bill's hospital room's door.

"You won't hurt him, right?" Her own panic rushed through her mind, but once again, it had no effect on her body. No racing heart, no quick breaths, nothing.

"No, I'll heal him and then I'll go."

"With or without me?"

"With you."

"You can't stay in my body forever."

"I know."

An image flashed through Ciara's mind—or rather, Theo's. An image of Liam's face.

"What—"

"Don't finish that thought if you want me to heal your friend."

She had a hard time shifting her thoughts back to Bill. She focused on Bill's pale skin and pained expression. He looked half-dead. Perhaps even more dead than alive.

"I'm sorry I did this."

"Me too."

Theo moved closer to the bed, Ciara's body obeying him unconditionally. With one hand, he grabbed Bill's left hand, and with the other, he grabbed his wand from Ciara's pocket.

It was his wand, not hers, even though she had one too.

Despite being unable to control her own body, Ciara could feel how cold Bill was. She hadn't lost her senses; she shared them with Theo.

"He would have died within a week. I'm sorry."

"Is he healed now?"

"Not yet."

Ciara tried to calm her thoughts, so Theo could focus on healing Bill. She wasn't sure if it helped, but a bright light blinded her for a moment.

Bill gasped for air like surfacing from below water.

Before Ciara could even see his eyes open, Theo ran out of the room.

"Theo, I need to see him!"

"No!"

Liam's face flashed through Theo's mind again.

"Theo?"

He flicked his wand, and they—in her body—appeared just outside the safe house.

Anger and worry mixed in Ciara. "What the fuck are you planning to do to Liam?"

16

Liam couldn't believe Ciara! How could she?

She had every right to be angry with Liam, with Henry, with Jenna, with their mother Mary, even with their father...but Gabe hadn't lied to her. He was one of the few people Ciara couldn't hold responsible for any of it.

Gabe had invited her to his birthday dinner, eager for her to join them like she had so many times before in the past, but she failed to show up. Ciara's absence left Gabe visibly disappointed, despite his efforts to hide it.

Gabe skilfully dodged the subject whenever someone accidentally brought up Ciara in a conversation. Even Henry steered clear of mentioning Ciara. They were both hurt that Ciara hadn't shown up, their anticipation having turned to disappointment.

If Ciara had come, Liam wouldn't have forced her to talk to him. He would have let her be. A no was a no, and she didn't want to talk to Liam. He could respect that even if it broke him.

She should have showed up for the younger Rosslers.

"I can't believe she didn't show up," Liam grumbled when he walked Henry and Jenna to the door.

Jenna gave him a pointed look, ready to defend her long-time friend. "She's not in an easy position."

"I can talk to her," Henry suggested, his arm wrapped around Jenna.

"Do that."

With a beep coming from his pocket, Liam pulled out his phone. Mistaking it for a work-related message, he muttered a curse. The moment he saw Ciara's name on the screen, his body tensed up.

"Actually, I can talk to her," he said and looked back up.

"You?" Henry shook his head, frowning. "I don't think that's the smartest idea."

"She texted me." Liam glanced at the words on his phone's screen. "She wants to talk, or so she says."

Jenna smiled as if seeing right through him. "And you're still angry?"

Liam tried to be. Ciara should have come to the dinner—for Gabe. Despite being hospitalised, even their father had been allowed to come for a few hours.

"Depends on what she has to say."

It didn't depend on anything. He was dying to talk to her. She had been avoiding him since that wretched night—the warehouse mission.

The memory of that warehouse—of what had happened in there—still made him shudder. And still filled him with regret.

"Will you be okay on your own?" Henry frowned. "After all, it's Ciara. I doubt she'll go easy on you."

Jenna rolled her eyes and turned to her boyfriend, the sound of her exasperated sigh filling the air. "Oh, please. Your brother can handle himself."

Liam smiled at the couple. "I'll be fine."

"Don't get your hopes up," Henry warned.

"I won't."

They finished their goodbyes, and Henry and Jenna left. Polly and Poppy had already gone upstairs, but their mother and Gabe were in the living room. Their father was already back at the hospital, because it wasn't safe for him to be away from surveillance for too long. He wouldn't even have been allowed home if it wasn't for Mary and the fact that she worked at the hospital.

Liam walked to the living room, lingering in the doorway. It was still Gabriel's birthday. He didn't want to leave, and yet he did. In the worst case, it was his last chance to prove himself to Ciara.

The words stuck to his throat as he hesitated. Eventually, though, he knew what he had to do. "I need to go somewhere. Is that okay?"

It was still Gabriel's birthday, and Liam felt like he was abandoning his brother on his special day. Liam wanted to blame it on Ciara, but he couldn't. Ciara wouldn't intentionally spoil Gabriel's day. Liam refused to believe that. Even if Ciara could be selfish, she always put people that mattered before herself. People like Gabe, who didn't let her down.

Liam's mother frowned. "I thought we would watch a movie or—"

"Where are you going?" Gabe asked.

Liam pondered on telling the truth, and in the end, he told just that. "Ciara asked me to talk with her."

His brother's brows rose. "When?"

"Now." Liam held up his phone, the message still open on the screen.

"Oh."

Liam sighed, his brows creasing with worry. "Why is everyone so surprised?"

"I talked to her yesterday," Gabriel admitted.

Liam and their mother both turned their gaze towards Gabe. "What?" they said in unison.

"I went to see her yesterday."

"And you two talked?" Liam blinked, trying to shake off the fog in his head. "About what?"

Gabe shrugged. "A lot of things. But I tried to tell her she should talk to you."

"Looks like it worked," Liam mumbled, glancing at the message on his phone's screen. He glanced back at his brother, chest filling with hope. Dangerous hope. "T-thank you."

Gabriel shifted in his seat, eyes cast down. "You should know something, though."

"What is it?"

"It's about what happened at the warehouse. About what she did to get you all out of there." Gabe grimaced, his lips twisting into a pained expression.

"What are you talking about, Gabriel?" Worry painted their mother's face as she glanced between her sons.

"She stabbed Theo, and I don't think she told anyone about it. At least she didn't tell everyone," Gabriel said, glancing from Liam to their mother uneasily.

"She what?" Liam and his mother spoke in unison.

"She—"

"Did he die?" Liam asked.

Gabe's arms wrapped around himself, even if he didn't realise it. "I don't know. I don't think she knows either."

"She killed Theo?" Blood rushed off Liam's face, and worry filled his guts. He hadn't known. That night—the night they had broken up—he had loaded all his problems on her.

He had never realised what she had done—and everything she had gone through.

He had been angry with her for comparing him to Theo. But she had been mourning someone she had once loved. Despite discovering that her friends and Liam had lied to her, she had still chosen to save them by killing Theo.

Liam had never been so sorry in his life—and he had to tell Ciara.

"Apparently." Gabe nodded. "I shouldn't have told you, but…"

"I'm glad you did."

"You're going now?" Mary asked.

"Yes." Liam stopped and swallowed. "I must apologise. Properly. I never realised…what she did in there. Hell, she probably saved all our lives." His fingers raked through his hair as blood slowly returned to his cheeks.

"At quite a price." Mary's lips thinned into a line. "Make sure she's okay."

"I'm planning to. But I have to go now."

Ciara had texted him again. He hastily replied, telling her he would meet her wherever. Right after she texted him an address of a pub.

"I need to go." Liam forgot to say goodbye to Gabe and his mother before he rushed out.

Perhaps he still had a chance with Ciara.

Liam spotted her dark hair swaying in the wind. She stood in front of a pub on a quiet street, looking around, waiting for him.

"Ciara." He didn't mean to sound so desperate, but he didn't care. She needed to know how he felt. How sorry he was.

With a quick spin, Ciara faced him and smiled. It didn't quite reach her eyes, but even the effort surprised Liam. She hadn't looked at him like that since that horrendous night at the warehouse.

"Y-you wanted to talk." Only she could make him stumble over his words like that.

"Yeah." Her voice was softer than the last time they had talked. As if she no longer hated him as much as she had.

He knew he shouldn't have got his hopes up. But standing there in front of her was the closest thing to a conversation they had had since that mission. He was dying to fix what he had broken. It was already a promising start.

Liam knew hope was dangerous, but he couldn't help it. He would fight for Ciara.

"I know I suggested this place." Ciara gestured at the pub's door, a frown crossing her face. "B-but do you think we could talk at the nearby motel?"

Liam's eyebrows rose. The word *motel* raised new thoughts in his mind. They had barely talked the past seven weeks. She couldn't want to sleep with him. Could she?

"I...uh..."

She bit her lip, trying to hold back a smile. Liam loved when she did that. "Based on that look, I can practically hear your thoughts. I just want to talk in private."

"I know. Of course." He wanted to punch himself for letting his thoughts show through. "I'm sorry, Ciara." *Sorry for everything.*

She nodded, and her smile dropped. "Shall we?" She gestured ahead, towards the motel where they would finally talk.

"Yeah."

17

"Theo, stop!" Ciara screamed inside her head. "Theo, I'll never forgive you. Fuck! Just stop."

She tried to move, but her body refused to cooperate. Theo was still in control, no matter how hard she tried to fight it—to regain control over her own body. He refused to stop. She had already begged for hours. For nothing. He didn't listen.

"Theo!"

"I'm sorry."

Her feet kept moving towards the motel, along the pavement.

"The fuck you are!"

"I have to do this for you!"

"I will kill you myself if you even touch him."

But both Theo and Ciara knew it wasn't true. She *couldn't* hurt Theo again.

But if something happened to Liam because of him, Ciara wasn't sure what she would do—or could do.

Liam walked beside her—or him. Her body, but under Theo's control.

Liam didn't have any idea about what was going on. Not the faintest clue. He sincerely thought it was Ciara—and that she wanted to talk to him.

And she wanted to. She was dying to tell him to run for his life, but she had no control over her body. Her screams only echoed inside her head, her lips unmoving.

She should have never trusted Theo.

Hurt rushed through her. She had learned the odd waves of feelings weren't hers, but Theo's.

"You better be hurt!" she screamed in her mind. "Don't you get what you're about to do?"

"I know exactly what I'm about to do."

Ciara couldn't quite explain it, but a memory ran through her mind like a clip from a movie. It wasn't her memory, but there were two people she recognised. The memory had to be Theo's. Theresa was also in it.

"They want me to do this," Theo said inside her head.

Ciara's mind went blank for a second. "Who wants you to do this?" she demanded hastily.

"I heard you talked to Gabe." That was Liam's voice, talking to her. But she couldn't answer.

Only Theo could. He moved her head, making her nod. "I did."

"Theo, what the hell is going on?" Ciara screamed inside her own head.

"I'm doing this for your safety. Stop asking questions. I can't lie," Theo said in her head.

"Which is why I'm not stopping!"

Ciara tried to regain control, but she wasn't powerful enough. She wasn't trained enough. Being trapped in her own body was worse than being paralysed. After all, she was moving, but she had no control over her body.

She was like a puppet that Theo was using in his own game.

The motel was already in sight, and panic built up. It wasn't just Ciara's panic. Theo was panicking, too.

Another memory—like a scene from a movie—rushed through Ciara's mind. It was from the same moment as the earlier one. There was a man speaking—a man she didn't recognise.

But that man threatened to gut Ciara with a dull dining knife if Theo didn't do what he was told to.

"Who was that?" Ciara asked Theo. It was his thought—his memory—so he knew what she was referring to.

It was all in his thoughts. He couldn't lie, nor could he hide his thoughts from her. It seemed to be the only perk of the situation. They shared their minds as they shared her body. It was an odd experience. It was as if Ciara could read Theo's mind. Everything he thought about was in her head, too.

"Elliott Hardy, the founder of witch hunters. He hates the name, though. Witch hunters are not like the Salem hunters, which the name comes from. He claims the media is full of dimwits for coming up with such a name."

Elliott. The man Jesse had talked about. That man was blackmailing Theo.

Elliott Hardy was behind everything. He was the man Ciara had tried to hunt down for years and years, and still she had never found him.

Ciara—and Theo—and Liam made it to the motel's parking area, walking in silence. That was enough for Ciara to momentarily set aside thoughts of Elliott.

"Theo!" Overwhelming panic and fear rushed through Ciara—both her and Theo's panic and fear. "Theo, please, don't do this. I'll be fine. I don't know what they're threatening to do, but I can handle it. You don't have to do this. *Please*, don't do this."

"I can't lose you, Ciara."

"Theo, don't do this, or you will lose me forever."

"I'll be fine as long as you are alive."

"Fuck! Theo!" It was like trying to break a dome made of unbreakable glass. Nothing worked. Ciara was trapped inside her own body—her own head.

"This way," Theo said to Liam, speaking with Ciara's voice.

Ciara tried to find his presence within her, so she could push him out. She was running out of time if she wanted to save Liam.

She had to save Liam.

"You can't," Theo told her through his thoughts.

"Fuck you, Theo! Stop this right now!"

"I faked my death to keep you safe."

"Fuck, Theo! Fuck!" The cursing wasn't helping, but she couldn't think straight anymore. There was only panic.

And determination to get Liam out of the situation alive. It didn't look good for him—or her.

"Theo, please, I'll do anything," Ciara begged.

"I don't want to do this, but I have to keep you safe."

"I don't want you to keep me safe!"

Theo led Liam towards a motel room, looking for keys in *her* pocket. Liam still hadn't realised it wasn't Ciara.

Liam, please. He had to realise she was acting odd. Theo was a great actor because he was inside her head, but Liam had to see through the act. Liam had to know she wouldn't have asked him to leave Gabe on Gabe's birthday.

"You already have a room?" Liam asked.

This time, Theo played his role well. He fidgeted with the keys, acting nervous. "Y-yeah. I wasn't sure if I'd want to talk in private or not. So, just in case."

"I'm glad you want to talk. It means a lot."

Theo smiled at Liam in Ciara's body. Their gazes met, and Ciara could see Liam's hazel eyes twinkle with hope. Her heart broke, knowing Theo's plan.

Hope had blinded Liam, and he wouldn't see through the act. Liam would think it was her, and somehow that was the worst part.

Theo unlocked the door and opened it, gesturing for Liam to go in first. Ciara tried to push Theo out, but her efforts were for nothing.

"Theo, please." If her voice had been audible, it would have been high-pitched and hysterical.

"They threatened to hurt my mother."

"We'll get her to safety. I swear!"

Ciara couldn't lose Liam. If she had been in control of her own body, she would have been a screaming, sobbing wreck.

"No, Ciara."

Theo locked the door before following Liam into the dimly lit room. The furniture displayed a variety of muted red tones, ranging from burgundy to maroon. The walls, painted in a vibrant shade of yellow, stood in stark contrast to the earthy brown floor and ceiling.

Soon, though, everything would be tainted with red.

"Let me talk first." As Liam spun around, his eyes connected with Ciara's, their intensity evident. "Gabe told me something."

She trembled, but not from her emotions. It was from Theo's anxiety. He didn't *want* to kill Liam.

"He said you stabbed Theo. T-that you possibly killed him." Worry seeped into Liam's voice, making it quiver.

Ciara's mouth opened, but Theo didn't have words for the situation. Liam misread the situation, likely thinking her voice got caught in her throat. He moved closer. His hand reached out, but he pulled it back to his side before he touched Ciara.

He respected her boundaries while Theo had violated every one of them, even invading her mind.

"I'm so sorry, Ciara." His voice was low, quiet, and full of sorrow. Sorrow for her. He thought she had killed Theo.

Regardless of Theo being alive, her feelings about the situation remained unaffected. She regretted hurting Theo.

But the moment Theo would lay a finger on Liam, that

would undoubtedly change.

"I know he meant a lot to you." Liam cleared his throat, keeping his eyes fixed on Ciara's. "You loved him. A lot."

Theo froze as Ciara's mind filled with memories. Memories of her sorrow, of sharing that sorrow with Liam and her friends, and of the sorrow shared with Theo's mother.

"I lied to you about how Doherty died, because I knew the truth would break you. It would have broken your heart. I didn't even want to believe it myself. For a while, I tried to deny it. I never...I should have realised you would find out, and you would have deserved to find out some other way. *Any* other way."

Ciara wanted to cry. If only she had been in control of her body, she would have reacted. But she couldn't even move. All she had were her thoughts and feelings, swirling like a storm in her mind.

And Theo inside her head, controlling her.

Liam had come to make things right with her. That meant the world to her, but she wished he hadn't shown up. She would have rather seen him hate her than die for caring.

"I saw Theo kill him. You were so broken when you...saw Doherty lying on the floor. W-when we brought him back. I just couldn't tell you." Tears formed in the corners of Liam's eyes.

Image of that night flashed in Ciara's mind. Her crumbling to the floor. Liam catching her and taking her upstairs. Her state of shock. The numbness that followed.

She still wasn't over it. Losing Doherty had been too much. Losing Liam would be worse.

"Theo, don't do this," Ciara begged in her mind. She knew Theo had seen her memories.

In his mind, Theo said, "If only I didn't have to do this."

"I know I should have told you, and I'm so sorry. Hurting you was never my intention. I...I didn't want *him* to hurt you, so I tried to keep you in the dark. But that was wrong, and you can't even imagine how sorry I am. I was a fool, and that's on me. My only intention was to keep you from getting hurt, Ciara. I love you and I'm sorry I wasn't there for you when I should have been." Silent tears slid down Liam's cheeks. "You don't have to forgive me. I wouldn't expect you to. All I want is for you to know how sorry I am." He swallowed, pausing. "I never meant to hurt you," Liam whispered, the words like a caress.

If only Ciara had control over her body, tears would have streamed down her face. She had never given Liam the chance to explain. Now that he did, his words hit home.

"It's time." The thought—Theo's thought—echoed through Ciara's head.

"Theo, Theo, Theo. Please, stop!" She tried to push him out, but he wouldn't budge—as if he was glued to her.

"I'm sorry." Her voice, Theo's words.

Liam blinked away his tears. "You—"

Theo pulled Ciara's dagger from her belt.

"I'll kill myself if you kill him!" Ciara screamed in her mind. The problem was that it wasn't true, and Theo knew it, as her thoughts laid it all bare. Thoughts that he forced her to share with him.

Her hand moved, gripping the knife, under Theo's command.

"Ciara!" Liam's eyes widened. He tried to jump back, but she—or rather Theo—moved too fast, cutting Liam's arm. The deep gash was a gruesome sight, and the metallic smell of blood filled the air as it quickly soaked his sleeve.

"Theo!" Ciara screamed. It felt as futile as trying to break through a concrete wall with bare fists.

Ciara's body moved, kicking Liam in the face and sending him to the ground. She jumped on him and punched his face. Except it was all Theo.

"Theo!" Ciara was shaking.

"I'm sorry."

"Stop! Stop! Stop!" She was shaking.

Theo, controlling Ciara's body, punched Liam in the face again.

"Ciara." Liam's voice was nasal. Theo had already broken his nose.

But Liam thought it was *her*.

"You can't do this to me!" Ciara wanted to throw up. The thought of Liam dying and the possibility of being his killer left her feeling nauseous and unsettled. Even the thought of losing him *killed* her.

Ciara's hand moved, raising the knife. Her other hand's knuckles ached from punching Liam.

Liam's gaze shifted from Ciara's knife to the steely determination in her eyes—Theo's determination. Panic, terror, and confusion mixed on Liam's face.

"Theo!" she screamed in her head. She had to make him stop.

"Ciara, please." Liam's voice was barely above a whisper, as if he couldn't believe what was happening.

She pushed harder, desperate to get through. She had already lost enough. Losing Liam would be too much. Even if they weren't together, he meant the world to her.

Stop.

Theo, stop.

Stop, stop, stop, stop, stop!

STOP!

Her hand moved against her will. The knife sunk into Liam's abdomen, her fingers wrapped around the handle. Her hands coated in sanguine liquid—Liam's blood.

"Theo, stop!"

The room turned white, but only for a second.

When her vision cleared, the first thing Ciara saw was her hand holding the knife. The red liquid warmed her hands, and she wanted to hurl her guts up. Her hand, stained by Liam's blood. She let go in an instant.

Theo—in his own body—lay flat on the floor.

Liam was blinking, as if struggling to stay awake.

Ciara was back in control of her body. Her hands shook. "N-no. No, no, no."

"Ciara?"

Her hands hovered over Liam's wound. "I have to..."

"Ciara?"

"T-the..." She couldn't form words.

There was blood everywhere.

It was like a replay from that night at the warehouse. She had stabbed the man she loved.

The only difference, this time it was Liam.

And there was more blood.

18

Ciara cried out, and the lights flickered. The lamp hanging from the ceiling swung in the air, threatening to fall.

Her magic pulled out the blood-covered blade from Liam's abdomen.

The lights turned on as Ciara's mind emptied. The next moments were bright flashes—like images flashing through Ciara's mind.

The knife dropped to the floor, Liam's blood dripping off of it. His blood soaked his shirt, pooling out of the stab wound. His lips were turning white. Pain was all there was left on his face. He screamed.

Then her hands were on the wound, pressing on it.

"Ciara."

His shirt was wet with the crimson liquid.

"Ciara."

It was all over her hands.

"Ciara."

It was warm.

"Ciara."

His skin was cold.

"Ciara."

Ciara blinked as she realised the blood had stopped pooling out of the wound. The light bulb burst out, snapping Ciara back to her senses.

The only light in the room came from the streetlights outside, dimmed by the thin curtains.

Liam's bleeding had stopped. Even the wound on his arm had...

It looked healed. Scarring remained, but the wound had shut itself. Ciara traced her sticky fingers along the scar.

Liam's fingers tightened around Ciara's arm, and she immediately locked eyes with him. Worry twisted his face into a frown. "Has this happened before?" He tore his gaze from her, eyes moving down to his stab wound.

Ciara's eyes followed the suit. She saw what he saw. His non-existent wound. Only fresh scarring—almost like burns—remained.

Ciara's breath hitched. "Did I—"

"I'm sorry about this," Theo said, standing up behind Ciara.

She was on her feet in an instant. She spun around and faced Theo, who held his wand. That wand had been in Ciara's pocket until it had fallen during the fight—when Theo had tried to kill Liam.

Liam scrambled up to his feet behind Ciara, but she remained in front of him—between the two men. She was Liam's shield and wouldn't let anything happen to him.

"Theo, stop," she said.

"I can't." His face had lost its colour and warmth. All that was visible was panic and worry.

"We'll get your mother to safety. I'd never let anything happen to her," Ciara reasoned.

"They'll kill you too, Ciara!" Theo's voice rose. "You don't understand what they're capable of!"

"I'd rather die than let you hurt Liam."

"Maybe you should just stay away from her." This time Liam spoke, his voice filled with anger.

Ciara glanced at Liam to see his wand in his hand. Glancing at Theo, she knew he noticed it, too.

Just as they were about to raise their wands, she stepped in, fists clenched and sent their wands flying away. "Stop!"

Using magic made her realise how tired she was. Her knees buckled. Theo grabbed her before she toppled to the ground, keeping her upright.

"Ciara!" Liam and Theo said in unison, both hovering over her. They glanced at one another, eyes narrowed.

"We need to go to Canada." The exhaustion hit Ciara like a brick wall. She could hardly summon enough energy to speak out loud.

Liam's worried eyes moved from Ciara to Theo, hardening. "What is going on?"

Theo sighed, rolling his eyes, and met Liam's gaze. "Your life will cost hers."

Liam's brows furrowed, and his eyes moved back to Ciara. "What—"

"Theo, no more killing." It was an order, but it sounded more like a plead.

Theo's eyes softened. "I can't—"

"Fuck that!" Ciara pushed him away, standing on her own. "I'm right here. I'm safe. I'm not being gutted by a dull dining knife."

Theo winced at the thought.

"Can someone explain what the fuck is going on?" Liam eyed both Theo and Ciara, understandably freaked out.

"They're blackmailing him." Ciara moved his gaze to Liam, but gestured to Theo.

"Black—"

Ciara moved her gaze back to Theo, not having finished yet. "And Theo doesn't realise I can take care of myself."

"Like a moment ago when you lost control again, huh?" Theo gestured to the bloody spot on the floor where Liam had laid before. "You drain your energy with no control over it, and that puts you in more danger than you realise. One day, you'll drain your life source."

Ciara's brows furrowed. "It rarely happens."

"But it's been happening more and more often." Theo clenched his jaw. "You're not safe."

"I'd be more worried about your mother."

Theo let out a long, frustrated sigh. "You don't get it, Ciara!"

"I get that you're being blackmailed by the witch hunters. You wouldn't even be one of them if they hadn't threatened to hurt me. You would have never faked your death if it wasn't for them, and I know that. I was inside your head just as much as you were inside mine. I know *everything*."

She knew a lot, but not everything—all thanks to Theo's trick. She knew why the witch hunters had come to Europe to begin with. It was safer and easier to pretend to be defeated in countries where they weren't hunted down. Besides, they had still managed to cause harm. They couldn't have done that in the US or Canada.

Theo shook his head, running his hands through his hair. "Not everything. Only what I thought about."

Ciara frowned. "You're still hiding something?"

"This." Theo took a step towards Ciara, but Liam blocked his way before he could get to Ciara.

"I think you've done enough harm as it is."

Ciara moved past Liam to stand between the two guys who were having a *glaring* contest. "Guys, stop." She still didn't trust them so close to one another.

After all, Theo had tried to kill Liam. Ciara didn't want to give him another chance.

"At least I didn't lie to her out of jealousy or whatever," Theo snarled.

"It had nothing to do with—"

"Guys, stop!" This time, both men looked at her, stopping their argument. Ciara sighed, shaking her head, and faced Theo. "What are you still hiding?"

"The mark on your shoulder."

"The witch hunter mark."

"I thought Jesse did that," Liam said, eyes glued on Ciara.

She shook her head and shifted her gaze to Theo. "He did."

"I didn't do that. I hid it with a spell, so you wouldn't start investigating it further. You were unconscious when *they* did it." Theo's hands were shaking, and he had a hard time controlling his voice. But anger shone through as he spoke.

"I don't know what you're talking about. You left it on my shoulder at the warehouse." Ciara pointed at the mark on her shoulder.

"No, I unveiled it at the warehouse."

"So when did I get it?"

"Our second to last mission together. You passed out from draining your energy because you couldn't control your outburst. They got you and they did that." His eyes moved to the mark before returning to meet her gaze. "They would have done a lot more."

The puzzle was complete.

She felt as if someone had hurled her against a wall, knocking all the air out of her lungs.

"They started blackmailing you back then, didn't they?" Ciara's eyes widened. "That's why you were so nervous before our last mission, why you didn't want me to even come. You knew what would happen. That you would pretend to die. That—"

"Yes. They think you can either be a threat or an ally. I told them I would handle it, but I needed time." Theo sighed. "You're not just another hit witch to them, like everyone else."

"How soon will they go to Canada?" Blood rushed off Ciara's face, thinking about Estella.

"Soon if I don't go to them with his corpse." Theo didn't turn to look at Liam, but he pointed at him.

"We need to get your mother to safety."

To Ciara's surprise, Theo nodded. As if he had finally given up on hurting Liam. Hopefully, he had.

"I need to talk to you, Ciara."

She turned to Liam but didn't get a chance to say anything. Theo beat her to it.

"I'll wait outside. Get rid of him," Theo said, heading for the door.

"Liam's coming with us."

Ciara's words made Theo halt and turn around. "I'm not letting him anywhere near my mother, not knowing what he'll do."

Liam glared at Theo. "Frankly, I'm not the one who tried to kill the other."

"No one is going to hurt anyone." Ciara looked between the guys to make sure neither had such plans in mind. "If you were told to kill him, he's not safe on his own."

"What about his family?" Theo crossed his arms. "There's no guarantee they won't be in danger when the witch hunters realise what's going on."

Theo was right, but Ciara already had a plan. "I'll alert Kellan."

"Fine." Without another word, Theo headed out.

"Are you okay?"

Ciara took a deep breath and faced Liam. "I'm pretty sure I should ask you that. I stabbed you."

"*He* stabbed me." Liam pointed towards the door. "You... you healed me." He blinked, glancing down at the healed wound. His eyes held mesmerisation as if he couldn't believe what he saw.

"I guess." Ciara wasn't sure what had happened. If Theo was right, it had been another outburst. Just not the violent type this time.

Ciara wasn't a medical expert, but she could tell the

wound hadn't been bad enough to kill instantly. Even so, she shouldn't have been able to seal it. She shouldn't have been able to save him with magic. It was a miracle he didn't need proper medical treatment.

Healing magic wasn't real. Magic could do a lot, but she had only shut the wound. Potions were for healing. She wasn't great with potions. But evidently she was skilled enough with spells to seal a wound shut. At least during one of her magical outbursts.

"I'm fine, though." Liam frowned. "Or at least I am now."

"Good."

"Are you sure you can trust him?" Liam's eyes moved between Ciara and the room's door. "He killed Doherty."

Ciara shuddered. Liam was right. Theo had killed Doherty—someone dear to Ciara. Regardless of the reasons behind his actions or any potential regret, Theo had still committed the crime.

"Against his own will," Ciara said, even though it wasn't that simple. "He was protecting me and his mother. And yes, he's done other horrible things. But he knows that. I...*we* can trust him."

"I don't trust him." Liam's eyes narrowed. "You do realise he tried to kill me? He killed Doherty. He faked his own death and lied to you for months."

"I know. All of that. I was inside his head, Liam." She shook her head. *And you lied to me for months too*, she thought, but didn't say that part out loud. It wasn't the right time. "Trusting and forgiving are different things. But he's not some mindless psychopath like you think."

Liam's eyes widened in disbelief. "He tried to kill me."

"I haven't forgotten, nor will I ever forgive him. But Elliott Hardy threatened to gut me with a dull dining knife if he didn't do it. He shou—"

"Who is Elliott Hardy?" Liam's gaze hardened, fixed on Ciara.

Ciara frowned. She finally knew who to go after, but

instead of going after him, she would have to run away to Canada to save Estella. "The witch hunters' actual leader. The one and only. He has somehow stayed in the shadows until now. I still don't know the entire story, but he's the first witch hunter."

"He's their leader?"

Ciara nodded.

"A-and he threatened to..." Liam winced and didn't finish the sentence.

"He threatened to kill me and he also threatened to hurt Theo's mother. He has done so multiple times, if I'm right."

Liam sighed, as if he hated every bit about the situation. "So Canada?"

"You wouldn't hurt Estella, right?" Ciara had to be sure. She trusted Liam, but she also knew how tempting revenge was. Theo had hurt him, and Liam had every right to be furious.

Ciara had longed for revenge for a big part of her life. It felt like an old friend rather than something unwelcome. She was the last person who could blame another for that same longing.

Liam's gaze didn't falter as he looked Ciara straight in the eyes. His expression was serious but sincere. "I would never."

"Good." Ciara pulled her phone out of her pocket. "I'll get Theo. We'll have to leave the instant I end the phone call."

"Why?"

"We can't have Kellan or the others follow us. Too risky with spies and everything." Ciara still hadn't recovered from Theresa's betrayal. She wasn't going to let there be a rerun of that.

19

When Ciara, Liam, and Theo landed in Vancouver, city lights greeted them in the dark night. There was nothing they could do until the morning when Ciara could finally execute her plan. Yet again, she would need Josh's help.

She hadn't had a chance to warn him, but she knew he would help. Josh always helped her.

Ciara, Liam, and Theo got a room in a motel because they all needed the night's rest.

"You got just one bed?" Theo asked, being the first one to step in the room.

Ciara stepped in right after Theo, followed by Liam. She stared at the double bed in the middle of the room. Taking a quick look around, she cursed in her mind. There wasn't even a sofa.

"I said three."

"I'll take care of it." Liam was out before Ciara could even utter a word.

"Tense, huh?"

Ciara shot a glare at Theo. "You tried to kill him," she hissed at Theo, not in the mood for any humorous comments.

The glimmer left Theo's eyes. "I'm sorry." He sighed. "And yes, I know no number of apologises will make you forgive me. I don't expect you to forgive. Like you said, I tried to kill him."

"You won't hurt him again, right?"

Ciara had trusted Theo to be smart enough not to try anything in an airplane. But they were on the ground now. Just the three of them. She couldn't be sure the guys wouldn't try to hurt one another.

But she had more trust in Liam than she did in Theo.

"I swore on it, didn't I?" Theo raised an eyebrow, expecting Ciara to reply.

"You did." She looked around the room, grimacing at the lonely double bed.

"If this is the only room we can get, you can share the bed with Liam."

Ciara frowned. "I don't...I don't think he'd be okay with that."

"It would be awkward."

"You said it yourself."

Theo hummed. "I doubt you'll share it with me, either."

"No."

"We could try a threesome."

Ciara shot another glare at Theo. "Not funny."

"You don't want to share a bed with two of your exes?" His brows rose, and a smirk formed on his lips.

He was pushing her buttons, but she refused to snap at him. It had been a long day for all of them.

And it wasn't over yet.

Ciara couldn't wait to get some sleep.

There was no way they could share the bed *and* get some sleep. She couldn't think of anything more awkward than sleeping between two of her exes who were plotting each other's painful ends.

"We could just skip sleep."

Ciara shook her head. "I think we all need sleep after tonight." The time difference between London and Vancouver didn't help with that.

Theo didn't argue. Instead, he nodded, for once agreeing. "I bet he'll try to get a room for you two, and a separate room for me."

"Your jealousy is shining through," Ciara teased, but her voice didn't come out as light as she had meant it to.

Theo's lips thinned, his stormy grey eyes fixed on Ciara. "You love him."

"It's not that simple."

"I know. In fact, I know *everything*."

She held his gaze. "You do."

"Except one thing."

"Like..."

"When did you stop wearing the engagement ring on the chain?" Theo's eyes moved to Ciara's neck.

"After I found out you're alive. But I still have it at home."

"Will you throw it out when you get home?"

"No."

"So you don't...hate me."

"I'm angry, if that's what you're asking." She crossed her arms across her chest. She was furious, to be honest, but there would be a better time to talk about it. Later.

Estella came first. They needed to get her to safety, and they needed one another until then.

Theo looked away. His eyes moved to the door, waiting for Liam to appear. "I wouldn't expect anything less."

"But I don't hate you." Ciara's voice softened.

His eyes snapped back to her, the storminess easing. "I'm glad you don't."

Ciara smiled. She knew she had lost Theo. But maybe he hadn't lost himself yet.

Just when she was about to reply, Liam walked in. He

didn't have a new key in his hands. "The guy claims they don't have another room. And the cleaner said someone trashed the other free rooms last night. They won't let us stay in either."

Ciara's throat closed. She couldn't believe her luck—or lack thereof.

"So it's this or nothing." Liam glanced at Theo, but then his gaze returned to Ciara.

"Great," she muttered sarcastically. She didn't bother to hide her annoyance. She had expected to get a good night's sleep, but it looked like that wasn't going to happen. "Guess it's our only option, then."

Liam nodded and closed the door behind him.

The room felt even smaller with the door closed. The air filled with tense silence. Ciara didn't dare to turn around to look at the stupid bed. The only bed they had for the night.

The guys had to be thinking about the same thing.

Ciara wanted to scream at the universe. There was no way she would share the bed with Theo and tell Liam to sleep on the floor. Not after what Theo had done. She still wasn't sure if her healing spell would even last, so she preferred to keep an eye on Liam. She was still worried.

But sharing the bed with Liam and telling Theo to sleep on the floor didn't sound much better.

Even with everything going on, she cared about them both. She had once been planning her future with Theo. They had even owned a house together.

She didn't know how they had ended up in the mess they were in.

She sighed, hating the words before they came out of her mouth. "Three can share a bed, right?"

It had been a long day, and it wasn't like she hadn't shared a bed with both guys at some point. In fact, she had shared a bed with them plenty of times. Just not at the same time.

It was going to be deadly awkward, but she wanted to sleep. She had never been as tired.

Liam didn't look comfortable with the idea, but Theo just shrugged.

"Fine by me."

After getting Theo's answer, Ciara turned to look at Liam. "This once and never again?"

"Guess there's no other option."

It was going to be one hell of a night, and Ciara already dreaded it.

⚜ ⚜ ⚜

Both guys were standing, arms crossed, on different sides of the room, when Ciara walked out of the bathroom. She had taken off her jeans, but she wasn't going to take off her shirt. The situation was already awkward enough.

Theo headed to the bathroom after her, and she walked over to the bed.

Standing next to the bed, she turned to face Liam. "Are you...uh...okay with this?" Her cheeks turned red. Even thinking about sleeping in the same bed with both guys had that effect on her. She was praying to be swallowed by the earth, so she wouldn't have to make it through the night.

"It's our only option." Liam shrugged, walking closer to Ciara. He stopped in front of her. "But never again."

Ciara grimaced. "Agreed."

"Are you okay?" Liam asked, both his voice and eyes softening.

Ciara looked up at him, dying to brush his hair behind his ear. But she kept her hands in check, forcing them to stay at her sides. She didn't want to make the situation more awkward—if that was even possible.

"I've been better," Ciara admitted.

Liam snorted lightly. "I know the feeling."

"Does the scar hurt?" Her eyes travelled down to his abdomen. A new, intact shirt covered his body, but she could remember the exact spot.

"No, it's fine." Liam's face brightened a smidge, a small

smile appearing. "I feel fine."

Ciara nodded, letting out a sigh of relief. "Good. I was worried."

"I could tell." Liam reached into his jeans' pocket. "But I guess this works then." He held up the lucky charm Ciara had given her before their mission at the warehouse. "I'm pretty sure it worked before. That night."

Ciara looked between the charm and Liam. It made sense. In every deadly situation he faced, he avoided severe injuries.

"I think you should have it. After all, it's yours." He pried her hand open and placed it on her palm.

"You sure you don't need it? You've been in a lot of dangerous situations lately." Ciara swallowed, worry seeping back into her heart. "I don't want anything to happen to you."

"You need it more." His brows furrowed, creating a shadow over his piercing eyes. His voice was rough—raw with feeling. "I'd rather not see you wheeled off to a surgery again."

Liam saw that? Ciara hadn't known. She hadn't realised how worried he had been. But there it was, right in front of her, the raw feeling clear in his eyes.

He still cared, and that warmed her in the pleasant, tingly sort of way.

Theo walked out of the bathroom, and Ciara didn't want to go on with the conversation. Especially when Theo's eyes fell on the lucky charm. It had been a gift from Theo to her.

She hadn't realised why he had given it before. After the recent discoveries, she did. He had seen the witch hunters burn the mark on her while she had been unconscious. He had given it after that mission.

Theo cleared his throat. "I'm dead tired."

"Same." Ciara twirled her fingers for a spell and the charm floated onto the chair where her jeans were.

Liam didn't say a word. He hummed a reply that seemed to be a reluctant yes. At least Ciara interpreted it as such.

Both guys kept their clothes on. They were still as statues. Ciara was too. No one in that bed was going to sleep much that night.

The bed was wide enough for three, but it wasn't comfortable. Not in that situation. Ciara was dying to turn onto her side, but she wouldn't. It was already awkward enough. She didn't want to face either guy—nor turn her back to the other.

And to add to her bad luck, the middle of the bed had sunken. Thanks to the sunken middle, the guys were pretty much pushed against her on both sides.

Liam lay on her right side—closer to the motel room's door. She could hear his breaths. He wasn't asleep, but he kept his eyes closed when Ciara peeked at him. She couldn't blame him. Sleeping on the same bed as Theo after what had happened couldn't be ideal—to say the least.

Theo had tried to kill Liam. She hadn't forgotten, nor had she forgiven.

But she had no doubt Theo had given up on that plan. Perhaps she was a fool, but she trusted him.

Her own breathing reached her ears, and it sounded too loud for her liking. She thought about her past with Theo. They had been in love before he had faked his death. Now that she knew he had done it to protect her, she wasn't sure what to think. She had been angry—and she still was for what Theo had planned to do to Liam. But she was also heartbroken.

And angry as fuck. The witch hunters had taken him from her, even if it wasn't in the way she had first thought. They had ruined what she and Theo had had.

Because there was no going back. Everything was too fucked up for that.

Ciara's feelings for Theo weren't burning with passion anymore, but the embers were still there. She longed for what they had once had. Something she couldn't have. Not after everything he had done.

The thought of what Theo had done nauseated her.

Ciara had to close her eyes and try to focus on something else.

She let her mind drift to Liam, who lay still as a statue on her right side. He cared. He was sorry. They needed to have that conversation, but they still had hope.

At least Ciara had hope for her and Liam.

Theo pretended to yawn and stretched his arms as he did. Then he relaxed on Ciara's left side.

She allowed her muscles to relax too, and soon she felt Liam relax beside her as well. The awkwardness lingered, but she had hope of getting some sleep. She had slept with both guys before—in more than one sense. She could share a bed with them this one time.

With that thought in her mind, she allowed the warmth of the bed and the company to embrace her and finally fell asleep.

20

Ciara tapped her arm with her finger, her nerves driving her insane. She kept looking around, trying to spot the person she was waiting for. Her hair kept flying onto her face, covering her view, thanks to the windy winter weather.

Perhaps he hadn't understood her message. Or perhaps the prepaid phone had been faulty. She sighed, air passing between her lips.

It looked like smoke as it rose. A signal. Perhaps a warning of what was to come.

"Something really *that* wrong?"

Ciara spun around and came face to face with a familiar, bald African-American man in his thirties. Josh stood right in front of her.

It was about time. Every minute was a minute wasted.

"You have no idea," she said, running her hand through her hair. She struggled to keep her hair off her face. "It's complicated, to say the least."

Josh's left eyebrow rose. "You're undercover or something?"

Ciara hesitated for a second. "Something." She took a quick look around, scanning the mass of people. "No one knows you're here, right?"

"No. What's going on?" His voice grew more serious—more demanding—but the worry shone through as well.

"I need you to trust me." Ciara gave Josh a long look, so he would know it wasn't as simple as he had likely imagined.

He nodded, the movement oddly slow, as if he hesitated. "I'll try my best."

"*Do* your best." Ciara started walking and Josh followed her.

Liam and Theo were waiting at a nearby alley. It hadn't been Ciara's brightest idea to leave them alone, but it had been her only option. Josh would have grown suspicious if she asked him to meet her *and* Liam. But Josh also couldn't see Theo out in public, where it was crowded.

Josh still thought Theo was a witch hunter. He, like most others, didn't know the whole truth.

"You're acting weird, you know," Josh said. He surveyed the area carefully.

Ciara couldn't blame him.

"You'll see why soon. I just need you to wait before you do anything...harsh or abrupt. Just know you're safe, no matter what you may think of this. You can trust me."

Josh gave her a weird look, but nodded. "Alright."

Sweat coated Ciara's palms as the pair of them walked away from the crowded streets, nearing the remote alley. Her heart thudded and worry gnawed in her chest. It wasn't just Josh's reaction she was worried about. She was also worried about what she would find around the corner. Theo wouldn't try to kill Liam. Not again. But that didn't mean Theo and Liam got along.

Ciara shuddered, thinking how she had nearly lost Liam. She would have lost him without the outburst of magic. And

Ciara didn't even remember what had happened during said outburst. It was all hazy in her head.

She hadn't healed the wound. She had sealed it, but apparently that had been enough. At least Liam was fine.

"Don't...touch your wand." Ciara eyed Josh. "I know your first reaction will be to do that, but you don't need your wand. No one is going to hurt you. You can trust me on this, even if it might not seem like it at first."

"What are you on about?" Josh's forehead creased. "You've never acted this weird. I'm beginning to..." Josh's words drifted off when they stopped at the alley, his gaze finding Liam and then falling on Theo.

Josh's breath hitched. His hand flew to his pocket upon instinct, but he didn't draw his wand out. He trusted Ciara enough to do as she had asked him to.

"Let me explain." Ciara moved to stand between Josh and Theo in case something went wrong.

"You know he's..." Josh's eyes flickered between Ciara and Theo. He had once been Theo's colleague. He had to feel betrayed, like Ciara had felt.

Ciara nodded, showing Josh she understood his reaction. "That's what we need to talk about."

"It's good to see you, Josh." Ciara had told Theo to stay quiet until she had explained the situation to Josh, but Theo hadn't listened—or he just didn't care.

Josh turned his gaze to Ciara, not saying a word to Theo. "I'd like that explanation now."

"You know Theo faked—"

"His death. Yes, I know, Ciara," Josh hissed, eyes narrowing as his gaze moved back to Theo. "What is he doing here?"

"Theo isn't one of them. Not like we thought."

"The hell—"

"Listen, he's not. December 2016, we, I mean me and Theo, had a mission, remember? I passed out, and he brought me back, still passed out. I was in the hospital under surveillance for an entire day."

Josh nodded. "I remember. But what does that have to do with anything?"

"This." Ciara pulled her shirt and coat off her shoulder, revealing the witch hunters' branded mark. "This is from that mission. Theo hid it with a spell until recently."

Josh frowned, eyes fixated on the mark.

"They threatened to do much more. Worse than this." Ciara pulled the shirt and the coat back up to cover her shoulder. "They threatened me, and that's how they've been blackmailing Theo ever since."

"Is this true?" Josh faced Theo. He wanted his confirmation.

Theo nodded. "Yes, all of it. But that's not everything. They've also been threatening my mother."

"And that's what we're here for. We need your help with that," Ciara said. "You're the only one I could trust with this."

Josh had been present more than the others when Ciara had lost Theo. Even if she had pushed him away too, he had put in the most effort. He had seen her at her very worst. He knew what she had been through when Theo had died. Better than anyone, in fact.

"Are you willing to take a truth potion?" Josh directed the question at Theo. Josh hadn't even glanced at Ciara since turning to face Theo.

"Of course," Theo said.

There was no way Josh had a truth potion. Even though Ciara had been the worst at potions during her school years, she knew that truth potions were hard—almost impossible— to make. They were almost solely used in unsure court cases, and that was it. Some ingredients—like many magical herbs—were rare, too, and that made the potion expensive to brew, and even more so to buy.

"Then I believe you," Josh said.

Ciara had to bite her lip not to smile. She had expected worse. Much worse.

Theo didn't bother to hide his smile. He walked up to Josh, giving his old colleague a hug. Josh chuckled, clapping

Theo on the back.

"Good to know you haven't lost your mind."

"Not just yet," Theo said, also chuckling.

Josh smiled, but it faded when he faced Ciara. "So your team doesn't know?"

"No, not everything. They know something is going on because I told them to put Liam's family under protection."

Josh frowned, glancing at Liam.

"Long story," Liam said, crossing his arms across his chest. He had been unusually quiet since the previous night.

"So what exactly do you need me to do?" Josh turned to Ciara again.

"Get Estella somewhere safe, like my mum." Ciara swallowed. It had been a while since she had talked about her mother—and even longer since she had seen her or talked to her.

"You want to meet her before?" Josh asked Theo.

Theo shook his head. The words that followed had to be painful for him. "I don't think that's smart. It would be too risky."

"Alright. I'll have to put up an alert, saying some witch hunters crossed the border. Otherwise, I'll have no explanation for taking Estella to safety. You three best get back to Europe before I do that." Josh looked at all three of them in turns to make sure they all understood they didn't have time to waste.

"Thanks for doing this," Theo said.

"Of course." Josh smiled. "It's great to see you. And to know you're good."

"You too, man."

"I just need to talk about one more thing in private, Josh," Ciara said, gesturing away from the alley. Both Theo and Liam gave her a look, but she didn't explain herself.

Josh nodded. "Alright."

They walked around the corner but far enough for it to be a private conversation.

At the end of the conversation, Ciara placed her hand on Josh's arm.

"Thank you. For everything, I mean. You have no idea how much this all means to me."

"My life's mission is to help you. But don't worry, it's rewarding." Josh grinned. "And I know you'll have my back when the time comes." He placed his hand on Ciara's shoulder and squeezed. "Let's do this."

Ciara nodded. For a moment, she wanted to hug Josh. "Let's do this."

She didn't hug him, and they parted ways. Next time she was going to, even if she wasn't a big hugger.

21

Liam had never felt so out of place. Theo stuck to Ciara's side. Liam wanted to remain by Ciara's side, but he couldn't stand to be near Theo.

He wasn't angry with Theo like he had once been. His anger had eased, knowing Theo had done everything just to protect Ciara. Ciara meant the world to Liam, and he would have done a lot for her, too. Except Liam would have never hurt Ciara by killing Doherty or by faking his own death. He would have found a better way to protect Ciara if he had been in Theo's place.

Even if Liam no longer despised Theo the same way he once had, Liam couldn't wipe away the memory of seeing Theo kill Doherty. It had been brutal and cruel. Liam shuddered, just thinking of the final spell that had killed Doherty. It had come from Theo's wand. Even if he had done it to protect Ciara, Theo had killed a person. And not just anyone. It had been Doherty—someone Ciara had cared about deeply. Doherty had been like a father to Ciara.

And Theo hadn't even been there to pick up the pieces after he had shattered Ciara, taking Doherty from her.

Liam liked to think Ciara still cared about him and that meant Theo had tried to do it again when he had tried to kill Liam. Theo had tried to take more from her.

Liam wasn't confident that Theo's plan wasn't to take everyone but himself out of the game. Perhaps all Theo wanted was Ciara to himself.

Liam hoped his fears were as irrational as he tried to tell himself they were.

But a lot had gone downhill in one day.

The trio headed for their departure's gate, ready to return to Europe. They had left in a hurry the previous night, so they didn't have any luggage. It was better that way. After all, they weren't exactly on the right side of the law. Not with Theo tagging along and everything.

In the eyes of the law, the guy was still a terrorist and a murderer. Even in Liam's eyes, he remained a murderer.

"We have twenty more minutes. Come here." Ciara took an abrupt turn to the right, leading them to a narrow corridor.

"We can't hide in the staff area," Liam whispered. They would stand out. If someone was looking for them, they would be found.

"It's not...just that." Ciara stopped at a door, her eyes moving from Liam to Theo. "Come in." She pushed the door open and led the way in.

Liam realised her plan the moment they walked in. A woman with brown hair and small wrinkles around her eyes stood in the middle of the room. The moment she and Theo looked at one another, Liam knew who the woman was.

Theo's mother, Estella Boucher.

"M-Mom." The second Theo had gasped out the word, his mother scooped him into a hug.

"Oh, Theo." The woman tried to hold in her sobs, but her voice cracked. She hadn't seen her son in over a year, and

Liam assumed Ciara hadn't even told Estella that Theo was alive.

After all, there had been a time when Ciara had thought that she had killed Theo.

Josh wasn't in the room with Theo's mother, but he had to be nearby. Theo getting to see his mother had to be Ciara's plan. That had to be why Ciara had talked to Josh in private.

Ciara stood beside Liam, but her full focus was on Theo and Estella. There were fresh tears in her eyes, threatening to spill. Happy tears, undoubtedly.

That had been Ciara's life once. Liam looked at the hugging mother and son and then at Ciara again. He was the only one who didn't belong there.

But he was dying to belong in her life. With everything they had found out about Theo and the witch hunters, he wasn't sure what was going to happen with Ciara. Would she want to be with Theo again? Liam didn't have the faintest clue.

It took a while for Estella to calm down. Then she turned to Ciara, smiling and opening her welcoming arms for her. Ciara stepped closer and hugged Estella.

"It's so good to see you," Ciara said.

"You too, Ciara." Estella smiled warmly, eyes closed, enjoying the embrace.

Watching the scene made Liam sick. That should have been Ciara's future. A future Liam wasn't included in.

Selfishly, Liam was glad that the future he saw hadn't happened. If it had, Ciara wouldn't have been there to save Liam from a dreadful future with a cheating wife.

"We have to go in just a minute." Theo's voice was oddly soft when he talked to his mother. He didn't even talk to Ciara like that. "Josh will get you to safety."

"Josh?" Estella turned to frown at Theo. "Who's Josh?"

Something was not right.

"The guy who took you here." Ciara paused, her lips thinning. "Joshua."

Liam dashed for the other door leading out of the room. He pulled out his wand, pointing it at the person in that room. *She* wasn't Josh.

Theresa broke into a run, but Liam was faster. He blocked her way with an invisible shield, swinging his wand. She spun around, wand ready in hand.

But then the wand flew across the room, landing on Ciara's palm. It rose and floated above Ciara's hand for a mere moment. Then she snapped it in half with a spell. Even the stone core of the wand broke. Ciara dropped the useless pieces to the floor, the clatter echoing through the room, and aimed a deadly glare at Theresa.

At that moment, Theresa's intimidating image was shattered for Liam as he witnessed her shaking wide-eyed. Theresa feared Ciara.

But to Theresa's credit, even Liam hadn't seen Ciara look so lethal.

Ciara strode up to the brown-haired part-Hispanic, part-Caucasian woman. She shoved Theresa to the wall. "Where is Josh?" Ciara's voice dropped dangerously low, and icy chills ran down Liam's spine. Her eyes were thunderous.

That was a Ciara that Liam wasn't familiar with.

Liam glanced at Theo and his mother, who stayed in the other room. Theo was explaining something to his mother. They were fine.

Liam turned back to look at Ciara and Theresa. The witch hunter appeared to be alone, which was odd. Theresa wasn't stupid and still she had come with no backup.

The only explanation Liam could think of was that Theresa had assumed Theo to be alone. Theo wasn't a risk to Theresa, not with everything the witch hunters had against him.

Liam walked up to where Ciara was standing, keeping a short distance from the scene.

"Where is Josh?" Ciara's hand flew up, punching Theresa in the face.

Theresa winced but recovered fast. Her eyes were still wide, terror written all over her face.

Ciara snapped her fingers, and her new knife flew up to her hand. It looked like the blade would be bloodied soon, even though it hadn't been yet.

"Wait, wait! Stop!" the tattooed woman screamed out, voice breaking.

"You got Bill half-dead. So guess what? I don't have to wait." Ciara pressed the knife against Theresa's neck. The previously unused blade was sharp enough to draw blood.

"Josh! J-Josh is—"

"Yes?" Ciara urged, only easing the pressure on the blade a little.

"She killed him. Claimed to have killed a witch hunter." It wasn't Theresa.

Both Liam and Ciara turned to face Theo, whose face had drained of blood. Liam's eyes flew to Ciara, but she had already turned back to face Theresa.

"Ciara, wait!" Liam grabbed Ciara by her wrist, stopping her hand mid-air. He reached for the knife in her hand, but she pulled it away from him. His next move was to force it out of her hand by twisting her wrist. The last thing he wanted was to hurt Ciara, but there was no way he would let her kill Theresa.

Ciara's eyes were stormy when they met Liam's gaze. "If she killed Josh—"

"She will pay." Liam turned to Theresa, voice low. "Either way."

Theresa's eyes grew bigger, but it only took a split second for her to regain her composure. Her tough façade, which Liam remembered from that night at the warehouse, was back.

Ciara's muscles relaxed under Liam's touch, but the bloodlust in her eyes didn't fade. It was no surprise, given the circumstances. She had once trusted Theresa. They had been friends.

Theo had to step forward, wand in hand, to cuff Theresa. Liam let go of Ciara, but remained between the two women. Ciara still refused to look away from Theresa, and Liam feared what was going through Ciara's mind.

Theresa was a traitor, and Liam hated her as much as Ciara did. But killing the witch hunter wasn't an option. Not when they had no idea where Josh—or his body—was.

The thought filled Liam with an icy sensation. He prayed they would find Josh alive. Josh didn't deserve any of the things Liam could imagine Theresa putting him through. Especially not for helping Ciara and Theo—and Liam.

Guilt already gnawed inside Liam, even though he hadn't been the one to ask for Josh's help. He could only imagine how Ciara felt.

He knew how she felt. He could see it in her eyes—the panic, the despair, the guilt. She tried not to show it, but Liam saw right through her.

"Where's Josh?" Theo's voice hardened when he talked to Theresa.

"His corpse?" Theresa tried to smile, but it didn't work. The fear shone through her eyes, and the smile turned into a grimace. A worried grimace.

Theo's jaw clenched, and he struggled to keep his cool. After all, Josh had been his friend, too. They had just rekindled their friendship, even if barely so.

Liam glanced at Ciara, whose eyes shifted to Theo. Josh had been *their* friend and colleague.

Liam was still the outsider. He was there for his own safety and for that only.

Ciara shook her head as if to clear her mind by doing so. "We need to get out of here."

Theo met Ciara's gaze, and the intensity of it bothered Liam. Not that it was any of his business, but he cared about Ciara. And he wasn't convinced Theo could be the man for Ciara after everything the guy had done—no matter his reasons.

Liam could live with Ciara walking away and finding another guy. But Theo had killed Doherty and had committed various other crimes. Ciara didn't deserve to be hurt like that—not even for her own protection.

Liam was glad Theo had kept her safe.

But Liam wasn't convinced she needed to be kept safe. She was more than capable of doing it herself. Even if seeing her in danger made Liam uneasy, she was an incredible, powerful witch.

"*The* place?" Theo's eyes didn't leave Ciara's, waiting for an answer, but his wand stayed on Theresa's throat.

Ciara nodded. "I'll take your mother and Liam?"

"See you there."

It wasn't time to go home after all.

22

Ciara rushed to the next room to find Estella slumped against the wall, her head buried in her hands. Ciara walked over to the older woman, brushing her hands on the woman's upper arms. "Estella, we need to go."

"Where exactly?" Liam moved to stand beside the two women.

Ciara met his eyes. "It's a safe place, trust me."

Liam's eyebrows furrowed, and he reached out to touch Ciara's arm. "I trust you. But do you trust me?"

"Yes." Ciara fought her urges, dying to roll her eyes. Obviously, she trusted Liam.

But there wasn't time for that conversation.

She turned her attention back to Estella. "We'll get you somewhere safe soon."

"All I care about is Theo's safety." Ciara had never once seen Estella look so serious. The woman's gaze was hard, showing no glimpse of amusement or uncertainty.

It was the look of a mother who had just got her dead son

back.

"He'll be safe with me," Ciara swore, placing her hand over her heart as a sign of a promise.

Estella nodded, her muscles visibly relaxing. "I know."

Ciara offered a hint of a smile. "Let's go?" After receiving a nod from Estella, she turned to meet Liam's gaze again. He, too, nodded.

Both Estella and Liam grabbed Ciara's hand, and she teleported them to the cabin she and Theo had bought in the past. The scent of pine and fresh earth filled the air as they appeared in the middle of the Canadian woods. She had never sold the cabin, nor rented it.

But she also hadn't planned to go there again. Not after Theo's death. She had abandoned the place when Theo had abandoned her.

The forest view with snow-covered trees surrounded them. A small cabin, built with wood that had later been painted, stood amidst it all. Ciara and Theo had painted it light brown to blend it into the landscape in the summer.

The big, wooden front door was open, meaning Theo was already inside with Theresa.

Ciara let out a breath. She hadn't dared to even dream of returning to the cabin. The overwhelming number of memories ran through her mind, and she struggled to keep her composure.

A lot had happened in that cabin. Theo had proposed during their stay at the cabin. They had gone for a walk by a beach, and he had proposed there. Afterwards, they had returned to the cabin. Just the two of them.

So much had changed since then. Ciara had changed, and so had Theo.

"Are you okay?"

Ciara jumped back to reality from the depths of her memories, turning her attention to Liam—who had spoken. "I'm fine."

He didn't buy it, but she didn't have time to explain. She

didn't want to explain. Not to him.

Ciara cleared her throat. "Let's go inside."

They still had to find Josh, so the day was nowhere near over.

Trying to maintain composure, Ciara clenched her teeth to prevent herself from cracking. Josh had been helping them. If he had died doing so, she would never forgive herself.

Pushing the thought aside, she took her first steps forward. Estella and Liam trailed after her.

"You two came here when you weren't home, huh?" Estella looked around, mesmerised by the place.

Letting out a deep sigh, Ciara said, "We did."

She had to keep herself from running her hand along the railing as she walked up the few snow-covered stairs leading up to the open front door.

Stepping inside, she was greeted by a coolness that contrasted with the rush of warmth brought on by memories. The memories were like a welcoming warmth of a home. Like an embrace.

The feeling was quickly tainted by Theresa's frustrated scream. "I hope they find her and gut her!"

"If you don't shut up, I swear—"

Ciara rushed to the guest room—which they had never used. Theo had placed a chair in the middle and had tied Theresa to it. With his temper running short, his fingers clenched tightly around his wand. His grip on the wand was so tight that his knuckles had turned pale.

"Theo." Ciara kept her voice calm, striding over to him. She nudged him gently, making him step away from the smirking Theresa. *That bitch.*

Theo's eyes were murderous, staring at the tied up woman, but the look softened when he faced Ciara. "I'm going to kill her," he hissed lowly, seething.

"Calm down."

"If she says one more thing that—"

"Theo." Ciara snapped her fingers, gaining Theo's full attention. She pointed to the door. "Out."

"I'm not leaving you alone with that freak." He glanced at Theresa, but quickly returned his gaze to Ciara.

"You don't have to." Liam leaned against the doorframe, arms crossed. His expression was somewhat neutral, but Ciara could see through that. He was jealous because of Theo, and his anger was reserved for Theresa.

They were all angry.

"Go talk to your mother." Ciara lowered her voice. Theresa didn't have to hear what she was saying. "You both need that."

Theo couldn't argue with that. With one last look at Ciara, he tore his eyes off her and walked out.

Liam slid the door shut, the soft thud filling the air. With the door closed, he locked eyes with Ciara. They nodded to one another, then faced the witch hunter woman.

"What did you do to Josh?"

Ciara's eyes flew back to Liam, taken aback by his initiative. He, however, kept his eyes on Theresa. Ciara was relieved to have him there, seeing how natural he was as a negotiator.

Theresa smirked at Liam, trying to push his buttons. She didn't let the smirk waver even when Liam didn't react.

Liam tilted his head to the side.

Ciara had never seen him look so intimidating. So tough and cold. It wasn't the Liam she was familiar with; it was a façade.

He was good, and she was *damn* impressed.

"What did you do to Josh?" There was no impatience in his voice. Somehow, he remained calm, despite the situation they were in.

All Ciara wanted to do was stab the bitch, so she was glad he handled the talking. She wouldn't have been able to stay calm. Not this time.

Usually Ciara was the one who could keep her cool, no

matter what. This time, it was clearly Liam.

"Maybe I stabbed him." Theresa shrugged the best she could, being tied up to a chair.

"I doubt that."

"Smart." Theresa's smirk grew. "I didn't stab him."

"What did you do?" There was a complete absence of emotion in Liam's voice, leaving it cold and indifferent. His expression had hardened, like a stone wall, revealing nothing. Not even to Ciara.

Ciara spotted the glimpse in Theresa's eyes. The moment of fear when Liam spoke.

"I..." Theresa cleared her throat, annoyed by her loss of composure. "Maybe I gutted him." Her eyes moved to Ciara, meeting her gaze. "Like Elliott will gut you."

Ciara was tempted to steal a glance at Liam, curious to see his reaction, but she resisted the urge. Theresa glanced at Liam, though, amused by whatever she saw on his face.

"I'll handle him." Ciara didn't want to sound arrogant, but she was busy trying to find her possibly dead friend. There was no time to talk about Elliott Hardy—the leader and founder of the witch hunters, the man Ciara had spent years looking for. "So don't worry." Her eyes narrowed into slits.

She still struggled to understand how she had once trusted the woman tied to the chair. She had gone out for drinks with her, never realising what was going on.

"I'm not worried, but you should be." Theresa's eyes shifted to Liam, and her grin widened. "He sure looks worried." Her eyes returned to Ciara, twinkling with amusement. "I bet Theo is just as worried."

"Lucky for you, that's none of your concern." Ciara kept her eyes on Theresa, refusing to glance at Liam—no matter how much she wanted to. "Where's Josh?"

"The obvious place. Figure it out." Theresa rolled her eyes. "I'm giving you *nada*."

"You were always a bitch to work with. The others were

so much better."

Ciara froze, spotting the look on Theresa's face. The woman's fiery eyes contrasted with her unusually pale face.

Ciara had hit a soft spot.

"I'm glad Kellan and I didn't have to fire you." Ciara shoved her hands in her pockets to appear more casual. "It would've been a mess. This is easier."

Every single word was a lie. Theresa had been one of the best in Ciara's team, after all.

Ciara didn't know what she would achieve with the lies, but the idea of hurting Theresa enticed her to go on. Even if she hated what she was doing—belittling a female colleague—she couldn't help but keep doing it.

Theresa wasn't her colleague anymore. Nor was she a friend. She had taken a side. The enemy's side.

"Fuck you!" Theresa screamed out, her façade shattering into tiny pieces. The waterworks opened, angry tears glimmering in the corners of her eyes.

It was Ciara's turn to smirk. "You thought you were good at your job?"

A small twinge of guilt hit Ciara. There were too few hit witches, and even the few had it hard enough amongst the loud and arrogant hit wizards. Ciara hated using that as leverage against Theresa, but it was all she had.

Besides, Theresa had picked her side. She was a witch hunter because she wanted to be—not against her will, like Theo. She wasn't a hit witch and had never truly been.

"I hope Elliott guts you slowly!" Spit flew out with Theresa's words.

"Well, someone must do the work that you can't. Why not let the terrorists who, as you know, named themselves after Salem's misogynist wizards do the work for you?"

"The media named us that." Theresa's eyes narrowed.

"And you seem to enjoy using the name, *witch hunter*."

"Fuck you. You're playing games with me."

"And you are stupid enough to play along."

Ciara already had an idea where Josh was. If he was in the obvious place, it had to be Estella's house.

She turned away from Theresa, grabbed Liam by the arm on her way to the door, and pulled him out of the room. She closed the door, sealing it with an enchantment in case something happened and Theresa tried to escape.

Finally, out of the room, she looked at Liam. His eyes were a mix of worry and anger. His worry for her created a soothing warmth in her chest.

Ciara had to clear her throat and look away from Liam's intense gaze. "Josh is at Estella's house."

"You sure that's not *too* obvious?"

"We should find out."

"Fair enough."

Ciara led the way to the living room where Theo and Estella were talking. Both had their faces covered in tears, their eyes swollen and bloodshot.

"I and Liam have to check your house, Estella," Ciara said.

"My place?"

"Josh is likely somewhere there."

"But I didn't see anything." Estella's eyes widened. "Wouldn't I have…"

"I don't know." Ciara glanced at Theo, noting the worried look he gave her.

"Theresa could have hid Josh." Liam's lips pursed together, thinking the same as everyone else in the room.

Or his body.

"Will you be fine here?" Ciara looked at Theo, expecting his answer.

Theo nodded as a yes. "Be careful."

"We—"

"We'll be fine." All eyes turned to Liam. He rarely spoke to Theo, not unless he had to. Ciara didn't miss the subtle exchange of glances between the two men, nor the piercing stare Estella directed at her.

She needed to get away from that cabin. And more than

anything, she had to find Josh.
 "Let's go."

23

Ciara let go of Liam's hand the moment Estella's house morphed into view. The cool winter air bit at her skin, but it didn't bother her as much as it should have. She felt cold with or without the weather's effect.

The house and the back garden brought back memories of different days. None of those memories included Liam, and being at the house with him didn't feel right.

But Ciara was happy to have him by her side. Even with her worries about him being there, his presence also brought her a sense of ease.

Liam exhaled loud enough for Ciara to hear. "Plenty of memories from here, I bet."

Ciara hummed. "Yeah."

"Let's hope they won't be tainted."

Despite looking at the house, Ciara sensed Liam's eyes on her. She desperately wanted to look back at him, but focusing on the task was more important. Finding Josh was *all* that mattered. She couldn't let anything distract her.

"Are you ready?"

"No." Ciara shuddered. "But waiting around isn't going to help us find Josh." She stepped forward, only for her path to be blocked. Liam had stepped in front of her, his hands already moving up her arms.

As his palms pressed against her arms, they radiated warmth, yet an icy coldness persisted inside her."I can go. Alone," Liam said.

Ciara raised her gaze and locked eyes with him. "No. I have to do this. I asked him to help and—"

"Don't blame yourself. There's nothing you could've done differently."

Ciara nodded, but they both knew she hadn't taken Liam's words to the heart. "Let's find Josh."

The obvious place was Estella's house. Still, Josh could be anywhere—or his body if Theresa had killed him.

Ciara refused to believe it. She couldn't. Josh had been her colleague since the start of her career. He was one of the few she had remained close with through everything.

She had always been prepared to lose any of her colleagues. Death came with the job and it came without a warning. She had to be prepared. Every hit witch or hit wizard had to keep a distance from their colleagues, knowing one day they would certainly lose some of them. But even thinking of Josh's death made Ciara's head spin.

He couldn't be dead.

Ciara walked ahead, leading the way. She headed for the backdoor, the hinges creaking as she pushed it open, and walked in with Liam.

It was evening, so there was hardly any light coming in through the windows. Ciara reached for the light-switch, afraid of what she would see with the lights on.

When she turned the lights on, she flinched. For nothing. There was nothing out of the ordinary. No bodies, no blood. Just the regular furniture there always had been.

But it didn't ease her mind; they still had to check the

other rooms downstairs and all the rooms upstairs.

"At least this time we get to search a house with the lights on." Liam lowered his voice to a hushed whisper, even though they were likely alone in the house.

The memory of their previous house search flooded Ciara's mind. They had found Mr Tubbs's body. An image she couldn't get rid of even after all these months. The witch hunters had killed him.

As always, they had done it for publicity. They wanted the media's attention. And when they didn't kill to get their point across to the media, they killed to wipe out those who dared to oppose them. They spread terror; that was their mission.

"Let's pray this time is better," Ciara whispered with the image of Mr Tubbs's body still in her mind. She didn't want to see Josh like that. Dead. Murdered.

Liam reached his hand to her shoulder and squeezed lightly, his fingers warm against her skin. "Everything will work out."

There was no way he believed his own words.

But Ciara didn't voice her doubts. There was no point. So, instead, she nodded.

Shuddering as if it was cold, Ciara took a step forward. One step after another, heading to the next room. They would check the rooms downstairs first.

It wasn't cold in the house, especially not with their winter coats on. Ciara's insides grew colder and colder, a chilling sensation creeping up her spine.

But it had nothing to do with the temperature in the house. And everything to do with the fear, wrapping around Ciara's heart like a fist.

If Josh died, she would be the one responsible for his fate.

She peeked into the bathroom and then checked the empty room filled with boxes. One by one, she and Liam looked through each room, finding nothing downstairs.

Josh wasn't there. Not dead, nor alive.

"Upstairs?"

Eyes glued to Ciara, Liam waited for an answer until she raised her gaze. Taking a shaky breath, she nodded, and her eyes drifted to the wooden stairs.

She wasn't ready, but it didn't stop her. It never did. She strode to the stairs, fighting against her hesitance with all her might. Her foot hit the third step when a thud interrupted her panicky thoughts. Her eyes flew to the top of the stairs, and she saw nothing.

But something had to be up there. If it was Josh, he had to be alive.

Sparing a hurried glance Liam's way, she rushed up the rest of the stairs. He followed right behind her. Her eyes flew from doorway to doorway until settling on the end of the hallway. The only light they had was the bit of light coming from outside through the windows. But it was enough.

Theo's old room's door was open, and despite how little light got in, Ciara could see inside the room.

Her knees wobbled, barely holding her up, and the weight of a million boulders crumbled down from her shoulders. She could hardly feel her feet as they moved on their own.

Josh's dark eyes widened with relief, and his shoulders sunk down. He tried to say something, but no sound came. A cloth gag covered Josh's mouth. But it was no ordinary cloth. Not even a grunt got past it, so it had to be enchanted. Josh realised it too and struggled against the binds.

Ciara had never been so happy to see her old colleague.

Her feet carried her through the doorway. But no further. She tripped over something.

Her hand flew up to reach for anything. Her other hand flew forward to deal with the impact, expecting to hit the floor.

But she never did. Strong arms wrapped around her, pulling her up before she fell.

Her gaze snapped up the moment something *cut* the air. She registered the glint of metal rushing through the air, and it was too late.

"No!" Her voice had a will of its own, coming out as an earsplitting scream.

She pushed at Liam, rushing away from his arms and throwing herself forward. Her hands flew up to Josh's neck, a clean slit running from the right side to the left.

Josh's eyes rolled back.

"Josh!"

A raspy sound, not a breath, nor a word, came out of his mouth, his head falling back. The gash on his throat opened up wider, and Ciara raised his head, supporting it from the back.

"Josh!"

Wet, warm liquid coated her hands, drops running down her arms. Josh's gaze was unmoving and unfocused. Still.

"Ciara!" Hands gripped her shoulders, ripping her away from her bleeding friend. Panicked, darting eyes came into her view. "Dammit, Ciara, breathe!"

She frowned, not understanding the words. Liam shook her by the shoulders, not bothering to be gentle.

Coming to her senses, she gasped for air. Her head spun, and so did the surrounding room.

Real.

The sticky crimson coating her hands knocked her back to reality. Her chest tightened, and her heart stung.

"No." Her eyes moved to Josh.

His head hung down, covering the wound. The blood tainted his brown skin like red wine spilled on a shirt. It was still dripping down, having already coated the front of his clothes.

Her eyes flew back to meet Liam's. "No," she rasped out.

Her legs buckled, but Liam's grip tightened, so she didn't fall. He pulled her to his chest and hid the view from her.

Icy sensation washed over her as if cold water drowning her. But the slowly drying liquid still warmed her hands and arms. It was on her shirt too, the fabric clinging onto her skin.

Like when she had stabbed Theo. Images of that night at the warehouse came rushing back, mixing with the fresh memories of her dead friend. Josh had definitely been more than a colleague, and Ciara had just lost a friend.

Bitterness evaded her mouth. She had to close her eyes not to hurl her guts up. Her fingers clung onto what she assumed to be Liam's coat.

"Let's get out of here." Liam's voice wavered, but his muscles remained unmoving—stable and supportive.

"No." The words came out hoarse.

"Ciara—"

"Y-you have to go back. I-I..." Her teeth chattered, even though the temperature hadn't dropped. "I have to call...to call Brody or...or someone."

"If you think I'm leaving you for one second—"

"N-not here. Not in this room." She opened her eyes, looking up and meeting his hazel eyes. Tears glazed her eyes, threatening to slip out.

Liam nodded. Shielding Ciara from the gruesome view, he led her out of the room. While still helping her stay on her feet, he slipped out of his coat, wrapping it around her.

She blinked when they were downstairs, not having registered walking down the steps. Everything was a blur.

"I'm never again leaving you alone with something like this." His hands hadn't left her arms, his fingers still wrapped around them to support her.

He was talking about Ciara stabbing Theo in the warehouse. Liam hadn't known until later.

Just like that time, Ciara was the one to blame. "I asked Josh to—"

"This isn't your fault." His hands tightened around her arms. On purpose or on instinct, Ciara couldn't tell.

Ciara winced. She didn't deserve to hear those words. They held no truth in them. Josh had been there because she had asked. She had triggered the trap.

"I'll call Brody or whoever you want me to call," Liam said.

"I have Brody's num..." Her sentence fell short, realisation dawning on them. They didn't have their phones, so they wouldn't be tracked down.

"We'll go back to the cabin and—"

"I can't leave him!" Her arm shot up. She pointed her finger upstairs, where Josh's still bleeding body was tied to a chair.

"Ciara." Liam swallowed, struggling with his next words. "He's dead. He doesn't need you to be here."

The first tear escaped, promptly followed by a dozen more. Her hands covered her mouth, smearing blood onto her face, and sobs rang through the house.

Liam wrapped his arms around her, bringing her back to his chest again. She didn't push him away, and she didn't bother to keep in her tears and sobs. She couldn't.

The sobs echoed off the walls until little by little they died down. Ciara reached up to wipe the tears but stopped herself before she could. Blood coated her hands, and smearing it all over wasn't ideal.

"We'll come back."

She didn't fight this time, merely nodding.

Liam gripped his wand, flicked it in his hand, and the surrounding house turned into a snowy forest.

Ciara's gaze fell, looking at the snow at their feet. Red had already ruined the white with the blood on their shoes.

24

"Ciara!"

Liam's eyes flew up, and Ciara's grip on his shirt loosened. A certain dark-haired man came running to them. Ciara's fingers let go of Liam's shirt, and she flung herself into Theo's arms.

Something tightened around Liam's heart, and for a second his hand clenched into a fist. But he wasn't angry. Not with Ciara. She needed all the comfort she could get—and perhaps she didn't want it from Liam.

Theo's eyes were wild, moving between the woman in his arms, the blood on the snow, and Liam. "Are you okay?" His question was for Ciara, but his eyes flew back to Liam.

Liam nodded, confirming Ciara was okay—at least in some sense. Theo was worried about the blood, and it wasn't Ciara's.

It was Josh's.

"J-Josh." Ciara's voice shuddered, the word coming out with a gasp.

The name was enough for it all to dawn on Theo. His eyes grew round, his muscles freezing. For a moment, he remained unmoving and out of it. Like he wasn't present.

Liam was about to step in when Theo's eyes moved back to Ciara, whom he was still somewhat hugging. His fingers moved restlessly, and little by little he gripped onto Ciara tighter, bringing her closer to his chest. His jaw clenched, and his eyes seemed remote. He was there—at least enough to acknowledge Ciara was there.

Josh and Theo had been colleagues once, too. Even Liam had known Josh, but they had never been that close. They hadn't known each other that long.

Still, a frosty feeling rushed through Liam when he thought about the way Josh had bled out. How his corpse was still there. Liam's stomach twisted.

Josh had been a great guy. Someone who wouldn't have deserved to go in such a way. In any way.

"H-how?" Theo's voice broke, and it snapped Liam back to reality. He had never seen the guy show any emotion with anyone except Ciara. This was a new side of Theo—for Liam, that is.

"It was a trap." Liam knew Ciara would answer, so he beat her to it. "Theresa's trap." His eyes moved to the house, and anger filled his chest. That bitch had done more than enough, and Liam was dying for her to pay for all of it.

Something changed in Theo's eyes. They remained remote, but the emotion turned colder. And for a moment, he looked like the killer again. The killer Liam had thought him to be.

"She's going to—" Theo let go of Ciara and spun around.

Liam saw it coming and jumped in Theo's way—between him and the house. "No." His eyes flickered between Theo and Ciara.

Ciara's eyes widened, registering what Theo was planning.

"We need to deal with this the right way." Liam focused his gaze on Theo, so the guy wouldn't slip past him.

"Tell me you don't want that bitch dead!" Theo screamed at Liam, pointing at the cabin.

"I can't tell you that." Liam wanted Theresa dead as much as Theo, perhaps even as much as Ciara. But they couldn't go around killing people like the witch hunters. He wouldn't let Theo do it. The guy was already a criminal, and Liam wouldn't let Theo pull Ciara deeper into his bullshit.

"Then move!" Theo pushed at Liam, eyes narrowed, but it did next to nothing. Liam had expected it.

"Stop, Theo!" Liam raised his voice too, knowing he needed to get the guy's attention. "She'll get what she deserves, trust me. But we're not killing her. Not like she killed Josh."

"I'm kill—"

"The fuck you are!" Liam was done with Theo—and even more so with his bullshit. "I get you did bad things to protect Ciara, but this isn't for Ciara. This isn't for anyone. Not even Josh! Revenge isn't right, so back off before you do something you regret."

Theo's eyes grew wider, the words sinking in.

"You're already a criminal. Don't make this worse for all of us." Liam pointed a finger at Theo and glanced at Ciara, but he couldn't read her face. It was like she was wearing a mask again. She did it when things got *bad*.

"We need to call Brody." Ciara's voice came out hoarse, yet strong enough to gain both of the guys' attention.

"We can't let him know about Theo."

Theo spun around, turning to look back at Liam again. "Excuse me?"

"Josh understood. We were lucky he did. But let's be real, he's more understanding. And I bet he was closer to both of you. Brody might not listen, even if we try to explain everything." Liam looked between Theo and Ciara, hoping they would see his point. "So do you, honestly, want to go to jail?" Liam stopped to look at Theo when he finished his question.

Theo didn't answer, but it was enough for Liam to continue.

"Brody will start to wonder if he even sees Ciara here. He might know you've vanished from England." Liam let his eyes linger on Ciara, heartbroken by how good she was at turning on the mask-like stare. The stony stare.

As if she didn't care, when in reality she was dying inside. It broke Liam's heart to see her so strong for everyone else.

Ciara nodded. "That's true."

"We need your mum to help us." Liam turned back to Theo. "We have to say she came home, and Theresa was there waiting. Josh was dead. Does your mum know Josh?"

"Not well, but she would know who Josh is. She'd recognise him. She'd know he's my old colleague." Theo cleared his throat, eyes watering. "Or was."

"Do you think she can call Brody or someone? Anyone from your work? Could she have their numbers?"

"I think she has Brody's number."

"Good."

"You need to call him and say Theresa was there and killed Josh," Theo explained to his mother.

"He's really dead?" Theo's mother Estella looked around the room, scanning the three younger adults' faces. She stiffened each time she looked at Ciara, who still wore her *mask*—the stony façade.

"Yes." Ciara's voice hadn't returned its strength, but she wasn't the wreck she had been a moment before. She was calm and collected—unlike the woman Estella knew her as.

"And what about t-that woman?" Estella's eyes moved to the door, which was the only thing between them and Theresa.

Liam stood near the door, knowing Theo would take any chance at revenge.

"What about Theresa?" Theo joined in, turning his gaze

to Liam.

It wasn't Liam who spoke; it was Ciara. "Even trapped, it's too dangerous to bring her there. We'll figure something out later."

Estella's eyebrows furrowed, but she nodded.

"You need to make sure Brody takes you to a safe house." Theo turned his full attention back to his mother, still kneeling in front of the sofa where Estella was sitting. "Insist on it being Brody. Don't trust anyone else."

Estella exhaled. "So only Brody?"

Theo nodded. "Yes, and insist on it. He'll know *he* needs to do it if you insist."

Liam frowned and turned to Ciara for answers, but for once Ciara looked as clueless as him. Did Brody and Theo have a pact or something?

"And remember not to mention any of us." Theo glanced around, his eyes lingering on Ciara before he turned to look at his mother again. "You never saw us. Especially not me."

"Theo." Estella's eyes filled with tears, looking at her own son with heartbreak.

Liam wondered how his own mother was, not knowing what was going on. Liam had vanished after he had left the house to go talk with Ciara. His family had to be worried, and he didn't even know if they were safe. Kellan was supposed to take care of them, but Liam couldn't know for sure.

If the witch hunters had his family...

No. He couldn't think like that. He needed to prioritise more urgent matters.

They finished briefing Estella, and afterwards Ciara insisted on taking Estella to the house.

Liam shook his head. "No, I don't think that's such a good idea."

Ciara's eyes snapped to him, narrowing a little. "I'm going."

"You can go *with* them." The message behind Theo's words didn't go unnoticed by Liam.

"So you could kill Theresa? No."

Estella's eyes widened at Liam's words, but she didn't voice her worries. "I can go on my own."

Liam nodded. Ciara and Theo seemed to hesitate, so he talked first. "I think that'd be for the best. I'd advise you not to go upstairs, though. You don't want to see it."

Estella shuddered but nodded. For such a gentle and caring soul, the woman was tough. Liam had to give her points for that.

"Okay. I don't think—"

"I'll be fine." Estella placed a hand on her son's forearm. "Don't worry about me. You have enough to worry as it is."

Theo sighed and pulled his mother into a tight hug. "Don't go…there. Upstairs. And remember to insist on Brody. Don't forget that, no matter what. If something goes wrong, get away. Come here or something. Anything."

The witch hunters were still a threat to Estella. They could only pray their plan worked, and Estella got to safety before it was too late.

"It's time to go. The longer we wait, the more dangerous it gets," Ciara said reluctantly—as though she didn't want to part ways with Estella.

But she was right. The witch hunters could go looking for Estella. The sooner Estella got to safety, the better.

Estella finished her goodbyes with her son and then hugged Ciara. She thanked Liam, looked at Ciara and Theo one last time, and took her wand. Flicking it, she disappeared.

Theo exhaled shakily and ran his hands through his hair.

"She'll be fine." Liam's words didn't do anything—and he knew it—but it was the best he could offer.

"I can't believe Josh is gone," Theo breathed out.

Liam struggled to wrap his head around the fact that the killer in the room could be so upset about death. Rationally, it made sense. But Liam had seen Theo kill Doherty—the man who had trusted Theo. Theo had even tried to murder Liam. Sorrow for another's death didn't change any of that.

Theo was still a cold-blooded killer.

A killer that Ciara loved.

"I'll go see our *guest*." It was Liam's way of excusing himself. He wanted to get away from the pair.

He and Ciara had broken up, but he still loved her. It was his fault; he had messed up. She had every right to be angry with him and he half-expected her to be. But he hated the thought of her rushing into Theo's arms.

Yet that was exactly what had happened earlier that day. She had chosen Theo to be the one to comfort her.

25

Ciara watched Liam disappear into the room where Theresa was tied up. She wanted to tell him how much she appreciated having him there. She wouldn't have been able to handle herself after what had happened to Josh. Not without him.

Theo let himself fall onto the sofa. Not in the way you'd fall after a hard day of work, but the way you fall when your legs can't carry you. When it's all too much.

"H-how are you?" Ciara sat down beside her ex-fiancé, a lump forming in her throat. She couldn't keep in all her emotions for much longer. At any moment, her mask was going to crumble.

"Not good, but I'd imagine you're worse." Theo's eyes glossed over with tears. "It's just...Josh. Out of all the people on this planet."

Ciara swallowed. "I can't even remember how many times he saved my life."

"I can't remember how many times I thanked him for it."

The first tear slipped, rolling down his cheek. "Hell, I would have lost you years ago if it wasn't for him."

Ciara reached up to wipe away his one slipped tear. "I know." Her voice shook, and her own eyes pooled with tears. "I should've...I wish..."

"Not your fault." Theo shook his head. "Theresa killed him, not you."

"I saw him die." Her voice cracked, and her sorrow seemed to crush her from within. "I saw him bleed out." The tears flooded her eyes and slid down her cheeks. "H-he looked up. A-at me. I swear he looked so relieved. Like he had feared for his life the entire time in there. A-and then...and then..."

Breathing was hard, like something was tightening around her chest, cutting her airways. She bit her teeth together and shut her eyes tight.

"Fuck." The word came out as a sob, and Theo's arms flew around her.

"I know." His voice cracked, and his hands began working on Ciara's hair, brushing it softly. "I know."

"I tripped over the fucking thing." Ciara's voice broke, and the words came out hoarse.

"It's not your fault." Theo's fingers untangled from her hair, sliding up to her neck and then to her face. His thumbs wiped away some tears, and he looked deep into her eyes. "It's never your fault, Ciara. You always do the good thing. You tried to save him."

"But I couldn't." More tears slid down her face. "Like... like when I thought you died. Like when...you know." She couldn't say Doherty's name out loud. "O-or at the...at the warehouse. When you nearly...when Liam..."

Theo's lip quivered. "I'm sorry. I'm so—"

Ciara's hand flew up to rest on top of Theo's hand, which was still cradling her face. "I just...I wish I could save someone."

"You've saved your mother from all of this."

"She probably hates me for it."

"No, she loves you." Theo's face remained wet with tears. "I love you too, Ciara."

Her eyes watered more, blurring her vision. She threw her arms around Theo, clinging onto him. "Theo, I—"

The guest room's door burst open, colliding with the solid wooden wall. Echoing through the cabin, the sharp thud made Theo and Ciara quickly move apart and stand up from the sofa.

Liam's eyes were wide with bewilderment, remaining close to the guest room's door. "We have a problem!" He held up an object, and they all recognised it.

A stone with a locating enchantment on it.

Ciara wiped her tears away harshly. Her thoughts were a blur as she tried to readjust to the new revelation. "Fuck."

"We need to get out. Right now." Theo rushed into action, pulling out his wand and running to the windows. "It's too dark."

"Get down!" Liam flung his wand, tripping Theo. Ciara dropped flat onto the floor on her own.

Shards of glass flew in, and Ciara's hands flew to the sides of her face for cover.

The second the shards stopped raining on them, Ciara rushed to where Theo was, remaining low. She helped Theo up and turned to look for Liam, but she didn't see him. "Liam!"

He stepped out from behind a pantry door. "Right h—"

The door flew off its hinges, slamming onto the ground. It shattered into wooden shards. A man in a cloak stepped in. "Theresa?" He didn't wait for an answer and cast a spell directed at Ciara and Theo.

Ciara raised her hand, shielding the pair of them. Theo sent a curse at the man at the same as Liam did. It was teamwork at its finest.

The man blocked the curses, a smirk forming on his face. "Oh, Theo."

Another witch hunter flew himself in through the

window, and Ciara recognised him. It was Jesse. Liam sent a curse at Jesse without a second thought, but Jesse was fast enough to block it.

Two more witch hunters followed Jesse inside, leaving Ciara and the guys outnumbered.

Panic set Ciara's heart on fire, her gaze fixed on Jesse. Flashes of *that* night rushed through her mind. Her hand instinctively brushed against her abdomen, where the scar lay beneath her shirt. Jesse had stabbed her there. He had nearly killed her.

But she couldn't freeze. Not with Theo and Liam in danger, too.

Jesse's eyes settled on her, a smirk growing on his face. "Long time, no see."

Don't freeze. And she didn't.

Ciara sent a curse at one of the other witch hunters and tried to pull Theo further away from them with her, but he didn't budge. He started sending curses at Jesse and one of the other freshly arrived witch hunters.

Ciara's eyes scanned the room, seeing Liam fight with the cloaked man. There was no way she could grab both Theo and Liam. But they had to get out or they would die in there.

She raised her hand and shielded herself from another curse. It crashed into the shield, disappearing with a flash.

A hiss from her side—from Theo—grounded her. She didn't need to see more than some red on his trousers, and she jumped into action.

Grabbing Theo, she teleported out.

The warm cabin with its yellow lights morphed into a beach. The one where Theo had proposed to her.

"Press on that wound." She turned around, ready to go back for Liam.

Theo was faster, and he grabbed her by her wrist. "You're not going back!"

She spun around. "Liam is there!" Yanking wasn't enough to free her hand. Theo's hold was like a death lock—too determined.

"He knows how to teleport!"

"But if he—"

"Going back would be suicide!" Theo screamed, his eyes wide. "You're not going back."

He hissed in pain, his other leg buckling beneath him. Ciara rushed to aid him, easing him onto the ground.

There was a shard of glass sticking out from his thigh, and the blood was slowly coating most of his jeans around the stab wound.

Had it been Jesse who had hurt him? Ciara hadn't paid enough attention. Either way, there was no way she was going to lose Theo because of the witch hunters.

"Fuck. Fuck. Fuck!" Ciara screamed out the last curse, her hands shaking.

Liam wasn't with them. He was dead, kidnapped, or he had escaped. And there was no way for Ciara to know which was the case.

"I'm sorry. I—"

"It's not your fault." Ciara shook her head. "But we're screwed. With your leg and—"

"Just pull it out."

Ciara's eyes widened. "Just pull it out? And let you bleed out like Josh did? I'm not a healer!"

"And I'm a criminal. You can't take me to a hospital."

Ciara cursed under her breath, going through her options. The only healer she could think of was Iris. If she could get Theo to Iris...

The only problems were that Iris could be hostile towards Theo and that she wasn't in Canada.

"If I teleport to England—"

"That's impossible."

"Hard, not impossible. We know there's witches and wizards who've done it." Ciara had listened enough in history classes.

"Using that much power is not safe." Theo shook his

head. "Fuck no! Do you want to kill yourself?"

"I want you to stay alive." Saying those words out loud hit Ciara like a truck of reality.

Theo was *bleeding out*.

Her eyes watered again, and her heart pounded against her ribcage. "We need to get you there now."

"No, Ciara. I can—"

Ciara took Theo's hand in hers, clinging to him. Afraid she would lose him again.

There was no way she would let that happen. Not after Josh. Not after everything.

Sharp pain rushed through her spine as she focused on thinking about an alley near the magical hospital in England. Her chest felt as if it was on fire, flames dancing on her skin. She could feel the rush of her own blood.

Next nausea hit her, and she wanted to hurl up her insides. Everything burnt. Yet everything around her was black. No light, nothing to see.

The feeling of Theo's hand in hers was faint. Barely even there.

"Fucking hell."

Ciara's eyes flew open, taking in Theo, whose hand she was still holding. She looked up, taking in the familiarity of her surroundings. The brick walls. She recognised the place.

"Don't touch the glass." She gave Theo a murderous warning look, so he would realise how serious she was. "I need a prepaid phone."

"Ciara—"

She didn't stay to listen and ran to the grocery store nearby. Her movements were a blur in her sight. Not having money on her, she used an illusion spell to pay for the phone with money that didn't actually exist.

Running back to the alley, she dialled the right number.

"Ciara," Theo said.

She looked up, blinking. She sort of saw Theo on the ground in the alley, but it was all hazy.

"Who is this?" The voice coming from the phone was more feminine.

"Iris," Ciara spat out. "Alley near the hospital." Her words sounded like a slur, but Iris had to hear them. "He's hurt. Please—"

"Ciara!"

The foggy view of Theo vanished, replaced by oozing blackness.

26

"Where the fuck is Liam?" A high-pitched scream pierced through the air, and the sound echoed in Ciara's head.

She hissed.

"If you so much as—"

"Fuck." The soft curse passing Ciara's lips was enough to silence the brightly lit room.

Ciara heard wood creak under someone's foot.

"You'd better stay still, or I'm killing you right there." Iris's voice.

Ciara frowned, fighting to open her eyes. She reached to touch the soft material beneath her. Was it a duvet?

She forced her eyes open, staring at a painted ceiling. Wood, painted dark brown.

"Ciara." Relieved male voice.

"Stay still!" Snappy, high-pitched female voice.

Ciara forced herself up. "What the—"

"Stay down." Iris's voice softened, her eyes on Ciara.

"No, I need to—"

"You fucking passed out." Iris shook her head, as if she could hardly believe what Ciara had done.

"Wait. Did you..." Ciara's eyes flew to Theo, who stood near the wall with his hands up in a sign of surrender. Her eyes scanned his body, even more so his leg. There was no glass shard anymore. Only a hole in his jeans with something white peeking through.

"Yes, I treated him. You said *he* was hurt. Did you mean this murderer or—"

"I meant *Theo*." Ciara struggled to keep a blank face. After all, Iris had helped her—and Theo. It wasn't time to argue with the woman.

"And where the fuck is Liam?" Iris raised her voice again. "Something is going on. They are holding his family somewhere for their safety, and you disappeared with Liam. Where the fuck is he?"

"Are you sure she's an ex?" Theo asked Ciara, having the worst possible timing.

"You shut up now!" Iris raised her wand, pointing the tip at Theo.

"Stop!" Ciara hurried up from the bed. Her feet turned out to be more wobbly than she expected, and she had to grip onto the bed for support.

Theo rushed past Iris—and her wand—and helped Ciara back onto the bed. But she remained sitting, refusing to lie down.

"How long was I out?"

Iris crossed her arms. "I was about to call Kellan to tell you're in a coma. It's the next evening."

"It's been about thirteen hours since the cabin," Theo clarified. Vancouver and London were in different time-zones after all.

"Thirteen?" Ciara shrieked, eyes widening.

"Where is Liam?"

"That's a freaking fantastic question." Ciara breathed out,

shuddering at the thought of all the possibilities.

Was Liam even alive?

Iris's eyes widened, and she pointed her wand back at Theo. "If you tell me he—"

"Theo didn't do anything! We were ambushed. The last time I saw Liam, we were in Canada and—"

"Canada?" Iris shrieked. "And you flew back home *without* him?"

"We didn't fly back." Theo narrowed his eyes at Iris.

"Then how..."

"I told you," Theo gritted his teeth, "she tired herself."

The words sank in, and Iris's eyes grew wide. "Blimey, Ciara. That's...a lot."

"I'm fine."

Ciara tried to stand up, but both Theo's and Iris's hands pushed her down. The two shared a look at their simultaneous reaction.

She sighed—or half-growled—in frustration. "We need to find Liam!"

"You can barely stand," Iris said. "How do you think you'll do that?"

"She's right. Surprisingly." Theo's eyes stayed on Ciara, even when he talked about Iris.

"I'll stab you with the fucking—"

"Stop! Stop! We need to find Liam. Can you two stop bickering for a second?"

"This is the last time I help him," Iris warned, eyeing Theo.

"Can we just focus on the issue?" Ciara snapped at her.

Liam could be dead. The witch hunters could be torturing him. But Ciara prayed he was safe. She hadn't meant to leave him behind. She had wanted to go back.

"We need to go to the cabin." Ciara glanced at Theo, her eyes filled with a desperate plea.

"The hell we do. It's not safe."

"What if he's dead and—"

"Dead?" Iris spat out. First her eyes widened, but the worry swapped into rage within a second. She spun around to face Theo. "If you—"

Theo narrowed his eyes at Iris. "I didn't do shit to him."

"The witch hunters attacked us."

"He is one of them!" Iris jabbed a finger into Theo's face.

His jaw clenched, and he pushed Iris's hand away from him. "You don't know anything, so shut up and listen for once."

"Theo had nothing to do with what happened." Ciara struggled to keep her calm. There was pounding in her ears. It had to be from the frustration. She was already tired of Iris—even if she had helped her and Theo.

"Yet the witch hunters have Liam." Iris rolled her eyes and then narrowed them—this time at Ciara. "He should've never got involved with you."

"Whatever you say." Ciara's hand clenched into a fist. The moment she realised, she released it. "We don't even know if they have him. He might have made it out of there."

"So, what's the plan now?" Iris asked, crossing her arms across her chest.

"We need to go to Canada."

"How?" Theo frowned. "They know witch hunters are a threat again with everything that happened. The flights and everything will be under surveillance."

"I can do the same as—"

"No!" both Theo and Iris yelled at Ciara.

"What choice do we have?" Ciara's voice raised, panic picking up on her. Liam had been gone for hours. *Anything* could have happened.

"You'll kill yourself." Surprisingly, it was Iris who said it.

"Like you care."

"I care about Liam, and he cares about you. You know the drill." Iris pursed her lips together.

"I don't have a better plan." *And I need to find Liam.*

Darker scenarios of Liam's fate entered Ciara's mind,

and the surrounding voices faded close to nothing. She had already lost Josh. The moment of death repeated in her head. Only this time it wasn't Josh; it was Liam.

Ciara jumped up from the bed, running for the bathroom. Except she didn't know where the bathroom was. Picking the door by luck, she found it.

Next she was hurling her guts up, trying to hold her hair up. The acidic scent filled her nostrils, making the nausea worse.

"I've got it." Theo's hands gathered her hair, keeping it away from her face.

"Thanks." She gagged, but nothing came up this time.

"Yeah, teleportation is out of the question," Iris said, remaining in the doorway.

"Then I'm going to fly there." Ciara's hands shook, and her vision blurred from the sides, but she didn't throw up again.

"Kellan has an inside search on you. They are monitoring places like airports, so you have to explain everything to them first."

Ciara wiped her mouth and moved to the sink to freshen up. "So not an option."

"Unless you ditch the ex."

"Also not an option."

"Fine. Pay for my flights, and I'll go find Liam."

Ciara frowned, eyeing the other woman carefully. "You serious?"

"Yes." Iris smiled. "Do you want mouthwash before I go?"

"That'd be nice."

27

"She hasn't called yet." Ciara paced around the motel room, her eyes flickering back to the phone waiting on the coffee table. "She should be at the cabin." She and Theo were in a motel room.

"Calm down." Theo stood up from the sofa and stepped in front of Ciara, stopping her from pacing. He ran his hands down her arms and took her hands in his. "She'll be there soon. She has to check the surroundings and everything. Besides, it's in the middle of the woods. For someone like her..."

"She helped you."

"And she treats you like trash." Theo's lips pursed together. "I'm not a fan. Yes, I'm thankful for what she did. But still, not a fan."

Ciara sighed. Pulling her hands from Theo's grip, she ran them down her face. "I'm losing my mind." She gritted her teeth, unsure how she felt about everything.

Her thoughts were scattered all over the place. She

couldn't stop thinking about Josh—nor Liam. She was dying for the phone to ring. For Iris to call her. She wasn't sure what to do after they found Liam. *If* they found Liam.

She shuddered at the last thought.

"I can see that." Theo wound his arms around Ciara and pulled her in for a hug. He ran his hands up and down her back.

She had to admit it worked. It soothed her and eased the panic.

At least Theo was fine.

But for how long? What would happen if he got caught by her colleagues? What would she do then?

"Stop worrying so much," he whispered the words in her ear, and his hot breath hitting her skin sent tingles down her spine. She had missed that feeling.

"Theo—"

The ringing phone interrupted them. Ciara dashed for the phone, picking up the call with trembling hands. "Iris!"

"There's blood near the windows, and it's a wreck." Iris's breathing shook, and her voice rose high with panic.

The memory of Theo being stabbed flashed through Ciara's mind. He had bled on the floor too. "That's Theo's blood."

"Then I don't have a clue about Liam. He's not here. There's no one here. So where can I look for him?"

Ciara pinched her nose, trying to think.

"My mother's house," Theo said loud enough for Iris to hear.

Ciara turned the call on speaker.

"Where does your mother live?"

"I'll give you the address. No one should be at the house, because that's where..." Theo cleared his throat. "Josh died there, so it's under surveillance. You can't go in, but he might be around there."

"Very helpful. If I can't go near the house, then what the fuck am I supposed to do?"

"Walk along the street and look around like a dimwit." Theo smirked, but it didn't show through his voice.

"Wonderful." Sarcasm dripped off Iris's voice. "I'll call when I've done that."

Ciara's eyes widened, thinking Iris might hang up. "Iris, wait!"

"Yes?"

"There's no sign of Theresa, is there?"

"No."

"Be careful."

"Of course." Then Iris hung up.

"That wasn't helpful."

Ciara rolled her eyes. "We know Liam's not dead. Or if he is, they didn't kill him there."

"Does that comfort you?"

Sighing and shaking her head, Ciara fell onto the sofa. "No. Maybe? Not enough."

Theo followed suit and took a seat beside her. "Liam's smart and capable. I think he got out."

Ciara hated *the reason* Theo knew that. He had tried to kill Liam more than once. "I'd like to know for sure," Ciara said.

"Me too."

Ciara glanced at Theo, taken aback by the honesty in his voice. She scoffed and rolled her eyes. "You don't care about him."

"Let's just say he's important to me if he's important to you." Theo didn't turn to look away. He didn't even blink. "You love him, don't you?"

"We don't have to talk about it."

"So you do."

"I said—"

"I know what you said, and I want to talk about it." Theo's eyes softened, admiring Ciara's face. There was even a faint smile making its way onto his lips. "I think he makes you happy."

"Stop."

"I'm *glad* he makes you happy."

"Theo, for real—"

"Let me talk."

Ciara frowned, not quite understanding the eagerness in Theo's eyes. She didn't want to talk about Liam, her ex-boyfriend, with Theo, her ex-fiancé.

"I did wrong by you."

"He's done wrong by me, too."

"Maybe, but—"

"Why are we talking about Liam?" Ciara raised her voice and jumped up from the sofa.

"Because I'm trying to tell you it's fine if you pick him."

"I'm not picking anyone!"

"So the two of you will never get back together, huh? Nor the two of us?"

"I don't know. Honestly, none of that is on the top of my priority list right now." Ciara exhaled. "I just want to deal with everything that's going on. I want to get rid of the witch hunters and clear your name. Then I can spare this...all this some thought." She gestured to the space between her and Theo. "But not now."

"Fine."

"Fine?"

"You know where I stand." Theo stood up, still holding Ciara's gaze.

She nodded. "I'm sorry."

"Nothing to be sorry for."

Ciara ran her hands through her hair. "I don't know what the fuck I'm supposed to do."

"For now, we wait for Iris to call and—"

"I'll lose my mind before that happens, Theo!" Ciara snapped. She didn't mean to even raise her voice, but the panic seeped back in. Her hands shook, and the images of Liam's dead body invaded her mind again. She needed a distraction.

"What do you want me to do?"

"I don't know." Ciara shook her head. "I need to stop thinking, because I'm this close to going crazy." Ciara pressed her thumb and index finger together. "What if—"

"Stop." Theo's hands moved to either side of Ciara's face, gently brushing against her skin. "Do you need a *distraction?*"

"I..." Theo's closeness sent her heart into a thunder match, and her breath hitched.

"Do you want it? If you tell me to, I'll back away and I'll keep my hands to myself. For good."

"Shady motels aren't the most clean."

"You mean the bed?" His eyes scanned the stained cover on top of the double bed. Returning to meet her gaze, his eyes darkened. Mischief glimmered in them. "I don't think we need the bed."

Her cheeks heated, and she tiptoed to press her lips on his. He tasted like toothpaste—the one they had bought from the motel's reception. It was a mix of mint and something sweeter.

Oh, how she loved those lips. Even when they were rough from the frosty weather.

He pulled away just a fraction, lips still brushing against hers. She needed more. Grabbing onto his shirt, she kept their lips connected and led Theo to the sofa. Even when they sat down, Ciara climbing onto his lap, their lips remained connected.

His hands found their way to her sides, caressing her skin. Her hands roamed on the sides of his neck until moving up to his tangled hair.

"Do you ever brush this thing?" she joked breathlessly, fingers raking through his hair and her lips hovering over his mouth.

His lips twitched, forming a grin. "Sometimes. You can brush it if—"

"Not now." Her lips crashed back onto his, tasting the mintiness in his breath.

Theo's hands stopped at her waist, his fingers tracing

figures there. The touch sent tingles all over her body, and she was hooked.

She had missed him. Even if it was just a distraction...

Ciara stopped, pulling away the tiniest bit—but enough to pull their lips apart.

Theo's eyes fluttered open, and the awe turned into concern. "What is it?"

"Nothing. Just..." Ciara didn't meet his gaze, moving off his lap to sit beside him.

It wasn't fair. For either of them.

"You don't want to give me false hope? I don't expect anything from you, Ciara."

She nodded and dared to meet his eyes again. "It's not fair. Not for you, not for me."

He nodded. "Then we stop."

"It's not that I wouldn't enjoy—"

"I know. Trust me, I do." He bit his lip to hold back a grin.

"Oh, shut up!" She couldn't help but blush at the suggestive tone of his voice, thinking back to when they had still been together.

"Sorry. I will." He took a deep breath and leaned his head back against the sofa. "We good?"

"Of course." Ciara smiled at her ex-fiancé. The tingling on her lips tried to tempt her to continue, but her head told her no. It wasn't right.

He wasn't Liam.

"Why are you still staring at my lips?" Theo teased, with a cocky grin crowning his lips.

"I'm not!" She totally was.

He grinned. "Sure, sure."

It had been a while since the last time they had smiled like that or had enjoyed each other's company like that. Ciara missed it more than she could admit to herself.

But then the reality dawned on her.

It wasn't real. It was a distraction. Theo was still trying to keep her mind away from Liam and everything that was going on.

"Thank you." She pushed herself closer, leaning her head on his shoulder.

"I don't know what you're talking about," he claimed, clearly lying, and wrapped his arm around Ciara.

"Whatever you say."

He hummed. "How are you?"

"Worried."

"About Liam?"

"And about what's going to happen to you if we get caught."

"Let's not get caught?"

"I like that idea."

28

"Why the fuck hasn't she called yet?" Ciara's hands gripped on her hair. She was close to pulling her hair off her scalp. It was nearing morning, and they hadn't heard from Iris since the previous evening.

She heard shuffling behind her on the bed, followed by Theo's voice. "You need to sleep. You are going to kill yourself with your habits."

"Insomnia is better than drinking."

Theo stood beside Ciara, who was sitting on the floor beside the coffee table. "Agreed, but it's not good." His brows formed a crease between them. "You need to stop drinking, though. And smoking too."

"Let's just get all this handled first. Then we can talk about that."

Theo sighed. "You need to sleep."

"No. I need Iris to call me and tell me what the fuck—"

Theo kneeled beside Ciara and cupped her face. "Calm

down."

"I can't." Her breathing quickened. "What if he...what if he's..."

The worst scenarios flashed through Ciara's mind as images. She never wanted to witness any of those images. Liam, bloodied. Liam, dead. She had to trust that he was fine—because he simply had to be. He meant too much to her.

"Don't think about that. Anything but that. Iris will call soon and—"

The ringtone cut Theo off. Relief and panic washed over Ciara at once, and she reached for the phone, pushing Theo aside. "Iris!"

"Look, Liam wasn't there, so I had to call Kellan. He—"

Ciara's heart stopped for a second, and her muscles stiffened. "You did what?"

"Kellan. They have the resources to search airports and—"

"No, no, no. Are you kidding me? Fuck, Iris!"

"What's the matter? He's your boss, Ciara. He—"

"Well, he can't know!"

"Oh, about your fiancé? Not my problem. I'm here to find Liam, not to protect your murderer boyfriend."

Ciara wished she could punch the woman through the call. Instead, she took a deep breath, trying to calm herself down.

"Liam's—"

"Fuck you!" Ciara's hand shook as she flung the phone at the wall, smashing it—and thus ending the call.

"Ciara—"

"What?" she snapped.

"I need to go."

She spun around. She wasn't ready to let Theo go, not knowing if she would ever see him again. "*We* need to go. If you think I'm leaving you for even a second, you're wrong. My team might come here and—"

"And that's why I have to go."

"And I'm coming with you."

"Ciara, you'll never find out if they find Liam."

"If they find him, he's safe. If not, I'll find out, eventually." She swallowed. A part of her wanted to go and find Liam, but another part of her wasn't prepared to let go of Theo.

"We can't run away forever." Theo shook his head. "Me, I'll have to. But I don't want you involved in my mess. Not any more than you already are."

"It's a good thing I suck at listening to anyone telling me what to do." Ciara grabbed her coat from the sofa and flung Theo's coat at him. "Let's go?"

Slowly pulling his coat on, Theo shook his head. "I'm serious."

"So am I."

"This way." The loud voice came from outside, a couple of rooms away from Ciara and Theo's door. It was distant but recognisable. *River.*

Ciara hadn't realised her team could be so fast. Iris hadn't been in a hurry to call, it seemed.

Ciara cursed in her mind, rushing to grab Theo's hand, and she teleported them out.

As the motel room morphed into rural England in the middle of nowhere, Ciara lost her balance. She stumbled but never hit the ground, thanks to Theo keeping her upright.

"What was—"

"It was River outside the room. They must have tracked the phone."

"Your team?"

Ciara nodded.

"You should have told me to teleport. You're still..."

"I'm fine." Ciara pushed herself off Theo's arms, standing on her own. "See? I am."

His brows furrowed. "You're gonna be the death of me, Ciara Jareau."

"You've said that before."

"Plenty of times."

"Ciara!" The scream echoed off the tall walls as the building rumbled from the earthquake.

She coughed from breathing the dust. "Fucking witch hunters." The words came out as a slur.

She had hit her head. Or rather, someone had hit her to the back of her head, knocking her out for a second.

"Ciara!"

She recognised the echoing voice as her boyfriend's. She tried to call out, but no voice came out. Instead, a coughing fit took over her. "Fuck this dust," she croaked out in-between coughs.

"Ciara!"

The building was going to collapse. Soon. She had to get out before it was too late.

"Ciara!"

"Over here!" This time she got the words out, only to be taken over by coughing right after.

"Ciara!" This time he was closer.

"Over—"

Theo ran through the archway, his eyes landing on Ciara. He sprinted. His arms wrapped around her, gentle but firm. "Let's get out of here." His voice was shaky.

"Were you worried?" Ciara teased.

He chuckled breathily. "You're going to be the death of me, Ciara Jareau." He sighed, relief shining in his eyes. "I nearly had a heart attack."

"Glad you didn't."

Theo chuckled again and tapped the air with his wand, teleporting them out of there.

"It's true though," Theo said and smiled. "No one else has that effect on me."

Ciara smiled back. "You said you'd be fine even if I

picked Liam." She hated that word. "So you know, if you had someone—"

"I don't."

"Well, I wouldn't mind if she'd be good for you. And as long as she would be nothing like Iris." Ciara grimaced, saying the name out loud.

Theo chuckled. "I don't think she's my type."

"Good."

"Okay, so what now?" Theo looked around. Fields surrounded them as they stood on a dirt road. There was nothing else for miles.

"This was just the first place that came to my mind." Ciara shrugged. "But we should come up with a plan."

"Plan for what?"

"Well, my team, Kellan, and Iris are searching for Liam. If they can't find him, neither can we."

"Go on."

"The witch hunters are searching for you too by now."

"I know."

"We need a plan to fix that."

"When they want someone dead, they don't stop."

Ciara shoved her hands in her coat's pockets to warm them. It was still February, so it was chilly outside. "That's why we have to stop them."

"Just us two?"

"We can at least make a plan."

"Last time you tried to fight the witch hunters, you had a power outburst. Last time you had one of those, you literally collapsed and passed out. I'm not taking any risks with you, Ciara."

"So what do you propose, then?"

"I'll lie low and you'll go back to your life."

"Theo, you're a part of my life."

He sighed, shaking his head. "Why are you so stubborn?"

"I still love you."

"You love Liam, but you gave up on finding him."

"Wrong. I didn't give up. I trust my team and I know they will find him...if there's something to find."

"Don't always assume the worst."

"It's not always that simple."

"I know."

"So how do we handle the witch hunter problem?"

29

uck. Fuck. Fuck.

Liam pulled the cap lower to hide more of his face from the people passing by. Any of them could be a witch hunter *hunting for him*.

Ciara had vanished with Theo. Liam had teleported out of the cabin too, but it had been a tough call. Liam had been close enough to kill Jesse, and he hated himself for not taking the chance. Jesse had nearly killed Ciara.

If Liam was sure about one thing, it was that one day Jesse was going to die by his hand. Jesse would pay for ever laying a finger on Ciara. That Liam was sure of.

Even the thought—the reminder—made him seethe in rage.

Liam wondered if Ciara had gone back for him and, more importantly, if she was okay. He didn't go back, aware of the suicide mission it would have been, and he hoped that Theo had successfully kept Ciara from returning.

Ciara would have tried to go back for Liam. Even if things

were twisted and warped—even between them—Ciara cared about him. Liam knew that.

He had gone to the motel they had stayed at. It had been the only place that he knew in Canada—on top of the cabin and Theo's mother's house. The cabin hadn't been an option, obviously, nor had the house.

Ciara had to be fine. She just had to. Liam kept telling himself that Theo had stopped her.

He sighed. Everyone had always told him that the best couples brought out the good in one another. Did Theo bring out the good in Ciara? Sometimes, perhaps.

And Liam? He had ruined everything when he hadn't been honest with Ciara.

Not that Theo had been honest, either. But Liam tried not to compare himself to Theo.

"Sir."

Liam prayed it didn't mean him, and he kept walking. He couldn't let himself get caught. The discovery of his body would shatter his family's hearts. He couldn't let them go through that.

"Sir!"

Fuck.

Liam picked up his pace, trying to vanish into the crowd.

"Sir!"

He kept moving, pretending to be late for a flight rather than running from someone. But it had to be obvious to the man trying to reach him.

The man had to be a witch hunter.

He would have recognised Theo's voice, and it wasn't him. The only other reasonable option was a witch hunter.

Unless they had reported him missing. But even then, they wouldn't have been searching for him in Canada.

"Liam."

This voice made him halt and look up from beneath his cap. "Trixie?" What the hell was she doing in Canada? Liam hadn't seen her since Ciara's housewarming party the previous autumn.

"Sir?"

Trixie didn't say a word. She grabbed Liam's hand and led him aside. She pulled him through a crowd of people, helping them disappear. Looking around to make sure they had lost the man, they walked into a nearby men's room.

"What are you doing here?" Trixie's eyes widened, scanning Liam from head to toe.

"I could ask you the same."

"I have a flight leaving for England soon." Trixie started going through the bathroom stalls to make sure they were empty.

Liam didn't say anything until she confirmed the room was empty—except for them. "I have dangerous criminals after me. You know, they want me dead and stuff."

Trixie's eyes grew round, completely fixated on Liam. "Are you serious?"

"It's the witch hunters." They had been all over the news in England. Considering Trixie was a journalist, she had to know about them.

She sighed. "Charlie had to rush to work because of an emergency with them last night."

"Charlie?" Liam's eyebrows rose. Charlie was one of Ciara's American colleagues. He had been at the housewarming party too—and had left with Trixie.

"We're dating." Trixie paused. "Did you have something to do with the emergency?"

"I might know something."

"The man who was following you—"

"I think he could be a witch hunter."

"Fuck," Trixie cursed. "You're not safe then."

"I know."

"I'll call Charlie."

"Wait!" Liam's eyes widened. Theo had told his mother to ask for Brody. The guy had been hellbent on it. Could Liam trust Charlie?

Charlie couldn't be as bad as the witch hunters. He was a hit wizard and had once been Ciara's colleague. He had to be better than the other option.

"What is it?" Trixie asked Liam.

"Are you sure?"

Trixie nodded, placing a hand on top of Liam's. "He'll help you. We'll help you."

That was the best Liam had. Trixie hadn't always been the nicest of girls—not back in school—but Liam had no reason not to trust her.

It didn't take more than thirty minutes for Charlie to walk into the men's room. Liam had only met him once, but he recognised Charlie. Light olive skin, ink black hair, dark eyes, and a defined jawline.

Before Liam even opened his mouth, Charlie said, "Let's get out of here." He offered his hands to Liam and Trixie. Trixie clung to Charlie's side, smiling at her boyfriend, while Liam grabbed his hand.

Charlie teleported them to an asphalt-covered field. For a second, Liam mistook it for the airport. And it appeared to be an airport, just not Vancouver's airport. This airport had only one small, old building.

"Why are we here?" Liam frowned. "Wherever *here* is."

"Kellan is on his way with a private jet." Charlie's gaze shifted to something behind Liam. "And she's here."

"Liam!"

Liam spun around, only to be engulfed in a hug by a familiar blonde woman. "Iris?" He hugged his ex-fiancée in shock, having no idea how she, too, was in Canada. And even more so, *why* she was there.

"I'm so glad you're alright!" Iris hesitated to let go, but eventually she did.

Liam's frown deepened. "What do you know?" He was more interested in finding out how Iris knew anything. Had

Theo been caught? If he had, Liam hoped Ciara hadn't been there. She didn't deserve to be blamed for anything Theo had done.

"I know what happened at the cabin."

"How?" Liam wasn't ready for the answer, but he had to know. If something had happened to Ciara...

"Ciara and Theo told me," Iris said.

Liam glanced at Charlie, whose gaze fell on Liam.

"I have a feeling you know even more than we do." Charlie crossed his arms, eyes narrowing. "Kellan knows as much as I do."

"Wait. Where's Ciara?" Liam shifted his gaze to Iris. Nothing mattered more than Ciara's wellbeing. She had to be okay.

"She and Theo are on the run."

Liam clenched his jaw. He was tempted to kill Theo for taking Ciara with him. She didn't deserve to suffer for his choices.

"You said you're in danger." This time it was Trixie who talked.

Liam faced her. "It's a long story. Just, everyone, hear me out." He turned back to meet Charlie's gaze. "It's not what it looks like."

He frowned, unconvinced. "It looks like Ciara switched sides."

"No, she didn't." Liam shook his head, his tone turning defensive.

"She sure seemed to have switched sides when I treated her *and* Theo," Iris said.

Liam's eyes snapped to Iris. "What do you mean? Treated Ciara?" His mind clouded with worry. He hadn't seen Ciara get hurt. But everything had happened so fast at the cabin, so he could have missed it.

Unless Ciara and Theo had run into trouble again after the attack...

"She teleported all the way to England with Theo and

passed out soon after," Iris said. "Theo had been injured at the cabin, and they couldn't go to a hospital. She called me before she passed out. Apparently, it was like the outburst at the warehouse. Just...this time, it was worse."

Liam's eyes widened. Theo had been right about the outbursts. They could turn out to be lethal. "She had one of those again?"

"She's had more of those?" This time it was Charlie who asked.

"Wait." Liam shook his head, as if that would clear his hazy mind. Theo had joined the witch hunters to keep Ciara safe after they had found out about her outbursts. If they were getting even worse, it couldn't be a good sign.

Charlie, Trixie, and Iris were waiting for Liam to explain everything when the sound of a plane interrupted him. He spent the extra seconds making sense of what was happening.

Once the private jet had landed, it didn't take long for Kellan to walk out and hurry over to where the four of them stood.

"You found him," Kellan said to Charlie, eyes on Liam.

Charlie nodded in answer, even though Kellan didn't see that. "Trixie did."

"I was trying to get back to England," Liam said. "Is my family okay?"

"They're safe." Kellan frowned at Liam, disapproval and confusion mixed in his eyes. "But why are you in Canada?"

"I came with Ciara and Theo." It wasn't the smart answer, but Liam wasn't going to lie.

"Wha—"

"Let me explain *everything*. There's a lot you don't know."

Kellan nodded as if to tell Liam to go on.

"They blackmailed Theo into joining the witch hunters. And wait until the end before you question me." Liam knew how absurd he was going to sound. "The witch hunters were going to kill Ciara, and that was their leverage on Theo." Liam couldn't believe he was standing up for that killer. "I'm not saying he isn't a criminal. I saw him kill Doherty. But he's on the run from the witch hunters because he failed at his task."

"His task?" Kellan asked.

"He was told to kill me. The witch hunters, or their leader Elliott, threatened to kill Ciara and his mother otherwise."

"Theo's mother was taken to a safe place today." Charlie frowned. "A witch hunter killed Josh in her house today."

Liam sighed. "I know."

"How?" Charlie's eyes hardened as if he blamed it on Liam.

"It was a trap. Theresa set it up. She threatened Theo's mother. And..." Liam paused. "If I tell everything, what are you going to do with the information?"

"Find Ciara," Kellan said.

"What about Theo?" Liam didn't care about Theo, but Ciara did. She cared about him more than Liam wanted to think.

"If you're telling us the truth, his punishment won't be as bad." This time, it was Charlie who spoke. His voice gave away just how conflicted he felt. He had been Theo's colleague once. Liam couldn't imagine the hell of a day he was going through. Charlie had lost Josh as well.

"I'm telling the truth. I don't like Theo. He's done a lot of bad things, but he's done them to keep people safe. What he's done is wrong, but he's not our enemy. Not the way we thought." Liam shook his head. "And we told Josh that, too. We asked for his help."

Pain crossed Charlie's face.

"Josh was there to get Estella. He was going to let Theo meet his mother and then Josh was supposed to take Estella to safety." Liam shuddered, thinking about how wrong everything had gone. "Theresa showed up with Estella. We caught Theresa and took her to the cabin. Then I and Ciara went to find Josh. There was a trap, and we triggered it. And..." Liam didn't want to even think about it. "He was alive before that." He turned to look at Charlie, who had tears in his eyes. "I'm sorry. I know you were friends."

"What happened then?" Charlie asked, lower lip quivering. But he didn't cry—didn't let himself cry.

"Estella went home and called Brody. And then we found a locating enchantment on Theresa, and right after that, the witch hunters showed up. Jesse was there, too. There were too many of them and they had the element of surprise, so they forced us to flee. That's when we parted ways."

"Ciara and Theo were in Scotland, but they escaped when River and Declan went looking," Kellan said. "Where are they now?"

"I have no idea. I haven't seen them since they got out in the middle of the attack."

"Then they teleported to England, and Ciara passed out for half a day," Iris said.

Liam's stomach twisted. "Half a day? But she—"

"She was fine the last time I talked to her," Iris reassured.

Liam shifted his attention towards Kellan. "I know Ciara's safe with Theo. He's not the monster you think he is." He turned back to Charlie. "Ciara had an outburst on a mission back here in America over a year ago. Before Theo faked his death. The witch hunters nearly killed her, and they burned their mark on her. That's what made Theo do everything he's done."

Charlie's face was easy to read. The sorrow and hurt were all over his face, out there for everyone to see. "Will you say that in court under the influence of a truth potion?"

"Yes, it's the truth."

"I believe every word then," Kellan said. Clearly he didn't have a truth potion. Considering how expensive and hard it was to brew, Liam wasn't surprised he didn't have one.

Charlie nodded. "Me too."

"But right now, we need to find him and Ciara," Liam said, worry gnawing at his insides. His hand tightened into a fist. If he didn't know where Ciara was, he couldn't look out for her.

30

"Even if we get rid of the witch hunters, it's not like I'll be free to go as I like." Theo stared at the ceiling of their new motel room.

Ciara sat on the other side of the double bed. She turned to glance at him. "Just don't get caught."

"Simple." Sarcasm dripped off his voice.

"No, but—"

"Ciara, even if I was to run, you couldn't stay in my life." He faced her. "I've done horrible things and I'm going to be locked up for that."

A part of Ciara wondered if she should feel guilty for Theo's actions. He had done it all for her. A part of her wanted to even blame Doherty's death on herself. "But you did it all for me!"

She would have never done what Theo had done, though. Not even for him. Not even for Liam. She could have never even considered hurting Doherty.

"Do you think anyone will care?"

Her voice caught in hesitation. But even if she hated it, she cared. "I care." Ciara reached to take Theo's hand in hers and gave it a squeeze. "I'm a superior hit witch. My word has to weigh something."

"I've killed." Terror flashed in Theo's eyes. "I killed *him*."

"Doherty."

Theo flinched at the name. "You have no idea how sorry I am."

Doherty clapped his hands, earning the attention in the entire room. "Alright, wake up. We're finished for today."

"Finally! Research—" Theo stopped himself from finishing the sentence.

Doherty raised his eyebrows, waiting for him to finish—but knowing Theo wouldn't. "Thought so," he muttered.

Everyone packed their bags and paperwork neatly before leaving the room one by one.

Ciara was the last one there with Doherty. She was about to say goodbye when he began to talk.

"You and Boucher becoming a thing?" he asked, eyeing the doorway. Theo had just walked out.

"Maybe one day." Ciara glanced at the doorway too, unable to bite back her smile. She couldn't see Theo anymore. He had already gone. "But no, nothing yet."

"He sure likes to flirt with you."

"I'll try to make him keep it to a minimum."

"No worries. It's entertaining." Doherty chuckled. "Glad to see you have something more than work on your mind."

Ciara smiled. "Yeah, it's nice."

"With our job, you'll need to work on keeping a balance. Perhaps he'll be that balance for you. As long as you keep work and love lives separate, that is."

"I promise, if something is to come out of this, it won't affect our work."

"I know."

Doherty had cared about Theo, too. Ciara couldn't imagine what Doherty had gone through right before his last breath.

"I..." Ciara swallowed. She turned to look away, but continued to hold Theo's hand. "I wish you had never done that." She sighed. "I don't know if I would have done the same for you."

One thing was for sure: she would have never hurt Doherty.

Ciara stared at the grey stone before she lied down beside it. Tears blurred her vision when she thought about what she was doing. Lying on the grass beside her fiancé's grave.

It had to look baffling for anyone passing by, but she didn't care. She needed to talk to him—even if he wasn't there to hear her anymore.

"I miss you, Theo." Her voice came out as a whisper. Like how one would whisper into their lover's ear. Something she could never do again. "I love you."

Most people said they had loved people they had lost. But even if Theo was gone, Ciara's feelings for him weren't. She still loved him, and even his death wasn't enough to change that.

"I wish it had been me, not you."

Theo squeezed Ciara's hand. "I've done horrible things. Unforgivable things. And I've hurt you. I know how much you cared about Doherty."

"You did it to protect me." That didn't change it. Not even for her. Doherty had been like a father to her.

"Yet I hurt you."

"I should hate you," she said, nodding. "And to some extent, maybe I do."

Doherty's death still weighed on her. It always would.

His death seemed to be a burden for Theo as well, and rightly so. It would likely haunt him for the rest of his life.

But even if Ciara was angry with Theo, she was more angry with the witch hunters. They had made him kill Doherty. They had put Theo through hell.

Because of them, Theo was no longer the person who Ciara had planned to marry once upon a time.

Ciara had allowed herself to live in a bubble for a little while. In her dream, Ciara envisioned a life where she and Theo were never separated. But in reality, it was inevitable. If it wouldn't be the witch hunters, it would be the law. Something would separate them one way or another, and Ciara hated the mere thought of it.

She had let herself get too used to the past that they were trying to relive.

"You need to go find out what happened to Liam." Theo pulled his wallet out and went through his coins. But whatever he grabbed wasn't a coin. It was tiny. He shoved his wallet back in his pocket and grabbed his wand. With one tap, he morphed the tiny object into a knife.

Ciara's knife. The one she had stabbed him with.

"You should have thrown that away," she hissed.

"It's yours."

It was hard to meet his gaze. "I don't want it."

She had hurt him, too. She had tried to kill him. Everything about their situation was messed up.

"If this is about the stab—"

"I could have killed you!" Ciara had to bite her lip to keep herself from crying. She bit hard enough for it to sting. The pain in her chest grew as well.

"I forgive you." Theo placed the knife in her hand. She would have dropped it if he hadn't wrapped her fingers around it.

"You shouldn't." Her voice shook as the memory of that night replayed itself in her mind. She would never forgive herself for what she had done.

"I already did."

"Theo, I nearly killed you!" She looked straight at him, fresh tears blurring her vision. The memory of that night was still enough to make her throat feel tight. The knife in her hands weighed on her as if it was a boulder, not a simple knife.

"You didn't know the truth."

"I would have never found out if..." She couldn't finish that sentence. She stood up and placed the knife on the bedside table. "You should be angry with me."

"You want me to be angry?" Theo raised his eyebrows, but his lips thinned. Ciara didn't know what was going through his mind.

"Yes."

"Fine, I'm angry. But that has nothing to do with what happened at the warehouse." Theo stood up and raised his gaze back to Ciara.

The only thing between them was the bed. But with Theo's eyes so intense, Ciara felt as if there was barely even air.

"I'm angry that you went crazy with revenge after what happened to me. If it had been real, if I had died, do you think I would have wanted you to risk your life for something as petty as revenge?" The all-too-familiar storminess built up in Theo's eyes. "I wanted you to be safe, Ciara! You were supposed to live your life!"

She couldn't tear her gaze away. She wanted to, but Theo's eyes were too intense for her to look away.

"I didn't want you to erase yourself from all our friends' lives. Dammit, I wanted you to live! Like *actually* live." Theo shook his head, and his hands twitched with frustration. "You were so hellbent on getting revenge that you became blind to the real danger." Theo paused, taking a deep breath. "Jesse could have killed you! Even before the stupid speed dating thing."

"Theo—"

"No!" His eyes narrowed at her. "Don't come up with excuses! You didn't check his background. You trusted him blindly. He broke into your hotel room, Ciara, and you didn't even realise it was him!" Theo shook his head again. "You should have been smarter. You should have figured it out. But no, you went and slept with the guy. Hell, you moved in with him for a little while." He threw his arms up. "What were you thinking?"

"I wasn't."

Theo clenched his jaw. "If something happened to Liam, you have to promise me you won't go crazy with revenge again."

Her eyes widened. She hadn't let herself consider the possibility. Liam had to be okay. "Theo—"

"I'm trying to keep you alive, and you're making it unnecessarily hard right now! You always do. What do you think I would have done if you had come with me that night at the warehouse?" He paused, but not for long enough for Ciara to answer. "I would have taken you to safety!"

He was right, and that was the worst part. Everything he said was true.

Theo grunted in frustration and strode over to Ciara, who was standing on the other side of the bed. He cupped her face with his hands, stroking her cheeks. "I know how much you love him. You gave him the lucky charm."

He was letting out his built-up anger, jealousy, frustration—all of it.

Ciara's breath hitched at the sudden closeness. The physical contact was so familiar it was almost painful. Because even if their connection had stayed the same, nothing else had.

"Promise me you won't do anything reckless for him." Theo looked into her eyes to see if she hesitated and said, "Ciara, promise me."

"I can't. You know that. I'd go to Hell and back for you... and I'd do the same for him." Ciara swallowed, tempted to look away. "Stay safe and I will too."

For a moment, Theo hesitated. He looked conflicted—as if he didn't know whether to be furious or glad she cared.

"Fuck it." Then he leaned in, lips crashing onto hers.

Her arms wrapped around his neck, making sure he wouldn't pull away. She had missed Theo so much. Kissing him again was surreal. After thinking he was dead, it barely felt real.

But it was. It had to be. She could feel him right there under her fingertips. His lips were on hers. His stubble scratched her skin.

He was real and alive.

In the middle of the heated kiss, her hands travelled to the hem of his shirt. She wanted to get it off him. She wanted to feel him.

One last time, she told herself. It was like saying goodbye to an addiction. Perhaps he had replaced alcohol or cigarettes for her. Maybe even both.

"Ciara," he rasped out breathily, his lips still hovering over hers. He was speaking into her mouth.

"Theo."

"Are you—"

"I'm sure." She pulled the wretched shirt off him in a hurry.

Theo wasn't dead, and she was going to enjoy that for once.

Her back pushed against the wall, and her front touched Theo's bare chest. She was about to run her hands down his chest when he gripped her shirt and pulled it off.

His lips returned to hers, hungry for more.

For a second, she wondered if it was a mistake. If it was wrong when she still loved Liam.

But for a moment, there was only Theo. She inhaled his scent, letting him hook her. He intoxicated her like a drug.

When Theo's lips moved to her neck, it was easy to forget everything outside their little moment. His hands worked at her bra. Then her jeans.

His touch was like a drug she had been deprived of for the past year. She was addicted again, and she needed more.

So much more.

She would never get enough of him.

"I love you, Theo." Theo—the man I wanted to marry once.

"And I love you, Ciara." His mouth covered hers again while he slid off his own jeans. He kicked them away without breaking their kiss.

His touch on the sides of her neck was delicate and soothing, like a gentle breeze on a summer day. The tingling sensation travelled through her body, making her hairs stand on end. Then his hands moved lower, tracing a tantalising path along her waist.

Ciara wished they could have stayed like that forever. In their own little bubble, reliving their past.

31

Theo's unruly hair stood in contrast to the radiant morning sun that flooded the room, enhancing his overall appearance. He looked so calm when he was asleep.

His bare chest was warm. Ciara lay half on top of him, their legs tangled together. Like it had always been when they had lived together.

Ciara wasn't ready to pop that bubble. She would have to soon, but she was going to cling onto it for as long as she could. She and Theo would have deserved a life together.

But it was too late for that, so she savoured every detail of the one precious moment she got.

"Morning." His husky morning voice sent chills—the pleasant kind—down her spine.

She looked up, a smile forcing its way onto her lips. "Morning."

He smiled back. It had been a long time since she had seen that exact smile. A genuine smile of pure joy. He hadn't looked so happy in a while.

When Ciara and Theo got up, they showered together. After that, Ciara stopped by at a nearby café to get them breakfast. They sat on the bed, eating croissants, when Theo broke their bubble.

"You have to go."

Ciara stopped mid-bite and shifted her attention to him. "What?"

"You have to go back and figure out what happened to Liam."

Liam's name had an unusual effect on Ciara. She felt *wrong*—guilty. She didn't know if he was okay and still she was hooking up with a guy who had tried to kill Liam. Ciara was running away from her problems, and that was wrong. "Theo—"

"I don't expect anything from you, Ciara. Not even after last night or this morning." He smiled at her, but this time it wasn't a cheerful smile. "Things are complicated for everyone involved."

"I meant what I said."

"I love you too. But I also know you love Liam."

He was right. "Theo—"

"Let me speak." He looked at her, seriousness covering the smile on his face. "You need to find out what happened to him. You don't even know if Kellan took his family to safety. And with me as a burden, you can't find out. So, please, just go."

"And what are you going to do, then? Run away and leave me for good?"

Theo shook his head. "I'll be around."

"Theo—"

"You know I'm right."

Of course he was, but Ciara hated it. She didn't want to leave him now that he was back in her life. It was hard to see past her old grief when he was there right in front of her. She had longed to get him back for so long.

Ciara gritted her teeth, looking down at the floor. "You're shoving me out after last night?"

"This has nothing to do with what happened." Theo raised his hand to stroke her cheek. "We can't stay hiding forever. Well, I'll try, but I'm not going to take you with me."

"I need a way to contact you."

Theo smiled. "I already told you, I'll be around."

"I don't know what that means."

"You'll hear from me."

She rolled her eyes. "So I'll only meet you on *your* terms? I'll only be able to contact you when *you* want to talk to me?"

"For your safety."

"Stop, Theo."

"No." His face hardened. "I will not. You need to go to Kellan. Go see Bill. Go find out how Liam is."

Ciara had been dying to see Bill since Theo had undone the curse. She hadn't talked to him in what felt like a lifetime, and she missed him. She wouldn't stop feeling guilty about what happened at the warehouse until she got a chance to talk with Bill.

And as for Liam, she had to know what had happened. She had to find out if he was okay.

And if Liam's family was okay. In the worst case, even Henry could be in trouble. Ciara had to find out how the Rosslers were.

She didn't want to leave Theo. But after everything Theo had done, she wanted to see Bill and Liam more than she wanted to stay.

"This evening," Ciara said. "I'll leave this evening. Until then, we get to ignore the rest of the world." She needed it for her sanity. It was selfish, but for a moment, she deserved to be selfish.

Theo's lips twitched, and soon he was smiling. "Sounds good to me."

It was hard not to think about how limited their time together was, but they both did their best to ignore that. And Ciara did her best not to think about Liam, Henry, Bill, and everyone else. She didn't want to taint their last hours with worrying.

It was like they would have never separated. As if Theo would have never faked his death. Of course, it wasn't real, but Ciara didn't let that bother her. She wanted to enjoy the time they had until it was gone.

That evening Ciara kissed Theo goodbye and slipped the lucky charm in his pocket. She had to close her eyes before she teleported away. It was too painful to see his face when she vanished.

She wanted to cry the moment she appeared at her workplace. Reality hit her like a boulder rolling down a hill.

She prayed she could find Kellan—or someone. It was late, so she couldn't be sure if anyone was working anymore. But with hopeful thoughts, she headed for Kellan's office. He always worked overtime. Hopefully, this time wasn't any different.

The moment she set her foot in the Hit Department area, the alarms went off. About a dozen officers surrounded Ciara, wands pointed at her. They were yelling orders at her and at one another. Ciara raised her hands, showing she was unarmed—not that it mattered with her wandless magic.

"I'm unarmed," she tried to say calmly through the commotion, but the officers seemed more focused on yelling at her.

Ciara wasn't sure what was happening. She had taken one step, and chaos had surrounded her.

"Wait!" It wasn't Kellan—but River was better than no one. "Lower your wands. She's not a criminal."

The officers did as River told them, but they hesitated to leave, eyes staying on Ciara and her every movement as she slowly lowered her hands.

"I'll handle this." River grabbed Ciara by her arm and led her to her own office—away from the officers.

"What the fuck was that?" Ciara asked, gesturing back to where they had left the officers.

River shrugged. "Kellan doesn't always have great ideas."

"He set alarms for me." Ciara couldn't resist the urge to roll her eyes. "Of course he did."

"Where's Theo?" River asked.

"I don't know." Perhaps it was better that she didn't; at least she could tell the truth.

"You *were* with him."

"Is Bill okay?" Ciara asked, nerves making her stomach twist. Theo had undone the curse, but Ciara still wasn't sure if it had worked. He hadn't let her see him wake up—another reason she should nothing but hate him despite their past together.

"He's still in hospital, but he's been awake for a week now."

"So it worked." Overwhelming relief washed over Ciara, and she didn't watch her words.

And River clung onto that. "You had something to do with it?"

"Yes, and no."

"Ciara!" River snapped. "I'm not your enemy!"

She was going to have to work on getting back to reality. She couldn't make everyone her enemy, even if they were Theo's enemies. "I know, I'm sorry."

But would River hurt Theo if he got the chance? Who was really Ciara's enemy anymore? Everything had been black and white before—witch hunters against her side.

Theo didn't belong to either side. Ciara was unsure what that meant for her, even though it shouldn't have changed anything. Her team was on the same side as she was.

"Theo undid the curse," Ciara revealed, even though she wasn't sure how much information she could trust River with.

"Curse?" River's brows furrowed. He was the team's curse specialist, so he knew plenty about curses. "It was a curse?"

"Yes. A slow, lethal curse. But Bill is fine now if he's awake."

River frowned, falling silent for a moment. "Do you want to see him?"

"Yes!" She was already about to grab River and teleport, but then she froze. "Wait."

"The Rosslers are safe. Liam included."

She didn't need to know more than that. Nodding, she grabbed River's hand and teleported them to the front of the hospital.

She rushed in and headed for Bill's room. The people passing by were a blur as she ran to Bill's room and yanked the door open.

Ciara halted for a second when she saw Bill. His green eyes were open, and he was smiling. He was awake *and* fine. Paul was sitting beside him on the bed, and even he looked better than he had the last time Ciara had seen him.

Ciara dashed for Bill and pulled him into a tight embrace. "Dammit, I missed you!"

Bill chuckled and wrapped his arms around Ciara to hug his friend. "Glad to see you're back."

For a while, Ciara didn't pull away from Bill. But when she couldn't trust her senses, she pulled away to make sure he really was there—eyes open and everything. And he was.

"I'm so sorry, Bill, for everything that happened and—"

Bill shushed her, smiling. "I'm fine now."

"Thanks to the same guy who did this." River had joined them in the room, and he didn't sound too delighted.

Ciara grimaced. She loved Theo—or who he had once been—but she also hated him for the things he had done. Theo had hurt Bill. He wouldn't have had to undo the curse if he hadn't cursed Bill in the first place.

There were no excuses. Ciara's and Theo's bubble of dreams had burst, and it was time to focus on the reality.

"Theo?" Bill frowned, looking at Ciara.

"It's complicated. I'll explain some other time, okay?"

Bill nodded. He didn't even hesitate. It was one of his qualities that Ciara had always admired. Even with their job, he remained understanding.

"Well, at least I have some experience in my own field now." Bill grinned. He was the team's terrorism expert. "I've had to endure a terrorist attack firsthand now."

Ciara squeezed Bill's hand, ecstatic to see him. "Yeah, I think you have had enough experience for one lifetime now." And Ciara meant it. She never wanted to see Bill get hurt again.

"I agree!" Paul said.

Bill smiled, glancing from Ciara to Paul. "If you say so."

River didn't leave, and soon Ciara realised he wasn't going to leave. He was monitoring her. It probably hadn't been River's own idea. Ciara was convinced Kellan had ordered him to stay with her.

She wasn't even sure if she still had the safe house in her use. And if she didn't, she didn't know where everything she owned was. After all, she was no longer renting the flat Jesse's friend owned. Not after Jesse's attack.

Ciara stayed with Bill for a couple of hours. River remained at the hospital, but at some point, he left to get himself a coffee. Paul stayed too. Apparently, he had been hanging out at the hospital a lot with Bill. Ciara only just saw them together for the first time, but Paul seemed like someone who deserved Bill. They were both so genuine and so caring.

"Alright, we have to go." River didn't sound as bitchy as Kellan would have. Ciara had a hunch the words had come from Kellan.

"Don't let Kellan get to you," Bill said.

Ciara smiled at him. "Don't worry. I can handle him."

Bill smiled back, but he didn't look convinced. "I know."

This time River was the one to teleport them because Ciara had no idea where they were going. As the surrounding hospital morphed into green, Ciara realised they weren't going back to work.

The lack of light meant that it was already past eight. It was also chilly, and the ground was damp. The lush greenery of the forest enveloped them, accompanied by the soothing melody of water gently flowing nearby.

As Ciara spun around, her eyes widened at the sight of a lake stretching out before her. On its shore, there stood a quaint cottage nestled among the trees. The thatched roof of the cottage provided a gentle rustling sound as the wind whispered through the reeds. The outer walls were made of rough, weathered stone. It was like straight from a fairytale.

"Kellan is here."

"Please, don't tell me he lives here." Ciara loved the place, but it didn't seem Kellan's style.

River chuckled and led the way to the cottage. "It's a safe house."

"Wait..." Ciara's eyes widened, hope already creeping in. "Are the Rosslers here?"

"Yes. And Jenna. Along with Kellan and a few more guests."

32

efore Ciara and River made it to the door, Kellan walked out. His gaze was thunderous as he marched up to Ciara and River. He pointed a finger at Ciara, the rage shining through his eyes.

"Kellan," Ciara said tightly. She knew to expect a scolding.

"I demote you!" Kellan yelled at her. His expression softened the slightest bit as his eyes snapped onto River, meeting his gaze. "River, you got a promotion."

"Fine." Ciara had never wanted a promotion to begin with. Still, it stung, but she wasn't going to let it show.

"Um..." River cleared his throat, eyeing the two others with discomfort and worry.

"Go ahead, and congrats," Ciara said and smiled at River. There were no hard feelings between them. It was between her and Kellan.

River frowned and looked at Kellan, waiting for him to say something. Kellan just gave a nod to tell River could go in. Then River left without another word.

"I can't believe you ran off like that! You know, the witch hunters were hunting Liam in Canada when you abandoned him!" Kellan yelled at Ciara.

Ciara had to fight every inch of her body not to show how the worry engulfed her. "I tried to go back but..." Ciara didn't want to tell Kellan Theo hadn't let her go back. "I didn't have enough power. Teleporting drained all of it."

"Iris said something along those lines."

Ciara's eyes widened upon hearing Iris's name. *That bitch.* She had been the one to reveal everything. She had almost got Theo caught.

"Is Estella Boucher safe?" Ciara asked.

Liam was safe. The rest of the Rosslers were safe. Theo was, hopefully, safe. Estella was the only one left to worry about.

"Yes. Your American colleague Brody took care of that. I don't know where she is, but I suppose that's for the best."

Ciara's shoulders relaxed. Everyone was safe. At least everyone who was still alive.

Josh. He was gone.

The thought nauseated Ciara, but it wasn't the right time to mourn. She could cry her eyes out later.

Kellan took a deep breath, shoulders slumping visibly. His stern gaze shifted into a look of pity. "I'm sorry about your friend." So Kellan knew about Josh.

"Thanks." Ciara didn't want to talk about Josh. Not with Kellan, nor anyone. But Kellan was closer to the end of that list.

"You bitch!"

Kellan's eyes widened—an unusual look for him. He turned around, stepping aside in the process. A red-faced Iris was stomping her way over.

"You abandoned Liam in Canada!" Iris screamed at Ciara. "You know what? Those sickos followed him. He could have died, and that would have been on you! You're no better than your fiancé. What are you even doing here? Go back to him. And stay away!"

Ciara ignored Iris and faced Kellan, keeping up a blank expression. "Did you want to discuss something about work?"

"I'm talking to you!" Iris screamed at Ciara.

"We'll talk later." Kellan sighed and headed inside.

Ciara's gaze returned to Iris. "I did what I had to. Everyone's fine now. Not thanks to you, though." Guilt gnawed inside Ciara, knowing Iris was right. Ciara had left Liam behind and she shouldn't have. But Ciara refused to admit that to Iris.

"I'll kill Theo myself if I ever get the chance," Iris hissed.

Ciara raised her eyebrow, surprised and furious simultaneously. Her protective instincts kicked in. "Will you?" She lowered her voice and leaned in a little. "I dare you to try."

Iris took a step back, a worried look flashing in her eyes. "You're insane and just as much of a killer as he is."

"Then you should know when to take me seriously." Ciara narrowed her eyes at Iris and walked past her, heading for the house. She was seething, and Iris was the last person she wanted to see—or talk to.

She stepped inside, instantly greeted by a hug. "Ciara!" She had expected it to be Henry, but it was Charlie—her colleague from America.

"Charlie! What are you doing here?" Ciara embraced Charlie tightly, her heart pounding with astonishment. She hadn't seen him since her housewarming party. Seeing him brought back memories.

Those included Josh too. Fighting back the urge to break down, Ciara bit her lip, determined not to let her emotions show in front of others.

Charlie pulled away. He tried to smile, but the sadness shone through and it looked more like a grimace. "I was at Estella's house. Then Kellan contacted us about Iris."

Ciara shut down. She was in that room in Estella's house again. She could have sworn she heard the blade slice through the air. Her hand tightened into a fist, and she pushed her nails against her palm, trying to ignore the grief. Anything was better than the grief.

She had asked for Josh's help. It was all on her.

"I heard about..." Charlie cleared his throat.

Ciara hugged him again, throwing her arms around her old colleague. "I'm so sorry."

"It's not your fault."

She didn't agree with Charlie, but she was too tired to argue.

When the two pulled away from one another, Kellan stepped into the hallway. "You ready here?" He wasn't talking to Ciara. He didn't even glance at her.

Charlie nodded and looked at Ciara again. "I have to go back to Canada."

"W-will you let me know about the funeral?" Ciara's voice came out hoarse, despite her greatest efforts to sound strong.

"Of course." Charlie hugged Ciara one more time. "I'll see you then."

"Thanks. See you."

She and Kellan didn't exchange words. He nodded at her when he passed by and left outside with Charlie.

"These people better be done now!"

Ciara turned around just in time to see Henry rushing towards her, arms wide open. "Henry!"

She had never been so happy to see her best friend. Despite how raw she felt after seeing Charlie, a smile made its way onto her lips.

Henry pulled away from the hug too soon. "Everyone will be so happy to see you," Henry said and pulled his best friend with him to the next room. Cosy sofas were arranged around a warm, flickering fireplace. The walls were painted in a soft, peachy orange hue. It was as if the space had a soothing energy that instantly made her feel at home.

Ciara noticed the house was definitely bigger on the inside

than it was on the outside. There had to be an enchantment.

"Ciara!" Jenna rushed to hug Ciara the instant she spotted her.

Ciara beamed and hugged her back, not wanting to let go. Seeing her friends safe was what she needed after the past week.

It had been exactly a week since Theo had taken over her body. It had been the longest week of her life.

After Jenna, Polly rushed to hug Ciara. "I'm so glad you're okay," Polly squealed.

"Better than okay now, seeing all of you." Ciara smiled at Polly, who stepped aside.

Poppy hugged Ciara next. "Wait until Liam gets back! He'll freak out." The younger Rossler chuckled. "He was so worried."

Ciara had been worried about Liam as well. No matter how hard she had tried to remain in her stupid bubble with Theo.

But she had trusted her team. They had found Liam— with the help of Iris, apparently.

The jealousy was a sure sign of Ciara's feelings that she had been doubting lately. With Theo more or less back, things were weird between her and Liam.

She had broken up with Liam when he had needed her the most. But he had also lied to her when it had mattered the most. They had both wronged each other. But not the same way she and Theo had wronged one another. She and Liam weren't that far gone—or so she hoped.

But she had slept with Theo when she should have been out looking for Liam.

"Don't tell that to Iris." Henry grimaced.

Had Iris done something? Was she fawning over Liam again? Ciara didn't ask, but she couldn't help but wonder.

At the very least, Iris still cared about Liam. Otherwise, she wouldn't have threatened Theo. She was still protective of Liam.

Theo had hurt Liam, and Ciara hadn't forgotten—nor forgiven.

Mary pushed Ray into the room in a wheelchair. Her eyes widened when her gaze landed on the young hit witch. "Ciara!" Mary rushed to hug Ciara, leaving Ray in his wheelchair beside a sofa.

Ciara hugged Mary tighter than ever before. "I'm so glad to see all of you."

Especially Ray, who was finally out of the hospital.

"Wait. Gabriel needs to see you too." Mary pulled away and rushed out of the room to get her youngest son.

Ciara turned to Ray, her face brightening with a warm smile. She had never been as happy to see him. "It's good to see you."

Ray smiled. "You too."

"Are you better?"

Ray nodded, but glanced at his wheelchair with a look of disdain. "I am, thank you."

That was a relief.

"Hi."

Ciara spun around to see Gabriel in the doorway with Mary. Ciara stepped ahead, standing in front of Gabriel. She had promised to be at his birthday dinner. To help him tell his family about Tim. But she hadn't kept her promise.

"I'm so sorry I wasn't at your birthday dinner. Something happened to me, and I couldn't come. But I wanted to. I really did." Ciara let out a heavy sigh, her shoulders slumping. "Things just took an unexpected turn."

"It's fine." Gabriel nodded, his eyes filled with understanding. He knew what Ciara meant. "Don't worry about it."

Ciara smiled and hugged the 18-year-old boy—or rather, a young man. "I'm so glad. Thank you for understanding."

"Birthdays come and go."

She would be there when he would be ready to tell his family about Tim. She would kill to be there if that was what it took.

"You honestly disappeared to Canada with Theo and Liam?" Henry asked. A slight frown tainted his expression. A frown of worry. Ciara could understand why Henry had been worried. He had been through so much in just a few months. What had happened at the warehouse—his father's accident included—had to affect him.

Ciara took a deep breath. "It's not that simple."

"The most important thing is that everyone is fine now," Ray insisted.

"You are still in danger." Ciara looked around the room. "Anyone who knows me is. That's *their* leverage." The witch hunters' leverage.

She should have known better than to care. But she couldn't help it. Not with these people.

They had lied to her once. They had hidden the truth about Theo. But that was the past. They were in trouble because of her. The least she owed was forgiveness. The secrets and the lies wouldn't matter anymore.

Or so Ciara hoped. She wanted to learn to forgive them all.

"There's an international alert for witch hunters," Mary said. "Kellan has multiple teams on it here in the UK, too."

"Good." Still, it wasn't enough. Not when they had no spies inside the witch hunters.

"Besides, no one would look here," Jenna said, clinging onto Henry's side for comfort. "We're safe here. Kellan or River," she gestured to River who was sitting on a sofa, shooting him a smile as she did so, "has been getting groceries and everything for us."

Kellan wasn't a spy. That much Ciara was certain of. She also trusted River. Perhaps the Rosslers were, in fact, safe wherever they were.

The safe house was probably in Scotland, but Ciara didn't know for sure.

The heavy front door slammed open, and everyone in

the room jumped a little.

"Stop!" It was Liam, yelling at Iris.

"You can't be serious!"

"I am!"

Next, Liam was standing in the living room doorway. A few stray strands had fallen in front of his eyes, but there weren't enough to cover the enchanting shade of hazel. The rest of his hair was in a ponytail, and Ciara realised how much his hair had grown recently. There was also the stubble that Ciara loved.

Ciara's hands twitched at her sides. She wanted to run her fingers through Liam's ponytail. She wanted to touch him, to feel that he was there—safe and fine, in one piece. Not once before had she been so relieved to see him. Her knees felt unstable, as if they were just air under her, about to let go.

If it had been just the two of them, she would have run into his arms. But his entire family was watching, along with Jenna and River.

Liam's eyes settled on Ciara. "Hey." His breathless voice revealed his disbelief.

Ciara smiled, ecstatic to see him with her own eyes. To see that he was fine. There wasn't a scratch on him. Not one she could see, at least. "Hi."

His eyes drank her in as if he was relieved to see her, too. "Can we talk outside?"

Ciara hesitated. Iris was outside the cottage, and Ciara had had enough of her for a little while.

Liam saw right through her hesitation. "Iris left."

Ciara nodded. "Sure," she said, answering his earlier question. She and Liam excused themselves and left outside.

"What happened?" That was the first thing Liam asked, his gaze glued to her.

"At the cabin?" For once, it was hard to look at him. She was so ashamed of herself for leaving him behind.

He nodded.

"Theo got injured, and I panicked." Ciara shuddered. She had done wrong by leaving Liam behind. "I didn't mean to abandon you. I would have come back, but Theo wouldn't let me and—"

"No, I'm glad you didn't go back there. I got out. I'm just happy you did, too." He meant that. It showed in his eyes.

Ciara breathed out. "I was worried."

"And I was worried about you."

He had been worried about her when she had closed all her troubles out—and had slept with Theo. It wasn't like she had cheated on Liam. They weren't together. However, something about it didn't sit right.

"Theo was bleeding, and it was bad." Ciara sighed. "I couldn't think of anyone other than Iris."

"So you teleported to England and passed out for it." Liam's brows knitted together. "What if it had been worse? What if—"

"I'm fine."

"But Theo was right to worry about those outbursts. You can't control how much you drain your energy."

Both Theo and Liam were right, and surprisingly, they seemed to agree on something for once.

Ciara sighed. "I know. I'll be careful."

"You better be."

"How did you get back?" Ciara asked.

"Witch hunters were following me. Then I saw Trixie at the airport. She and Charlie are dating, so she called him. Charlie had already talked to Iris by then. Kellan picked us up with a private jet. I didn't know your department even had one of those."

Ciara had known. "It's for emergencies."

"W-where's Theo?"

"I don't know."

Liam raised his eyebrows as if he didn't believe Ciara.

"I don't," she said. "He told me to come back, so I did. For all I know, he's somewhere fighting witch hunters on his own. We tried to come up with a plan, but I had to make sure you got to safety." Ciara glanced at the cottage's front door. "And your family, and Estella, and I had to see Bill."

"Kellan won't let me leave."

"You're not safe." For once, Kellan and she agreed on something, too. "Not yet."

"Yet?" Liam's voice rose. "Don't tell me you're planning something reckless."

"I'm not," Ciara assured. "I'm just trying to come up with a plan. A safe plan. Or, however safe is possible."

"I want to come with you if you attack the—"

"No. Absolutely not."

"You *can't* tell me no. They nearly killed my father. I get to fight like you do, Ciara. I don't want you to go without me." His words were infused with passion, fuelled by the intensity of his unwavering gaze.

"Liam, stop," Ciara said sternly. "Your father nearly died. Don't put your family through that again."

"That's not fair."

"You need to stay here. Stay safe."

Liam let out a deep sigh, his frustration clear. "Ciara—"

"I mean it."

"Will you come visit?"

She hesitated, wondering if she should just say yes. "Do you...do you want me to?"

She loved Liam. Theo was right about that.

"Of course I do."

"Then I will."

33

Kellan returned to the cabin late—around midnight. River had already left by then, but Ciara was still there. But she had to leave with Kellan. He took her to the same safe house she had lived in before leaving for Canada. She didn't invite him in, but he still stepped inside.

"If I could have done things differently, I would have," Ciara said, breaking the tense silence between her and Kellan.

He sighed. "The demotion is more about what others will think."

"It's fine."

"It's late."

"I know."

Kellan leaned against the wall in the hallway. They had stopped there after walking in. "Will you come to work tomorrow, so we can talk? Around noon, perhaps."

"That sounds good."

"I'm not your enemy."

"Nor am I yours," Ciara reminded. The mutual respect was wavering, and Ciara wanted to fix that. Even if the tension remained, she wanted to regain the respect they had once had for each other.

"You really don't know where Theo is?"

"No." She held Kellan's gaze, so he could see that he could trust her. "But I know he's not the bad guy. At least, not out of his own desire."

"Liam told us so. He said he'd prove it in court if needed."

Ciara's eyes widened, her eyebrows shooting up in surprise. "He did?"

Kellan nodded. "I know how much Liam despised Theo before. If he can now trust Theo, on some level at least, that already tells me a lot, even if some of it is just for your sake. I believe you and Liam. Your fiancé isn't the monster we thought him to be."

Ciara wasn't sure how to reply. Theo had done horrible things, and he was a criminal, but his reasons had been more or less right.

"I'll see you tomorrow." Kellan turned around, heading for the door.

"See you tomorrow."

Next day Ciara went back to work. She had hoped her—or after her demotion, River's—team would have found more about the witch hunters, but they didn't have anything new. She told the team everything she knew, but it wasn't much.

Still, it was better than what they had had before. At least they had a name: Elliott Hardy. They also knew Theresa wasn't being blackmailed, thanks to Theo. Theresa had chosen to support the witch hunters, and it had nothing to do with any sort of threats.

Ciara also told the team about the outbursts. They were going to be working with her. For everyone's safety, it was better they knew.

Bill wasn't back at work, but he was the only one. Owen and Declan were back. Still, they were missing two people. With Bill still recovering and Theresa revealed to be a traitor, they needed a recruit—someone new.

Kellan had been trying to go through different candidates, but none of them had struck his interest—or trust. Ciara wondered if he was too careful after what had happened with Theresa, but she said nothing. She would have been careful too, especially knowing what Theresa was like—and what she was capable of.

It was past ten in the evening when Ciara was ready to head home. She had just changed and walked out of the women's changing room—that was now her private changing room without Theresa there—when she ran into River.

He sighed, as if relieved to see her. "You're still here."

"You were looking for me?" Ciara asked.

"Yes. I wanted to talk about the entire team leader thing and—"

"It's fine." Ciara placed a hand on River's arm. "No hard feelings."

"Still, it's not fair. You were a great team leader. Kellan is just being...a dimwit." River shook his head. "He's extra careful, and even paranoid. Honestly, it's getting out of hand."

"Talk to him."

"Even if I'm the team leader now, I can't challenge him like you do."

Ciara raised her eyebrow. "Why not? You've known him longer than I have."

River sighed, switching his weight onto his other leg. "I don't have the guts, to be honest."

It was a little funny. River was almost twice the size of Ciara. Yet he was afraid to talk to Kellan.

"You want me to talk to him, then?" Ciara asked.

"Someone has to, and I feel like he might listen to you."

"Or I'll just end up arguing with him." Ciara ran her hand

through her hair. "I think he's angry with me."

"Should I ask Owen then?" River frowned. It was clear he was worried about Kellan.

Ciara sighed. "No, not yet. I'll try my best. Then we can ask Owen. Does that sound good?"

"It does, thanks."

"No problem."

River smiled at Ciara, his brown eyes almost sparkling with delight too. "It's good to have you back." River paused and cleared his throat. "For a moment, we were worried."

"Worried about what?" Ciara frowned.

"That you had gone rogue."

"In a way, I did."

River nodded. "True, but your reasons seem valid."

Ciara smiled a little. "Were you afraid I was becoming the enemy? After Theresa...I wouldn't blame you."

"You're better than Theresa."

Ciara's smile grew. "I'm glad you think I'm better than a witch hunter."

River laughed. "Yeah."

Next morning Ciara went back to work already at seven in the morning. She had barely slept the previous night, but she wanted to talk to Kellan.

She suspected he would be at work early. When she made her way to his office door, she found out she was right. Kellan spotted her and opened the door by flicking his wand.

Ciara stepped in, and the door closed—with magic—behind her. "Hi."

"Hi." Kellan looked her up and down. He didn't bother to hide his surprise.

"May I sit down?"

"Go ahead."

Ciara took a seat and faced Kellan. "How are you?"

"Why does this sound like an interrogation?" Kellan

raised an eyebrow. "Are you here to beg me to give back your position?"

"No, I don't want it."

"Oh."

"I want to talk about you."

"Me?"

Ciara nodded. "Yes, you. So first, how are you?"

"Busy." His annoyance shone through. Kellan liked to be the one in charge, but he seemingly had no idea why Ciara was there. But she was going to let him know soon.

"I think you need a break."

He rolled his eyes, glancing at some papers on his desk. "Can't take one."

"Can't or won't?" Ciara challenged.

Kellan frowned, meeting her gaze. "I'm fine."

"So, have there been any interviews? How many potential recruits have you met so far?" Ciara asked.

"No one has been good enough so far."

"Or is it your trust issues?" Ciara was pushing it, but she didn't care. She needed answers out of Kellan. She also had to make him see he had trust issues.

River was worried, and that made Ciara worried too. Kellan had to stay sharp for what was coming. The witch hunters were relentless and wouldn't stop until they were defeated.

"I don't have trust issues. What happened with Theresa won't happen again."

"No, it won't. But you'll have to hire someone. We need more people, Kellan. The witch hunters are growing bolder, and we're not ready. So stop wondering if every person is going to betray you and man up. Hire someone now. I bet you've found at least one qualified person."

"We can't afford more spies."

"The witch hunters are ahead of us either way. No, I don't like it either, but it's the truth. We need more people. Not everyone is a spy."

"You betrayed us, too. How are you better than Theresa?"

"Don't you dare!" Ciara snapped, jumping up from her seat. "You don't get to compare me to her. She killed Josh. She killed my friend, and she enjoyed it. Theresa aspired to be a witch hunter, and I think I know why. But she's insane. A monster. I'm nothing like her. I did what I did to keep people safe. To keep Liam safe. To keep Estella safe. And yes, to keep my ex-fiancé safe as well."

"You talked to Theresa?"

"I tried to break her, so she would have told me where she was keeping Josh. The only subject that made her crack at all was telling her she wasn't good enough at her job. As a woman in this field, she's been put down enough times to make her doubt herself. That's her weakness, but I can't tell what exactly made her choose to become a witch hunter."

Kellan nodded, letting the words sink in. "I heard about the trap. Theresa killed Josh, not you."

"*I* triggered the blade out of sheer stupidity."

"*She* killed Josh."

Ciara wasn't sure how she always ended up having such deep conversations with Kellan. They always tried to point out the wrongs in each other. They challenged one another and drove each other half-insane. But Ciara liked that. Somehow, Kellan helped her stay sane.

"Thanks for saying that."

Kellan's eyebrows rose, and surprise filled his eyes. "Did you just thank me?"

"Yes." Ciara leaned forward. "Now, let me help you pick a recruit."

Kellan hesitated, but eventually he sighed, giving in. "Fine."

week went by fast. Ciara spent every day at work.
When she had time to spare, she visited Bill or the
Rosslers—Jenna included. There wasn't much time to
spare, though.

On Thursday, Kellan told her to take the rest of the week
off. She was going to fly to Canada that evening for Josh's
funeral, which would be on Friday.

If the situation would have been any different, she would
have argued to stay and work. This time, for once, she didn't
mind having a few days off.

Josh's death had hit closer than it should have. Ciara had
let herself care too much. Josh had always been there for her
to save the day. She had promised to be there for him and
she had failed. She had triggered the trap. If she had been
more careful, she could have saved Josh.

"Tomorrow's the funeral?" Henry asked.

He, Jenna, and Ciara were sitting in the cottage's kitchen,
talking together. Ciara kept picking at her nails, already

worried about the funeral. It was going to be tough to get through it.

Ciara nodded. "Yes."

"You're going alone?" Henry asked, as if he didn't want to let Ciara go alone.

"Yes, but I'll be fine." That was a lie. Ciara wasn't anywhere near sure she would be fine on her own.

But Henry didn't need to go through a funeral. He had already been through enough recently. Ciara knew he wasn't holding together as well as he tried to make it seem. Nearly losing his father had left an impact on him. He didn't realise anyone noticed, but he still looked at his father as if he was going to die any moment.

When he looked at Ciara, his eyes had the same expression. She could only imagine it was because of the stabbing. Henry had been one of the people to find Ciara at her flat after Jesse had stabbed her. Based on what she had been told about the situation, it had been rough. Even Kellan had said so, and he had seen a lot worse.

Jenna frowned. "If you need to talk, just call us."

Ciara smiled at her friends. "Of course, but I'll be fine. So don't worry if you don't hear from me. I might just go straight to bed after the...whole thing."

Henry nodded, an almost permanent frown remaining on his face. "You sure you won't take Liam or—"

"No, I won't take anyone with me." Ciara's gaze dropped to her hands. She couldn't help but fiddle with her fingers.

She had talked to Liam, but there was an awkwardness between them. Still, a part of her was considering telling him about her night with Theo. On the other hand, she wasn't sure if he wanted to hear. He hadn't done anything that would imply he wanted something from her—or *with* her.

Not since Canada.

Ciara had thought about asking Liam to go to Josh's funeral with her. She would have if it would have been safe for Liam. But it wasn't.

"He would come if you asked him to," Henry said.

"I know."

"Then why won't you?" Jenna lowered her voice and leaned closer. "You don't understand how much he worries about you. He hates being stuck here, unable to help. I bet he'd want to come with you."

"We broke up." Ciara gave a sharp look to Jenna and Henry. "In case you two forgot."

"Well, he loves you." Henry sighed. "Neither one of you just says anything."

"Now is not the time."

"It's never *the* time."

"Henry." Ciara shook her head. "Just let it be. I'm an adult, he's an adult. We know what we're doing."

"I doubt that."

"Henry's right," Jenna said, humming. "He goes running every freaking day. Like he'd go insane if he just stayed here at the cottage. Not knowing what's up with you."

"I doubt it has anything to do with me. I'd go crazy if I couldn't leave this cottage, either."

"It's not that bad." Jenna shrugged. "Henry's family is the best."

Henry groaned. "Yes, it is bad. There's a reason I moved out."

"If things go well, you won't have to stay here for much longer," Ciara reassured.

"I know what that means." Henry's lips pursed together momentarily. "You're trying to find the witch hunters. And when you do, you'll go after them."

"Not alone."

"Still."

"I'll be fine."

"Yet you never actually are. You never die, which I support, but you can't claim to be fine." Henry's eyes softened. "You've been through a lot."

It reminded Ciara so much of Doherty's words. The pity in Henry's eyes was the same pity that had been in Doherty's eyes.

Before Theo had killed Doherty, that is.

Ciara missed Doherty. She couldn't believe she had to attend another hit wizard's funeral. It had only been about six months since Doherty's funeral.

Ciara swallowed, a tightness forming in her chest. "I'm fine."

"No, you're not." This time Jenna spoke, shaking her head. "It's a mask, Ciara, and you know it too."

"I'll take it off when I can." *But that'll take a while.*

"You can trust us enough to take it off now," Henry said.

"Can I?" Ciara didn't mean the words to come out so sharply. But she still wasn't over the fact that Henry and Jenna had also lied to her. Those lies had been enough to separate her and Liam. It was going to take more time before Ciara could look at Henry and know she could trust him with anything.

"I'm sorry," Henry said, voice barely audible.

"We're sorry," Jenna said.

"I-I know."

"Well, anyway," Henry cleared his throat, "I am going vegan!"

Ciara's brows rose. She was glad to move on from the earlier subject. "You are?"

"Yes." Henry nodded, a proud look on his face. "Animals are like creatures. I don't want to hurt either, so no more meat for me."

"He's been googling vegan blogs and everything," Jenna said. "I might give it a try as well."

"I think that sounds great," Ciara said. "Definitely on brand for you two."

"I wonder how it took me this long to consider it," Henry said.

Ciara shrugged. "What are you going to feed carnivore

creatures then? Does the veganism apply to them?"

"No." Henry shook his head. "They require meat to survive. It's our job to provide them with whatever they need. Sometimes, that means meat."

Ciara nodded. "I like that. Do you think eating vegan will be a challenge?"

"Challenge or not, it'll be fun." Henry smiled. "And definitely a change. A good change!"

Ciara stayed for as long as she could, but Liam didn't show up. She would have liked to see him before she left for Canada, but he was still on his run when she left the cottage.

Perhaps it was for the best.

Ciara wasn't sure what she would have said. She was already a mess because of the following day's funeral—Josh's funeral—and she wasn't even in Canada yet.

The flight to Canada was going to be pure torture.

Before her flight, Ciara had to stop at the safe house. She walked in and closed the door. She was about to shrug off her coat when a sharp blade pressed against her neck.

Her breath hitched, and she froze.

"You're not being careful enough."

When Ciara heard his voice, relief washed over her. The instant the knife lowered, Ciara spun around and threw her arms around Theo. "Where have you been?"

For a moment, their bubble was back.

"Around." Theo sheathed the knife and hugged her back. "Where were you today?"

Just like that, their bubble popped again. They both had to face the reality.

"Henry and the rest of the Rosslers are sta—"

"I don't need to know."

Ciara pulled away to see Theo's face, and her brows furrowed. "You're not the enemy, Theo."

"I know. I just don't want to risk anything."

"If you plan to do something—"

"I don't have a plan yet." Theo smiled down at Ciara and brushed her hair behind her ear.

"I need to go soon."

Theo frowned. "Where?"

"Canada."

"Josh's funeral." Theo's voice shook, and all warmth left his face. He had lost Josh too, but he couldn't go to the funeral.

Except he could. There was one way Ciara could think of.

"Come with me." Ciara took Theo's hand in hers. "Come to Canada with me. You deserve to be there, too."

"Ciara, I'd be arrested before we got there."

She shook her head. "No, you won't. You'll just have to use my body again. Like you did when you saved Bill and..."

Theo raised his eyebrows. "Tried to kill Liam?"

Ciara flinched but nodded.

"But—"

"I know you want to be there."

Theo's brows furrowed. "Ciara—"

"Theo, come with me. Please."

"I'd be in control of your body and—"

"Yes, and I'm asking you to do that. It's not like you'd be forcing me into anything."

Theo sighed. "Are you sure?"

"Yes, I am." She didn't want to go alone. Not really. And she knew Theo wanted to be there just as much as she did for the last goodbye.

This time Ciara cooperated with Theo. When he was unsure what he should say *as her*, she gave him the answer. When they arrived at the funeral in Canada, no one suspected anything.

Not even Charlie, who rushed to hug Ciara.

Ciara's old boss was there. Brody too. In fact, many of

her American colleagues were there. But the front rows were saved for Josh's family and friends who had known him outside his work.

Ciara—or Theo—kept looking around, already seated. Brody's knee kept going up and down, the pace only quickening with time. He was already biting his lip to keep the tears at bay.

Josh had been more than a colleague to all of them. He had always been so genuine. He had always put others before himself. Ciara missed that. She missed Josh.

The ceremony began. Someone talked at the front of the room. Ciara felt as if she wasn't even there, even though she was there just as much as Theo was—just as much as anyone was.

Even Ciara's old boss—Alan Torres—shed a few tears. It was a rare sight. They knew what their job meant. Losing a colleague happened at least once in a career—even a short career.

They should have all been prepared yet none of them had been. Not when it came to Josh.

Josh's mother cried the hardest, and it reminded Ciara of the way Estella had cried at Theo's funeral.

Theo flinched, hearing Ciara's thoughts.

"I'm sorry," Ciara said—inside her head—quickly. She should have kept her thoughts to herself.

"You can't keep your thoughts to yourself right now," Theo reminded. He didn't talk out loud; he was talking to her inside her head.

"I know. But that was uncalled for. This situation...it's already bad enough."

It was horrible, watching the closed coffin where Josh's body lay. He had been all alone. Ciara wasn't sure what she would have done if she had been there alone, tied up to a chair in a dark room. Guilt gnawed at her. After all, she had triggered the trap. She should have switched the lights on. She should have noticed it. There had to be something she could have done differently.

"You didn't kill him, Ciara."

"I asked for his help and I triggered the trap."

"You did not kill Josh."

She still couldn't let go of the guilt. Josh had saved her dozens of times, and she had let him down. She had let him die.

"You didn't *let* him die, Ciara," Theo said, voice stern inside her head.

"Still."

"You're getting through the spell."

"What?"

"Your fingers. You're fidgeting."

Theo looked down, making her look down as well. She was fidgeting, and apparently it wasn't Theo's doing.

"Sorry."

"No, it's fine."

The funeral didn't feel real. It was like a blur.

Ciara had been to too many funerals to count, but she couldn't picture Josh inside the coffin. Her mind refused to accept that Josh was dead. That he wasn't coming back like Theo had come back.

Josh would never pick up his phone again when Ciara called. He would never save her life again. She would never get to hug him like she should have the last time she saw him before his death.

⚜ ⚜ ⚜

"Theo would have killed me if I hadn't been on time. You would have a lot more than a few bruises." Josh glanced at Ciara and smiled, glad he had been on time.

Ciara was glad too. "I definitely would. Thank you. Again." Ciara tried to relax her muscles that ached like crazy. It was the bruises. They hurt. Even walking—and keeping up with Josh— hurt.

"I'm glad to be of help."

"Maybe, but I should really learn not to need your help so often."
Josh tilted his head as if to ponder. "You're too focused, maybe?"
"Sometimes, for sure."
"Well, we'll work on that. Until then, I'll be around to save the
day when needed." Josh grinned at Ciara.
"That sounds like a plan." She smiled too. "Thanks again."
They reached the team's meeting room's door and stopped
outside for a second.
"Anytime," Josh said before he opened the door.

Towards the end of the ceremony, Ciara wasn't sure if the tears that slipped down her face were hers or Theo's. Her best guess was they were both of theirs, mixed together.

After the ceremony, Josh's parents approached Ciara—and unknowingly Theo. His mother thanked Ciara for trying her best, and Ciara's guilt only grew.

She hadn't done enough.

After the funeral, Ciara had cried herself numb. First Doherty, then Josh—it was too much for Ciara.

It was too much for everyone. Ciara hadn't seen Charlie or Brody cry at anyone's funeral before. They both had cried this time. Especially when Josh's father had held a speech in his son's memory. Well, after the first couple of sentences, one of Josh's cousins had continued, but the words had still been Josh's father's. He had had the speech written down.

Even after the funeral, Ciara couldn't stop thinking about a part of the speech.

Josh was always there for you when you needed him.

Josh had been there for Ciara whenever she had needed him—and she still would have needed him.

"I'm sorry."

Theo left Ciara's body when they made it to the safe house in England. He had been in her body since Thursday, and it was already Saturday. Ciara had to lean against the wall to remind herself how to stay standing on her own. After so long, it was odd and even exhausting to be in control of her own body.

"About what?"

"For ever faking my death." Theo snaked his arms around Ciara and kissed her forehead. "I'm sorry."

Ciara frowned. "I forgive you. I thought I already told you that." That was one thing she could forgive. The rest were a different story.

"I just wanted to make sure you knew." Theo held her gaze, and Ciara knew there was a lot going on inside his head after the funeral.

Ciara had tried to control her thoughts, but the funeral had brought back memories. On top of reminiscing about her moments with Josh, she had accidentally thought about losing Doherty and she had also thought about Theo's funeral.

Ciara placed a hand on Theo's shoulder briefly. "I do." She could forgive Theo for faking his death. As for Doherty's death, there was no way. It was too much for her, and the feeling was still too raw. It likely always would be.

Theo nodded. "I have to go now."

"Where?"

His lips twitched, and soon he couldn't hold in his smile. "I like it when you show how much you care. Sometimes you hide it. Sometimes you don't let anyone see how you feel."

Ciara frowned. "You didn't answer my question."

"I'll be around. Just not right here."

"You could just stay here and—"

"Too risky. I can't get caught just yet."

Ciara's frown deepened, a shadow casting over her face as her mouth turned downwards. "What are you planning?"

"I already told you I don't have a plan yet. But when I do,

I can't be in jail."

"I wouldn't let them—"

"I don't want you to have to stand up for me. Not now." Theo shook his head. "Besides, someone is at your door."

The doorbell rang. Theo kissed Ciara's cheek before he grabbed his wand, flicked it, and teleported out of the house.

35

Ciara ran her hands down her face. Then she sighed and headed to the door. She opened it, and her eyes widened. "You can't be here!"

Liam smiled as if he wasn't worried in the slightest and was only happy to see her. "Let me in then, so I won't have to stay standing *here*."

Ciara hesitated, but she let Liam step in and then closed the door.

"What the hell are you thinking? It's not safe for you to be here. The witch hunters are after you. And alone? Something could happen!"

Liam's eyebrows rose. "You sound worried."

"Of course I'm worried," Ciara hissed.

He smiled as if she had told him how much she loved him. And somehow, that smile only reminded Ciara of how much she loved Liam.

But it only made the time she had spent with Theo feel more and more like cheating. She wasn't with Liam, nor was she with Theo.

Still, all of it felt wrong.

For a moment, Ciara regretted not asking Liam to go with her to the funeral. But she didn't regret letting Theo come for a last goodbye. Josh would have wanted Theo to be there.

"How are you?" Liam asked, his voice softening.

"I've been better." Josh's funeral had been tough. Ciara wasn't sure if she could have gone through it alone.

"I'm sorry."

"I should've known this would happen one day. Josh has saved my life so many times I'm surprised he didn't get himself killed doing that."

Liam shook his head. "You lost a friend. You should never be in a position where you expect to lose a friend."

"But I am." Ciara brushed her arm, her fingers moving up and down on her skin. "People die around me all the time."

Saying it out loud made her shiver, as if a gust of icy wind had blown through the room. Saying it out loud made it seem more real. It was already real, but saying it out loud made it *feel* real as well. People around her kept dying.

She had put the Rosslers in danger. They had to stay away from their lives and their friends because of her. Because they mattered to her. Ciara was afraid they were going to have to move abroad like her mother had. All because of her.

And if something happened to them...

Ciara didn't dare to think about it.

"That has nothing to do with you and everything to do with those monsters." Liam's warm arms brought her back to reality from the dark corner of her mind she had lost herself in. He embraced her tightly, her head resting against his chest as he gently kissed her forehead.

She felt safe in his arms, and she wished she could have stayed there forever.

Why does everything have to always go wrong?

Tears blurred Ciara's vision, and she clung onto Liam. Her

silent tears left his shirt wet. His arms tightened around her ever so slightly, providing a sense of security and comfort.

They stayed still, standing near the front door, for a good while.

How had they ever drifted apart? Ciara remembered living with Liam. She had loved that. Her best days from the past twelve months were from that time. Most of her recent good memories included Liam. Especially the best ones.

He always made her feel safe. No one else made her feel as safe.

Not even Theo.

"Liam, I—"

Her ringtone cut her off. Liam pulled away, and she grabbed her phone from her back pocket.

It was Kellan. Calling her in the middle of Saturday when it was just past noon. He knew Ciara had just come back to England after Josh's funeral. He wouldn't have been calling her if it wasn't important.

Ciara's eyes widened as panic flooded her insides. Something had to be horribly wrong.

She picked up the call and raised her phone to her ear. "Kellan?"

"Get here. Now! Ian Connell is dead."

The news made Ciara's blood rush. Ian Connell was one of the best protectors in their time. The absolute best.

"Was it the—"

"Yes! Get here *now*."

Ciara hung up, forgetting to say anything to Kellan. She shoved her phone back in her pocket. "I have to go." Her gaze fixed on Liam. Her hand had a will of its own, brushing down his arm. She wasn't sure if it was more to comfort herself or to comfort him. "Stay here and do *not* go wandering alone." She hoped Liam saw how serious she was.

His brows furrowed, worry clouding his gaze. "Is something wrong?"

"I'll explain everything when I get back." Ciara tiptoed,

her lips brushing against Liam's. Then she pulled away and teleported to work.

It was only then that she realised she had kissed Liam. But there was no time to stop and think about it. She would talk to him later when she got home.

Ciara ran all the way to the meeting room. River ran in a little after her, and then they were all there. Except for Bill, of course.

They would also have a recruit coming in for training, but he hadn't started yet.

So everyone was present.

"Ciara, sit down." Kellan's voice was oddly grim. But the oddest part was that everyone was standing, and he didn't tell the others to sit down.

It wasn't a good sign. The news was going to be *bad*.

Ciara hesitated, unsure what to expect, but then she sat down. Her fingers wrapped around the metal armrests of the chair. She had to stay grounded, no matter what she was about to hear.

After the funeral, Ciara wasn't ready for bad news. It was already one of the worst weeks of her entire life.

Kellan hesitated. When he finally spoke, his gaze remained only on Ciara. "Ian Connell was attacked while protecting your mother."

It took longer than it should have for Ciara to understand what Kellan was saying. When she did, her hands flew up to her mouth. Her eyes stung, but there were no tears.

"Where's my mother?" Her voice came out raspy and high. Like a screech.

Her mask was stripped just like that. After the funeral, she was already a mess. And after the news, the storm only grew inside her head.

Kellan hesitated, but raised his gaze. He shook his head, looking for the words. But the answer was already written on his face.

"Is she dead? Kellan, tell me!" Ciara was shaking, waiting

for the worst news of her life.

"They took her. The witch hunters have her."

Ciara wasn't sure which would have been worse: the reality, or her mother dying.

"No. Kellan, stop." Ciara shook her head. She gripped onto the table, knuckles turning white.

It couldn't be real. She had kept her mother safe. Her mother had always been safe.

"How would they even—"

"I don't know." Kellan sounded like a police officer bringing the worst possible news. And in a way, he was exactly that. But he was also her friend.

"She was supposed to be safe! I didn't even contact her and—"

"We are trying to figure it out," Kellan said.

Ciara realised her cheeks were wet. She was crying, but this time she didn't bother to wipe away the tears. It was her mother who was in danger. The one person who was supposed to be safe.

She couldn't even keep her safe.

Ciara looked up at Kellan. "The Rosslers—"

"I sent a team there just in case."

Her veins turned cold, the sensation rushing through her body. Her throat tightened as if ice shards got stuck there.

"Liam's at my house." Her usually firm voice came out raspy again, and she had to gasp for air as if she was drowning.

The room fell silent. Everyone shared the same thought, but none dared to voice their worries out loud.

The witch hunters had found Ciara's mother. They had found a safe house they shouldn't have been able to find. The safe house Ciara had been staying at couldn't be any safer than that. Liam wasn't safe there.

"Let's go!" Kellan said, even though everyone was already reaching for their wands.

Ciara appeared outside the safe house first, running straight in. Her mind was blank, and her feet had a will of their own. She had no plan. All that fuelled her was one thought. One of her worst fears.

Not Liam.

"Ciara!" Kellan called after her.

"Liam!" she screamed, panic choking her. She ran to the living room. "Liam!"

The room swayed, or so she thought. It was a mess. The coffee table had shattered into wooden shards. *No.* Someone had shattered it and trashed the place.

That someone had taken Liam too, and it wasn't hard to guess who was to blame.

Ciara's ears rang from her own blood rushing in her veins. It was utterly silent, yet so loud. In her head, at least.

"Ciara." The man's voice sounded distant, as if coming from a mile away.

She couldn't move. She wasn't sure if she even remembered to breathe.

How could she have been so stupid? She had left Liam alone, even when she had known it wasn't safe for him to be there. Especially not on his own. Her judgment had lacked when it shouldn't have—when it had mattered the most.

She had failed someone she cared about again. Only this time, it was the man she loved.

Someone grabbed Ciara by her arms.

Her hands trembled. Thoughts of what could have happened to Liam invaded her mind. He could be dead.

For all she knew, her mother could be dead.

Ian Connell, the best protector of their time, was dead, without a doubt. All protectors were trained to keep the good, but wanted, people safe. Ian Connell had been the best of them. No one had ever died under his protection.

He had died first.

And the two most important people in Ciara's life could have been just as far gone.

A cry broke past Ciara's own lips, and Kellan had to tighten his grip to keep her up and on her feet. Her limbs were numb. The pain pulsed in her head, and cold seeped into her veins.

Images of her mother's pale corpse flashed through her mind, only to be followed by a similar image of Liam. Lifeless, pale, and cold. Eyes staring at nothing.

Ciara's insides twisted. She had to rip herself free of Kellan's grip to rush to the bathroom. She hovered over the toilet, wondering if the nausea had passed.

But it was wishful thinking, and within seconds she was retching over the toilet. The acidic taste burned her mouth and the sharp stench scorched her nostrils while the tears stung her eyes.

They had barely buried Josh. And then *this*. It was too much.

Tears blurred Ciara's vision by the time she stopped vomiting. With a wave of her hand and a simple spell, she brushed her teeth; the toothbrush was floating in the air and doing the work for her.

When she no longer tasted vomit in her mouth, she let the toothbrush drop into the sink. She couldn't care less about anything anymore. No matter what she did, she would lose.

She looked up, meeting her own gaze in the mirror. Seeing her veiny eyes didn't faze her, but she remembered that she still had people to lose.

The rest of the Rosslers were also at a safe house.

36

Ciara was the first to appear at the Scottish cottage—the Rossler family's safe house. Right after, Kellan and the team appeared.

There was already a fight. Ciara could see a hit wizard—a man her age—lying dead on the ground. She couldn't remember his name because she had never worked with his team. But she recognised him. She had seen him when he had still been alive.

He definitely wasn't alive anymore, and that made Ciara think of Josh.

The other team was struggling. There were too many witch hunters for them.

Ciara's eyes darted around the area until she spotted Henry's dark brown hair and Jenna's blonde waves.

"Get the Rosslers out of here now," she ordered *her* team right before they all ran to help with the fight.

Ciara headed straight for Henry and Jenna, who were fighting against two witch hunters. She moved her hand, sparking her magic, and let her knife float out of her boot. Without touching it, she threw it at one of the witch hunters that was casting curses at Henry and Jenna.

"Ciara!" Henry got distracted by her sudden appearance.

Fucking idiot, Ciara cursed in her mind and blocked a spell directed at him.

Henry tore his eyes off her, also realising his mistake. He, Ciara, and Jenna all attacked the witch hunter at once, blasting him against the ground. Ciara finished him, using her magic and her knife.

She didn't even blink. Her mask was building itself back up.

Ciara spun around to look at Henry and Jenna. "Get out of here now." She didn't mean the words to come out so desperate.

"Where's Liam?" Henry asked, worry already filling his voice. "He—"

Jenna gasped before Ciara even answered. "Don't say they—"

"They have him." Ciara's eyes moved to Henry just in time to see the news sink in. His face twisted in pain. "They have my mother too."

"No." Henry's voice cracked. The news broke him. After everything he had been through, the witch hunters had also taken his brother. "No way. Liam's—"

A loud bang interrupted Henry as a witch hunter's spell blasted off one of the cottage's walls. Ciara raised her hands, shielding herself and her friends barely in time. She heard the rock smash into one of the already dead witch hunters. It was like smacking at a jelly with a hammer.

Red jelly.

"You need to get out of here now." Ciara didn't want to see Henry or Jenna become smashed jelly.

"I'm not going anywhere without you, Ciara!" Henry yelled, but Jenna grabbed his hand.

"For your mother," Jenna said to her boyfriend. She

glanced at Ciara, and that look was enough to reassure Ciara. Jenna would get Henry out of there and to safety.

Henry's shoulders dropped as if he gave in. But then he turned to his best friend. "Ciara, you have to—"

"I'll be right behind you," Ciara said with a quick glance at Henry. Then she ran off to help a hit wizard from the other team. She spared one more glance at Henry and Jenna just in time to see them teleport away.

She sighed, relieved they were safe. If she made it out alive, she would get to see them again.

Another spell smashed into the cottage. Half of it crumbled down.

"No!" a man screamed. Ciara looked around but couldn't tell who had screamed. Had one of them been inside? She hoped not, but hope did nothing.

While fighting side by side with the hit wizard, Ciara tried to count the witch hunters—as well as all the colleagues she could see. It seemed even enough, but she couldn't see all her team members.

Where were Kellan and Niles?

A thunderous boom echoed around the area. The sound thundered across the lake and even the water trembled. The rest of the cottage had collapsed, leaving a cloud of dust behind.

Once the dust settled, Ciara spotted a man floating in the air above the rubble.

He had to be a witch hunter because Ciara didn't know him—had never seen him. Unlike the other witch hunters, he wasn't dressed for a fight. Not with his long, black men's coat and immaculately styled blond hair.

Ciara had a hunch about the man's identity.

He scanned through the fight, still floating above the collapsed cottage. His gaze stopped on Ciara, and she saw his lips curl up.

That's him.

Ciara's insides burned with rage, and she flung herself

into the air. The floating witch hunter let her fling them both onto the other side of the rubble. They hit the ground and rolled in the mud and grass before they could stop.

Ciara stood up in an instant, ready to strike. He did too, but instead of attacking, he brushed the dirt off his coat. He looked so calm and collected that it bothered Ciara.

His hair was no longer immaculately styled. It was all over the place. Yet somehow, he looked effortlessly stylish.

"What are you waiting for?" His lips twitched upwards as he tried to hold in his smirk. He was cocky. Sure of himself.

Of course he was. He had the upper hand. He had Liam and Ciara's mother. They were leverage.

Ciara didn't dare to initiate. She couldn't risk Liam's and her mother's lives like that.

If they even were alive anymore.

The man could no longer hold in the smirk. "Don't you want to kill me? Think about what I made your beloved Theo do to keep you safe. To keep you alive."

Ciara's blood boiled. Energy surged through her, but she forced it down. She had to force her breathing to calm. She couldn't lose control of her powers with this guy. Theo's sacrifice couldn't be for nothing.

"Trust me, I want to kill you." Her voice didn't come out as strong as she had meant it to. She didn't want to anger the man, knowing what was at stake.

"You know who I am then."

"Elliott Hardy," she spat out.

"Theo told you?"

"No. You can thank Jesse."

"Ah." Elliott's smirk grew. "It's quite ruthless what you did to him. Killing his cousin..." He shook his head, forehead creasing, as if to tell her off. "Ex-girlfriends are the worst, but you must be at the top of the worst of them."

Ciara didn't feel sorry for doing her job. But shivers ran down her spine, cold seeping into her bones. She thought of Jesse, or rather, what *he* had done to *her*.

Elliott sighed, unamused when she didn't reveal her reaction to him. "You're as cold as they get."

"You're no different."

"Your mother is still alive."

Liam! Her mind was screaming. Blood rushed off her face, and her façade broke.

Elliott smirked. He got what he wanted out of her. "Liam is alive too. For now."

"What do you want?"

"Well, I can tell you what I wanted before I got it." Elliott's eyes calculated every movement and expression Ciara made. Like a hawk, but he wasn't the attacking type. He liked to watch her squirm.

Ciara hated his type. One day, she was going to hurt the blond man in front of her.

"Someone who's alone and unaware might get hurt unless you stop," Elliott cited.

A lump formed in Ciara's throat, and her eyes widened. Those were the exact words she had read from one of the notes. The note left at her flat door when Liam had been alone in there.

It had never meant Liam. It had been about...

"My mother." It was no use to hide her shock. He was already too far ahead. Everything had been planned for months, and the witch hunters had merely been waiting for the right time.

"I've been keeping tabs on her for a long while now." Elliott tilted his head, observing Ciara as if she was his prey. "Had a hard time keeping all the information from Theo at first, but then he ran off. Do you happen to know where he is?"

"Fuck off."

"So, you do." Elliott clicked his tongue, nodding. "Tell him I said hi, will you?"

Ciara pursed her lips together.

"Fine. Enough of small talk."

"Why did you kidnap my mother and Liam?"

"So you can try to find them. Consider it a game of sorts."

"This isn't a game." Ciara's hands clenched into fists. Her power roared inside her, dying to roam free. But she couldn't lose control. It was what he wanted, and she refused to give him that.

"Yes, it is, and I make the rules." Elliott's eyes twinkled with excitement. Sickening excitement.

"And the rules are?"

"Try and find your mother and Liam before it's too late. The clock is ticking. So, just some advice, but you should hurry." His smirk didn't fade as he flicked his wand and faded away.

Ciara tried to attack him, but it was too late. He had already vanished.

Ciara looked around frantically, trying to spot her team and Kellan. All she saw were witch hunters leaving one by one, vanishing as they teleported away. They followed their leader like lost puppies—and that worried Ciara, especially now that she knew what their leader was like.

Owen and River dropped to the ground in exhaustion. *Two.* A glimpse of red hair told Ciara Niles was fine. *Three.* Next, she spotted Declan. *Four.*

Kellan was nowhere to be seen.

Ciara ran over to where Owen and River sat by the lake shore. "Where is he?" she screamed.

River's eyes widened. For a moment, Ciara wanted to punch him for sitting there speechless. But then it hit her.

Her team hadn't seen her in the state she was in. Tears streaming down her face, her usually collected expression far gone. Elliott was slowly breaking her, tearing her apart piece by piece.

He had been doing it for a while, too. One blow at a time, hidden behind the curtains, never entering the stage.

Except now the curtain had been pulled aside. The play had begun.

"I'm here."

Ciara spun around and rushed to Kellan. She hugged him—something she had never done if the fake dating situation didn't count.

Kellan didn't hug her back at first, but eventually his arms wrapped around her. "Let's go see the Rosslers."

37

"We need to get my brother back." Henry rushed to Ciara and Kellan the moment they opened the meeting room's door. "They'll kill him."

"You're staying here," Ciara said, leaving no room for discussion. "Let others handle this."

"It's my brother we're talking about!" The rage and despair shone through his voice, and his eyes gave away the panic he was in.

"Exactly my point!" Ciara raised her voice as well to get her point across. "They're already using him *and* my mother against me. This is a direct attack on me. What do you think I'd do if they held you hostage, too?"

Ciara couldn't lose her best friend.

Henry's jaw clenched, and his eyes narrowed in a way they never had. Ciara had never seen him so serious. "My brother could die." His words came out in a low, wavering voice. Rage and grief mixed on his face.

Ciara snapped out of her shock at seeing her best friend

so grim and yet so furious. "And he wouldn't want you to die with him."

The words hurt her as much as they hurt Henry. But she had to get her point across.

Henry's deadly expression washed away, and his eyes shone with tears of realisation. Jenna reached out to place a hand on his shoulder, knowing he needed all the comfort he could get. Mary clutched onto her husband's hand, a quiet sob escaping her lips. Poppy and Polly held onto one another, sitting down on chairs, and Gabriel stood still and silent near the back of the room. Kellan's expression remained blank as he stood behind Ciara.

Everyone in the room shared the same thought. *Liam might die.*

They all tried not to think about it, but it was clear. If they didn't find him soon, it would be too late.

One half of Ciara's mind was fuzzy and panicked. Her thoughts were scrambled all over, and it was hard to form coherent words in her head.

Except three. *Mum. Liam. Dead.*

She needed a plan. Elliott had told her to find Liam and her mother, but Ciara didn't know where to start. Not when there wasn't a map or a guide. Not even one clue.

Elliott had left Ciara in a panic. Likely on purpose. He wanted her to lose or to bend to his will. She was a puppet, and he held the strings.

Even for the witch hunters, the move was bold. However, it had also been meticulously orchestrated and had still caught everyone off guard.

Stupid, Ciara cursed herself. She should have been prepared since the first note that had been left at her flat's door.

"I..." The hesitant word made everyone turn to Ciara, expecting a big plan or an idea that would save the day. She didn't have either. "I need to talk to you, Kellan." Her heart broke, looking at each of the Rosslers and Jenna. With a shaky breath, she still forced herself to turn around and look at her boss.

Kellan nodded. "We'll be back," he said to the Rosslers and Jenna. Then he reached his hand out, placing it on Ciara's shoulder, and led her out of the room as if she couldn't walk without the guidance.

She was in a weird state in her mind, and she gladly accepted Kellan's odd-but-comforting behaviour.

"I know it wasn't my place to give orders today at the cottage."

Kellan frowned, eyeing Ciara as if she had lost her mind. "I don't mind. You were in shock. Besides, I just demoted you. And I'm not sure I had the right to. Especially the way I did."

"Is this an apology? Because I didn't exactly follow the rulebook."

"Well, sometimes the rulebook is just...guidance to keep in mind. But next time, you stretch the rules...please, let me know."

Ciara's eyes widened. "You're not angry? Disappointed? Furious?"

"I have a feeling you're too deep in this...*shit* with your personal life. I understand why you're acting the way you do. This is more than just work now." Kellan dragged a hand down his face. "I can't let you go off the rails but consider your position as the team leader given back to you. River hated being promoted, anyway."

Ciara's mouth opened, but for a moment no words came out. Kellan was right. The situation wasn't just work, but also personal. The witch hunters were targeting Ciara and the ones she loved.

"T-thank you."

"Now, I need you to tell me everything you found out about Elliott Hardy."

Ciara exhaled, trying to calm herself. Not that it worked. "He is the leader. He's behind all of this. I think he does most of the planning. A-and his plan," Ciara lowered her voice, even though no one could hear them from the meeting room, "has been under works since...I don't even know."

Worry painted creases on Kellan's forehead. "He told you?"

"He told me that the first note wasn't meant to be about Liam." Elliott had tricked Ciara and her team. Even Theo had thought the letter had meant Liam.

"The first note?"

"Someone's who's alone and unaware might get hurt unless you stop." The wretched words made Ciara squirm. She couldn't believe she still remembered them.

"Your mum."

Ciara nodded. "She wasn't literally alone, but I suppose that's just a reference to being away from me. A-and she was unaware of most of this."

Kellan's lips thinned into a firm line. He didn't hide his worry from Ciara.

"Elliott told me to find my mum and Liam before it's too late." Ciara's breaths came out as gasps. "I-I don't know what to do."

"We need help to locate any witch hunter." At least Kellan was calm enough to think rationally. Something Ciara wasn't.

"How—"

"Well, the public. Unless you have a better plan. I just hope they'll realise how serious this is. We need to get the word out *now*."

Ciara's expression eased, and the panic faded to the back of her mind. Finally, she had at least a part of a plan. "I think I can get that done."

"Mia, you have no idea how much this means to me." Ciara's voice broke, but even with Mia on the other end of the call, she didn't bother to hide it. It had been a long day.

Ciara had needed Mia plenty of times. But never as much

as she did then and there. Mia, as a journalist, could get the news out faster than Ciara could if she tried to contact some dimwit contact person representing the press. Not that they all were like that, but many of them were too busy to do anything as quickly as was needed.

"I'm glad I can help." Mia's usually bright voice was grim this time. "If there's anything else, ever, that I can do to help, let me know."

"For now, just this." Ciara sighed. "And hopefully that'll be it for a while."

"I hope so." Mia's voice shook. "I hope your mother and Liam will be fine. Let me know when…when something comes to light, please."

"I will, I promise." Ciara clutched the phone, fearing she would drop it with her shaky hands. "I know I have been distant and away, but I'm so glad you're helping."

"Of course. It looks like you have a lot going on in your life. Definitely more than I realised."

"Thank you."

"Well, I have work to do and an emergency like this can't wait. Be careful and try to stay safe, Ciara."

"I will. Thank you again."

"No problem. Bye."

"Bye, Mia."

Ciara hung up and slipped the phone in her pocket. The situation was dire enough to have Mia's bubbly personality diminish to nothing, and that made Ciara somehow worry more.

38

Ciara stared at the newspaper on her desk in her office with her mother's and Liam's faces plastered on the front cover. Below the pictures was another one: an illustration of the witch hunter's mark. Ciara's hand rose to where her mark was on her shoulder. She hated the flame-like symbol so much she sometimes wanted to cut her skin off to remove it.

Mia was a lifesaver. Ciara didn't know any other journalists who could have had everything done in such a short time. But Mia had done it, and that could save either Liam or Ciara's mother.

Hopefully both.

If anyone spotted Ciara's mother or Liam, they were to call Kellan—the Head of the Hit Department. And if they spotted the witch hunter mark on anyone, they were also to call Kellan.

One day had already passed, and it couldn't mean anything good. Each passing hour made Ciara's nausea worse. She had tried to sleep in her office, but she couldn't.

The Rosslers were staying in the training area. Kellan had provided them with camping cots and such to make it a little more comfortable for the nights. There was also a television in the meeting room.

Ciara hadn't gone down to speak with the Rosslers. She felt at fault for Liam's kidnapping, and somehow she feared facing his family.

None of it was rational. The Rosslers weren't blaming her.

She blamed herself.

A knock woke Ciara up from her thoughts. She raised her gaze to see Henry through the window of her office door. She motioned with her hand, opening the door with a spell.

Henry stepped in. He looked as bad as Ciara did. Dark circles under his eyes and face ghostly pale. He hadn't been sleeping either.

"Any news?" His voice was scratchy, as if he had been crying all night. He probably had been.

Ciara shuddered, wishing she could have lied to Henry. "Nothing yet."

"How are you?"

"Not good."

Henry nodded. "Same."

"I-I've been trying to figure out what to do, but—"

"You'll just have to wait."

Ciara shook her head, refusing to sit and wait for the news—even though that was what she had been doing. "I can't. I think I'll lose my mind if we don't find them soon."

Henry blinked, but his eyes remained glossed over. "Do you think he's still alive? O-or your..." He cleared his throat, trying to keep his voice from breaking.

"I don't know."

The words pierced through Ciara's own chest like an invisible knife. But it was the truth and she couldn't run from it.

Ciara cleared her throat to keep her voice stable. "H-how is…"

Henry understood the question without Ciara even having to finish it. "Not good. We just got Dad back and now…"

"I'm so sorry."

"This isn't your fault," Henry said, frowning at Ciara. "We were fighting them even before you came back to England."

"But they took Liam because of me."

"You think he'd ever stay away from you?" Henry's brows rose. He waited for an answer that never came. Then he sighed. "Even if you tried to push him away, he wouldn't budge. I can confidently say that even right now, if he's alive, he regrets nothing. He loves you."

"And I love him," Ciara said, her voice breaking. She hadn't said it out loud in so long it was almost weird to admit it. But it was the truth.

Henry rushed to the other side of the desk to hug Ciara, and they leaned against one another for comfort and support.

They needed Liam. And she needed her mother, too.

Ciara returned to the safe house she had been staying in. The sight—the trashed living room—was revolting. But she didn't have to stare at it for long before a gasp alerted her.

She spun around, ready to attack the intruder, until she saw who it was. "Theo." His name passed her lips as a gasp, and she clung onto him, arms wrapping around his neck.

She had been worried, not knowing if the witch hunters were trying to catch him, too.

"Ciara." His arms snaked around Ciara in an instant, as if she would otherwise slip away and vanish.

"They have my mother and Liam."

Theo's entire body froze from the words, and he went rigid like a statue under Ciara's touch.

Ciara's eyes stung with fresh tears. They still didn't know where Liam and her mother were held. Time was slipping through her fingers, and with it, her mother and Liam.

"Do you have a potion storage in here?"

Ciara's grip loosened, and she blinked. Taking a step back, she frowned at Theo, wondering how he could think about potions after the news.

But his eyes were dark with worry and his mouth a thin line. He had a plan, or he was working on a plan.

"What are you going to do?" Ciara asked. She didn't want to risk losing Theo, too. She couldn't lose him again.

Enough was enough.

The safe house had potions in a storage room, but Ciara wasn't sure she wanted to give them to Theo. First, she wanted to hear what he was planning.

"It's nothing. It might help, but I can't tell you."

Ciara shook her head. "You're planning something. If you think I'll let you risk your life—"

"Nothing like that." Theo's hands rose to Ciara's shoulders, and he brushed his fingers down her arms, trying to soothe her. His grey, stormy eyes held worry, but the corners of his lips turned up, forming a tiny smile.

"I can't lose you too," Ciara said. Her voice broke and new tears surfaced.

Life without her mother would break her. Life without her mother and Liam would be enough for her to lose herself. But life without her mother, Liam, and Theo...

She wouldn't get through that.

Theo embraced her with his arms firmly around her figure. "I'd never let that happen."

"I have potions here, but we both know I don't know a thing about them."

"Lucky for us, I do." Theo's voice softened. Ciara expected there to be at least a hint of humour, and yet there wasn't.

They untangled their arms from around each other, and Ciara led Theo to the hidden basement. At first there wasn't any light. But when Ciara clapped her hands, the entire room lit up.

She led Theo down the metal stairs. The room was about the size of an average bedroom, and there was a cot in the corner for emergency situations. There were also a lot of cabinets in the room.

Ciara walked to the one with the potions. She opened it, revealing shelves filled with metal boxes. All locked one way or another. She didn't have to open all of them because there was a list on the side of each box.

"Go ahead and have a look," Ciara said and stepped aside.

Theo's eyes scanned the lists of the boxes. When his eyes landed on the fifth box's list, he halted. "This one." He grabbed the box and handed it to Ciara.

She opened it with a spell and revealed the bottles and tubes inside of it. "What are these for?"

"Even if I told you, you wouldn't remember in a minute," Theo teased, but most of the humour was still absent from his voice.

Ciara hummed and gave in.

"Mind if I take two?"

"Go ahead."

Theo grabbed two bottles and shoved them in his pockets. Then he closed the box and placed it back in the cabinet. "I need to go now, or this might not work."

"Go where?" Worrying about Liam and her mother was enough. Ciara didn't want to have to worry about Theo.

"Don't worry."

Ciara didn't bother to hide the eye roll. "Theo, don't be—"

"I mean it." He stroked the side of her face, trying to soothe her again. "Everything will work out. You just have to trust me on this."

She could trust him with this. Whatever this was.

"I just..." Theo hesitated, but his gaze didn't falter. "I know you won't let others handle the fight when it comes to it."

"I need to—"

"I know." Theo smiled. "You're so stubborn. And I know you can handle yourself, but I still worry."

Ciara swallowed. "You said yourself that everything will work out."

Theo chuckled, and for a moment, his eyes twinkled with amusement. But worry soon replaced it. "But just in case, I have one request."

"Anything."

"Let me kiss you one more time."

Ciara hesitated for a split second, her thoughts slipping to Liam. She and Theo had no future, despite their feelings. But she and Liam...

Theo was helping enable that future.

A final kiss—a kiss out of gratitude—wouldn't hurt anyone.

Ciara's hands flew up to Theo's face, stroking his scratchy stubble, and her lips landed on his. His mouth tasted like iron, as if he had been biting his cheek until he was bleeding. Or maybe she had bitten her own cheek.

Theo's hands found their place on Ciara's waist and shoulder, holding her in place as if he feared she would escape. She wasn't going anywhere, though. Instead, she pushed her body closer to his, old memories painting the world beautiful in her mind.

He squeezed her shoulder as if he didn't want to let go of the moment. She felt light-headed for a moment. She could almost forget all the worries that tainted her days.

But that image only lasted a moment. The second their lips parted, Ciara was back in the present and the worry came crashing down on her.

"I need to go now. I love you." Theo gave her one last, longing look before he teleported.

The words hit Ciara like a kick in the stomach. Had she made a mistake by giving Theo the potions she knew nothing about?

39

Ciara returned to the headquarters, heading for her office, after Theo left. Her mind was clouded by more worry than when she had left the office. Theo was up to something, and she didn't know what that something was.

It bothered her.

Ciara raised her hand to open her office door until a voice made her freeze. "Ciara!"

She spun around and came face to face with River. "What is it?"

He looked both grim and excited—an odd expression on his face. "We got a clue."

Ciara's eyes landed on a cut on River's cheek. A fresh cut. There was red blood smudged on his brown skin. "What happened?"

"We found a witch hunter. You want to do the interrogating?"

Ciara's eyes widened. *Finally!* After what felt like an eternity, they were getting somewhere. "Yes, please."

River led Ciara to the interrogation rooms. During her time in England, Ciara hadn't interrogated anyone there. It was about time she got a chance.

Kellan stood outside the interrogation room. He turned to River and Ciara when they were heading down the dark corridor leading to the interrogation rooms. "Thanks, River. You can go."

River frowned at the unusual order but nodded. Turning to Ciara, he said, "Good luck."

Ciara turned to look through the window into the interrogation room as River turned and walked away. She recognised the bulky man sitting in the chair, chained to it. He had been at the warehouse at the beginning of the year— the night Ciara had found out Theo wasn't dead.

"You recognise him?"

Ciara nodded. "He was at the warehouse with Theresa."

Kellan hummed and crossed his arms. "Go ahead then. I turned the cameras off."

Ciara's eyes snapped back to Kellan. "You want me to..."

Killing someone during an interrogation wasn't approved. Not even in the States, not anywhere in Europe, perhaps not anywhere in the world.

"What you do is up to you, but we need information. I'll step in if you need me to." Kellan's gaze was so cold it made him look deadly. And Ciara didn't doubt he was. That look Kellan had in his eyes gave a whole new meaning to icy blue eyes.

She turned to the door. If she got enough information from the witch hunter, perhaps she could stop Theo from going through with his plan. The plan that he had seemingly made out to be less risky than it was.

And to be honest, she was willing to do anything for her mother and Liam at this point.

Taking a deep breath, she twisted the doorknob. The door closed with a heavy thud as she stepped inside, creating an eerie silence in the room.

The room she was in was all black. Even the ceiling was black, and somehow that added to Ciara's worry and anger.

The man in cuffs wore a tight tank top, revealing his muscular arms. And more importantly, the witch hunter mark tattooed on his upper arm.

Ciara's lips thinned at the sight of the symbol. She wanted to burn it off his skin.

"Where did Elliott take them?" Ciara asked through gritted teeth. Playing nice wouldn't work on this guy, and she wasn't going to waste her limited time.

"Who?" The guy smirked. He knew what was going on but chose to play dumb.

"Fine." Ciara clapped her hands as the show was about to begin. "What's your name?"

The witch hunter rolled his eyes, but this time, he answered. "Zach. But trust me, I've seen this. First you're a bad cop, then a good c—"

Ciara clenched her hand into a fist and let the flames form around it. She slammed her fist against the witch hunter mark on the man's—Zach's—arm.

The witch hunter roared. "Bitch!"

The smell of burning flesh was nauseating, but Ciara held her hand there for a little longer. Long enough that Zach's eyes filled with tears from the pain.

Her mouth formed a smile, and she couldn't help it. She enjoyed seeing the piece of shit in pain. He had once caused Bill pain.

"I am not a good cop. Nor am I like any interrogator you've met before." Ciara twirled her fingers in the air, letting a small flame dance in the air. "I don't need a wand. I can punch you and burn you at the same time. So, if I were you, I'd talk."

He kept his lips pressed together in a thin line.

"This one is for Bill." This time, she punched him in the face hard enough to hear a crack when his nose broke. A satisfying sound.

"I'm not telling you anything," Zach spat out, his voice going nasal. Blood poured down his shirt from his bleeding nose.

"No worries." Ciara clenched her hands into fists. "I can keep going for however long you want me to." She lit her fist up in flames and then punched the man in the face.

She burnt off his other eyebrow and left a red mark on his skin. It covered most of his forehead and the corner of his left eye.

He screamed, but the sound grew distant. Ciara didn't care about the screams. She didn't care if the man died as long as she got answers. Finding Liam and her mother was all she cared about.

Ciara kept going. Whether it was a punch or a spell, she tortured the man. She twisted his fingers until he howled in pain. She burned his skin off. He screamed and cried but gave no answers.

Even if it would take hours, she was going to break him.

Ciara cut the man's jaw, blood pouring down his neck. He roared in pain, and for once it sounded like a word. She kept going with another cut.

"Stop!"

She didn't.

"Stop!"

She wouldn't stop until she had answers. She raised her hand, and using a spell, choked the man.

He gasped for air, struggling against the shackles. "Rosslers."

Ciara hesitated, only easing the spell but not yet lifting it.

"Rosslers. Home."

"The witch hunters are at the Rosslers' house?" Ciara asked.

"Y-yes!" the witch hunter gasped.

Ciara stopped strangling the man. Glancing at the time shown on the wall, she realised the man had wasted an hour of her precious time. Letting out a yell, she lost control and punched the man in the face again.

The force was unnatural, fuelled by an unintentional spell, and right after her fist hit the man's face, there was a snap. His head lulled back, eyes going still.

Ciara had broken his neck. She stared at the man, his head hanging in an unnatural position. It was the first time her outburst had killed someone—and still, it had been her smallest outburst recently.

She rushed out of the room, gasping for air. *Fuck.*

"You did what you had to." Kellan's voice wasn't as cold as it had been when Ciara had gone in. In fact, it had gone a lot softer. He sounded worried. Not about the witch hunter, but he worried about her.

She had lost control again, and this time the outburst had caused a death. Kellan seemed to realise that, too.

"I'm fine," Ciara said, still catching her breath. "But I didn't mean to..."

"I know."

She really hadn't.

Or had she? She wasn't sure. Recently, she hadn't been sure about a lot of things.

She wasn't sure she still killed people purely out of revenge.

Kellan placed his hand on Ciara's shoulder briefly. "You wanna tell the news to the Rosslers' family? I'll get the team and meet you in the meeting room."

Ciara looked up at Kellan. Despite their arguments, when it mattered, he had her back. She was forever grateful for that.

"Y-yes." Ciara swallowed. "See you soon."

They headed separate ways. Ciara went straight to the training area where the Rosslers were living until it was safe—or at least for the time being.

"You bitch, this is all your..."

Ciara looked up, seeing that Iris had joined the Rosslers. She had started yelling, but the sight of Ciara with her bloody clothes was enough to stop her. Luckily. After just killing a man, Ciara wasn't in the mood to talk to Iris.

"We might know where Liam and my mum are." Ciara's own voice was cold enough to send chills down her spine. "You have to stay here." Her gaze slid from Jenna and the Rosslers to Iris. "Perhaps you should, too."

"I'm coming with you," Henry and Iris said in unison.

Ciara shook her head. "No, and that's final." She looked at Henry, hating how bitterly he looked at her. Then at Jenna, who was looking at Henry with worry. Mary and Ray were sitting down, holding hands. Gabriel and the twins were all sitting together on one of the cots.

Ciara prayed she would get to see them again. Even after *her plan* was finished.

"I'm sorry," she said. Spinning around, she rushed out of the room. If she was going to go through with everything, she needed to hurry.

Her vision was a blur. She barely registered what was going on around her. It felt as if the doors opened themselves to make way for her. Perhaps it was her magic, perhaps her imagination. She didn't have to think about moving her feet. It was as if she was gliding.

All that mattered was her plan—and saving Liam and her mum.

40

Ciara stopped at the safe house and left her phone there. She wouldn't need it at the Rosslers' house.

Her clothes were still bloody, but she didn't have enough time to change. They would have to do. And if everything worked as planned, there would be more blood on them soon.

Henry would hate her. Not that she would mind, as long as he wouldn't blame himself for whatever was about to happen. *Please, I need you.* It was his voice echoing in her head as if Henry was right beside her, trying to talk sense to her.

Henry had admitted that he still hadn't recovered from Ciara's stabbing. He had told her himself that the image of her lying in a pool of her own blood haunted him.

I can't go through that again. It was Henry's voice again.

This time, hopefully, he wouldn't have to be there to witness it.

Kellan would be angry. Perhaps, if Ciara survived, she would be kicked out of the team. But she didn't have time to wait for a plan. She had the location.

It was time to act.

Her chances of succeeding were better than her chances of surviving. Ciara hadn't lost hope for herself, but things didn't look good.

And she didn't care as long as she saved Liam and her mother. She was willing to die for them.

She had no way of contacting Theo, and she regretted not having the chance to tell him she loved him, too. But he should have already known. She hoped he also remembered.

And she hoped Liam and her mother knew how much both of them meant to her. She loved Liam, and her mother was *everything* to her.

As long as the witch hunters didn't win, it was a victory. Hopefully, the others would understand that, too.

Perhaps they would realise that she had to hurry, so the witch hunters wouldn't win. So that she would get there before it was too late for her mother and Liam.

Gripping her wand, Ciara was ready to teleport. Just as she was about to, though, someone rushed in.

She refused to let her plan be ruined. Not when it was working so well.

"Ciara!" River yelled.

She was too close to the finish line to let him stop her.

He gave her no choice. Stepping around the corner, she took him by surprise. She twisted his arm and cast a binding spell to tie his wrists and ankles together.

"Ciara, you can't do this!" Anger and despair mixed in his voice. "It's suicide to go alone!"

"I'm sorry," she said, pushing River onto his knees. "This is my fight."

"Dammit, Ciara! Think about Henry! You—"

Ciara didn't have time to listen. In any other situation, those words would have torn down her mask. But this time, there was too much to lose and too little time.

River's eyes were pleading as if the mere look could

knock someone sense into her. But she refused to let that affect her.

She stepped back and teleported to the Rosslers' house.

She appeared in front of the house, far enough not to see anything through the windows. It didn't matter. The windows were covered with curtains, so she couldn't see inside either way.

The Rosslers' house had always been a happy, safe place, but this time there was a certain gloominess in the air. Ciara's heart thudded against her ribcage, and for once she couldn't get her nerves under control.

Too much to lose, she thought to herself.

The front door opened, revealing her gagged mother with a knife held to her throat. Theresa held the knife, and Ciara swore to murder Theresa the second she got the chance. Ciara wouldn't even blink. There would be no mercy for Theresa. Not from her. Not again.

Theresa had already crossed the line when she had killed Josh.

Theresa smirked as she led Ciara's mother down to the open area at the front of the house. "Hello, Ciara."

Ciara's mother—Sarah—had blood on her clothes, but Ciara couldn't see any big, open wounds. There were also blood stains on her light brown curls.

She had a tan too, and Ciara tried to imagine her at a beach where it was sunny—where she was smiling. Ciara wanted to give that back to her mother.

Her mother deserved happiness and more.

Elliott Hardy would pay for what he had done. All the witch hunters would. Ciara wanted to kill every one of them. If she got the chance, she would. No hesitation.

Her hand clenched into a fist, but she knew losing control wasn't an option. She eased her muscles as well as she could.

Dragging Liam, who had been beaten and gagged, Jesse appeared in the doorway. Jesse's eyes stayed on Ciara to see her reaction as he pulled Liam outside. Ciara tried not to give away how worried she was, but her reaction was enough to amuse Jesse. He smirked in a disgustingly pleased way.

Liam looked at Ciara from under the hair that had fallen on his face. He was trying to say something with that look in his eyes. But Ciara didn't know what it meant. Not when her mind was barely functioning.

She could only focus on the plan. There was no room for errors.

It had to work.

Her gaze moved back to the door. "Come on out!" Elliott Hardy yelled, a wide grin plastered on his face already. He was in charge, and everyone knew it—and he enjoyed that.

Witch hunters popped out of nowhere, forming a large circle around Ciara. Most of them wore black—some hoodies, some leather jackets, and some even cloaks. They blocked her escape, trapping her.

Not that she planned to escape.

She was there to save her mother and Liam. Ciara staying alive would be an unlikely bonus, not a requirement.

"Lover boy would have been beaten to death if you had come even a little later," Elliott said, shaking his head in disapproval. "I told you to *hurry*."

"Your guy wasn't the chatty type," Ciara said, her voice void of emotion. Inside she was screaming, thinking about what Elliott had planned to do with Liam—and thinking about the witch hunter's neck snapping.

She had killed before—but never accidentally because of her magic's outbursts.

Elliott's smirk wavered. "Zach?"

Ciara nodded.

"And where is he?"

"I don't know."

Elliott's smirk dropped, and his gaze moved across his followers—the witch hunters who had formed the circle. "Don't let ideas of vengeance cloud your judgement. Not today."

That likely didn't apply to Jesse. At least Elliott didn't even glance at him.

Jesse's eyes were glued to Ciara. If he was happy to see her, it was because he was going to try to kill her again. Which was likely, based on the wicked smirk on his lips and the insanity shining in his eyes.

Ciara had once cared about him. Now he held a wand against Liam's head while dreaming of her murder—or perhaps both hers and Liam's—and Ciara had never despised someone so much.

She shuddered, fighting the fear and anger.

As long as she kept her emotions in check, there wouldn't be any outbursts. She had to stay calm and collected until the job was done.

"You made a mistake coming alone, Ciara," Elliott said.

Ciara turned her attention from Jesse and Liam back to Elliott, sparing a glance at her mother. Her mother—Sarah—looked so worried. Ciara prayed her mother wouldn't have to see her own daughter die. It would be cruel.

"You hoped I'd come with my team then?" Ciara asked.

"I don't care, to be honest." Elliott took a few steps closer to Ciara, but he still left at least eight feet between them. "The end will be the same either way."

"And what is *the end*?" Jesse killing her? That was the worst Ciara could think of.

But as far as she was aware, Elliott didn't want her dead. He wanted something from her first.

That wouldn't stop Jesse from trying anything, though.

"You do as I say, or your mother dies. Or Liam dies. Or they both die." Elliott smirked. "It's a simple game, isn't it?"

"You told me to hurry. I already did that." Ciara hated playing a puppet in the sick man's game. But as long as there were lives to be lost, she would.

Anything to save Liam and her mother.

"And next you'll help me attack the government. It's about time they learn what they're really up against. It's time they learn their weapons are useless."

Ciara's brows furrowed. The witch hunters attacked people, but so far, all individual attacks had been relatively small. The witch hunters had never attacked the government directly. Not even in the States or Canada. They had attacked civilians, wreaking havoc across America and later Britain.

"Wasting your talents by killing you would be insane." Elliott shook his head. "You're alive because you will be useful."

"I'll help you once you release Liam and my mother." Ciara glanced at her mother and then at Liam.

Theresa still had a knife pressed against her mother's throat, and Jesse's wand was pointed at Liam as it had been before. Ciara couldn't even try to fight, or at least one of them would die. She had no doubt Jesse would gladly kill Liam the second Elliott would allow it.

Elliott laughed at Ciara's suggestion. "I'm not going to release anyone. I don't need to. You'll help me no matter what I do."

Ciara's hand clenched into a fist. "If you hurt either—"

"You'll still help me." Elliott's eyes sparked up. Ciara's threats excited him.

"You're insane if you think so."

"I'm a genius."

Ciara's brows furrowed. There had to be something she didn't know. Something she hadn't realised when she had come up with the plan. She had planned to give herself in exchange for her mother and Liam. That plan was going to fail, and it could cost more than Ciara's own life. She wasn't ready to lose Liam, and especially not her mother.

She needed a new plan. Fast.

Think, think. Fuck!

She regretted running off on her own until her eyes fell on Liam. Elliott had said Jesse would have killed Liam if Ciara had arrived even a little later.

She had made the right call, or so she tried to tell herself.

"You'll do exactly as I say." Elliott walked closer to Ciara, leaving two or three feet between them.

She refused to take a step back.

"Everyone," Elliott said with his gaze locked onto Ciara, "kneel."

Ciara's eyes widened, seeing every witch hunter in the circle kneel like a robot. Not out of fear, but loyalty. It was a terrifying sight. Even Jesse and Theresa let go of Liam and Ciara's mother. The two witch hunters kneeled like the rest of them.

And so did Ciara's mother.

Ciara's gaze flew to Liam. He was on his knees, but Jesse had shoved him on his knees, so he hadn't *kneeled*.

Liam looked around, eyes wide, and then his gaze landed on Ciara. Neither of them knew what was going on.

Ciara turned back to Elliott, whose eyes grew round, gaze fixed on her. His forehead creased, and he gritted his teeth together. "How?" He scanned the crowd, spinning around in rage, until his eyes landed on Ciara's mother.

Just then Ciara's mother grunted as if she was in pain.

"Mum!" Ciara's hands shook from anxiety, but she didn't dare to rush forward. She didn't know what Elliott had planned, but she knew he wouldn't let her get to her mother. Not without consequences.

Her mother cried out, and her hair changed. The caramel brown shade took a cooler tone at first, and then little by little it darkened a shade at a time. Her body morphed until there was no longer anything feminine in her figure.

Ciara wanted to cry the moment *he* looked up. The

weight of worry lifted only for new worry to crash down on her. *Theo.*

Theo had used a transformation potion.

But that didn't explain what had happened to Ciara's mother. The witch hunters had kidnapped her, not Theo. So where was she? And how had Theo taken her place?

Elliott laughed at first, and then he clapped his hands together three times. "What a surprise, Theo!"

Theo looked up, but he didn't say a word even when he took off the fabric blocking his mouth. His eyes moved from Elliott to Ciara and back.

"Come here."

Theo stood up like a dog obeying its master and walked up to Elliott. He didn't even glance at Ciara.

Elliott grabbed Theo by his shirt and ripped the fabric. Theo stayed still as a statue.

"You're going to die for this," Elliott snarled at Theo.

Theo couldn't die. Ciara's mind filled with fiery rage, and she grabbed her wand, clinging to it.

Then she saw the mark near Theo's shoulder. It hadn't been there before, and it looked exactly like the one Ciara had had. A burnt witch hunter mark.

Had they marked him too?

Ciara hurried to glance at her mark. But it was gone.

Theo had taken her mark. She tried to figure out when that had happened and how she hadn't even noticed.

And she remembered the kiss in the hidden basement. Theo had squeezed her shoulder. Had it been then?

Ciara's gaze snapped back to where Elliott was. His eyes were now on Ciara. He had seen that she didn't have the mark anymore. And for some reason, he smirked.

Ciara was ready to rush forward to save Theo, but she stayed in her spot when she heard the next words coming from Elliott's mouth.

"Kill her." Elliott looked at Theo but pointed at Ciara. Clearly, he didn't realise that Ciara wouldn't kill Theo.

Theo's eyes widened, and blood rushed off his face. "*No*," he grunted, as if saying anything would have physically hurt him.

"Jesse, grab the other guy."

Jesse jumped up from his kneeling position and grabbed Liam before he could get up from the ground. Liam struggled against Jesse's grip. "Ciara!" Liam yelled. He had managed to get the gag off.

Theo pulled out a wand from his pocket and faced Ciara. Panic painted over his face as he took the first step.

Ciara didn't know what to do, nor what to say. Would Theo really kill her?

It had to be the mark. Ciara had always assumed the witch hunters had their mark tattooed on their skin because of some cult thing. But it was more than that. Elliott could control everyone with the wretched mark on their skin. It didn't matter whether it was a tattoo or a scar.

Ciara's breaths came out shaky. Even her hands shook. "Theo."

"Ciara, go." He struggled to say those two words, and they came out as a mix of a cry and a groan. Speaking hurt Theo.

Resisting Elliott's power hurt him.

"I can't." Ciara couldn't leave Theo and Liam. Elliott would kill them both if she did.

"Now." Theo's eyes begged as he stepped in front of Ciara.

She didn't move. Not until his hand shot up with a knife. She jumped aside, and Theo followed her movements with ease.

Despite his pained expression, he made calculated and swift moves. His expression was truly his, but his actions were Elliott's doing.

"I forgot to say I love you, too, Theo," Ciara whispered when Theo got close enough again.

Theo's eyes watered. But his hand—the one holding the knife—cut through the air. Ciara moved aside just in time. But then Theo moved his other hand—the one holding his wand—and she flew onto her back.

She jumped up. Barely in time, she turned to see the knife flying towards her. She raised her wand and made the knife fly in another direction. It cut through air, landing on a kneeled witch hunter's chest.

Ciara's eyes moved rapidly between Elliott and Theo. Elliott didn't even twitch from one of his followers collapsing dead onto the ground. And Theo sent a spell at Ciara.

She blocked it and then glanced at the bleeding body. Horror seeped through her.

Another death that was on her. Another ruthless kill.

"Theo, how about you use your fists?" Elliott said, a pleased tone ringing in his voice.

Ciara wanted to crush that man. She wished the knife had hit him instead of his follower.

Theo slipped his wand back into its pocket. He gritted his teeth as if trying to fight against Elliott's commands. But it didn't matter. He still charged at Ciara. This time with more force.

Ciara jumped aside again, but Theo was quick to follow. He was doing everything to hurt her. To kill her.

But she couldn't hurt him.

Theo's fist hit Ciara's cheek. She stumbled a step back. Right then, someone pulled at her feet, tripping her over. Theo jumped on top of her, and his fist landed on her again. This time he hit her ribs, and they both heard a crack.

"Fuck," she mumbled as the pain shot through her.

A drop fell on her face, and her focus came back. "You have to kill me," Theo said. She looked up at him. He was crying in panic. "If you want to get yourself and Liam out of here alive, kill me."

Ciara shook her head. "No."

She had tried to kill him once. She had never regretted anything as much in her life. Theo's life was worth more than hers.

"Fuck, Ciara," Theo cried through gritted teeth as he

punched Ciara in the face again. "Grab your wand or knife!"

Elliott was laughing in the background. His followers, however, remained silent as if they were in a trance. They were like robots that only worked with commands.

"Theo, it's okay," Ciara said, reaching her hand up to caress his face.

"Don't you dare give up," Theo hissed, more of his tears falling on Ciara.

"Not yet." Ciara pushed Theo off her and onto his back. She warmed her palm with fire, reaching for Theo's shoulder. But he kicked her off him before she could burn the mark off his shoulder.

Ciara rolled onto her stomach, but she couldn't stay like that. She jumped up, and the movement shot a surge of pain through her. It was enough to have her knees buckle.

Her ribcage hurt.

"Ciara, watch out!" It wasn't Theo who was talking to her; it was Liam.

Ciara turned around and dodged the knife, barely in time. Theo tried to stab her again. She grabbed his wrists, holding the knife away from her. But even that hurt.

She cried out from the pain, and out of nowhere, a surge of energy sent Theo to the ground. He dropped the knife.

Ciara was losing control. She glanced at Elliott to prove her predictions correct. He wanted her to lose control.

That was his plan.

Less than an hour before, Ciara had lost control, and she had killed a man. She couldn't live with herself if she let that happen with Theo—if she killed Theo.

Ciara tasted iron in her mouth and realised her lip was bleeding. She wasn't sure how bad it looked, but Liam's expression was more worried than she had ever seen. And he always worried.

There was no way out of the situation. Not one Ciara knew of. Not one where she, Liam, and Theo would all live.

Theo was standing again, and he grabbed his wand.

Before he could cast a spell, Ciara cast one. The wand flew off his hands.

"No," Theo breathed out, with his voice barely audible.

Ciara realised Elliott hadn't allowed Theo to take the wand. He had fought against the mark's control.

Theo had been planning to kill himself to save Ciara.

"Theo, use your fists," Elliott growled. He had also noticed his control slipping.

From the corner of her eye, Ciara saw Elliott flick his wand. Next, she was on the ground. She tried to get up, but it was as if she was bound down. Invisible ties held her down from her wrists and ankles.

Theo dashed for her.

"Ciara, get up!" Liam screamed.

But even if Ciara could have, it would have been too late. Theo jumped at her, and his fist connected with her face again.

She didn't mean it to happen, but a whimper escaped past her lips. "Theo—"

He punched her again, cutting her off. His expression was wavering, and the tears had begun to dry. Elliott's grip on him had to be strengthening.

Theo wouldn't forgive himself. Ciara knew it too. She couldn't let Theo live with guilt like that.

"This isn't you, Theo. It's okay," she whispered. Her head throbbed with pain, and so did her ribcage.

Theo cried out, slamming his fist into her stomach. An involuntary cry left Ciara's mouth, and she had to bite her teeth together. Her ribs were in flames—or so it felt.

"Theo—"

He hit her stomach again. Ciara wasn't sure how much more she could handle. Her vision was blurring. She could barely make out Theo's stormy grey eyes. The eyes she had once tried to tattoo in her mind.

She couldn't kill him. She refused to even hurt him. And either way, she was tied to the ground with nothing left to do.

Ciara heard Liam trashing against Jesse's hold. Jesse laughed along with Elliott. Liam was screaming. Ciara could make out her name, but not much else.

She tried to turn her head to see Liam, but her body refused to move at her will. The pain was wearing her off.

She was close to giving in when, out of nowhere, Elliott's and Jesse's laughs stopped and so did Liam's screams. For a moment, Ciara pondered if she was that close to dying.

It wasn't that.

A spell blasted Theo off her. She tried to move, but the earlier spell still held her down.

"Fight!" Elliott roared, and the witch hunters obeyed him, hands already reaching for their wands.

Had River got himself free?

42

Liam rushed to Ciara and pulled her up, releasing the spell. "Fuck, Ciara," he mumbled, cradling her face in his shaky hands.

"I can't look much worse than you," Ciara said, looking at Liam's split lip and black eye. There was also a cut running along his cheekbone.

"I'm fine." Liam pulled Ciara onto her feet, arms securely around her.

Ciara summoned her wand, which she had dropped during her fight with Theo. She looked around and the slightest movement made pain shoot through her body.

Her team had come. But so had Henry, Jenna, and Iris.

The last three shouldn't have.

Ciara's eyes landed on Elliott, who was heading for her and Liam. Rage filled Ciara's heart, and her fingers tightened around her wand. She would kill that guy.

Power crackled in the surrounding air, and Liam had to jump away from her. He called out her name, and she almost didn't hear it.

Her ears were roaring, and her eyes remained on Elliott. She couldn't control her power anymore. She didn't care anymore. As long as Elliott Hardy died for what he had done.

But when she raised her wand, it cracked and shattered. The splinters of wood scattered with force. Some of them cut through the skin on Ciara's forearm, and she hissed as blood trickled down her arm.

Elliott's eyes widened in awe until he recollected himself. His usual smirk replaced the amazement. "Your powers are too strong for your wand."

Elliott was right. But even without a wand, Ciara could wipe off that disgusting smirk from his face.

Where's Theo?

Ciara didn't have time to search the crowd. Her team and some members of the MPG—at least Henry, Jenna, and Iris—were there. But there were also a lot of witch hunters. She wasn't sure how even the fight was.

So far, the only body bleeding on the ground was the witch hunter Ciara had killed. But even with one casualty, the stench of death was already enough.

"Get out of here." Ciara knew her order had no effect on Liam, but she left him standing and rushed towards Elliott.

Pain shot through her ribs, and she hissed. Gritting her teeth, she kept going. Her injuries would have to wait.

Without warning, Elliott turned around, his smirk never leaving his face. Ciara frowned, watching the man run for the front door of the Rosslers' house. She rushed after him, even though every movement put her in more agony.

She still couldn't spot Theo when she rushed to the front door. Sparing one last glance, she stepped inside where Elliott was waiting for her, tapping the floor with his foot.

"I will end you." Ciara's hands tightened into fists.

"Will you?" With his wand, Elliott summoned a powerful gust of wind. Enough to push him up the stairs. He stood tall at the top of them. "I thought this place held precious memories."

Ciara glanced around to see that everything had already been trashed. There were plates shattered on the floor and some of the furniture was in pieces. The mess was all around, scattered everywhere.

Ciara ran after Elliott. He ran too, and Ciara knew where he had to be heading.

Liam's room.

Ciara rushed all the way up the stairs and she didn't halt until she was at Liam's room's door. Elliott stood in the middle of the room next to a bloody spot.

They had beaten Liam up in his own room. Ciara felt sick, thinking about all the tainted memories. That was his childhood room. Even the two of them had shared endless— and precious—memories there.

A flame danced near the tip of Elliott's wand, which he was moving around in the air. Teasing.

He was going to burn the place down.

"This is a particularly aggressive flame, you know." Elliott's smirk grew—something that was surprisingly possible. "We wouldn't want to burn the house down, would we?"

"Stop."

Liam's room was untouched—except for the bloodied spot—unlike the rest of the house. Probably all part of the plan. Somehow Elliott had to know that the room held memories.

But Henry's room did, too. Elliott didn't know how much Henry meant to Ciara. Elliott hadn't figured that out, and it was best to keep it that way. The less Elliott knew, the better. He couldn't use Henry against Ciara when he didn't know how much Henry meant to her.

Elliott let the flame grow. The light danced on his face, enhancing the curve of his lips. "I already have Theo. Who knows what I'll do to him or what I'll have him do to himself if you don't do as I say."

Ciara cursed in her mind. She needed to get out and

somehow erase the witch hunter mark on Theo's skin.

Until then, Theo was under Elliott's command.

"I won't kill innocents."

"Innocents?" Elliott spat. His smirk dropped, replaced by uncontrolled fury. "The magical governments are all rotten, and you know that as well as I do!"

"You're worse than them."

The flame grew again, and Ciara worried what would happen next. But she was so close to getting answers. Elliott's coolness was long gone. Calling the government innocent had triggered him, and that had to mean something.

"Worse?" The word came out as a hiss. Elliott was like a snake trying to talk. A furious, deadly snake. "They kill children as long as the magical world remains a secret. There are no limits to what they'll do. They'll kill everyone if they have to, as long as the magical side of the world remains hidden. And let me tell you something, it's not for our safety. They just want to control us. I know you know that, too."

"And you worked for them." It was merely an assumption, but she hoped it would bring answers.

The moment those words left her mouth, Elliott's eyes widened. He was a mess—a mix of shock and rage.

Ciara's eyes widened, surprised. She had found her answer with just a guess. "Who did you kill?"

That drove Elliott over the edge, and he screamed. The bedroom ceiling lit up with flames.

Ciara had to jump out of the room not to be consumed by the fire. The moment her knees hit the floor, she looked up. Flames took over all of Liam's room. Ciara couldn't see Elliott anywhere, and she wondered if his own fire had been uncontrolled enough to turn him into ash so fast.

Even if Elliott was dead, the fire was far from it.

Ciara scrambled up, pain shooting up her ribcage. Tears stung her eyes because it hurt so much. She dragged her feet to the stairs. The first step was fine, but she miscalculated the next. She stumbled down the stairs, her screams echoing through the house as waves of pain consumed her.

When she hit the bottom, she pushed herself up.

"Ciara!" Henry ran in. His eyes fell on her first, and he hurried to help her up to her feet. He wrapped his arms around Ciara to help her stay upright.

Her feet and legs seemed fine, but she felt lightheaded from the fall. She clung onto Henry so she wouldn't drop on the floor.

"No," Henry gasped, his eyes fixed on the top of the stairs, where everything was already on fire.

"We need to go," Ciara mumbled. Her head kept spinning.

"No!" Henry let go of Ciara and tried to rush upstairs.

Ciara gripped him with all the strength left in her. "You'll kill yourself! We need to get out *now*!"

Her heart broke thinking about everything that would be lost in the fire. She couldn't even imagine Henry's grief. But if he made it upstairs, there was no way back. It would have been a suicide.

The fire spread furiously down the stairs, coming for them.

Henry stared but refused to move. Ciara pulled at him with all her strength, but the pain was wearing on her.

"Henry, fuck!" Ciara cursed.

"I can't—"

"I can't let you kill yourself!" Ciara screamed at Henry. "Henry, now!"

"I won't leave!"

"I won't watch you die!"

"Let me go!"

Ciara glanced at the main bedroom's door. Memories rushed back to her. Memories of Henry and Jenna lying there on the double bed, losing blood. Henry had barely survived back then.

And he sure as hell was going to get through the day this time as well.

"This is my—"

"This is for your family!"

Ciara tightened her grip on Henry and waved her hand for a spell. The two of them flew out of the house through the front floor, hitting the ground with a heavy thud.

"Ciara! Henry!" Jenna rushed to the two. Henry was up before Jenna could help him, so she helped Ciara stand up.

Henry stood still, staring at the flames that danced at the bottom of the stairs. He didn't try to rush back in. His shoulders had slumped as if he had given up.

The house was lost.

Ciara spun around, knowing that her best friend was safe. She tried to spot Theo in the crowd but couldn't.

"Have you seen Theo?" she asked Jenna.

Jenna only shook her head.

"Liam?"

Jenna looked around, and her eyes widened. When her gaze returned to Ciara, the answer was obvious.

Ciara spun around in panic, trying to spot Liam. Kellan was fighting two witch hunters, blasting curses at them. River was beating a witch hunter woman with spellwork. Declan and Niles were fighting side by side against a few more witch hunters. Ciara caught a glimpse of Owen, too.

"Ciara!" It sounded like someone was screaming for help, but it wasn't Liam. It was a woman. *Iris.*

Ciara ran towards the voice, blasting off witch hunters who dared to step in her way. She couldn't see Iris, but she heard her voice call out again.

Ciara ran past River and the witch hunter woman whom she now recognised as Theresa. She sent a spell at Theresa, giving River a little help, before her eyes fell on Iris.

A witch hunter held Iris back. She was struggling to keep a floating knife at bay.

And behind them were Liam and Jesse. Neither one was holding their wand. Instead, Jesse had Liam pinned to the ground. Something metallic glinted in Jesse's hands.

A knife.

Jesse was trying to kill Liam.

"We are done here!" A voice boomed, boosted with a spell. It was, without a doubt, Elliott's voice.

So, he hadn't died.

The witch hunters tried to leave. The ones that weren't targeted left their fellow witch hunters behind, fleeing the scene.

Jesse didn't budge. Nor did the ones still fighting.

"Help him!" Iris screamed at Ciara.

Ciara didn't have to be told that. She had already been running for Liam and Jesse, her hands shaking like crazy.

While running to save Liam, she summoned the floating knife the witch hunter tried to use on Iris and gripped it in her hand. Images of Jesse stabbing her made her nauseous, but Ciara kept going. Jesse's knife was too close. It nearly touched Liam's throat.

Before Jesse or Liam noticed her, she threw herself at Jesse, and the two of them rolled to the side. She made sure she ended up on top, so she had the upper hand on Jesse.

She raised the knife, but he was faster. His fingers curled around her wrist, and he twisted. She howled as the pain shot up her arm. Next, she was on the ground with Jesse on top of her. The knife was no longer in her hand.

Jesse punched her, straddling her to keep her still. Ciara tried to kick him, but his feet kept her legs still. He was heavier than her, and her struggles seemed futile.

It was like that night at her flat all over again. Expect this time she tried to fight back. She refused to freeze.

Jesse grabbed something from the ground beside them. Ciara didn't realise what it was until she saw the blade. The knife she had dropped. The witch hunter's knife—the one's who Iris was fighting against.

With his other hand, Jesse pressed on Ciara's ribs, making the pain worse. Her vision went blank, and she screamed. It didn't feel just like having her ribs on fire. It was worse. So much worse.

Worse than that night at her flat. The night Jesse had stabbed her.

When her vision cleared and the pain dulled, Jesse held his hand up, gripping the knife so tightly his knuckles were white.

Before he could stab her, Liam ripped Jesse off Ciara. But Jesse still held the knife.

Ciara struggled to rise, but the excruciating pain held her down.

Liam punched Jesse. Murderous blaze burned in his eyes as he punched Jesse again. Ciara recognised something in Liam. A dark glint of revenge filled his gaze, reflecting a part of herself that Ciara could see in him.

That both terrified and thrilled Ciara. She didn't want anyone to long for revenge the way she had for almost a year, but it thrilled her to see how much Liam cared. How much he wanted to avenge her.

Jesse attacked Liam, and Liam dodged.

Ciara had to get up.

Liam grabbed his wand before Jesse could and sent the knife flying in the air. It fell to the ground. Liam and Jesse used their fists then. Liam ended up on top of Jesse, beating him. Rage filled his eyes, but every punch drained him of the little energy he had left.

Ciara tightened her hands into fists and forced herself to sit up. The pain was everywhere. She wasn't sure if she was about to pass out or not.

Her knife was in her boot, securely resting against her ankle.

She looked up only to see Jesse punch Liam and push him off. Jesse was already bloodied from being beaten up. But Liam wasn't much better.

Liam had been beaten before Ciara had even arrived at the house.

She stood up, unsure if her legs could hold her up. But she already had her knife in her hand.

Jesse ended up on top of Liam again, and Ciara's mind was screaming at her to move—to ignore the pain and do something. *Not Liam!*

Ciara pushed Jesse off Liam, ending up straddling Jesse. She thought of everything Jesse had done to her and Liam, and then she slashed at Jesse with her knife before he could do anything.

Blood pooled out of his neck, forming a dark pool on the ground. He gasped, but the sound was more like a croak. His eyes were wide, and his hand reached up as if to caress Ciara's cheek.

It's odd. The things you remember when you're watching somebody die. Doherty had once said that to Ciara.

"You're beautiful." Jesse reached his hand up to brush his fingers down the side of Ciara's face.

Their lessons were over for the day, and they were enjoying the warmth of spring out in the fields. They had been lying in the grass until Ciara had climbed onto Jesse's lap for a make-out session.

Ciara smiled down at her boyfriend. "And you're cheesy!"

Jesse laughed. "Pfft! Girls love it."

"Maybe I'm not like those girls then." But it was a lie. Ciara loved seeing Jesse gaze at her with such tenderness.

Ciara let out a sob.

Or a shriek.

Or both.

Her hands shook as she scrambled away from Jesse's corpse. The blood formed a pool around him, painting his dirty blond hair crimson.

Ciara dropped the knife in panic, but the blood still coated her hand. Her eyes snapped back to Jesse, and she let out another sob.

She had loved him once. Not in a long time. Especially

not since the night he had stabbed him. But seeing his lifeless, bloody corpse in the grass broke her.

She wished she hadn't killed him. More than anything.

She could have cut off his tattoo.

She should have.

"Ciara." Liam's arms wrapped around her, but she barely registered it.

Her eyes remained staring at Jesse—cut up and lifeless.

"Don't look." Liam blocked the view, and all Ciara could stare at was his shirt.

She couldn't form words.

"It's okay."

Nothing was okay.

Ciara moved her head enough to see the house engulfed in flames. Her team, Jenna, and Henry were trying to extinguish the fire, but it was too late to salvage anything.

Theo was gone. All the witch hunters were.

Iris was heading to help with the fire.

"Where's my mother?" Ciara asked, looking up into Liam's eyes.

"She's safe."

The relief from the news was enough for Ciara to burst into tears. Despite all the blood covering her, Liam pulled her into an embrace—still making sure she didn't see Jesse's corpse.

43

Ciara had tried to rush off to see her mother, but Kellan had stopped her. He had claimed she couldn't go see her mother in the clothes she was wearing.

And he was right.

Ciara wasn't sure how much of the blood was Zach's, how much hers, and how much was Jesse's. But there was a lot of blood. The nauseating smell of her blood-soaked clothes overwhelmed even her own senses.

Liam took her to the safe house she had been staying at, but they both stayed silent. Her thoughts were jumbled, and Ciara struggled to make sense of them.

She had to go one step at a time.

First step was to change clothes. She did that but didn't bother to shower, despite the blood in her hair. Even with the clothes, she needed Liam's help, so she didn't want to know how hard showering would have been.

She needed to see a doctor because of her broken ribs and the split lip.

That was where Liam took her after the quick stop at the safe house. She refused to leave until the doctors had checked on Liam as well. Neither one had to stay at the hospital, but they got medication—mostly healing potions—for the pain and to enhance the healing.

As Ciara had expected, she had broken ribs and lots of bruises. She was told to rest for the next month.

There was no way she would, though. Not with Theo gone.

Liam led Ciara to a hospital room where her mother was sitting on a bed. Mary was also there, keeping Sarah company.

Ciara's mother, Sarah, burst into tears the moment she saw her daughter. Ciara did too and rushed to hug her mother. She hissed in pain when her mother hugged her back. Her ribs still hurt.

Her mother almost asked about it, but Ciara was faster with her answer. "I'm fine. Just a broken rib."

It was actually more than one broken rib, but the details didn't matter. What mattered was that she finally got to hug her mother. And that her mother was safe.

"Oh, sweetheart."

"Hi, Mum."

They both cried, but there were also happy tears. Especially on Sarah's side.

Ciara wasn't so sure. Not after she had lost Theo and killed Jesse.

It should have felt like a victory—at least a small one— but Ciara didn't remember hitting such a low in her life ever before.

She shouldn't have killed Jesse. She should have put him in prison. Nothing had forced her to kill him.

Jesse's parents would take the witch hunters' side if they already hadn't. His death could inspire more people to help the witch hunters, and it was her fault.

Except, most of that wasn't true. Jesse had been too far

gone for a long time, and his parents had likely already taken a side.

"Ciara?"

She snapped out of her thoughts and looked at her mother. "Sorry. It's been a long day."

"I understand, but I'd like you to meet someone if it's okay." Her mother gestured behind Ciara, and Ciara turned around.

A man in his fifties stood in the hospital room's doorway. He had light brown olive skin. His black hair was long enough to be pulled back with hair gel. His beard—longer but groomed—had light grey streaks here and there, like his hair. Parts of him looked Italian, but Ciara could have sworn he also looked part-Greek.

"I'm Enzo." The man offered his hand, and Ciara shook it.

"Ciara."

"I know. Your mother talks a lot about you." Enzo smiled with genuine warmth, and Ciara had a feeling she would like the man.

"It's nice to meet you."

"You too."

Ciara glanced at her mother. All she saw on her mother's face was love when Enzo and her mother looked at one another.

Her mother had been happy in Italy—happy with this man called Enzo. But that didn't mean he could be trusted.

What raised alarms in Ciara's mind was that Enzo hadn't been killed or kidnapped.

"Where were you when they killed Ian Connell?" Ciara asked him, her tears fading in an instant.

Enzo's face lost all warmth and colour. For a moment, he seemed like he would throw up. Dead people didn't seem as mundane to him as they did to Ciara. "I-I was picking up groceries, so I wasn't at the house. I found the house empty, except Ian was...d-dead."

Ciara nodded. "I just had to ask."

"Of course." Enzo nodded too. The warmth didn't return to his face and even when he tried to smile, it didn't quite reach his eyes.

He wasn't the bad guy; he had just been extremely lucky. The witch hunters would have killed him if he had been at the house with Sarah and Ian.

Sarah introduced her husband to Mary and Liam next. Soon after, Mary and Liam left. Enzo claimed to need another cup of coffee too, so Ciara got a moment alone with her mother.

All the Rosslers were taken to their house to see the damage. Ciara wanted to go there after the hospital, but images of Jesse's corpse running through her mind made her stop.

She couldn't go back.

With nowhere else to go, she ended up sitting in her office. Alone with her thoughts. It wasn't smart because her own mind was slowly driving her insane.

She had lost Theo to the witch hunters again. There was no way to tell if he was even alive anymore. An uneasy feeling lingered in Ciara's chest. She suspected Elliott wouldn't make his next move—not even with Theo—before he had an audience of witnesses.

That didn't comfort Ciara. It was more of a warning that something horrible was going to happen.

44

Ciara raised her gaze when someone walked in. Henry stood at her office door. His gaze softened seeing his best friend sitting on the floor.

"Hey." He closed the office door and walked up to her. Sitting down next to Ciara, he said, "We've been looking for you. Liam went to see if you were still at the hospital."

"I couldn't come to the house after..." Ciara paused and rested her head on Henry's shoulder. "I'm so glad you're okay."

"Thank you for getting me out of the house." Henry took in a sharp breath. "Without you...well, you know. I wasn't thinking. At all. Jenna gave me a scolding, and only then I realised how...reckless I was. It's just...the house...it's been there my whole life."

"I'm sorry about the house."

"It wasn't your fault." Henry wrapped an arm around Ciara and rested his head on top of hers. "And it's just a house. The memories won't go anywhere." Henry exhaled shakily. "It's just that recently nothing has seemed certain. The house seemed like the only thing that wasn't in danger. I never thought they would..." He shuddered. "I almost lost Dad, then you. It's too much. It's just a house, yes, but...it was my family's house."

"I pushed Elliott into doing it. I shouldn't have questioned him and—"

"No." Henry sighed, shaking his head. "He's a lunatic. He would have done it either way."

"For a moment, I thought he died. I hoped he had."

"The fight isn't over." Henry's voice lacked determination. He, too, was exhausted.

It was already the following morning. Ciara had stayed up all night, and it seemed Henry had as well. Ciara knew the doctor had told her to lie down, to sleep and rest, but she couldn't.

Jesse's lifeless face haunted her even when she was awake.

"I don't know what I would have done if something had happened to you," Ciara whispered. "It was like back when *they* attacked you and Jenna at your old flat. You lost so much blood, and I thought I was going to lose you then. And now, it happened so much faster, but I feared for your life, Henry."

"I'm sorry. I acted like an idiot. You saved me from a ridiculous suicide."

"No. I get it. That house held *so* many memories."

"It did."

"But it really hit me today. How easily I could lose you. And what a horrible friend I am. Pulling your family into this. Making them a target." Ciara looked up at Henry. "They have Theo because he took the mark from me. I was meant to be in his position. The one brainwashed. He saved my life again."

"We'll get him back. Alive and well. And my family, they're fine. We were all in this before you pulled anyone into anything."

"I wish that was true."

"Getting Theo back? We'll make it true." Henry hugged Ciara, and she hugged him back.

Words didn't change anything, but that didn't mean they held no meaning. Henry's words were a promise. Ciara wasn't going to have to fight alone. That was his promise, and it meant the world to her.

For once, Ciara didn't feel like she was on her own.

Ciara and Henry remained hugging one another for minutes until someone walked in. Ciara pulled away and looked up to see Jenna. She smiled at Ciara and Henry, her eyes teary, and then she joined the hug.

Ciara couldn't push everyone away. She needed her friends, even if she sometimes wished she could get through the fight on her own.

She regretted going alone. It had been a suicide mission— or it would have been without the team and her friends. They had saved her.

She owed a big apology to River.

Ciara walked into Kellan's office. "They're brainwashed." She dropped into the chair on the other side of Kellan's desk. "I'm no longer sure how many witch hunters have joined willingly."

"I saw." Kellan nodded.

"You saw the fight. But you didn't see how they knelt when Elliott ordered them to." Ciara shook her head, trying to shake the memory. "I had the mark too, but Theo took it from me. I think he had figured out what they could do with the mark, but I don't know how he did it. He didn't tell me what he was doing these last days. I didn't even know about his plan to save my mother."

"If you had come back with River, I could have told you." Kellan sighed. "Your mother teleported here and came straight to us, but you had already rushed away."

"I'm sorry." Ciara glanced down, sensing Kellan's

disappointment. "But I won't say that I regret it. They would have killed Liam if I had waited."

"No." Kellan shook his head. "He had a lucky charm. Otherwise, he would have been dead by the time you got there."

Ciara's eyes widened. "A lucky charm?"

"Theo gave it to him."

Ciara cursed in her mind. She had slipped that lucky charm into Theo's pocket when they had parted ways. Theo had given it to Liam. To save Liam *for her*.

Or had Theo begun to care about Liam all of a sudden?

Either way, Theo wasn't altruistic. He hadn't done it out of the goodness of his heart.

Ciara loved Liam. No matter Theo's reasons, she was grateful for what Theo had done. But even if she had Liam, she also needed Theo. Loving Liam didn't make her care any less about Theo—even if her romantic feelings for Theo were wavering. With her and Theo, the past seemed to hold more weight than the present, saturating their relationship with nostalgia.

"What did Elliott say to you? Anything important?"

Ciara exhaled shakily, memories swarming her mind. "He is angry at the magical governments. He doesn't want the magical side of our world to remain hidden. I think he called the governments rotten. He said something about them killing whoever, as long as the magic stayed hidden. I don't have more details, but this is personal to him. He wanted to use me against the government. That's why he was so angry when he realised I no longer had the mark on me."

Kellan's forehead creased, aging him by at least five years for a moment. "That's not good."

Ciara swallowed. "I know."

Kellan stayed quiet, still frowning. "Go home now. Come back once you've healed."

"I'm coming back tomorrow." Ciara could wait one more

day, but not more. Theo was in danger, and she had to find him as soon as possible.

"You have broken ribs."

"I'll skip training."

Kellan's shoulders slumped. "Ciara."

"Yes?"

"Their attacks are only getting worse."

"I know."

"This is far from over."

"But *we'll* end it." She still had a man on her kill list: Elliott Hardy. Only after his death, it would all be over.

To her luck, Ciara found River before she went home. She needed to apologise.

Even Jenna had made sure to remind her of that. Jenna had checked on River after the fight at the Rosslers' house. Ciara hadn't realised how close the two of them had grown after the mission at the warehouse—when River had taken Jenna to the hospital. He had saved Jenna, and that had created a bond between the two of them.

River had come back to work early. He had only gone home to change clothes.

"River, wait." Ciara walked up to him when he halted. Humiliated by her own actions, she looked up at him with a mixture of shame and regret. "I'm *so* sorry. I had no right to tie you up and leave you there. Your safety was at risk, and I should never, under any circumstances, put you in such a position. You were just trying to help and...there's really no excuses for my behaviour. I can't go back in time, but it'll never happen again. I'm sorry."

River nodded. "As long as you don't do it again, we're okay."

"I would never," Ciara swore. "It was wrong of me. I wasn't in my right mind. In the future, nothing of that sort will happen. You can trust me on that."

River tapped Ciara on her shoulder. "Good. Then we're good."

"Are you sure?"

"Absolutely. It was a crazy situation for you."

She didn't deserve his understanding, but she was glad he didn't hold a grudge.

Ciara went to the safe house—her temporary home.

But she couldn't bring herself to step inside. Her recent memories in that house weren't good.

Changing her blood-stained clothes, tying River up, helping Theo with his plan, finding out that the witch hunter had kidnapped Liam. It had only been two days since they had kidnapped her mother and Liam.

The witch hunters ruined everything for her. Even the safe house was ruined in her mind.

She sat at the front door and pulled out the knife in her boot. The knife she had once stabbed Theo with. The one he had given back. The one she had killed Jesse with.

She hated the knife with passion for what she had done with it. Still, it was the only thing she had that reminded her of Theo. On top of her engagement ring, of course. But she didn't want to use her engagement ring. She still had it, but she wasn't going to wear it again.

She and Theo didn't have a future. But that didn't change the fact she needed Theo to have *a* future.

Someone teleported right in front of Ciara and gasped in surprise, seeing her at the front door. Ciara looked up at Liam, and his brows furrowed in question.

"I can't go in," she said.

Liam's eyes fell on the knife, and Ciara's gaze followed. He sat down on the ground next to her. "I thought you lost this knife in January."

"Theo saved it after I stabbed him with it. After I tried to kill him." Ciara had to look at her hand to make sure there wasn't blood as the ghostly memory creeped into her mind. "I can't do it again."

"We'll find him and remove the mark." Liam's voice filled with force and determination, and that comforted Ciara. She wasn't alone, and this time she didn't even feel alone.

"I hope so."

"He told me to get you out of there, no matter the cost." Liam sighed. "But I think *you* got yourself out of there."

"I'm fine." Ciara looked up at Liam, meeting his hazel gaze. "H-how are you?"

"I'm fine." He held her gaze. "As long as you are."

Ciara smiled.

Liam's gaze dropped back to the knife, and the frown reappeared. "He gave me the lucky charm."

"I'm glad he did."

Liam looked back into Ciara's eyes. "If he had had it—"

"Then you could be hurt. Or worse." Ciara swallowed, disturbed by the thought. "And I couldn't lose you."

Liam frowned and took in a deep breath. "I saved this." He pulled out a green gemstone, shaped similarly to a wand. Except it was thinner. "The core of your wand. It didn't shatter. I found it in the grass when you ran to the house."

Ciara took the shiny gem from Liam's hands, admiring it a little. She had never held a bare wand's core in her hands before. "I don't think it can be fixed."

"It still worked when I used it against the witch hunters," Liam said. "Maybe it can be used without the wooden parts."

"Maybe it only worked right after it broke. I've never heard of anyone using just the core of their wand to cast spells."

Liam shrugged. "We'll have to find out."

Ciara liked his choice of words. *We.*

"Do you want the lucky charm back?" he asked, hand already reaching for his pocket.

"No." Ciara's hand stopped Liam's before he could reach for the lucky charm, and she looked back up into Liam's eyes. "Please, keep it. You might need it again."

Liam hesitated but nodded, and Ciara dropped her hand.

"Where's Gabriel?" Ciara asked and stood up.

Liam followed the suit and stood up. "At my family's hotel room. They got us a freaking penthouse." He chuckled, shaking his head. "It's ridiculous."

"Well, your family should stay together. It might be good for all of you."

"Gabriel and the girls will go back to school in a week."

"We'll add better security to the school."

"Do you think the witch hunters will still target us?" Liam asked.

Ciara swallowed, gaze fixed on Liam. "I-I don't want to risk it."

"Me neither." Liam frowned. "How's your Mum?"

"She and Enzo got a penthouse, too."

Liam nodded.

They stood in silence for a little while. Ciara inspected her wand's core. "Thank y—"

"Why did you come alone?" Liam blurted the words out as if he had been holding them in since the previous day. His face was twisted into a frown. The worried kind.

Ciara swallowed. Liam knew her better than anyone. Perhaps he already knew the answer.

"I wasn't thinking," she said, but it wasn't entirely true.

"So, you knew it was a suicide mission? You could have..." His frown eased, replaced by sorrow in his gaze.

"And I will never do something like it again," Ciara promised. "I should know by now that I need to trust my friends and my team. But at least I learned my lesson now."

"No more reckless, suicidal stunts?" Liam asked. "Will you promise me?"

"I promise. No more ridiculous, life-threatening stunts. From now on, I'll trust teamwork."

Liam smiled with relief. "That's a...development, for sure."

His smile brought a smile onto Ciara's face too. "Well, I think we handled the last bit of fighting well...together."

Liam's smile dropped, but his gaze remained on Ciara. "I wish you hadn't...I wish it had been me who killed *him*. For what he did to you."

Ciara didn't wish that. Liam didn't deserve the guilt. "It's done. Nothing we can do about it now."

"I went after him on purpose," Liam revealed, voice rough with raw feeling. "For what he did to you in January. I was *so* angry that I didn't think it through. All I could think about was you being wheeled off to surgery and something just snapped in me."

Seeing how much Liam cared made Ciara's heart swell."I know the feeling."

"But from now on, teamwork?"

"Teamwork," Ciara agreed.

"Do you want to come over? To the penthouse, I mean." Liam glanced at the house behind her. "Unless you want to go in after all."

Ciara shook her head, also glancing at the front door. "I don't. Not yet." She smiled at Liam. "Seeing your family sounds good."

Liam took one step closer. "And your mother? Is she out of the hospital?"

"She should be soon."

A smile crept onto Liam's face as well, and they smiled at each other. "Maybe we'll go make sure the penthouse is up to their standards, then. After we see my family."

"I'd like that."

Ciara wanted Liam to hear what she was going to ask her mother. But first, it was time to see his siblings and parents.

Ciara slipped the knife back into her boot and placed her wand's core in her pocket. Then she grabbed Liam's hand and gazed into his eyes.

Liam flicked his wand, his eyes never leaving Ciara's.

45

"It's more luxurious than the Italian house, for sure," Enzo said from the kitchen. He and Ciara's mother had grabbed groceries on the way home—to the penthouse—from the hospital.

Ciara's mother lay on the sofa, tired but much better. On the opposite sofa sat Ciara and Liam. Ciara was glad he had come with her.

"It is rather nice," Ciara's mother—Sarah—agreed. Then she turned to look at Ciara and Liam. "You didn't come just to see that it was up to our standards, did you?"

"I wanted to see you," Ciara said, biting the inside of her cheek. "But I also have a question. Maybe a few even."

"What is it, sweetheart?" Sarah asked.

"My father...he had wandless magic, right?"

Sarah sighed. "He did."

Ciara glanced at Enzo, but he kept filling the fridge silently. Then she turned back to her mother. "Did he...ever... kind of...lose control?"

Ciara's mother's eyes grew round. "I-I only saw it once. He broke all the windows when he got upset while we were fighting."

"Was it a bad fight?"

"It...it was, well, about...h-how he...he didn't want a child. That's...that's the reason he isn't around."

Ciara froze. Her expression must have changed because Liam's fingers moved to brush her forearm to comfort her.

"He said he didn't want to give anyone the power he had. He said it was a curse." Ciara's mother frowned. "You...have you..."

"I have outbursts," Ciara said and swallowed. Images of the dead witch hunter in the interrogation room flashed through her mind. "They're bad."

Ciara's mother opened her mouth, but she didn't have words.

"Do you know where my father is?" Ciara asked.

She had no one else to turn to. No one else knew anything about her magic. She didn't know anyone who could wield magic without a wand, and she didn't know anyone who had the kind of outbursts she did.

"No. Before he left, he said he was going to live quietly. In isolation. Those were his words."

"So he left before I was born," Ciara said.

"He didn't want anyone to have his curse. It had nothing to do with—"

"I...I don't need him in my life. This isn't about that. I just wish I had answers."

Ciara's mother frowned and shook her head. For a moment, she didn't know what to say. "I'm afraid I don't have the answers," she said eventually.

Ciara sighed. "Guess not."

"I'm sorry, sweetheart."

"Don't be. It's not your fault."

Ciara wasn't angry with her mother to begin with. She just wasn't sure what she could do about her outbursts. To prevent future accidents, she needed answers. And if her mother didn't have them, she wasn't sure where she would find them.

ᚹ ᚹ ᚹ

Liam took Ciara home after they had dinner with her mother and Enzo. Her mother kept apologising for her lack of answers, and Ciara kept telling her it was fine.

"Are you okay?" Liam asked when they stepped inside the safe house Ciara was staying at.

"At least I have more answers than I did before. Looks like this whole outburst thing is a family problem."

Liam ran his hand down Ciara's arm, and the skin warmed under his touch. "Your father shouldn't have left," he said.

Ciara leaned into Liam's touch and met his gaze. "But he did, and I don't blame him. I understand why he would consider this to be a curse. If I didn't have this kind of... power, things would be a lot different."

"We'll deal with the witch hunters." Liam took Ciara's hand in his, stroking the back of it with his thumb. "We'll get Theo back."

"At least everyone else is safe for now."

"And soon Theo will be too."

Ciara wrapped her arms around Liam's neck. "Can you stay here tonight?"

"Teamwork is hard when we're apart." Liam snaked his arms around Ciara, and for once, she felt safe. He kissed the top of her head and then rested his head on top of hers, engulfing her in his warmth. "I think I'll have to stay. For teamwork."

Ciara sighed, letting herself relax in Liam's embrace. "I think so, too. *For teamwork.*"

They stayed like that for a while, close to one another. Then Ciara remembered the leftovers her mother had given. They were in a plastic container that she had enchanted to be small enough to fit in her pocket.

She returned the container—and the food inside—back to the original size and headed to the kitchen. In front of the fridge, she halted, staring at a note on the fridge door. There was one magnet holding it in place.

There hadn't been any notes or magnets on the fridge door before.

"Liam!" Ciara grabbed the note in a hurry and rushed around the corner. Her heart raced in panic until she halted. Liam stood in the middle of the living room.

He was alone. He was unharmed.

"What is it?" His brows furrowed as he stepped closer to Ciara.

"There was a note on the fridge, and I thought..." Ciara swallowed. "I thought the worst."

"What does it say?"

Ciara opened the folded note and gasped when she recognised the handwriting.

"This..."

"It's from Theo," Liam said. "Do you want to read it alone or—"

"No. Please, stay." Ciara grabbed Liam's hand with her free hand. She needed him.

"I'm not going anywhere," he promised.

So, they read the note together.

I had to leave you a note in case this is my last chance to explain myself. When I figured out Elliott's plan, I had to make sure you didn't have the mark. The mark is like an enchantment on its own. I've heard they've been used on furniture and other enchanted objects. I read about witches who used the same mark on all their secret belongings, so they could turn them invisible all at once.

But Elliott has taken it further. Elliott can control everyone bearing the mark because it's essentially just an enforcer for his mind-controlling enchantment. I couldn't let him use you like that, so I practiced at a morgue. To practice the spell, I transferred scars from bodies onto myself and back.

I never got a mark of my own. Everything I did as a witch hunter was for you. But if it helps, I never took part in the family murders. I only did what was absolutely necessary for your sake.

Even that was too much.

I miss Doherty too and I'm sorry. Whatever happens, I hope you understand my reasons for everything else. If you can, try to remember me as the person I was when we were engaged. Try to remember me as I was before the day I died.

Theo

Ciara and Liam turned to look at one another, sharing the same thought.

The note was a suicide letter.

GLOSSARY

MPG: Magical Protection Group, the reformed group working against the witch hunters (see below)

HIT WITCH / HIT WIZARD: someone working to catch dangerous witches and wizards along with other criminals, excluding non-magics

CURSE BREAKER: someone working to break curses

WITCH HUNTERS: terrorists who want the secret of magic to be revealed to non-magics

NON-MAGICS: people without magical abilities

CRASHBALL: a magical sport reminding volleyball

WANDLESS MAGIC: magic when the caster doesn't require a wand

ACKNOWLEDGEMENTS

This book went through ups and downs with me. Luckily I had amazing people to get me through the process.

A big thank you to everyone who got excited about Revenge Undone and kept asking when the second book would be coming out. Here it is. Thank you for your excitement. It means the world to me.

Thank you to my mother who is always the first to read my books, usually in their early stages.

Thank you to my sister who always helps me spot ridiculous typos and weird sentences.

Thank you to my father who has taught me to do what I want.

Thank you to my fiancé who always supports me and cheers me on.

Thank you to all of you who were part of this book's journey from the first word to the last.

ABOUT THE AUTHOR

Senja Laakso is a fantasy author from Finland.
Her debut novel Revenge Undone,
a romantic dark fantasy novel, came out in 2021.

When she isn't lost in a fantasy world
of one of her books,
she's busy with university studies
or exploring and finding inspiration
from nature and historical sites.

To hear more about Senja, follow her on social media, check out her podcast and subscribe to her newsletter.

www.senjalaakso.com
Instagram: senja.laakso
TikTok: senja.laakso

www.ingramcontent.com/pod-product-compliance
Lightning Source LLC
Chambersburg PA
CBHW020902160726
47993CB00005B/1772